Sleeping with the MONSTER

ANYA MARTIN

Lethe Press
Amherst, Massachusetts

Published in 2018 by Lethe Press, Inc.
6 University Drive, Suite 206 / PMB #223 • Amherst, MA 01002 USA
www.lethepressbooks.com • lethepress@aol.com
ISBN: 978-1-59021-700-9 / 1-59021-700-4

Credits for previous publication appear on page 266, which constitutes an extension of this copyright page.

Set in Garamond and Monstice, with Bergamot Ornaments.
Interior design: Alex Jeffers.
Cover design: Inkspiral Design.

LIBRARY OF CONGRESS CATALOGING-IN-PUBLICATION DATA

TK

For my father

William C. Martin,

known to his friends as Bill,

who encouraged me to read and write things Weird *and* Wondrous.

"It is true, we shall be monsters, cut off from all the world;
but on that account we shall be more attached to one another."
—Mary Shelley, *Frankenstein*

"Real art must always involve some witchcraft."
—Isak Dinesen, *Letters from Africa: 1914-1931*

Contents

A Girl and Her Dog

Dear Diary,

(Read this with a slight southern twang and heaps of sweetness you could squish into jam in a jar, Daddy would've said back then.)

Today is my 10th BIRTHDAY!!!!! Mom and Daddy have got me the BEST present EVER—A PUPPY!!!!!!!!!!!! He is the cutest, most beautiful thing I have ever seen. He's a COLLIE, just like Lassie, but a BOY, and he doesn't have that white streak down his head. Mom says he's not show quality because his white ruff goes only halfway. Dora who we picked him up from says it doesn't matter. But I don't care. Now I have A REAL FRIEND. I love him. I will call him DANIEL!!!

—Cassandra Williams, May 22, 1979

"Bethany Rawlston, bitch!"

Cassie fumed silently, kneeling behind the thick trunk of an oak tree and scratching its bark angrily with her fingernails. Her black polish would be chipped, but she didn't give a flip when Bethany, her alleged best friend of fourteen years, was screwing around with Eddie "Munster" Wilkinson on top of his blood-red sleeping bag.

Well, they were not quite screwing yet. Bethany still had Eddie's black leather jacket wrapped tightly over her tits, but Eddie was working like hell to vibrate it off. And he was even playing the Clash for her—the tape she, Cassie, had given him for his birthday. The throb of machine-gun percussion ascended like crossfire through the woods. They were probably drunk off their asses, too, given the bottles of grape soda and Bacardi lying nearby. He probably stole that liquor from his dad's always well-stocked bar.

"Euuuuuum."

Cassie felt a damp kiss as a collie's nose brushed gently against her cheek.

"Hush, gorgeous," she whispered, fighting back tears. "Yeah, I still got you, Daniel. And you're ten thousand times better than any stupid Eddie Munster. So what if he can skate. So what if he's fronting the only hardcore band in this rotten dumbass city. He's a dickhead. And Bethany's a slut."

Cassie threw one last glance at Eddie's black liberty spikes and Bethany's platinum teased big hair. His jacket was off her now, his head grazing on Bethany's bodacious breasts.

"Boys always go for the tits, don't they?" Cassie said to Daniel.

The dog curved his head to the right as if trying to understand. Then he nuzzled her palm. She loosened the leash wrapped around her wrist and yanked gently to let him know it was time to go now.

"Maybe I should've bought Miss Clairol platinum blonde instead of Krazy Kolor electric fuchsia," Cassie grumbled.

Dog and girl stepped out of the woods onto the sandy playing field behind McArdle Elementary. The high school also had a forest area behind it, but the grade school woods had a reputation for being a more private and a discreet location for couples who wanted to get drunk and screw around. And there also was the thrill of busting your cherry just yards away from the rear window of Mrs. Chadwick, the gorgon of an algebra teacher whose house backed onto the McArdle playground.

Cassie paused by the log "creative play" fortress and knotted the loop of Daniel's leash around a thick wood post. Daniel obediently stood by as she plunked her blue-jeaned behind, crossed-legs into the sand.

"They didn't have this Davy Crockett shit when we were little, did they, boy?" She said, reaching out her hand to stroke Daniel's chin.

Daniel tilted his head again in short rhythmic shakes.

"Well, you'll be my sweetheart at least, won't you?"

Cassie gently eased the dog down. Daniel rolled onto his back and offered up mounds of snow white under-ruff. She responded to his clear request for a belly rub, and he moaned softly in pleasure.

After a few minutes of massage, she removed her hand and placed it onto her lap. Daniel rotated back onto his side, stretched his long legs, and closed his eyes.

What was so great about Eddie anyway? Yeah, he was one of the few punk guys at school, but what kind of romantic relationship would she have with a guy whose entire vocabulary consisted of "it sucks"? Christ, when she put it that way, he sounded as boring and pathetic as a fucking football player.

Cassie looked down at Daniel again. How peaceful he seemed, one paw shaking gently as if he was running in some doggie dream wonderland. She pictured him in some happy meadow chasing balls, herding sheep, playing with other dogs. Maybe she was there, too, in canine form, rubbing noses, frolicking with each other, and finally lying panting side by side. She couldn't help but smile at that thought.

Daniel's fur reminded her of a lion's mane with thick, wispy strokes of burnished red, goldenrod yellow, and charcoal gray—the hues of autumn blended with the soft white of winter snows that rarely descended on Georgia. The fragrant shades of seasons in the sun and of dreams.

Daniel's paw was moving faster now, and soon its rear partner was keeping pace. His eyes raced back and forth like manic pendulums.

"Ummmmmmmmm, owummmmm."

"Bad dreams," the voice said, startling Cassie out of her lost world reverie of watching the sleeping dog. "Bad dreams."

Old Crone, the suntan woman, loomed above her on the hardwood platform, a black plastic garbage bag trailing from her wrinkled dark brown fingers—all shiny in the rays of the setting sun and blowing back with the wind. She was wrapped in a tan suede jacket dripping with fringes, faded blue jeans with red bandana patches on each knee, and heavy brown hiking boots. Her gray hair was wound into tight braids under a cowboy hat.

Cassie pulled back and started to untie Daniel, who now had jumped up and started barking.

"Yes, good thing I came along," Crone said, biting her lip. "I can see that you love that dog. You love that dog a helluva lot more than that boy..."

She held the word long and slippery.

"...in the woods."

Scrapper, her Cairn terrier, was now scampering in circles at her ankles. The feisty little brown canine with the pink ribbon on his head hurled assault woofs like gunfire at the twin threat of strange girl and strange dog.

"No, Daniel, no," Cassie yelled at the collie. She hated raising her voice at him, but the noise, after Old Crone's accusation, was making her head throb. Daniel reluctantly fell silent.

"It's okay, baby," she continued, softer now. "She may be weird, but she won't hurt you. And you could eat Scrapper any day."

Old Crone bent down and clamped a leathery hand over Scrapper's mouth.

"There, there, Elijah," she soothed. "No one's gonna eat you. Now, sit."

Scrapper/Elijah obediently lowered his hindquarters and resigned himself to well-mannered panting.

"Now, Miss Rather," Cassie started.

Old Crone and Scrapper were kid-names for the old recluse and her exceedingly well-groomed dog. Mom had once told Cassie that their crazy neighbor was only thirty-four, but she looked at least in her sixties thanks to some disease that made you get wrinkled at a young age—like that guy in "Blade Runner."

"Yes, Cassandra Williams, isn't it? I've seen you every day walking that dog of yours back here. Elijah and I walk here, too. We've been walking here for a long, long time. Since before you were born."

"Miss Rather, you can't tell my mother about Eddie."

"Oh, yes. That's the boy's name, ain't it?"

"Miss Rather, I need to get home. It's Daniel's suppertime."

Why did today of all days have to be the one when Crone decided to start up a conversation? All Cassie wanted to do was lie down on her bed, dwell on her misfortune, drown herself in Cure and Joy Division tapes, and jab safety-pins into her arm just to feel the pain. She didn't have the patience today for eccentric old ladies.

"Daniel," Crone repeated, dwelling on the dog's name. She stepped down and petted the collie's head. He threw Cassie a questioning glance but allowed it. Scrapper watched, too, but mercifully ignored his high-strung terrier instincts and continued just to sit and pant.

"I'm sorry," Crone nodded, retreating up the steps. "It's just that I can see you love your dog. I love my dog. I tried loving boys, loving men, but the only love a woman can depend on is the everlasting affection of your dog. Not that you don't have to pay the price. You've got to put in your share for any love."

"Yes, Ms. Rather," Cassie said. "I do love my dog, but I've got to go."

"I'm sorry," Crone repeated. "But I saw your dog shaking and thought the Evil Man might be coming after him."

"The Evil Man?" Cassie winced at Crone's imagination. "He was just sleeping and dreaming like all dogs do."

"Yes, all dogs sleep, and most of them are unfortunate enough to have masters who allow them to be tormented by nightmares. I guess you don't really love Daniel as much as I thought. Go on home, little girl."

"Wait," Cassie was beginning to get angry. How dare this old witch—Mistress of Weirdness herself…

"Who are you to tell me that I don't love Daniel?" she demanded. "But what can I do? Dogs have nightmares. People have nightmares. It's a fact of life."

"Wake him up," Crone said, her eyes narrowing to slits.

Cassie stared at her. What did she mean?

"Wake him up," Crone repeated.

"I'd have to stay awake all the time," Cassie said. "He sleeps while I sleep. That's impossible. Oh, what am I talking about? Evil Man?! Come on, Daniel."

Cassie started to pull the dog away, but the sincere expression in Crone's eyes made her freeze. The creepy old woman really looked like she wanted to help.

"When dogs have bad dreams, it's because of the Evil Man," Crone continued. "There's nothing a dog fears more than that the human to whom he has devoted his whole life will turn on him, hit him, desert him, give him away to someone less tender. The Evil Man feeds on that fear."

"My daddy once said that for us not to dream is unhealthy," Cassie protested. "We work out problems in sleep. Nightmares are night therapy."

"Yes, but nightmares age you, too," Crone said, spreading her right arm out now like a giant bat's claw in the rapidly falling twilight. "If the experience of the day ages you, then why wouldn't the experience of the night age you as well? Think about it, girl. Long and hard. Men come and go, and dogs die in but a fraction of your lifetime. Don't you owe them something for their undying love? Elijah never has nightmares, and he's lived for over twenty-five years—twenty-five happy, happy years. Thanks to good dreams."

Crone bent down and stroked the dog's back.

The woman was crazy, Cassie thought. She looked at Scrapper. Sure, he'd been around as long as she remembered, but he wouldn't be charging at

Daniel if he was that old. She'd always heard a dog year equaled seven human years. If he was twenty-five, he'd be on dog crutches, wouldn't he? No, that'd be a hundred and seventy-five human years. That was impossible. He'd be dead.

"Wake Daniel enough times and the Evil Man will come to you, and maybe you can strike a deal, too," Crone said, her mouth curving into a yellow-teeth grin. "Come on, Elijah. The girl's got to think now."

The old woman headed back across the field towards the school, the little dog scampering past her.

"Elijah," Crone said loudly, striding after him. "Do you think she loves Daniel as much as I love you?"

The two disappeared around the front of the low brick building, leaving Cassie tending a new pit in her stomach.

"Of course, I love you, Daniel," she said, running her fingers down the dog's nose. "I bet you're hungry. I guess we better go."

Cassie started walking again, pausing whenever Daniel found an interesting scent or wanted to lift his leg and mark his territory. They climbed up the hill at dog-pace, wound down the block to Durand Falls Road, and hung a left on Chelsea Drive. She and Daniel charged up the driveway and across the open carport of her family's mid-'60s split-level home. She unlocked the side door and hung the leash on the collie-head hook inside.

"Cassie, is that you?" Mom called from the kitchen.

"Yeah, Mom."

Not wanting to chat and feeling the call of her Joy Division tapes more than ever, she started to duck Mom and just go upstairs. She looked back at Daniel, his tongue hanging out in exuberant pants. She'd always thought dogs looked like they were smiling when they hung their mouths open like that, but she also knew it meant he was thirsty and needed water. She turned instead for the kitchen.

"Mom?"

"Yes," Her mother looked back from the stove and wiped her hands on her apron.

"Mom, is it true that Miss Rather's dog is twenty-five years old?" she asked, picking up Daniel's metal water bowl off the floor and refilling it in the sink.

"Well, sweetie, that dog's been around for a long time. He was full-grown when your father and I moved into this house a year before you were born, so I guess he must be at least fifteen, sixteen. Terriers live a long time. Why?"

"How long does a collie live, Mom?" Cassie continued, as she set the bowl onto the floor. Daniel immediately started lapping at it noisily.

"I'm afraid they don't live as long, sweetie. But you needn't bury Daniel before his time. Rory, the collie I had when I was a girl, made it to ten years and four months."

"Ten years," Cassie said. "Only ten years. And you say you're sure that dog of Miss Rather's is past fifteen."

"I think so," Mom nodded. "But honey. Daniel's only four. You've got a lot of happy times ahead. By the time he gets old, you'll be in college and won't be thinking about dogs so much anymore."

"You cruel witch!" Cassie screamed. "How can you say that? I'll always care about Daniel. And he's going to live to be the oldest dog that ever lived. I won't let him die."

With tears streaming down her cheeks, Cassie ran to her room. She called for Daniel, and he romped up the stairs after her. Once he was inside, she slammed the door. She turned around to find him standing on her bed, his tail wagging eagerly—a flag of a country of pure warmth and affection.

Cassie pulled off her T-shirt and jeans and stood in front of the long brass mirror on her closet door. She touched her right hand to the lace that rimmed her size-A black bra and traced it across the two tiny hills that added a faint curve to the flat plain of her chest. Would more grow? Did it matter?

Cassie turned back to Daniel, still king of the bed, and knelt beside him on the mattress. She slowly wrapped her arms around the dog. Usually in a moment or two he would pull away as dogs do, but this time he seemed to sense how much she needed to hold him. They remained frozen, locked together, girl and dog. Crone's words echoed in her head—"the only love that you can depend on is the everlasting affection of your dog."

She closed her eyes and saw a room come back to her, a tiny sliver of a room with a metal bed in its center, a room she wasn't supposed to peek into. The soft purr of machinery. A green line bouncing up and down on a television screen. A tangle of colorless cords trailing underneath the white sheet—a head wrapped in bandages like a mummy and in between the strips of white, islands of charcoal crusted scabs and oceans of raw pink skin.

"No, Cassie, come back."

"Let me be with Daddy."

Her mother pulling her out of the doorway. The loud buzz like a police siren. The green mountains collapsing into a straight line.

As the memory receded, Cassie released herself from the dog-hug and ran her index finger slowly down Daniel's back. She laid her head down and rubbed her bright pink hair into his long, silky strands. She would be holding him just like this someday as a vet pressed a silvery needle into his limp paw—the needle of eternal sleep that gave human beings the power of life and death over their closest companions. She remembered the fit of rage Mom had after the accident because Daddy had never taken the time to make a living will. How she said that luckily he'd had the grace just to die.

Cassie closed her eyes again and imagined the fathomable emptiness of a world without Eddie, Bethany, Mom. And then she imagined the unfathomable emptiness of a world without Daniel.

Three months had passed since she had started the waking now. Inch-long brown roots crept out from faded fuchsia, and gaping black hollows lurked under her eyes. The only way she managed to sleep at all now was that Daniel slept on her bed. She encouraged it so that she could feel it if his paws started shaking and wake herself to rouse him.

Summer would be over soon though, making it much harder to safeguard his sleeping because she would be gone eight hours a day at school. She tried to remember Crone's exact words. She'd even gone to Crone's house, but although she could always hear a frenzy of woofs from Scrapper, nobody ever answered the door. How long would she have to wait until the Evil Man revealed himself to her?

Tonight, Mom had turned in early. Guess for a change she trusted her precious "little rebel" (always pronounced with the utmost of tender irony to emphasize her disapproval of the hair dye job and Cassie's punk wardrobe) to make it home okay from the night-time dog stroll.

Just to be on the safe side after walking Daniel, Cassie had crept upstairs and lain on her bed for a good half hour before slinking back down, with Daniel at her tail, to turn on the TV.

Maybe a splat-flick would be playing. She was crazy, she knew, to watch so many horror movies. That was probably the reason she got the nightmares, why this weirdo dude—cross between Michael Myers and Jason—kept chasing her with a bullwhip and that scary spiky thing she never got a clear look at.

Cassie went to the kitchen first, poured herself a large Coke and grabbed a bag of tortilla chips. Then it was back to the living room with Mr. Nose (Daniel) tracking every toss of the chips sack. She plunked down on the sofa, and Daniel leaped up beside her and laid his head in her lap. The "please, please, Cassie, give me some chips, please" tactic.

Even though Cassie knew that chips weren't healthy for dogs, those mournful brown eyes always melted her heart. Even before she grabbed the television remote, she was ripping open the bag and slipping the biggest chip she could find into Daniel's eagerly awaiting mouth.

Daniel gently pulled the chip from her grip and, with several crunches, devoured it.

Cassie reached finally for the remote, pressed the volume down to almost nothing, then powered on the television. It was past midnight now, so as she channel-surfed, she was met with an assault of used-car commercials, metal videos, a sex therapist (occasional laughs; she was now asking some guys whether they cared if a woman's breasts weren't both the same size), a David Letterman repeat with Teri Garr which she had seen twice, the Mascara Woman talking about fake nails that lasted two months, third-season *Star Trek* (the hippie episode; fuck, what a dweeb Chekhov was), and *Hallelujah!* Some dickhead on Cinemax who looked just like Eddie before he dyed his hair black and his blonde girlfriend were being axed by a mysterious masked killer.

"I sure wish someone would chop up Eddie and Bethany," she whispered, offering Daniel another chip and stuffing three broken shards into her own mouth.

About fifteen minutes or so into the movie, which turned out to be just as bad as Cassie thought it would be, they ran out of chips. Daniel raised his head from her lap, stood up, made a 180-degree turn. Then, as always, after a few paws at the cushion, he curled into a big, furry ball at the other end of the sofa, closed his eyes, and fell asleep.

Most of the time, his dreams seemed good. He'd twitch a little, maintaining the same adorable expression that drew "awwws" since puppyhood from all of her friends. But as the ginger-haired nerd hero crashed his truck into the crazed maniac, pushing him into the lake (water was the only thing he feared) and the credits began to roll, Cassie looked over and saw it begin.

It started slow as always. She didn't realize it was happening at first and even threw Daniel a smile. Then one paw loosened itself from his tightly wound knot and started twitching.

First, a slow jiggle, building rapidly to a fast thump. Then Daniel's eyelid would shake like something was trying to break free from inside the socket. His chest heaved up and down. All the legs were moving now and the moan, "ooooooo, ooooooo, owwwwwww."

Nightmare.

Cassie leaned over quickly and gently shook the dog.

"Daniel."

His body froze momentarily, then he opened his eyes and dealt her a soft glazed look.

"Oh, Daniel," she said, kissing his brow.

Cassie felt the rough wet rub of Daniel's tongue on her hand. She laid her head down lightly on his stomach.

Across the room in the shadows by the window stood a tall dark silhouette with a bullwhip in his hand. Cassie didn't see him at first, the ebb and flow of Daniel's breathing being so comforting to her. She felt a wave of relaxation waft over her, as if she could finally sleep. Then the man grabbed her hand and yanked her to her feet.

Daniel slept peacefully as long sharp spikes etched deep lines into Cassie's forehead and ripped across her fingers. She tried to scream but could make no sound—as if he had ripped her vocal cords, but he hadn't touched them. The spikes carved into her arms like razor blades, fretted her legs like broken glass, seared into her chest like sharp swords of burning metal. Blood gushed from her wounds, moist and slimy like a bath of strawberry syrup. And then just as she thought she was about to die, the pain ceased, and the man grabbed her head and forced her to look at his face.

His countenance was etched with deep furrows, as if he was the most ancient man alive, older than any friend's grandfather she had ever seen, the wrinkles extending back across his bald pate like the scars of battles fought long ago. His eyes descended into black holes, endless and with no return. His dry, chapped gray lips pursed into a leering grin.

Finally he spoke.

"I loved my dog once."

Behind him a giant black Rottweiler leered, white bubbly froth dripping from a hungry tongue encased in sharp teeth. Its back was colored with fresh red streaks, as if the Evil Man had recently beaten it to an inch of its life. And yet the dog seemed completely healthy, as if the wounds caused it no pain.

The Evil Man turned towards the creature, the two of them exchanging a look of pure hatred. Then they both vanished.

Daniel's collie bark woke Cassie. She found herself stretched across the couch, the lines of blood gone, erased, as if after all, all she had done was dream. Daniel prodded her with his nose, and she could hear Mom in the kitchen, the faint bubbling noise of the coffee machine and cereal pouring into a bowl.

"Yes, boy, you want to go outside, don't you?"

Cassie let Daniel into the backyard and went upstairs to get dressed for school. She looked in the bathroom mirror. She noticed the beginning of crows' feet next to her eyes that she could swear weren't there yesterday.

Cassie smiled, knowing now it was only a matter of time until the wrinkles came back to stay.

Dear Diary,

(Read this with a slight southern twang and a twist of wire, like the soft crackle of strep throat.)

I have tried everything, every miracle cream advertised in Vogue *or in* The Enquirer. *It doesn't matter. The wrinkles are getting deeper and deeper, coming faster and faster, the work of his fingernails and the whip etching away all remnants of my youth, arthritis numbing my joints. The nightmares come every night now, but Daniel wakes me when he hears me scream in my sleep. The Evil Man prods me to punish Daniel for making me this way, but I'll never hurt him even if no man will ever want me. Daniel is all I have now and he is so sweet. He's lying at my feet right now. We went to the park for frisbee yesterday with Dorothy and Elijah who just turned 38. If what the Evil Man says true—then we will continue to age as long as our dogs stay young and alive. But in this world, the only love a girl can depend on is the everlasting affection of her dog.*

—Cassandra Williams, July 22, 1996

Resonator Superstar!

"If you want to know all about Andy Warhol, just look at the surface of my paintings and films and me, there I am. There's nothing behind it"
—Andy Warhol (1968)

Curt clicked the keypad on the laptop.

"Here goes nothing."

Red strobe flash.

Blue strobe flash.

Rapid bursts of white light. DiDi felt the heat from the strobes on her back.

The music cut in. A steady drone in a single repeated chord.

In the original performances of Andy Warhol's infamous Exploding Plastic Inevitable, aka EPI, human hands would have had to switch on and off and maneuver each of the multiple lights, adjust the sound levels, run the 16-mm projectors, but thanks to twenty-first-century technology, Curt had developed a software program that executed it all with just one laptop tap, except for a live performance by the Velvet Underground, of course.

“Nothing comes of nothing, but you’ve really done something,” DiDi whispered as Curt leaned back and right towards her. Their chairs close already, he touched her hand, did that twisty thing with the thrift-store ring he gave her last week. It wasn’t an engagement ring, but after six months since they first met in a Sergei Eisenstein class, and then bonded over a mutual appreciation of Brakhage, the usual dance of we’re-fucking-but-are-we-a-couple-or-not, to her, it represented a powerful symbol. Punctuated by Curt slipping his hand down to her knee, sliding it slowly underneath the hem of her black leather miniskirt. She liked that, too.

Blue strobe blinks. Yellow strobe flash.

The first projector flickered on, fade from black to grainy black-and-white close-up pale hair in a ponytail, pussycat black eyeliner, full pouty lips. She looked down but then she smiled, maybe.

“You can really see in Nico’s face why they loved her and hated her,” DiDi whispered in Curt’s ear. But he put a finger to his lips. Why did she have to try so hard to be clever to impress him? She hated the times when she dared to do so spontaneously and he shut her down. Got to remember—less is more. Let him do the talking, listen, girl.

Yet this time Curt might just be protecting her from derision. Every one of the fifty seats was occupied, but no one was speaking, not even whispers. Not like the cineplex. More like a Catholic congregation, except its members bridged jaded aging once-punks-now-art-scenesters with self-consciously-attired hipsters not born until a decade or more after the original shows took place. The on-screen diva was their Madonna, years before another pop star actually pretended to that name. Guttural deep bass line and cacophonous guitar jangle, intentionally uninspired drum beat, as camera focused on her profile—pensive, speaking, sighing. Fade to black and back. Out of focus, in focus, out, in. Panned out enough to see she was banging a tambourine with a maraca—keeping the dull beat but an untrained monkey could do that—perhaps that was why she needed to dress like a Euro-Spy in black jumper and tight pants like she just stepped off the set of *The Man From U.N.C.L.E.* And finally the pan-out to the entire band, concentration, all serious intent on their instruments. The prophets of punk to come, the artists of anti-pop orchestrated by the King of Pop Art. At Nico’s feet, a blond toddler rubbed his eyes, sleepy, then shaking another maraca with a randomness only a child can accomplish amidst the wall of sound surrounding him.

More fades to black, pans, shaky cam and the window into the Factory expanded and contracted. Intimate, not intimate. Rehearsal not performance. Performance not rehearsal. Shake, rattle, machine.

Lou's ear peek-a-boo, his baby-cheek, DiDi wanted to stroke it—you could think he was just a cute-as-hell guitar player if not for the jarring metallica. Camera jerked from close-up to full rehearsal panorama. Sterling, she wanted to run her fingers through his hair. Why can't the lens ever focus on Cale, who had become her favorite as she found out more and more about his forays into film? They looked almost just boys, so young—even Mo Tucker, in her pixie cut and striped shirt, could have stepped out of a *Peanuts* cartoon. Everyone but Nico in dark sunglasses, eyelessness. Always back to her maraca banging on the tambourine. The beat blondtastique. Mother but not a nurturer, radiating discipline, that maraca could come down on a wrist. What she said to Iggy: "Poison is the essence of the performer."

A screech of feedback overwhelmed the incessant beat, scraped sonic burn over DiDi's eardrums.

"Look carefully at Nico's forehead," Curt whispered in DiDi's ear. It was okay when he wanted to share something. "How the camera technique makes it seem like her brow is vibrating as if something wanted to emerge from inside."

"Her super-ego?" DiDi asks; surely his initiation of dialogue was an invitation for some humor.

"No, Andy was fascinated with the pineal gland—it's kind of an evolutionary throwback but has been linked in rodent studies to the secretion of sexual hormones. It's stimulated by darkness but light dampens the effect. It's another thing Charley Tillinghast turned him onto."

DiDi wanted to roll her eyes. Charley Tillinghast again. In all her reading about Warhol, all the interviews she'd watched on YouTube and DVD with Curt as he researched his thesis, nobody ever mentioned a Charley Tillinghast. Yet after meeting some roadie out in San Francisco, Curt seemed obsessed with him, like he was Andy's right-hand man. Right-hand-jacking-off man maybe.

"So despite the implied sexuality of bondage and blowjobs in Andy's films, the EPI is an antisexual experience?" DiDi posed, unable to hide her skepticism.

"No, baby, you don't get it. It's all about turning off the sex drive and turning it back on again, except super-fast. The ultimate frustration. Like me touching you and then removing my hand rapidly."

He reached deep under her skirt now, touching her and then pulling out again, three times. Four.

"Stop it, or I'll have to take you back to the loft now," she said, giggling, forgiving him again.

"Point proven. Now shh, back to the movie," he said.

Mirror-shard sparkles swept across the screen. Disco wasn't even a thing then—what would they have called the ball in the sixties? Just mirror ball? Didn't matter. Pineal gland, sexual stimulation—Andy was all about the spectacle and the manipulation of his entourage. Sounded like typical Warhol BS. But Curt's playful prods stimulated anticipation of later tonight, a post-performance performance—his success transforming into her pleasure. She lifted fingers to play with his blond spiky hair. He looked to his side again, threw her a wink. Mission accomplished.

Two more projectors flickered on. When? That was the beauty of multimedia—the eyes, brain could not process it all, forced to make choices. On the left screen: the familiar images of *Vinyl*, which she'd viewed even in class. Gerard Malanga—all beatnik James Dean in white T—chest thrusting, elbows shaking, the punctuation of the crack of the whip, that guy in the suit laughing. Edie—big dark Boop eyes in tight little black dress—alternating between fashionably bored, puffing cigarette, and go-going without standing, like it was all just another hazy lazy day at The Factory.

Right screen: Beat incessant as *Blowjob* cuts in, head enraptured in receiving head and yet banal in its detachment from the act of pleasure looped over a half-hour. Curt had told DiDi that Andy varied which of his films showed up in the EPI like a mixtape which also included *Bitch*, *Restaurant*, *Eat*, etc., all his vignettes of the everyday human act or emotion stripped to monotone.

Green strobe—triple flash. Purple strobe—swam slow across the screens and flashed out.

"Lou used to wear sunglasses so he wouldn't be blinded by the strobes," Curt whispered in DiDi's ear.

She didn't quip back this time, remembering his last hush—repeating to herself, "less is more." She lamented that when it came to the EPI, at least a half-hour more. She loved the Velvets, but compared to sex later, or maybe he was right about the repetitive display stimulating her pineal gland. Whatever the cause, the whole production now chafed her eyes and ears like fingernails on a chalkboard.

A shadow of a girl dancing now projected high across Malanga's rattling body and above the screen onto the white wall behind. DiDi never saw the girl up until then nor saw anyone stand up from the crowd. Not even to slip out the back to the restroom.

At first she was just a wavy shape in a glossy sleeveless aluminum mini-dress, skinny but curvy at the same time—pale spidery arms and spellbound hands, twisting hips nurtured on Fats Domino down long model legs to shiny white boots of leather with solid heels—were there any other kind of boots in the sixties? She could have been part of the film except for the shadow she cast across Gerard Malanga, shifting the remaining light of the projector to Edie's perfunctory chair dancing.

Edie. The girl looked like Edie. Not just *looked*. Could have been her long-lost twin, up to her blonde bob, her darkly lined eyes, the eyebrows so smooth they seemed like lipstick.

Curt withdrew his hand fully from DiDi's leg, leaned in.

DiDi dropped her hand from his hair.

"Who's that? You didn't tell me you'd hired a go-go dancer. Good job though, spittin' image hair, eyes, clothes, she could be Edie's twin."

"I didn't hire anyone."

Gerard Malanga cracked whip onscreen behind proto-Edie.

"Well, she looks great, but I thought you didn't want any performers for this first run."

"If I pull her offstage, it'll disrupt the show. She's really good, obviously practiced on real footage. Makes it more like the real thing."

DiDi thought of Coca-Cola. Hadn't Andy painted Coke bottles like he did soup cans? Still, she didn't like the way Curt was watching the girl. The abrupt shift from affection to distance. What audacity to just jump up and start dancing, and yet exactly in synch with the exhibitionism that Andy had encouraged among his Factory groupies, feeding his and their addiction to fame. Still, DiDi had to admit the gal was good, especially since the footage was so damned obscure. One had to do some serious googling to put together any concept of the EPI and none of the YouTube footage was in any way really evocative given the light displays and the multiple streams of film that combined spontaneously for each performance, the fact that there were relatively few shows to begin with. This was one dedicated fangirl.

As the projector and strobe lights hit cosplay-Edie's body, which she grooved almost gear-like now from screen to screen, the dress glowed in different colors and DiDi thought she saw images, too, as film hit fabric—weird damage to the footage that wasn't visible on the screens. Squiggly lines and *x*'s—marks the spot, marks no spot—letters she didn't recognize,

Runic symbols perhaps. Then a man's face, each lens of a pair of dark glasses reflected on a breast, thick long hair spreading out into her arms—must be some mirage caused by the fabric itself or was this face sewn into her dress? She wanted to ask Curt if he saw a face in the dress. His eyes were still locked on the dancing girl, no, transfixed—had he taken some drug before the show and not told her? No, its success was too important to him—the culmination of his master's thesis, three years of intense research.

DiDi tried to turn Curt's head slightly with one hand, but he shrugged her off, shook his head.

Looking back at the dancer, DiDi almost jumped in her chair. Two red glows through the glasses right where her nipples should be. Eyes. Just above and perfectly centered was a third eye or at least a flesh-colored oval that resembled an eye inside a three-fingered hand. She thought back to Curt's description of the pineal gland. Was that it?

She shut her eyes, reopened. Just a girl in a silver dress go-go dancing. Was the effect of the EPI not just hypnotic, but hallucinatory? She recalled a previous animated speech Curt had given her about the EPI being able to induce a trancelike state, that Warhol took part of his inspiration from Heliczer's *Rites of the Dream Weapon* which sought to reduce the audience to lab-rats. Had she fallen for the experiment or maybe just fallen asleep, perchance to dream?

The center VU rehearsal film closed with the no longer unexpected arrival of the police responding to a sound complaint. One could empathize with a Factory neighbor, DiDi thought. Eventually the earworm would be too much. One might even long for an out-of-tune clarinet for variety. The two other reels pattered off into silence, the strobes continued to blink for a few minutes, a trickle out of the incessant sound and then quiet.

As the lights rose, the crowd clapped but did not rise. DiDi didn't expect they would—not the kind of crowd that gave standing ovations.

Edie's lookalike had vanished and yet DiDi never saw her leave the stage area. Hopefully she left the building like the proverbial Elvis and would offer no further visual stimuli to her boyfriend's penis or pineal gland.

DiDi again tried to give Curt a peck on the cheek as he rose, but once more he seemed oblivious to her gesture. As he walked to the front, she saw him scanning the crowd. He was looking for that girl.

"Thanks, everyone, for attending the grand premiere of this recreation of Andy Warhol's *Exploding Plastic Inevitable*. Thanks again to my landlord the Mattress Factory Lofts for allowing me to use their clubhouse studio in the basement. Sorry, we couldn't book the Velvet Underground to accompany."

Curt paused for a trickle of ironic laughter to cycle through the audience, then spoke again: "But this should give you some idea of what audiences would have experienced back in 1967. Underground film was as key an influence on the Velvets' sound as rock or experimental jazz. John Cale had been hanging around with filmmakers like Jack Smith and Ron Rice, through his association with La Monte Young's Theatre of Eternal Music. Even before hooking up with Warhol, Lou, John, Sterling and Angus MacLise had provided music for Piero Heliczer's multimedia presentations at the Film-Makers' Cinematheque. So when Andy, who by this time, had rejected art as his vocation, stepped forward to be their manager, they were not just open but enthusiastic to embrace his multisensory approach to performance. Keep in mind, folks, this was before the big light and prop shows that characterized arena shows in the seventies and eighties, a much more orchestrated type of spectacle. Each performance was different, and the EPI program I have developed takes all these elements and remixes them to mimic the same sense of spontaneity that would have occurred at the original shows. Any questions?"

An earnest-looking young woman with long straight red hair, dressed in a black turtleneck and jeans, raised her hand.

"You use the word *spontaneity*, but weren't John and Lou really about repetition, following the lead of Cale's work with La Monte Young in his Dream House ensemble?"

"Yeah, that's true but each show used different footage and effects to achieve the same effect of repetition." DiDi detected an edge in Curt's reply; she knew he hated restating what he thought was obvious. "Next?"

A bald older man with an obviously dyed black goatee and a British accent: "Andy always had a name for everything he did—a label even for the mundane. So have you got a name for your software program—it's not just EPI, I do hope?"

"I was going to call it the Transformer, after Lou's seminal album about his experience with Andy and The Factory, but in the end, I settled on the Resonator, after Charley Tillinghast's nickname for the whole sensory experience. Question for the audience to see how well you know your Factory players—who's Charley Tillinghast?"

Whispering first, then blinking on of smartphones. Furious googling.

"I know," a female voice said softly from the back.

DiDi looked to her right. Sure enough, it was the Edie lookalike. Her head tilted down, eyes to the floor.

"T-I-L-L-I-N-G-H-A-S-T."

Proto-Edie rattled off the letters machine-gun rapid face up, coy half-smile, nodded, dropped her head down again.

Weird that she spelled the name rather than answering the question. Surely Curt would think so, too. Instead, he clapped his hands.

"Very good!"

Sheesh, DiDi groaned silently.

"Now can anyone tell me who Charley Tillinghast is?"

Quiet fell back over the audience until proto-Edie lifted her hand.

"Charley Tillinghast helped Andy develop the EPI and ran the projectors."

"Hey, wait, how come we've never heard of him then?" asked a silver-haired woman in angular purple glasses.

Proto-Edie's eyes focused back on the floor, and she shuffled her feet back and forth. Was she still slowly dancing? Clearly she had reached the limit of what she was going to share.

When she didn't respond, Curt went ahead:

"When I was researching the EPI out in Frisco, I was able to track down one of the extra light guys who worked for promoter Bill Graham when he booked the EPI at the Fillmore West. As I'm sure all of you know, he pulled it after two nights. Official story was that Graham didn't like the VU's sound, but after a few drinks, this guy told me about Charley and how Charley was supposed to do something special during the show—some extra effect, he didn't know what it was—only it didn't work. And then on top of things, one of the dancers disappeared. Andy arranged for an extra show, a rehearsal with just the visuals and tapes of the band. After that, the guy never saw Charley again, nobody did. He was genuinely spooked. I mean looking behind to make sure no one was watching. There's no public record of Andy even saying Tillinghast's name before or after. Like he never existed. Should be one of the great mysteries of rock history. More questions?"

"If Andy never mentioned Tillinghast, how do you know that dude wasn't just pulling your leg?" asked a lean kid in Lou Reed T-shirt and jeans. DiDi smiled—right on, kid. She loved Curt, at least she thought she did, but sometimes he could be as pretentious as Warhol. He wasn't going to bring up the pineal gland, was he?

"I have to admit I was skeptical, but as I started doing my research on the EPI shows, I noticed there was a distinct difference between all shows leading up to the Fillmore and the ones after. So when I developed the program, I only used the shows before and including the Fillmore to generate the variations from the light and sound effects to what's onscreen. In a way, it doesn't matter if there was a Charley Tillinghast or not."

DiDi was disappointed when a black woman in a red leather jacket followed up with a routine question about Mary Woronov. Her mind rewound back to Curt going on about Tillinghast for hours after coming back from San Francisco, but she had to admit she had the same thought. Except suddenly this Edie-cosplay-chick knew who Tillinghast was, could spell his name. If Curt could find some hard evidence, he was set for his own place in rock history.

The Q&A continued for another fifteen minutes. More questions about the relationship between Lou Reed and Nico, technical intricacies about the Resonator's functionality, and underground filmmakers who might have influenced the EPI. Proto-Edie had retreated from the main seating area and was now cross-legged on the floor near the door, like a wind-up doll whose performance had stopped until someone twisted the key in her back. DiDi didn't like to think she was waiting for Curt, but if proto-Edie was a music box, she was sure that was the tune that would play—repeating like one of the tape loops of the EPI. Every bit of insecurity as to whether she and Curt actually were a couple ate back into her, and she hated herself for it.

As the audience rose and began to disperse, DiDi bee-lined to head Curt off.

"Well, that went pretty fucking amazing, don't ya think?" she asked him.

"Yeah, it was," he nodded, shouldering past her. Before she could spin around, he was already bent down and talking to that girl—and then helping her up.

People pushed past her, some pausing to say something congratulatory about Curt's accomplishment tonight—friends and neighbors and teachers who clearly considered them a couple. DiDi pushed down her anger and jealousy to make polite small talk. Then when the room had finally emptied, she saw with relief that Curt and that girl at least had not left together. He wouldn't have abandoned his laptop, his equipment. She should have known that.

The two were sitting, facing each other on the leopard-print couch at the back of the room. Curt was doing his usual, a soliloquy bound to impress, probably combining his knowledge of Warhol, the VU, his efforts to accurately recreate the EPI, and how it related to his master's thesis on the use of repetition in picture and sound in underground avant-garde film in the 1960s.

When DiDi approached, he broke away, enthusiastically declaring: "DiDi, meet Hester Tillinghast! Guess what, she's Charley's granddaughter. Who could have imagined that?! And she's going to show me some of her grandfather's notes. I was right about the pineal gland. Charley was a medical scientist at MIT before he hooked up with Andy. Isn't that fucking amazing? DiDi, can you be a doll and run up to your loft and grab us some beers?"

"Sure," DiDi nodded, not knowing how to react to this latest torrent of info-dump. Hester nodded, same polite but disinterested half-smile as earlier. Something in her eyes, a mix of everything and nothing all at once, made DiDi wonder if she'd ever said a word, other than what she said to the audience, maybe her name. As if Curt had made up everything he had just told her, or he'd learned it some other way than speech. But if Hester communicated through some kind of mental Star Trekkie brainy pineal method, she wasn't talking that way to DiDi.

DiDi found herself walking to the exit—as if Hester had dismissed her with that odd nondescript glance, more than Curt's request for beer. DiDi looked back from the doorway. Curt was still talking in monologue, but now he and Hester were holding hands. He had leaned in closer. DiDi didn't exist anymore, only Hester.

No, wait. Curt was looking at her. He'd realized she was watching, and the glare in his eyes was meaner than any she had ever seen from him.

DiDi rushed out the door now, pushing back tears. She ran for the elevator, punched the button like a trigger. It opened right away. Good, empty. It was past midnight, but in a building like this—full of artists and students—people kept all hours.

A few minutes later, she was in her loft. She slammed the door, threw the keys hard onto the concrete floor, making Trier, her Siamese cat who had been walking up to greet her, jump instead and run behind the sofa. She scooped up a pile of Curt's books and papers off the couch and hurled them in the air until they rained down across the floor. He didn't live with her, but lately he'd been there almost every night, studying and sleeping on her futon. Guess he wouldn't be doing that again. She ought to throw them all out in the hall.

What was she going to do? Was she going to just leave them alone to commune about Hester's grandfather's research on the pineal gland and test it all out with his penis? No way could she compete with Charley Tillinghast's granddaughter.

Trier had reemerged and was now meowing loudly from the pile of paper at her feet. She patted her lap to signal it was okay to jump up, but instead he just stood there.

"Silly cat," she muttered, reaching down to scoop him up. As she leaned over, she saw the word "Tillinghast" in Curt's messy handwriting on a piece of notebook paper and a rudely drawn diagram of a face with an arm-like protrusion extending out of its forehead and culminating in the three-fingered third eye thing she had seen on proto-Edie's chest.

She picked up the page, stroking Trier's back with her other hand, eliciting loud purring. She read further. "The pineal gland is stimulated by darkness." Okay, that was what Curt told her. "But rapid bursts of light and sound in the right combination can create a tension that awakens the gland to a new level of sexual arousal and release that opens a door to a higher consciousness, that frees the *id*. Andy Warhol wanted to be not just a leader in the world of pop culture, but a deity."

DiDi bent down to search for more notes, annoying Trier again, who disappeared to the kitchenette area after not getting the attention he wanted. His food bowl was probably empty, but it would have to wait. Ah, there, another drawing, men in robes, names next to each—Tillinghast, Warhol. Dollar signs next to Warhol's name. Did he pay Tillinghast to open the door for him, but somehow Tillinghast ended up going through instead?

Okay, so maybe Tillinghast was the face she saw in Hester's body. Was Hester the missing dancer? But then she couldn't be his granddaughter? Or Edie? Edie didn't die until 1971. Something wasn't right. No, nothing was right? Did Curt have another plan for tonight? Or did he unwittingly open that door? Did she need to go back and save him?

When DiDi got back down to the studio, the lights of the mirror ball were spinning, the colored strobes flashing but sleepily compared to the performance earlier. The repetitious beat of the VU throbbed loudly, but the groans permeated the wall of sound.

The two copulating bodies pulsed, rather than pummeled in and out of each other. Slow, the slowest she had ever seen. Their surfaces shiny, their skin seemed glazed over with a sheen beyond sweaty sex. They weren't connected just at the groin but at their heads, about a foot apart, tendrils intertwined and groping, massaging. The pineal gland had awakened not just metaphorically but physically.

"Curt!" DiDi yelled and ran towards them.

She pulled at Curt's shoulder, but as she touched it, her hand slid rather than gripped. His skin was slippery, no flesh to cling to—not rubbery plastic but hard plastic like a Barbie doll or in his case a Ken. She touched Hester's arm—also stiff, no give.

Neither showed any sign of recognizing her presence—as if she was invisible to them—just one conjoined blob. DiDi bent over to scan for any sign of life in Curt's eyes, then Hester's eyes. Both were rolled back, all white cornea, empty.

"Curt!" she yelled again, louder, top of her lungs.

Nothing.

Comes of nothing.

DiDi pushed against both again, trying to pry them apart by sheer force. No movement. They were soldered firm—locked at the head and at the groin, their shadow blocking Nico's emotionless onscreen visage, framed by Gerard dodging the whip on one side, male head appreciating head on the other.

Only one thing she could think of to free Curt—send Hester or Edie or whoever this Factory-manufactured doll was back into the whatever dimensional, id or super-ego doorway the EPI had opened. She had to shut off the Resonator.

DiDi ran back behind the rows of now empty folding chairs to find Curt's laptop, hitting the keyboard harder than she needed to wake it up. Now where was the icon? Damn, nothing called Exploding Plastic Inevitable, EPI, Warhol, Velvet Underground, anything that could be. Wait, in the far right corner was a folder called Resonator.

She clicked it open and saw the .exe file pulsating, clicked on it. A screen opened with rows of graphic frequencies, but how to stop it? Wait! She saw an icon for red strobe. She dragged it to the trash-bin. The red strobe blinked out. Then the blue, the green, the yellow. The light was now reduced to the spinning mirror ball. But that was still flashing light, the trigger for the pineal.

The music picked up in speed, and along with it Curt and Hester's coital undulation. Heads jerking, bodies jerking. From bare touch to *Arriba, Arriba, Ándale, Arriba!* Speedy Gonzales cartoon fast.

Fuck, what icon would turn the music off? She started clicking on them all, dragging every icon she could see into the trash bin, then the entire folder. With each drag, something did shut down, elements of the sound, a bang of drum, a drone of bass, a bar of guitar, Gerard faded to black, no more head, the mirror ball and lastly the VU themselves.

Curt and Hester's bodies ripped apart, backwards, the tendrils of the pineal gland pulling back into their heads.

DiDi breathed a sigh of relief, started to run up to Curt's side, to tell him he was safe. Safe with her.

But then the sound started to rise again, the strobes switched back on, the mirror ball, the projectors. Color everywhere now, not just at the front, the stage. How was this happening? She'd turned off the Resonator—did it no longer need the machine?

A beam of red crossed her arm like a blood stain.

Blue on her fingers.

Light so bright it blinded her. She needed to get to Curt, drag him out of here, away from Hester, away from the inevitable whatever was going to happen. But all she could see were flashing rainbow colors.

She remembered what Curt had said. Lou Reed used to wear sunglasses because…

She didn't have any sunglasses. She closed her eyes.

Somehow, feeling like a blind woman using the seatbacks to guide her, she made it to the screens. She kicked where the bodies should have been hidden by the lights, but her shoe found nothing.

She opened her eyes and found the lights faded back, the center screen visible again. No Nico, No VU, no kid with maraca. Just Curt in a white T-shirt and black leather jacket, dancing, all elbows, the crack of the whip. To the side, Hester smoking and go-going in her seat. Ultimate voyeur. Their pineal glands extending out from their foreheads in a dance of their own.

Hester smiled, winked, laughed.

No, the laughter came from the man in the suit. The camera panned in until Curt and Hester were no longer visible. Just the close-up on his face. Laughing.

The same face DiDi saw in Hester's dress.

From the middle of his forehead a long tendril shot out like a torpedo from a submarine.

She tried to duck but there wasn't time, felt her own pineal gland emerge from her forehead to meet it. And then the pull as her body entered the screen. And as she entered, she sensed his gland letting go and his body exiting.

DiDi wanted to scream, but she couldn't help but laugh as the whip cracked.

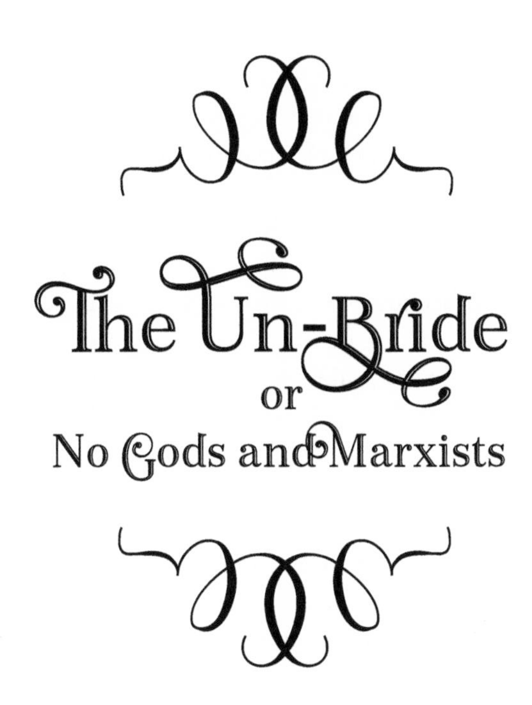

The Un-Bride or No Gods and Marxists

The first rule of telling a scary story is never to start with "It was a dark and stormy night." But I don't know how else to begin because if there ever was a dark and stormy night, this was it, and in Los Angeles no less, a city that almost never ever has dark and stormy nights. A place known for sunshine and moonshine, thanks to that nonsense called Prohibition; clear skies and maybe at most a layer of mist as you maneuvered your jalopy around the winding curves of Mulholland Drive up into the hills, towards the stars. Yes, it was a rare stormy night in Hollywood, the kind when a man might make a monster or a woman tell a tale about monster-making.

Charles and I were new to that scene in 1932 and renting rather lower but still cock-pointed up, the very last house on La Brea Avenue, that little stretch called La Brea Terrace. In other words, we were shielded by enough cliff and trees that we had no worry our humble estancia would be struck even though the thunder cracked as loud as the guns of war and lightning flashed like the neon lights of Mayfair through the silk drapes. You could scarcely get a peep out of Jimmy about his time in the trenches, but from the first martini of smuggled gin that night, he wouldn't shut up about how

Junior Laemmle was hammering him about making a sequel to *Frankenstein.* I empathized with his reluctance to be typecast as a horror director, but then who wouldn't? On the other hand, Biddy, my mother, taught me from the cot not to be surprised that money men always will pick a surefire blockbuster over art or any kind of social message.

"Nature at its crudest, most savage, and we, the very most refined of the London stage," Jimmy declared with his self-taught posh accent, lifting his pinkie before taking another sip of his cocktail. He paced, cigar in one hand, drink in the other, first to the window, pulling the shades to gaze out at the incessant sheets of rain, then migrated by the armchair where I sat in my green satin dressing gown nursing my gin and tonic, to the sofa where Charles sprawled with his legs up, his big head propped on a lacy pillow and knackered after a day on the set of Jimmy's current feature, *The Old Dark House*. He surely would be snoring away if not for the clatter of the storm and Jimmy's chatter. I had to stifle a giggle at us being "refined," but Jimmy had airs and ambition after his ascent from the poorest of the working stiffs. He kept his humble origins under wraps from the Americans, of course, who were as star struck by any affectation of British nobility as they were by any movie star. As the daughter of Edith Lanchester—socialist, Suffragette and insufferable—I wasn't going to out him for giving the finger to the upper crust. Not for that and not for that other matter either.

"I should wonder that an irate Junior Laemmle, God of Universal, was aiming those arrows of lightning right at the head of James Whale, Hollywood's greatest sinner. No, I shan't compliment myself so highly. Perhaps the bolts are meant for dear Charles, box office thunderclaps for England's greatest actor come to American soil."

Jimmy flicked his fingers quickly through Charles' hair, and I observed my husband twitch his neck ever so slightly, but whether from being shook out of a near-nap or discomfort at the sign of possible affection in front of me, I wasn't sure. I knew I needn't worry about replacing another couch, though, because Charles was, how shall I say delicately, too hefty to attract Jimmy's more personal proclivities.

"What of my Elsa?" Charles mumbled, sitting up momentarily to raise his own glass to his lips.

"She is a devil," Jimmy said, with a laugh, clinking his glass against Charles' with such force that some drops splashed onto a fuzzy swatch of the reclining man's pale pink chest peeking out from a partially unbuttoned shirt.

"You know me too well," I said with a laugh.

"Come, Elsa, watch the storm with me!" Jimmy said, grasping my hand now to pull me up to the window.

"You know how lightning bores me," I replied, nailing my bottom firmly to my seat until he laughed again and let go. At that moment the electric lights flickered and flashed off. This house wasn't old—nothing in LA seemed to be much more than a decade or two at most—but with no electricity, it now was most definitely dark.

"Charles darling, can you light the candles?" I asked, thinking I'd probably have to do it myself, but Jimmy jumped to it, igniting the five candles in the candelabrum above the fireplace with his cigar and then carrying it over to the coffee table.

"It hardly ever rains in Hollywood, and you know I am weary of Frankenstein," Jimmy said, turning back towards me. "And yet I cannot help but think of another stormy night when three gathered, a man and a couple, Lord Byron, Percy Shelley and his wife Mary Shelley, to weave weird tales. And how the most blood-curdling and creepy of all their stories was penned by that lovely, gentle, pretty young woman. How utterly astonishing."

"Unlike Elsa, of course, who will tell you to your face what she thinks and never worries about anyone's feelings," Charles said. "She's actually quite nice inside though." Even in the shadowy light of candles and lightning flashes, I could see he was sitting now. The opportunity to tease me had perked him up.

"So you both think I wouldn't tell a story of monsters and horror because I'm already so wicked on the outside," I said, rising to the bait. "What would I tell? Maybe a pretty little love story?"

Charles was snorting like a walrus now. He was tipsier than I liked him, so I chose to simply address Jimmy who after all was a friend in need. Besides, I had just what the Doctor ordered.

"As I recall, though, if you read the entire book by Mary Shelley, she thought even the monster needed love and bade Dr. Frankenstein create for him a mate," I said thoughtfully. "Mary wanted to deliver a moral lesson that man shouldn't meddle with the laws of God. But we know there isn't any God, don't we? And what if this new women made out of death didn't love, couldn't love? A man, after all, always expects a woman to love him. I've never understood why a man is so surprised when I don't."

Jimmy took a long puff of his cigar. Even in the dim light, I could discern the first look of excitement I had seen in him all evening—the mad movie director was alive again.

"Like Mary, you have a story to tell me, don't you, Elsa?" he said, perching on the arm of my chair.

"Elsa is quite the storyteller," Charles said. "You can never believe a word she says unless it's about somebody else."

"Shush, Charles," Jimmy said, swatting his hand in the direction of my husband with such force that Charles did something he rarely did—shut up. Then Jimmy turned back to me: "I'm all ears."

Thunder clapped outside.

"All right then, chaps, let me tell you a story, a story where there are no gods but there are monsters."

It all started with my older brother Waldo and me having electric shock parties with the neighborhood children, one of our favorite games the summer I was about ten. We got on rather well for siblings other than arguing over the gramophone. I wanted to play music and practice my dancing and Waldo wanted to take it apart to see how it worked. Anyway, I would devote hours to twisting green, silk-covered wire around a coil and setting out bowls of water in a circle. We'd stick our bare feet in the bowls and whoever was at the ends would hold the connected brass handles while waiting for Waldo to surprise us with the exact moment of the shock. The anticipation was scrumptious and you should have heard us scream with delight. Like every child, I suppose we liked the thrill of it and never thought about any danger.

But then came the frog. We found the little green thing happily frolicking among the rocks beside Leathwaite Road, a tree-lined avenue in southwest London near Clapham Common where we lived for a while. Lovers would hide under the shady low branches for a stolen kiss or a little more, and we kids would stifle our giggles when we spied them so as not to be told to shoo. Waldo and I often found frogs and took them home to a tank that we'd filled with water and some rocks. This little guy, however, would have none of it and jumped right out of my hands as I was trying to pop him inside. We couldn't find him and Biddy ordered us both to bed despite our protestations. So in the morning after she and Shamus, our father, left us alone, we moved all the furniture until finally we spotted the tiny fellow now brown, crusty, and flat as paper behind the heavy coal box. Waldo suggested putting him in the kitchen sink and running some water to provide a proper funeral at pond. An hour later though, the tyke had puffed right up again and was jubilantly leaping all over the kitchen. What I never told anyone—because Biddy made me swear not to—was how Waldo proudly announced that it hadn't just been the water that had brought the little bugger back to life. He'd dipped in some wire. The frog, henceforth named Lazarus, had been treated to his own electric shock party.

If Biddy hadn't come home and seen it with her own eyes, Waldo might have gotten into puppets sooner, or maybe he dedicated his life to puppetry because of what happened later, I don't know. We didn't have that kind of brother-sister relationship when we got older. I did my own thing and he did his. But after Lazarus rose from his watery grave, Biddy sent him straight off to apprentice with a scientific instrument maker. She had her own plans already then, though I didn't find out about them till a good ten years later.

In fact, I had rather forgotten about the shocks and the frog. I mean, why would I think about any of that when I was twenty years old and living a carefree dream of singing and dancing and my first real notice as an actress, playing the small but crucial role of the Larva in the London premiere of *The Insect Play* by that acclaimed playwriting pair of Czech brothers Karel and Josef Čapek. It was at the Regent Theatre, darling Nigel Playfair was producer and director, and he had taken a liking to my performances at the Cave of Harmony which is why he was willing to take a chance on me. Jimmy, I'm sure you remember, Claude Rains played the Lepidopterist that so vexes the lead character, that sensitive drunken tramp, by his killing and collecting of us bugs. John Gielgud was in it, too, quite a cutie, as well as my dear friend Angela Baddeley who played a beetle. You kind of hope to get your first critical recognition playing Ophelia, but I didn't mind being a squiggly wormy thing. I received some of the biggest laughs by whining loudly about my hunger while chatting up the tipsy Mr. Tramp, and then the greatest gasp of horror when my doting daddy Mr. Fly—quite abiding by Mr. Darwin's dictum of survival of the fittest—killed the rather delightful Mrs. Cricket just so his darling daughter could have some supper. Then, of course, nature caught up with me when the Parasite called Mr. Tramp "Comrade" for being uncomfortable with so much "eat and be eaten" and then ate me. After all, as the line went: "Nature's table is set for all."

I was living on Doughty Street in Bloomsbury, still performing Sunday nights at the Harmony with darling Harold and dating a handsome White Russian whom I met at the 1917 Club in Soho. You might wonder what a White Russian was doing in a place like that, but it'd become a dull joint by 1923 and I guess maybe he enjoyed the attention he received from the rather downtrodden civil servants and low-level Labour Party stiffs who were curious about what it really was like living under communism. They held out great hope that the Russians would get it right so they could convince the British to kick out our king, though most would settle for a polite exile rather than the messy firing squad that bloodied up the Romanovs. My tender White Russian didn't like it that the Bolshies shot the children, though he wasn't all that fond of tsars and kings and queens either. Probably he just liked a more comfortable life in London rather than those wretched winters and famines while the Reds got their act together. Or maybe he was a spy. I never asked because what's the point? If he was any good at being a spy, he'd never tell me.

What got me going to the 1917 was that you could run into E.M. Forster or Herbert Wells—I had to dodge quite a few passes from that philanderer—or someone else quite fascinating like Chaim Weizmann for fiery long afternoon chats while downing a gin and tonic. But now it was just doughy-eyed puppies lamenting how little progress socialism was making here and how instead all the young people in London just seemed to want to have a gay old time now that the war was over and they had money again. To be truthful, that's all I wanted to do—the night club frolicking that Biddy detested—and I didn't need that much money to have a good time, especially with a White Russian. He provided all the inspiration I needed to be a convincing, self-absorbed and well-fed little larva.

As I recall, it was right after the first Sunday matinee of the play's run. I should have known something was up when just as I was removing my antenna, Biddy, always my toughest critic, showed up in my dressing room with Waldo, whom I hadn't seen since a very uncomfortable Christmastime supper—as atheists, my parents never actually would confess to celebrating the birth of Christ but it was one of the few times a year Biddy let Shamus smuggle in a roast pig's head to her strict vegetarian household. As per usual, she hadn't told me in advance that she'd be in the audience. She greeted me with kisses on both cheeks, hugged me tightly with that somewhat clumsy gesture of someone who does not hug often, and then declared I was "terrific."

Waldo, looking more nervous than I'd ever seen him, extended a hand and nodded. "Yes, simply terrific, Belsa." He swallowed my childhood nickname instead of actually saying it.

Biddy then launched into how she admired the ruthlessly anti-war, anti-capitalist satire of the play, her usual litany of how the world would be better if all people were equal and vegetarians. I, of course, was impatient to change out of the rather tight sheath that was my larva costume, suitable for undulating on a stage floor but with my breasts and hips wrapped tight and flat so as to be childlike, quite uncomfortable when standing and even more so when humoring verbose relatives. Biddy didn't have conversations. She gave speeches. Meanwhile Waldo stood silently behind her, his hands fidgeting in his pockets.

"Well, my dear Elsa, again you did splendidly with the Larva, but then you have had plenty of practice being petulant and demanding and despite my best efforts, spoiled," she added, with her typical lack of any motherly diplomacy. As she turned to leave, I could have sworn she muttered under her breath how my training under Isadora Duncan was going to waste. But whatever she said was not loud enough for me to point out that it was Isadora who abandoned us girls and that sending me to a privileged Paris dance academy at all was a rather uncommunist thing to do. Believe it or not, I can let things go when speaking to someone like Biddy for whom there is no dislodging of any idea once set firmly in her head.

As soon as Biddy had turned her back and was proceeding rapidly out the door, Waldo stepped forward and reached his arm out to shake my hand again.

"Waldo, darling, I'm just your sister, you needn't be so formal," I started but he shook his head.

"Come along, Waldo!" Biddy said loudly. "I am sure Elsa needs her rest after such a strenuous performance, and we have much work to do."

"Goodbye," Waldo said, his mouth collapsing into a big staged grin. He bowed slightly and then turned and followed Biddy out the door with all the enthusiasm of a recently scolded puppy.

This wasn't the Waldo I recalled from the wild mischief of our youth, but he was a grown adult so if he wanted to be wandering around still tied to Biddy's apron strings, there was nothing I could do, I told myself. No, what I needed was a little inspiration, a little harmony in my own cave before heading to the Cave of Harmony for my late-night song and dance. I didn't have a dinner date that night with the White Russian, but he hadn't seemed to mind before when I showed up with a stray bottle of champagne ready for some nibbles.

I transformed from silk larva into a red silk dress which I hoped might remind the White Russian of how much he enjoyed eating red caviar. Then I donned my new burgundy spring cape and a rather large and trusty black men's umbrella because a smart woman will always sacrifice a little style over risking getting her hair wet. Mine already tended to frizz electrically in the perpetual London fog.

But when I turned the bend towards the White Russian's flat, I saw a sight that made me yank myself back around the corner. Because who should be walking ahead of me but Biddy. I assumed it must just be some unlikely coincidence. Maybe she was taking a back cut to Oxford Street or one of her socialist comrades happened to live nearby, too cheap to pay a proper rent. I crept ahead and ducked into an alley where I could keep hidden and still have full view of her movements. But no, with that determined Biddy gait, she headed straight up to my White Russian's building, inside she went, and five minutes later reemerged with him at her side.

I rather liked the loins on that White Russian so I cannot say I was not a little disappointed in seeing my impromptu "dinner" canceled. But I was simply aghast at either of the two possibilities. Either Biddy was outright trying to match me up with any Russian, but since she was opposed to love and marriage that seemed less likely than the other. No, she must be paying him to spy on me. Given that she was rather tight with her money, that also made me wonder now about the quality of his caviar.

The rain was picking up, but I was determined to follow and confront them face to face with my utter disgust. Curiosity, though, made me want to see where they were going first, so when they ended up at the taxi stand at Piccadilly, I hopped right into a rattly new Mk 2 Super parked three cars behind and popped the driver an extra shilling to jump the line and follow. Through the rain, the cabbie paced, keeping just far enough back that I hoped Biddy wouldn't suss that she was being pursued. At first, traffic was sufficient to mask suspicion as we veered down Haymarket towards Trafalgar, then cut over along Pall Mall to St. James Street and skirted Green Park onto Knightsbridge, but once we hit Sloane Street, the taxi had to hold back. We crossed the Thames at Albert Bridge. By then, I began to wonder, Battersea Park stretching on my left, if I was returning to old familiar territory.

Once Biddy's taxi turned onto Leathwaite Road, I bade the driver stop just round the corner and watched from the window until my mother's cab pulled up outside a house about halfway down the block on the left. I paid the driver, tipping him nicely for his extra effort, and stepped out. As he drove away, I observed the White Russian emerge first and then take Biddy's hand to help her exit their own taxi with leisure. They appeared to be chatting quite animatedly, or, well, as usual Biddy was doing the talking, and the Russian only laughing. I wanted to think he was just being polite, but when I saw him kiss the hand of my anti-class-elitist mother, another idea took hold in my head. Maybe I should just tell Shamus and he'd grab a few mates and teach a fine lesson to my White Russian. But then Biddy refused to ever marry him in the first place, even to the point when as all London knows, my grandfather and uncles famously kidnapped and placed her in a private loony hospital for a long weekend. With such an effort to avoid a wedding vow, was it even cheating?

After I saw them mount the steps and enter, I started down the street, determined to pound down the door if necessary and give them my mind. The low-hanging trees that the lovers liked had grown a bit taller in the dozen years or more since we played in their shadows and now offered some shelter from the worst of the rain. It being May, a gray luminescence still glowed through the clouds even now just shy of eight o'clock, but a tiny creature paid the price for my old habit of never looking at my feet. A little way down the block I felt my boot descend on something soft and heard a panicked squeak. I lifted my foot quickly and observed that I had stepped on one of Lazarus's descendants. As I kneeled to check the poor fellow's condition, he leaped away.

I looked carefully but saw no more frogs on the pavement between me and the front steps of the red brick two-story Victorian row-house that Biddy and the Russian had disappeared into. All the curtains were pulled shut, and the only lights in the building shone from two attic windows at the very top.

I rang the bell several times before Waldo opened the door. He was wearing a white lab coat and his hair was wild and uncombed.

"Well, hello, dear brother, are you in on Biddy's affair, too, and what are you doing all dressed up as a surgeon? You look absolutely daft," I said, wanting impulsively to pat down his crinkly locks, but he was already grabbing me by the arm and yanking me into the dark house. He paused to look up and down the street before pulling the door shut.

"Now, now, such melodrama to cover up for our mother dallying with my lover," I continued, chuckling a bit madly because if nothing else, the whole prospect still seemed utterly absurd.

"If only you knew, Elsa," Waldo said. "If I tell Biddy that it was just a salesman at the door, you might still have time to get away."

"Better yet, tell her I'm a Bible salesman, and you know she'll run down the street right after me to debate the existence of God," I whispered out of respect to Waldo's anxiety. Or more likely, I hissed.

"Elsa, really, it's not what you think, but if you don't go away now, she'll pull you right smack into it," Waldo said.

“Who is it, Waldo?” Biddy yelled loudly from above. “Hurry up and get rid of them. We’ve work to do.”

“Just a salesman,” Waldo yelled back. “I’m on my way.”

“Work? Is that what she’s calling it?” I hissed again so close to his ear that he flinched. “And I’m not leaving until I talk to her. You won’t begrudge a daughter bidding farewell to her mother, Waldo, will you?”

Waldo gritted his teeth and shook his head.

“You, Elsa, are the most stubborn woman next to Biddy on this whole bloody planet,” he declared. “I suppose you aren’t going to be sensible and trust me for once and just leave.”

“Elsa, sensible?!”

Biddy’s cackling laughter filled the foyer as I looked past Waldo to see the shadowy figure of our mother standing on the stairs. She also was dressed in a white lab coat, though I could see the skirt of her tweed theatre suit peeking out underneath.

“Waldo, dear, welcome Elsa inside, take her coat and umbrella. Since she took all that trouble to follow me and Sergei, I suppose it’s time we share our little project with her. I mean, what harm can it cause? It’s doubtful anyone would believe her anyway if she told. Who knows? Maybe she’d even enjoy doing something to better the world rather than simply entertain it.”

“Project?! Is that what they call it these days?” I shouted back. Biddy still had a way of making my head boil back then. Like an able mechanic at a factory, she knew every lever to pull. Meanwhile I let Waldo fold up my umbrella and place it in the stand by the door and help me slip out of my coat. Freed of my wet outer garments, I headed up the stairs prepared to punch Biddy squarely in the jaw. Then Sergei appeared. I hate to say I froze and that I let him kiss me, but I was twenty and yet foolish and it was too easy to let his lips upon mine erase my suspicions.

“Darling Elsa,” he said with his thick accent. “You have nothing to be jealous. I am simply assisting your mother and brother with a mission. I wanted to tell you—indeed it vexed my heart to keep anything from you, my sweetheart—but it required the utmost secrecy. Yet now that you are here, my *lapochka*.”

“Oh, hell, if there’s anything I can’t stand it’s the sentimentality of lovers,” Biddy said, throwing up her arms. “Just come upstairs!”

We all toddled after her like obedient ducklings. As we approached the first floor, it was apparent that the place was indeed lit after all and brightly, and the thick curtains were fully intended to hide that fact. We followed Biddy to the right into what most likely had been intended as a large master bedroom with attached sitting room but had been adapted for another purpose. The first thing that struck me was the humming and croaking—the unmistakable music of frogs. And indeed a shelf on the far wall was lined with terrariums containing the same little tykes that we used to gather years ago. It dawned on me how lucky the one I stepped on actually was, because these fellows had a rather more dreadful sight to watch. On a big table in the center of the room were several of their dead relatives, spindly arms and fat legs stretched on pins, heads and bodies cut open with organs in view and partially removed and stacked around them like petite hors d'oeuvres.

Lined up also on the table were six bird cages surrounded by large diagrams, scattered papers, and several notebooks. Inside each cage was a wooden marionette—a king, a queen, an archbishop, a devil, a ballerina, and a mermaid strung up to the cage lids. That part was the least of any surprise as my brother had always expressed a fascination with puppetry. He'd carved quite a few when we were children, and we used to put on shows for the neighborhood kids and any adults we could talk into indulging us.

The room's walls were lined with more shelves and tables containing books, stacks of paper, tools, and medical instruments and pickled specimens in jars. The chamber was a mishmash of puppetry workshop and laboratory at the Royal College of Surgeons. At any rate, I felt backstage to some kind of drama.

Biddy, however, made a beeline for the one object that she was clearly most intent on me seeing. She picked up a foot-high jar and presented it like a model showing off a new Paris hat.

"Elsa, meet Eleanor Marx," she said.

In the jar was a human brain preserved in some kind of clear liquid. I wasn't any fool and immediately understood the implication. Much of Biddy's stature among our London revolutionary crowd came from her employment as the last typist to the youngest daughter of Karl Marx.

Those crazy communists had saved the brain of the daughter of Karl Marx.

Now the only question was what Biddy, Waldo and Sergei intended to do with a hunk of dead body tissue. Then I remembered Lazarus. But all they had was a brain, no matter how famous, and Eleanor's body was cremated twenty-five years ago in 1898, four years before I was born. Poor unhappy thing publicly was deemed a suicide after being betrayed by her lover Edward Aveling. Biddy, however, had fluctuated between commending her employer for choosing a most "unmessy" method of suicide in prussic acid and suspecting that she had been tricked into swallowing it by the scoundrel Aveling.

I turned to Sergei, thinking maybe he could clear up this part of the mystery, and saw a tear on his cheek.

"Elsa, we don't have much time. Papa Lenin is very ill." Sergei was now sobbing as he spoke and laid his head on my shoulder. Not used to seeing a grown man cry, especially one so shall we say "manly," I held him and stroked his dark hair.

"I don't understand, what does an old brain of a dead daughter of a revolutionary have anything to do with Vladimir Lenin's health or lack of?" I said.

"Only the hope to finally unite the workers of the world!" Biddy declared, setting the jar back on the shelf. "For when we place Eleanor's brain in a new body, we will have created the perfect successor for Lenin, a woman ready to lead the Soviet Union to become the first real bastion of communism in her father's vision. Once Europe and America see that nation's success under the very daughter of Karl Marx, workers and intellectuals will demand change. Utopia is nigh! We must fulfill the destiny begun in October 1917!

"But we must work fast. Lenin has a powerful enemy in Joseph Stalin. Sergei will tell you how that villain plots to be the next leader of the Soviet Union and how disastrous that would be to our world communist cause. He may parrot the words and say he admires his Comrade Lenin, but the man is brutal and simple and only cares about his own power."

Sergei stepped back from me now, wiping his tears.

"When Papa Lenin received the letter from your mother with her proposal, he knew his friends are now few and fewer every day while Stalin makes promises and eliminates any who stand in his way. That pig even had the audacity to lie to the Politburo that Papa Lenin gave him instructions personally to administer poison if his pain became too severe. But Stalin would never be able to challenge the daughter of Karl Marx. She would have the love of the Soviet people from the moment her feet touched ground at Moscow Station. So Papa Lenin asked me, his most loyal comrade and personal guard, to travel to England to assist and bring Eleanor Marx home. Then he can die in peace, knowing that his dream of Soviet Russia is safe."

Jimmy, Charles, you know that absolutely nothing leaves me speechless. I hate to say I share that trait with my mother. But I was caught between the utter absurdity of a twenty-five-year-old pickled brain and the memory of Lazarus the frog. I turned toward Waldo upon whom the success of the whole crazy plan seemed to depend.

"All right, Elsa, I know it all sounds absolutely nutty, but—" he said, heading towards one of the terrariums which contained a lone frog. He lifted the wire lid and scooped it out. The creature struggled in his hands as he presented it to me. "Take a look at this fellow's head. Behold, Lazarus II."

I bent down and saw black threaded stitches circling the top of the frog's head. I'm no scientist but I'd spent enough time around them at the 1917 to immediately suss the implication.

"You killed the little sod, took out his brain, and popped it back inside?"

"Not the same brain, but another frog's brain to completely mirror the experiment," Waldo replied, placing the frog back in the terrarium where it issued a loud croak. "I also preserved it for three months in the same saline solution as Miss Marx's brain. I gently attached wires from the new brain to the frog's nerve endings, submerged the body in water and applied electricity. Of course, it didn't work the first time, and dozens of times after, but we finally achieved success just after Christmas and that's when Biddy wrote to Premier Lenin. What we discovered is that the body has to be freshly dead, the heart not stopped beating for more than a few hours."

"Elsa, I know you're thinking that the whole thing's batty," Biddy interrupted. "If it makes you feel better, we saved Eleanor's brain originally just for scientific study. Coroners don't make that much of a salary, so it's well known that for a little cash, they'll slip you an organ, and sew the body back up with nary a word. Poor Eleanor was going to be cremated and she had no living relatives who were likely to inspect her remains before they headed into the oven."

A frog was one thing, but was I really beginning to believe this "experiment" could work to regenerate a human body? Yes, of course, I'd read Mary's *Frankenstein*, but I always viewed it, like you, Jimmy, as just a moralistic horror tale—arrogant Man meddling with God's laws of nature and all that nonsense. Still I'd had a natter or few with a biologist or a doctor, so I knew science was advancing rapidly in extraordinary ways.

"And now all you require is a freshly dead body?" I said. "What are you going to do, murder someone for the great communist cause?"

"Oh, Elsa, you silly girl, of course not," Biddy said, shaking her head. "I took a collection from our comrades in the Communist Party of Great Britain—they paid for this house and every piece of equipment we've needed thus far. Sergei's here to pick up the cash and pay a visit tonight to the Battersea coroner. I was leaving your *Insect Play* when I received word that he just received a cadaver that sounds more than suitable. It's a sad fact, as you know, that young working women are always dying of foul play in London, and not all of them have kin who can afford a proper burial."

Somewhere in the house a clock struck nine loudly. I'd have to dial a taxi soon or I wouldn't make it to the Harmony in time for tonight's show. At this point, I realized I was going to phone Harold and tell him to make apologies to the audience that I was ill. The company had done without me on a few occasions before, and he knew I wouldn't skive off for any casual dilly-dallying. No, I was going to accompany Sergei to Battersea Mortuary to pick up the body and then watch my brother electroshock the brain of Eleanor Marx back to life to lead the world communist revolution.

As you may have predicted, Sergei wanted instead to drop me off at the Harmony, or if not there, home. He had some silly idea of me being a typical woman, a blushing flower who couldn't handle being around dead bodies.

Me?! Yes, I know you find that amusing, Charles. But you'll need to stop laughing if you want to hear the rest of the story.

Finally, Biddy threw up her arms and said there was no time to be wasted arguing with me. And Waldo chimed in that he could use another assistant in the operation. It was all in the family now, for better or worse, other than my White Russian, who had turned out to be a Red Russian after all. He was fun for a romp, so to speak, but I was not ready for a husband and he was heading back to Russia anyway if the experiment went as planned. Besides, as Charles knows, even if Sergei had been my fiancé, I wouldn't be taking his orders, and this little test of his character already was making me considerably less fond of him.

As it turned out, the Communist Party of Great Britain had also purchased a car. A taxi wouldn't do for the purpose of discreetly transporting a body, as Biddy pointed out. By this point, Sergei had lost any desire to speak and I could sense he was less worried about my delicate nature than quite angry to have a companion foisted on him for this gruesome task. We weren't in the car long before I ascertained why. The mortuary was next to the Battersea police station by the Thames, but instead of turning left towards the Albert Bridge once we hit the southwest corner of Battersea Park, Sergei turned right.

When I protested, he said only two words: "Short cut" and looped in through an open park gate. I wondered that the entrance was not locked so late and then remembered it still hadn't gone ten. We drove along a muddy road past dark trees and through incessant rain until we reached the edge of the lake which in sunlight and better weather would have been full of rowboats and lovers in straw hats. Then Sergei drove off the path onto the lawn behind a copse of foliage and turned off the ignition.

"You," he growled. "Stay put."

"Sergei darling, you're scaring me a little," I said, because he was.

"If you're going to come along when you are not invited, my lapochka, you need to learn to take orders," he said. "In Russia, women are comrades but they respect a man's word."

He glared at me, pulled his cap tight on his forehead, reached for a satchel in the backseat, and then stepped out into the rain. I waited until he was out of sight among some trees and then got out of the car myself to follow. And yes, I took my big umbrella, because if he found me back at the car soaking wet he'd know that I disobeyed his order. I thought I had lost him in the shadows and the rain, but then I spied a flash of light deep among the trees and a woman under an umbrella a good deal daintier than mine with a lantern in her hand. Sergei embraced her and they kissed.

We'd never had any agreement that we would not see other people, but nonetheless the whole evening had been shock upon shock. So he wasn't having an affair with my mother but another woman? And he liked her so much that he couldn't bear not stopping for a snuggle on the way to a mortuary? Obviously Papa Lenin wasn't his most beloved after all.

I should have realized that I was jumping again to a way too easy explanation, but I remind you I was but twenty—streetwise though hardly immune to jealousy. Just as I was about to pop out of the bushes and reveal to his lover that she was not his only paramour, Sergei lifted his hands from her waist to her neck. The movement was so rapid that the poor thing couldn't scream for help should there even be a guard patrolling this part of the park so deep in the greenery and in the pouring rain. I watched aghast as she struggled at first, clawing at his arms without success, even kicking at his legs. But I'd seen his muscles firsthand in the buff so I knew she had no chance.

Nor would I have any chance if he saw that I had seen him. His mission was quite clear now, not the one that my vegetarian pacifist mother intended. Biddy would have never condoned murder, and Waldo spent jail time during the Great War for his claim to be a conscientious objector. Sergei wasn't playing by the rules, and some innocent girl was paying the price of her very life for their idealistic scheme. As for me, the only sensible thing to do was to get back to the car as fast and quietly as I could before

Sergei disposed of me, too. As I scurried through the rain, thankful that wet leaves silenced my steps, it occurred to me that if he returned without me, he could so easily lie that he convinced me to let him drop me at the Harmony after all. So consumed with the cause, Biddy might even have been relieved.

I waited in the passenger seat about ten minutes until Sergei finally emerged from the trees, the body in his arms covered by a dark blanket that must have been in the satchel unless the unfortunate lady had hoped for more than a kiss in the grass. He placed it in the backseat and then got back in the driver's seat and turned to me.

"The coroner felt anxious about meeting at the mortuary, felt here in the dark would be more discreet," he said.

"That bears some logic," I said, adding "Messy business." If I wasn't a little saucy, I figured he'd be suspicious.

We drove back to the house on Leathwaite Drive with me prattling on about some backstage gossip among my fellow actors. Of course, the gears of my mind were all spinning. On one hand, I had seen a woman murdered right before my very eyes and by my very own lover. On the other, I had to tell my mother and hope she had the sense to abandon her noble cause and call Scotland Yard. If Sergei was this comfortable with killing, I had to wonder what more he would do for his Papa Lenin.

When we arrived back at the house, Biddy was keeping watch beneath the awning outside the front door. Sergei stepped out of the car, and she returned a hand signal to give the all-clear. When he went around the car and opened the passenger door for me, I wanted to laugh and say "such a bloody gentleman"—you know me—but danger gave me new common sense. I opened my umbrella, slipped out of the car, headed for the house, and after hooking my coat up in the foyer, I went straight upstairs in the hope of catching Waldo before Sergei carried the body in.

When I reached the frog room, I found it empty. However, I heard footsteps and other clatter above. Waldo must be in the attic. I spied another smaller set of stairs on the other side of the hallway and sprinted up them. Upon emerging, I realized that the room downstairs was no more than a research space. Here was the actual laboratory, or maybe better put, the stage for the strange production that was about to unfold.

The walls up to the rafters were lined with multicolored tubes and wires—red, blue and green. In the center of the room sat two tables. On one stood the jar that contained Eleanor Marx's brain and scattered paperwork—assumedly Waldo's experiment notes. On the other, a large metal operating table, was a white ceramic tub with low edges just the right size for a woman's body. More wiring and tubes extended underneath to a generator and across the floor hooking into the wall fixtures. The room was like a giant octopus, though with a hundred, maybe a thousand tiny stringy legs. At the far wall was a clear patch of wood floor with a series of levers, and that was where Waldo was poised, deep in concentration making various adjustments with what looked like pliers.

"Oh, Elsa, you're back," he said, looking up, his eyes covered by protective goggles and a surgeon's mask around his neck. "Can you hand me that screwdriver over by the door?"

I picked up the tool he was motioning towards from a table full of tools and medical instruments and started in his direction when he yelled: "Be careful! Don't step on any of the wires!"

I aimed my eyes down at my feet, tiptoeing carefully.

"Waldo, I need to talk to you," I said.

"Can it wait, Elsa? I need to be ready to proceed as soon as your Russian gent brings up the body."

"No," I said, and now right in front of him, whispered, "Sergei didn't get the body from the coroner. He murdered some poor woman in Battersea Park right in front of my very eyes."

Waldo froze. We might not have been close, but he knew that I don't lie.

Well, not about anything really important, Charles.

Then he buried his head in his hands and shook his head.

"This is what I was afraid of, that somebody was going to get hurt," Waldo said. "I figured it was likely to be Biddy or me."

"You've got to talk to Biddy, talk some sense into her," I said.

"Talk what sense into me?!" Biddy said loudly from the top of the stairs.

We both turned, as she pranced into the room, obviously practiced at watching her feet to avoid the wires. Behind her, Sergei entered with the body in his arms. The blanket was now removed, the body disrobed and naked. From the poor woman's face and perky breasts, she looked to be about my age. She had curly dark hair and thick brows—some attempt perhaps to match the look of Eleanor? I'd only seen my mother's employer in a photo kept on the mantel in every flat where we lived as children. Without clothes, her pale demeanor—no doubt enhanced by her deceased state—and the remnants of rouge on her cheeks gave no clue to her class or biography. Maybe she'd been naked already in the car. Under the blanket who could tell?

Sergei carried the girl's corpse, maneuvering carefully on the toes of his boots through the maze of wires. He then spread the body out in the ceramic tank. The display of tenderness churned my stomach. He stroked her cheek and brushed her hair away from her eyes. By now Waldo was frozen in fear. After all, Sergei was all muscle and Biddy was all Biddy. It was going to be up to me.

"Biddy…Mother," I said. "Please reconsider. Look at this poor girl."

"Yes, unfortunate dear," Biddy said, shaking her head. "If I could have prevented her from this ghastly end, but that's the reason we need a world without haves and have nots, where men view women as comrades, not as objects, not as chattel to be possessed and then violently discarded. But she will have a new life, bringing hope to all other women. She won't be fooled by love like dear Eleanor was the first time around. She will be wiser, stronger, a leader to make her father proud."

Sergei stepped back out of the wired labyrinth and was standing next to Biddy. He'd shown no affection to me since we'd returned. He just stared stonily in my direction, as if daring me to speak any more.

"No, you don't understand, Mother," I said. "Sergei didn't take your money and bribe the coroner. I saw him murder this woman before my very eyes. Your great experiment is already responsible for the death of an innocent."

Biddy stared at me. Waldo now was visibly shaking. Sergei reached into his coat and pulled out a black revolver which he pointed at the side of Biddy's head.

"My dear lapochka and clever clogs Waldo, if this procedure doesn't take place tonight as planned, I will shoot your mad, mad mother as dead as the lady before you," the Blood Red Russian said. "Waldo, you said the experiment only works when the body is fresh. How many frogs died before you figured that out? Already tens of thousands of men and women have died fighting. What is one more life for the greater good of the Soviet Union?!"

"Premier Lenin specifically instructed…" Biddy began. Even with a gun at her head, I was relieved to see she was at heart a diehard pacifist. But despite all my complaints about her, I didn't want to see her become a dead one.

"Quiet, Biddy!" Sergei yelled. Biddy shut up, but her eyes shot daggers. "Papa Lenin," he laughed then, a string of deep guttural guffaws. "Papa Lenin's hands aren't so clean as you think, my naïve British comrades. But I am not here for Papa Lenin. A man's tears win him the confidence of women so easily. No, Papa Lenin never received your letter. General Secretary Stalin intercepted it as he does all communications to the Kremlin. He also was quite entranced by your plan. He has a wife, Nadezhda, whom he loves very much. But if he took a new bride, the daughter of Karl Marx, then when Lenin dies—which will be soon—his victory will be assured not just in Mother Russia. Communists around the world will rally around him and his bride until all of Europe is a worker's utopia. The union of Stalin and Marx."

By now, Biddy's face had turned quite pale. Stalin was as much her nemesis as the King of England, maybe more.

"Waldo, cancel the experiment," Biddy said. "That's an order from your mother."

"Waldo, if you don't carry on, I repeat myself," Sergei said, "I will shoot your mother in the head, then I will shoot your sister. No, while you watch, I will take some of the instruments you have laid out here and remove her breasts and every organ inside until she is dead. While you watch. And listen to her screams. And then finally I will kill you, also slowly, maybe using your own electric shock devices. And then I will send to Russia for another scientist who will follow your notes and complete the experiment. Do you understand, Waldo? Nod if you do."

I looked back at Waldo. For a long moment, he stood frozen, his shaking now stopped, but eyes glazed in shock. Then he nodded.

I saw Biddy take a deep swallow and nod as well. She might have given up her own life for the cause, but listening to Sergei describe the cruel ends he had planned for her children had clearly scared her.

"Elsa?"

I nodded, too. What else could I do? He had us right where he wanted us. And somewhere thousands of miles away in the Kremlin, I imagined Joseph Stalin with his thick mustache lighting a big fat cigar and grinning, too.

For the next few hours, Sergei stood sentinel, his revolver pointed at Biddy's head. After a while he pulled up a couple of wooden chairs from the corner. Maybe he took mercy on making an old woman stand or maybe he wanted to save his energy. Killing a woman and hauling her body had to be somewhat exhausting. I wondered what was going to keep him from shooting us all anyway once the operation was completed and he could whisk Eleanor Marx off to Russia. Or worse, if it didn't work.

To keep my mind from macabre musings, I concentrated on helping Waldo prepare the experiment. He assigned me the task of wrapping thick white bandages around the body, "to protect it from electrical burns," he said. Meanwhile, he delicately cut an incision round the dead woman's skull with a bone saw. Once the top was removed like a fancy hat, he soaked up any blood that splashed onto the face with a sponge and delicately excised the current brain. Then he removed Eleanor's brain from its jar, attached some wires to its base and placed it inside the skull cavity, using a long pointy tool with a hook to attach the wiring to the nervous system as he had described previously. I tried not to watch that part too carefully, one, because the bandage-wrapping required concentration, and two, because I didn't understand how any of the science part worked anyway. It wasn't as if I needed to learn to reproduce the experiment. This was Waldo's talent, and I have to admit I was somewhat proud of him. Bringing dead revolutionaries or indeed anyone back from the grave seemed like quite an achievement.

If it worked.

Once I was done with the bandaging, Waldo proceeded to attach wires to the rest of the body until it was hard to see the bandages for all the mishmash of multicolored wires. I handed him tools upon request and obeyed whatever minor orders he gave me. "Hold this in place, Elsa." "Twist that blue wire slightly to the right."

Waldo inspected the body from head to toe, nodding and mumbling "check" and "yes." Finally he looked over at Sergei.

"Set to go but I need water. Can I send Elsa down to fetch a few buckets?"

Sergei grunted "da," and Waldo told me where the buckets were stored in the pantry. I got the impression not much cooking had taken place in that kitchen. I made several trips up and down the stairs lugging buckets of water, which Waldo then poured into the tank until the body was slightly submerged. Each time I reached the top of the stairs, Sergei would glare at me, though always keeping the pistol pointed at Biddy. I spread my lips into my sweetest smile just to annoy him.

The clock struck midnight, almost too appropriate for a grisly venture such as ours, and Waldo gave the go-ahead that it was time to commence.

"I need you to stay far back, Elsa," Waldo said. "I hate to say it, but you'd better go by the door with Sergei and Biddy."

I nodded. When I got there, Sergei kicked the chairs down the stairs and insisted that I stand in front so he could "keep an eye on" me.

"All right, everybody ready?" Waldo asked.

"No more wasting time, get on with it," Sergei said. I guess keeping a gun on someone's head for two hours can make even a big brute like him impatient.

Waldo flipped some switches, and the wires and tubes all around us began to sputter and flash. It was rather amazing that an ordinary house could sustain such power, I thought absently while waiting to see what would happen next. Waldo had mumbled something about the proximity of the Battersea Power Station and building extra generators such as the one underneath the operating table.

At first, all the activity happened on the walls, but then the floor began to shake and rattle as the current moved in one tremendous wave into the body. Sparks flew from the water in the tank and the body began to twitch, then tremble, thumping against its edges. I could see why Waldo wanted the bandages; smoke was rising until a small cloud hovered above. The momentum built until the water was bubbling and spurting sparks like a miniature fireworks spectacle.

Once most of the water had either splashed out or perhaps boiled down, Waldo pulled the levers back down and went to inspect the body.

"Well," Sergei said. "Is she?"

"We need to wait a few minutes to see," Waldo said. I could imagine he was nervous, knowing that lack of success was probably even more of a certain death sentence. He motioned for me. I glanced at Sergei, and he made a gesture with his non-gun-bearing hand that I could go.

I tiptoed through the wires and joined Waldo by the tank. We both stared in, waiting, watching, not sure what we wished for.

First her fingers moved. Just the right index and middle and the slightest tap. Then the left thumb did the same.

She opened her eyes and Waldo smiled.

"She's alive," he said, then shouted, "She's alive!"

Sergei's eyes widened but he stayed stiff as if waiting for more confirmation. Biddy actually grinned, seeming to forget for a moment that she had a gun to her skull.

In the tank, the newly awakened creature tried to stretch and flex her arms and legs as if testing their abilities. Restrained by the wires, her eyes communicated confusion.

"There, there," Waldo said, his voice soft like a doting father to a baby. "Elsa, help me loosen the wires so she can sit up. It's safe to touch them now. I turned off all the power to the generator."

He handed me some wire cutters and we both moved quickly, snipping, pulling away the strands and letting them fall into the tub, slide down onto the floor. We thought of speed, not of the mess we were making. We cared only about this new being, fully grown and yet like a child whom we had just brought into the world, of setting her free from her umbilical cords and seeing who she truly might be.

This "She" watched our every move, seemingly aware of our good intentions, patiently testing each limb as we liberated it. She lifted her head first slightly, and then as Waldo clipped the last tendril to her torso, she started to sit. It took her several tries, as if she knew to take each movement slowly. Or maybe this brain, after so many years asleep, was becoming accustomed to an unfamiliar new body further hampered by the bandages. I empathized with her from my own tight wrapping as the Larva, but I was only required to crawl on stage. Indeed, when she finally did sit up, her eyes focused on her arms, stretching them to their limits, twisting them side to side, bending her elbows.

Finally she flexed her legs, indicating she was ready to attempt to stand.

"No need to rush, let us help you," Waldo said. "Elsa, take one arm, and I'll take the other."

I approached her arm slowly, and then sensing she understood, I gripped it gently but firmly. Waldo and I helped her turn her waist and lift her legs off the low edges of the tub until she was facing outwards. Then a slight heave of her arms and her bottom slipped over its edge and her feet onto the floor. She looked at me as if she recognized something familiar, reached out and touched my hair with an innocent curiosity. It was then I fully noticed that the combination of moisture and static electricity had made her own frizz out to a wild state and on her right side, I saw a white streak, bleached perhaps from the sheer volume of power transmitted into her body.

Waldo was absolutely giddy with excitement. I hadn't seen him grin so much since we were children and he'd had a particularly scrumptious chocolate or…resurrected a frog. I almost forgot Sergei and his gun waiting to carry away this progeny of ours, for by now I was as charmed by her as if she were my own daughter. Apparently Biddy had forgotten the close proximity of cold metal, too, because she launched into one of her speeches.

"Welcome back to the world," Biddy declared loudly, commanding all our attentions. Our girl drew her hand away from her hair and turned for the first time towards my mother and Sergei.

"In the spirit of your rebirth, I rename you after the most important day of the year for the international worker. For you will bring a new spring for communism. Behold, my comrades, May."

"Welcome, May," I said, approving for once of a decision by my mother. I wanted to kiss May on both cheeks and hug her tightly, but I sensed

May's body tighten. I felt a pang of regret as she stepped away from me and Waldo.

The distance was only a few yards, but May moved slowly, stiffly, still unused to her legs, her mobility hampered by the bandages.

"She needs a comb through her hair, but I did well, didn't I?" Sergei said. I recognized the self-satisfied smirk that arrogant men make when they take responsibility for the smallest aspect of someone else's accomplishment, usually a woman's. "Look at her eyes, her brow, her lips. She could be a twin sister to Eleanor Marx. To think, I found her waiting tables in a coffee house."

When he said the name, May paused. It seemed logical that a brain unused for so long wouldn't remember everything all at once, but May's reaction surely indicated the triggering of some memory.

"I admit I look forward to presenting her to Stalin," Sergei went on, rapt in his reverie. "After he thanks me with a great big bear hug, he will pop open a bottle of the finest vodka. Then a hero's parade through Red Square. Well, after Lenin has passed. First, a funeral like none the world has seen, then a wedding."

By now, May was standing right in front of Sergei, tilting her head first to the right and then to the left. She was studying him, weighing him in her mind. I'd never heard him talk so much, boasting about what Stalin would do for him, a position on the Politburo, or maybe a general. The caviar, the women. He seemed to have forgotten that he'd killed a woman just a few hours ago, much less that she now had an exceptional brain. And if he didn't, well, all I can say is May, scarce minutes from her electric womb, already had the eyes of a woman who would not suffer a chauvinist murderer. Maybe we should send her to Stalin after all.

May straightened her head. Then in one quick birdlike motion, she twisted her neck and leaned torso and face forward at Sergei. She opened her mouth and let out what I can only describe as the longest, shrillest combination of a hiss and a shriek I have heard in my entire life. The only thing it reminded me of was the horrible sound made by the nasty swans at Regent Park, except ten times louder.

Sergei stumbled back as if hit by a stormy gust on the Brighton shore, the kind that can sweep you off your feet and out to sea. May followed Sergei, continuing to emit her shattering scream. He tripped and fell, then scrambled back up, pointing the gun towards May with a confused expression on his face. Clearly he was unused to being challenged by a woman. I savored the chaos that must be transpiring in his brain. If he shot her, what would happen to all that power and glory that he imagined Stalin was going to bestow upon him?

May quieted again, circling and stalking her prey silently now like a lioness on the hunt. He shuffled in our direction, so Waldo and I took the opportunity to scramble around the table and towards a free Biddy and the stairs. I didn't know how this duel was going to resolve, but I was betting on May. She had Sergei backed into the far wall against the switches. His eyes shuffled frantically, the pistol shaking in his hand, confusion clearly short-circuiting his simple brain.

With Sergei cornered, May shrieked again, stretched out her arms and pushed him. As he fell back onto the levers, he grasped one in an effort to steady himself, and I heard a sizzle of electricity switching back on. In a parallel movement, he waved the gun towards May's head and pulled the trigger, survival now trumping ambition. But the bullet missed and ricocheted into one of the now reactivated cathode tubes on the wall, a burst of flame rising from its shattered remains.

As the two struggled, Sergei fired more shots, all missing May. She had the advantage of position and it looked also like her electrical birth had endowed her with strength above and beyond an ordinary woman. As strong as I knew Sergei to be, he was like a flailing duck at the slaughter once her hands were around his neck. However, the flames now were spreading along the entire wall and onto the floorboards, making it harder to see. Smoke wafted in our direction, and Waldo had started to cough.

Then the epic battle was over. May straightened and turned back towards us, Sergei's body in a heap behind her feet. She had stopped screaming, and I could see the bandages had ripped open on her chest in the struggle, her breasts and white silhouette reminding me of the Delacroix painting, *La Liberté guidant le peuple.*

"We have to save May," Biddy said.

Waldo looked pleadingly in my direction, torn between his creation and his fear of the rapidly spreading fire.

"Come, May," he called. "Step carefully."

May started towards us, but scarcely had she taken two steps when the decision was made for us. The floor collapsed beneath her. As she fell, we saw her make a last grasp at the boards and extend her hand, but all gave way too fast for any of us to run forward. If one of us had, surely we would have plummeted also.

So instead we did the only sensible thing. We ran down the stairs and out the front door into the rain. The bell of a fire truck clanged in our direction, and several neighbors gathered around, throwing blankets over our shoulders and beckoning us across the street to safety in case of flying embers or if the house collapsed altogether. We stood and watched silently as the firemen battled the flames. Somehow they prevented the blaze from spreading down the row, perhaps aided by the rain, but by the morning, all that was left behind the brick were blackened beams and piles of ash.

It was only then that I remembered the poor frogs.

We all assumed that the creature we called May had perished in the fire, and Biddy, who usually could not let any topic drop, never said another word about the matter. Waldo abandoned his electrical studies, and along with his wife Muriel, founded the Whanslaw-Lanchester Marionettes, which became quite famous in puppet circles.

However, almost a year later, I was heading home from the Harmony very late on an April night, a young Irish actor friend on my arm. We decided to cut through Covent Garden. Most of the buskers had cleared out by that hour, except a pair of women, one playing what sounded from a distance to be a Mendelssohn concerto on a slightly out-of-tune violin and the other with a basket of flowers. My Irish friend insisted he wanted to buy me one, and giddy from a few glasses of champagne, we ran over.

The older violin-player was clearly a gypsy, black hair with streaks of gray, dressed in colorful shawls and bangles. The younger woman was also garbed like a gypsy, but her skin was lily pale. She had frizzy dark hair, and when she raised her head, I saw a white streak. Her eyes were empty, cloudy white, blind.

My Irish friend was still laughing and gay, but I put a finger to my lips to shush him, afraid he might say my name and she would remember it. I took the flower from her hand and placed a shilling in her basket.

The old gypsy stopped playing and bowed her head slightly. "Thank you kindly, mam," she said in a thick Romani accent. Then nodding to her companion and patting her on her head, she added: "Alas, she is quite mad, blind and mad, but she's very kind to an old woman."

"Friend," May said, grinning. "Friend, good."

I never told Biddy. I didn't want Biddy to get any crazy ideas about how she could make this poor thing remember a life she'd probably rather forget. If this and those terrible shrieks were the extent of her vocabulary, I had my doubts that much remained of Eleanor Marx. After all, her brain had been left pickled in a jar for twenty-five years. Or worse, one of Stalin's spies might find out and kidnap her to a more miserable fate. By then, Lenin had passed away, allegedly from a catastrophic stroke, and London's would-be revolutionaries were all convinced that Stalin had poisoned him.

I never saw May again. Who knows? Maybe I was mistaken and she just resembled May, or perhaps the perfect woman with the brain of Eleanor Marx is selling flowers somewhere in London.

Boisea trivittata

One insect slowly crept up the window glass. Another clung to the lavender wall, its six legs splayed. A third rode the computer screen. Little things, perhaps half an inch in length—black with two angled red stripes down their backs.

Ellie watched them go slowly about their business, whatever that was, then pause. And after a few minutes, they would commence wandering again until the next pause.

Where were they going?

Did they even know?

More importantly, where did they come from? She didn't ever remember seeing bugs of this kind before. Then a week after Christmas they started appearing—first one, then two—not enough to worry her. Now she was seeing an average of five to six inside the house every day.

Another insect crawled on her desk next to her keyboard. She grabbed the jam jar she kept at the ready, popped off the lid, and positioned the vessel sideways in the bug's path. It inspected the foreign object with its twitching antennae stretched in a wide V, and then strolled right in. She used the lid to scoop the pair from the screen into the jar as well and quickly sealed it. Then she headed down the stairs, opened the front door, popped the lid, and jettisoned its inhabitants out into the frigid morning air.

Boxelder bugs. A "*nuisance*" insect, or so a Google image search for the black and red insects informed her. They didn't spread disease like roaches. They didn't bite or sting. However, if you squished them, according to online articles, they secreted a dye that stained wood and other light-colored surfaces.

That was fine, because she didn't want to kill anything so completely harmless anyway. Vacuuming was recommended, but sucking them into a bag of dust to die slowly seemed even more cruel.

Boxelder bugs ate the leaves of a tree called a boxelder maple which apparently had the largest range of any American maple from the east coast to California and from Alberta to southern Mexico and Guatemala—so pretty much most of North America. Ellie had two Japanese maples in her front yard, but didn't remember any more maples of any kind—just oaks and pines and a dogwood. As she scrolled through the online photos, though, she observed that young boxelders' leaf configurations resembled the trefoil of poison ivy. Last summer she'd noticed plants like that growing among the pine straw, English ivy, pokeweed, and other assorted viney trespassers beyond the grass at the rear of her unkempt back yard. At one time, she'd really liked having a big garden, but at one time the half-acre was covered with grass and she had a husband who helped. And a dog.

From Ellie's sporadic online research, boxelder bugs didn't just eat maple leaves or seeds, but cherries, plums, peaches, apples, strawberries, grapes, and grass. The only fruit she had on hand was a bowl of apples, but she never saw any bugs in it. She did find a bug crouched on a garbanzo bean in a pan of leftover vegetarian chili in the kitchen.

One "fact," however, troubled her. She verified that they showed up on and in houses, but in spring or fall. No mention of winter. Maybe an unseasonably warm December and early January had awakened them early, but for the past two weeks temperatures had barely risen above freezing.

"...the Federal Security Institute has created a new containment unit in Visalia, California, that is projected to hold up to five hundred internees. The first buses are expected to arrive this afternoon..."

"Good morning, Miss Ellie," Jim said, stepping down from a ladder, paint-brush in hand, and lowering the volume on the portable radio. At over six feet tall, the bearded man towered over her five-foot-two frame, though his muscles were clearly compromised by beer and burgers.

"Good morning, Jim," Ellie said, wincing at the "Miss."

She shut the door quickly before he had a chance to reply and heard him switch the radio back up.

"The Prime Interrogator is headed to San Antonio to meet with the administrators of the Alamo Containment Facility..."

The announcer's voice faded to a metallic drone, thankfully undecipherable, as she headed upstairs.

....

Back in her office, Ellie tried to concentrate on work. She was behind on several editing jobs. She needed them to pay the mortgage and Jim, not to mention buying food and utilities. Sometimes she wondered why she was having home improvements done, but she'd been planning to do the work this year. She was tired of living in a house with peeling yellow paint and outdated green shutters. Sticking to plans was important.

Focus, Ellie, focus. Close your eyes. Count to ten and go!

Ellie reopened the file for the ninth chapter of a book by a Cambodian woman who escaped the killing fields of the Khmer Rouge and then returned years later to interview survivors of their reign of terror. The woman had a natural gift for weaving words together and once Ellie got back into the text, the passionate rendering inspired some kind of trance of productivity.

Zizzzzzzzzzzzzzzz.

Ellie looked up and sighed. A boxelder bug was hovering helicopter-like right under the shade of her desk lamp. Its body pointed upwards, completely vertical, and it lifted its wings to reveal a surprisingly shiny, fully red abdomen.

The boxelder bugs didn't seem to fly often. From three weeks of observation, she determined that they mostly only flew around light. When you're a bug, light might just be the most exciting thing ever, she guessed. Flies certainly seemed to think so.

Before she could make any attempt at capture, the creature dropped down behind her desk. Or so she thought. It was gone so fast, she wasn't precisely sure.

....

Luckily Ellie looked before picking up the water glass on her desk and saw the boxelder bug clinging to the inside two inches above the liquid before she took a swallow.

Her insect observation, however, was interrupted by the sudden rev of an engine outside. She looked out the window and saw a black Humvee, the third tonight, patrolling her neighborhood in the dark.

Ellie carried the jar into the bathroom and flicked the bug onto the floor, poured the rest of the water down the sink. It fell onto its back. Unlike cats, boxelder bugs never seemed to land on their feet. She stared at its frantically wriggling legs, then realized that her fascination was probably cruel. She squatted down to flip it over.

When she dumped the bugs outside, did they land on their backs, too? She hoped they were able to right themselves more easily with dirt and leaves and other yard refuse to climb onto, rather than a slick tile surface. But it still must be strange to go from a well-lit window screen or a mirror or the side of a cup to the great outdoors.

If they stayed inside, they'd surely starve—or drown, given their attraction to water. She had found several floating dead on their backs in the kitchen sink when she left dishes soaking overnight. Once a live one was clinging to the edge of the toilet, and she felt guilty when she flushed. But what could she do?

Stupid boxelder bug crawling into the toilet.

....

"Temperatures hit record lows up and down the coast last night. If you're in the nation's capital, there's an ice storm warning in effect with the storm expected to move north and develop blizzard-like conditions. In the south, it's just more clear and cold. Out west, look for the smog count to hit record highs in the big cities..."

The radio blared as Ellie, head groggy from sleeping almost to noon, crept out to the mailbox huddled in her leather jacket. Why hadn't she worn her long coat instead? Another day of clear cold Southern winter. It only warmed up when it rained and the last time had been more than two weeks ago.

She gave a quick wave to Jim, who was deep into removing a cracked pane of glass, the replacement piece leaning on the brick wall beside him.

"Whoa, little lady, you got that heat steaming full blast," Jim said as she passed him on her way back to the front door.

"Like the radio said, it's freezing," she said, not hiding her irritation.

"That's what's attracting them bugs," Jim said, gesturing to a quintet of boxelder bugs on the window sill beneath the empty frame. "Just like rats, when the weather gets cold, they try to come inside. If you give them a way."

He removed his work glove and swiped the bugs away with it, laughing, and then stomped his right boot down on top of them.

"You didn't need to kill them," she said, shivering.

"Just some stupid bugs," Jim chuckled.

"Why kill something that doesn't cause any harm?" Ellie asked.

"Got that glass replaced and I'll start glazing tomorrow, should get all the windows done in a couple of days," Jim said, returning to all-business. He had a knack for knowing when he was pushing it, probably because he also needed the money.

"Okay, thanks," Ellie said, nodding her head in his direction and making a beeline for the door.

....

Ellie watched as a boxelder bug slowly climbed up her computer screen. Their survival skills seemed to be improving, she thought. While it used to be easy to scoop them up into the jar, now they more often would avoid the lid and amble away.

She managed to knock this one into the jar, but it immediately attempted to scale back up the inside, meaning she had to clamp the lid down quickly, hampering her earlier strategy to capture more than one at a time.

Was that the sound of fireworks somewhere in her neighborhood? Or gunshots? Why weren't any dogs barking?

....

"Violence rocked the streets of Detroit again today, and police were forced to use tear gas and water cannons to subdue the protestors. At least two hundred and fifty arrests were made, police said."

Jim switched off the radio when Ellie approached and surprised her by bringing up the boxelder bugs again.

"I don't know if you know, honey, but those bugs are crawling all over the back wall of your house, especially in the cracks," he said. "But they should go away as soon as I fill up the spaces with caulk and apply the primer. They don't like fresh paint."

"Okay, thanks," Ellie asked, biting her tongue at his use of "honey" and unnerved by the unexpected revelation. "How many exactly do you think there are back there?"

"They're everywhere, swarming in every crack," he said with a chuckle. "Want me to go ahead and hose them down or just let the paint drive 'em off?"

Ellie paused to think. Jim's theory seemed to make sense in that the front of the house now was fully painted except for the second coat on one of the window frames.

"They have been coming in the house, but if you think the paint'll drive them off, that'll do," Ellie said. "When are you going to start on the back?"

"Oh, probably tomorrow, sugar," Jim said, adjusting his orange baseball cap.

"Well, guess those bugs'll be gone soon then," Ellie said and went back into the house.

Jim turned the radio back on.

Later that day after Jim left, Ellie stepped out onto the patio.

Boxelder bugs really were all over the rear of her house. Not every spot. In some places, the odd single bug clung or wandered by itself, but clusters of activity twitched in the cracks between bricks and the back door, around the windows, and under the eaves. She stepped backwards into the yard but couldn't get a full grip on the numbers with the glare of the afternoon sun on the sanded pale yellow wall.

Back inside, she checked the kitchen to see how soon she'd have to do the next food run. The shortages were making it challenging to stock up on staples, and she'd heard one of the announcers on Jim's radio mention talk of rationing. She'd gotten into the habit of prioritizing cans, boxes, bottles, jars, frozen vegetables, anything that would last. She took a quick inventory of the pantry and the fridge and estimated she might make it three or four more days comfortably, a week if she really stretched and wasn't too picky about what she ate.

Ellie probed one of the eight bugs on her desk with the point of a pen. She waited for it to climb on the pen but it froze stiff instead.

She didn't want to frighten the bug. She put the pen down and stretched out a finger. After a moment of hesitation and antennae-probing, the insect crawled onto it. She lifted her hand towards her eyes and watched its antennae twitch slowly.

Did it see her in color or black and white? Was she one clear image or broken into a mosaic effect as she had read happened with compound eyes common in aerial arthropods such as flies?

Ellie handed Jim the final check the following Friday.

As he headed for his truck, she was relieved to see the radio in his hand, leaving with him.

Stepping back from the front of the house, she had to admit that Jim was good at painting. She walked around to the back, inspecting his work from every angle. She remembered that time when she came home from a new salon with her hair dyed finally to the exact shade of blonde she wished that she had been born with and which her husband told her perfectly complimented her green eyes. If her house had feelings, she imagined it might feel that way now.

As Ellie circled back to the front, she heard the familiar rumble, except three Humvees were cruising down the street and it wasn't dark yet. The passenger window was down on the second vehicle, and a man in a helmet with dark glasses directed a stiff wave towards her. Reflexively, she waved back.

Heading back to the door, she paused to count the daffodils which had begun to bloom—mid-February right on schedule. She hoped the weather would warm up soon so they didn't freeze and die.

Inside, Ellie slipped off her shoes and stepped carefully on tiptoed stocking feet to avoid any of the dozen boxelder bugs crawling on the hardwood floor on the way to the stairs.

From her office window, she peeked out just in time to see the tail end of the Humvees as they circled back from the cul-de-sac at the end of her street and headed back up the hill.

Ellie stared at the boxelder bug slowly making its way towards her mousepad. She placed her left index finger in its path. When the bug reached it, she thought it might change its path to avoid the obstruction, but instead it climbed up onto it. She lifted her finger, and with her right hand, she positioned the jar towards her fingertip. The bug turned in the other direction. She reconfigured the jar, but it only clung more firmly to the digit.

Was its attraction to the warmth of her finger? Or did it somehow feel more secure?

Silly bug, do you think I'm your friend? I'm definitely not your mother.

She let the insect crawl along her finger and onto her hand, up to her elbow—its legs tickling slightly as it hiked across her arm hair. Finally, the odd sensation of its movement on her skin became too much, so she flicked the bug off her hand. It fell on its back onto the desk.

Ellie looked up and saw at least a dozen more bugs above her on the ceiling. Maybe she was a mother of bugs, at least metaphorically.

....

Morning ritual. Brushed off any boxelder bugs on her body or on the bed onto the floor. Shook her head because at least half landed on their backs. With her finger, flicked a few upright. Gave up because there are too many.

Life's tough, right, and you should be grateful to me that you are alive, not squished or stomped or vacuumed.

Picked up small broom by the bed. Gently swept away bugs on the floor and stairs as she walked to the kitchen so she wouldn't step on anyone.

Brushed bugs off counter. Checked coffee machine and removed a bug. Filled and brewed. Flicked bug out of bowl before adding cereal with yogurt, since she was out of milk. Stepped carefully all the way back upstairs to her office. Didn't need the broom because the bugs moved slow.

Removed bugs from keyboard. Why wasn't the Internet working this morning? Swore a few times. Assumed it would get fixed later. Played jazz. Worked on editing chapters she received yesterday.

....

The next day Ellie woke up cold. She reached over to turn on the light but it wouldn't switch on. Not only the Internet but now the power was out. Sunshine streamed in her back window. No rain and definitely no storm last night, nixing the most usual reason for an outage.

No stray boxelder bugs were wandering on her bed, and none on the floor either.

Shivering as she forced herself out from the warm blanket and comforter, she put on her flannel dressing gown and went to the bathroom.

No living bugs anyway.

She pulled back the shower curtain and saw some dead ones on the bathmat and around the drain.

No bugs on the steps or the banister or the floor at the bottom.

No bugs until she stepped into the kitchen.

On the floor in front of the dishwasher she saw them. A writhing mound almost a foot high and at least a foot wide.

What the hell?

She grabbed a broom and started sweeping them aside. Typically most of the boxelders didn't exactly scatter. They just rolled onto their backs, and some spun in the air, retaining enough of their balance to use their wings and land on the doors of the lower cabinets. She figured out by now they had been swarming over something.

Something they didn't want to abandon.

At the center of the former boxelder vortex lay a gray ball of fur. A mouse rolled into a fetal position.

She prodded it with the broom. It didn't move.

Was it dead?

She bent down for a close look.

Yet nothing that she had read about boxelder bugs explained this new behavior. The mouse's fur was intact, no blood, no indication that they were eating it like ants or maggots surging over a carcass. All the articles clearly identified boxelder bugs as vegetarian.

Meanwhile a fair number of the boxelder bugs had uprighted themselves and were crawling back in the mouse's direction. She thought a second about how her mother taught her never to touch dead animals because—*germs*. In a fast motion, she stretched her arm back and grabbed a plastic bag from the crack where she kept them between the refrigerator and the wall, stuffed it over her hand, and reached for the mouse.

She grabbed the little guy before the boxelder bugs could reach it, but as soon as she had it in her clutch, it squeaked loudly and began to wriggle so vigorously that she dropped it. Startled by the noise and movement of something she assumed dead, she let out a slight scream herself.

Before the mouse could run more than a few steps, the horde of boxelder bugs converged on it again.

Ellie swiped them away with her bag-covered hand, and the freaked-out mouse shot in her direction between her crouched legs. She slapped her hands to cover her face because it seemed like the bugs were heading right for her, but they separated into two waves and blew around her in a loud burst of *zizzzzing*. She turned and saw the mouse streaking out of the kitchen followed by the cloud of insects.

Mouse and swarm then disappeared down the steps to the den. By the time Ellie got downstairs, both had vanished.

Later she returned for a more thorough investigation and found the mouse in a corner of the downstairs bathroom shower stall, no longer merely paralyzed but dead. A few dozen boxelder bugs were scattered around the carcass which still showed no signs that the bugs had actually touched it in any way.

They must have smothered it so it couldn't breathe.

Jim's theory came back to her. Mice and rats come inside because of the cold. They're warm-blooded so they can retain heat, but insects are cold-blooded. They needed heat even more than the mouse to survive.

Ellie couldn't report the power outage because she had no cellphone signal either. By nightfall when the streetlights didn't flash on, she could see that the entire street was clearly affected. From her windows, she hadn't seen any activity around any of her neighbor's houses all day, though cars remained in their driveways. Nobody was outside, no children playing, no one walking a dog or riding a bike or returning from the corner grocery with bags of supplies.

She spent most of the day bundled up in bed because what else could she do? At least now she could catch up on that big pile of books on the floor next to it. A few times she heard what sounded like jets overhead, but no more daytime Humvee rounds.

In the evening, she put her bedside lamp on the floor and replaced it with a candelabrum.

Zizzzzzzzzzzzzz.

Ellie woke to the now familiar sound and flickering light. She should have snuffed out the candles for safety before falling asleep, but it'd been all she could do to close the book she was reading. Boxelder bugs hovered all around them, more arriving by the second. They crawled in through the doorway like an army of giant ants, then ascended in their helicopter vertical formations to join the firelight.

Pretty, she thought, dancing with fire, somehow keeping sufficient distance so as not to ignite their bodies.

Until one by one, each flame was overwhelmed by their sheer numbers—even fire needs oxygen to breathe—and blew out. As the room blinked into full darkness, it felt even colder.

Sometime after Ellie fell asleep again, she woke to the sensation of tiny legs crawling on her left arm. Her eyes squinted open and she saw a couple of boxelder bugs idling on her elbow. She swatted them off absently, pulled up her blanket to her neck and rolled back on her stomach.

A wintry wind tossed the trees and shrieked against the window glass outside. As Ellie huddled under the covers in the dark, she felt the bugs join her.

Minutes passed, hours. She wasn't sure how long without power and a working alarm clock, her cellphone battery long since expired. All she knew was she was lying in an undulating horde of bugs.

And without power, the only heat source in the house now emanated from layers of blankets and her human body. At least she was much bigger than a mouse, and their numbers were merely in the hundreds. Maybe low thousands. Some bugs felt smaller than others. Perhaps in the long weeks at the house, they had nested. No way to count, but the numbers definitely were growing.

She should carefully pull off the sheets and blankets and wrap them up and take all the bugs outside, now that they were all gathered in one place. Her mind puzzled on the best way to accomplish this task and be sure not to drop any insects.

She felt an itch on her nose where a bug must have been crawling on it. She swiped it away, but as she touched the rest of her face to remove any more insects, her fingers became coated in a glue-like film. Was it the sticky, staining substance that they supposedly excreted when squashed? Maybe she'd flattened some tossing and turning at night. Or like skunks, they excreted it when they were afraid?

Why did she think they were afraid?

Well, she was afraid.

Eventually Ellie drifted off to sleep.

When Ellie next opened her eyes, the bugs flushed into them. She tossed off another layer of insects on her arms so that she could wipe them away with her fingers.

The first light of morning shimmered into the bedroom—not sunlight but a silvery sheen. Through the window across from her bed, Ellie saw snow falling, the flakes drifting slowly at first and then faster in large puffy clusters. Tree branches and neighbors' roofs were quickly becoming cloaked in white.

The scene exuded calm, the sensation relaxing as the insects crawled around Ellie's body under the covers like an extra comforter. She recalled the electric blanket in her grandmother's guest room.

Then suddenly the tranquility was broken by the blare of a siren. She recognized it at once from movies—the old familiar emergency alert system used for air raids. She'd only heard it once before in real life when she was a little girl, a system test announced ahead of time with community flyers.

In one great mass, the boxelder bugs swarmed up her body and towards her face.

An unknown something else screeched like nails on a cosmic chalkboard above, outside.

Ellie opened her mouth and let the insects in.

Window

"This is not going to last forever," Michael said.

The words echoed in Angela's mind like the droning keys of an out-of-tune piano. Her eyes ached from the memory of tears.

"It's not working," he said. "I just don't love you. But I'll hold you because you're so very special and you deserve better than me. I'll hold you while you cry."

Something like that. His actual words had faded from her memory because she did not want to remember them.

"Why?" she asked him and hated herself for it.

And then she added: "Are you sure?"

His arms felt so good, tightly wound around her chest, the curve of his body curled around her back. She wanted to linger in his grasp. *Why not?*

The humming of cicadas melded with the Doors, the last notes of "Riders on the Storm," as Angela tried to let go of the recollection. She wanted to watch it fly out the window past the naked woman behind the glass, arms swimming open and closed. Her long black hair merging with the darkness behind, smiling milk-white teeth, just like in his photographs. *The woman before her.* Liza, who Michael said he could never forget, who he would always love despite the fact that she had treated him abusively and ultimately abandoned him. Liza who had thrown herself out a window but yet his heart remained preserved just for her—mummified and wrapped in her bed sheets, his dead body, only continuing the motions of life.

Angela's hands were soaked in clay and water, the clay hardening as the water dried in the night air that blew into the loft apartment from the open window. She was trying to concentrate on the half-finished pot that sat upon the wheel, but the woman in the window would not stop watching her, tanned breasts lifting up and down like signal flags, reminding her. She tried to rationalize the image away, tell herself it was just a figment of her paranoid imagination. She wanted nothing more than to exorcise that image, to slash it away from her consciousness. Angela wanted just to sit and make her pots. She wanted Michael just to come home and make love to her.

And he did.

An hour later, Angela heard his cowboy boots walking heavily across the wooden corridor, his key turning in the lock. She turned around just as the door creaked open. Michael, in his black leather jacket, walked toward her and kissed her lips.

He pulled away too quickly for her to catch his tongue, leaving a faint flavor of cigarettes and scotch in her mouth. She could taste that the thoughts on his mind were not about her.

"How was your day, dear?" he asked.

"Okay," she said, endeavoring to smile. "I made a horse. It's just waiting for the kiln tomorrow."

Michael walked over to the little wooden table and stared blankly at the equine figure, one hoof raised to mimic a Han Dynasty sculpture.

"Mr. Ed?" he inquired.

Angela could tell he was trying to make her laugh.

"Not exactly," she answered. "You'll see when I glaze it. I want the colors to be surprising, maybe a little jarring."

"Well, I'll be surprised then," he said, walking across the loft and lowering himself onto the black leather sofa.

Michael picked up a magazine and started to read.

"How was your day?" she asked.

"Oh, the usual shit," he said, not looking up from the magazine.

"Did Blake pull something?" she asked.

"No, I just kept to myself," he said.

"That's good," she said, wanting to stroke his shoulder, take all his frustrations inside her and set him free.

"Why is my life such a fucking hell?" Michael said suddenly, throwing the magazine down. He pulled a pint of Dewars from inside his jacket, unscrewed the cap and swigged deeply.

Angela saw he was crying.

She got up now, crossed the room and hugged Michael long and hard. He railed about work and promises that were made and Blake and Karen and everyone else. And how he wanted to be painting instead of working at the advertising agency. How he hated that he needed to just hold on a little longer and save more money. He couldn't give up the salary. Not yet.

"It has to get better," she said, feeling strength welling up inside her, her own strong belief in the power of human endurance. "We'll pull on through. Remember, we're a team."

Michael fell silent, then started swearing again. Sensing he wanted space, she released her embrace. He stared at the fireplace, at the floor. Then his eyes looked up towards the window.

"Oh, God, I miss Liza," he almost screamed, swigging again. "Why did she have to leave me, Angela? Why?"

Angela stared at him and started to say, "There was nothing you could have done; she chose to leave," but fear descended like the fall of an avalanche, and instead she said nothing.

Michael kept staring at the window.

Then suddenly he jerked his eyes back at Angela, hugged her, held her tightly on the sofa. The woman in the window laughed soundlessly as he began to kiss Angela on her cheek, her lips, her neck. He unbuttoned her shirt, sucked her nipples and glided his hands down to her skirt, slipping it off. She lifted and spread her legs and he bent his face to meet her. Later, after she helped him remove his clothes, he entered her, climaxed.

"You know how difficult it is for me to say the word again, but in my own way, I do love you," Michael said, his voice cracking. He pushed her hair back with his fingers and looked into her eyes.

Angela met his gaze and smiled.

"You never stopped loving her," Angela said, trying to understand seven months later when Michael told her again that it was over between them. They'd just finished dinner, and the air was scented with garlic and tomato sauce from leftover spaghetti. Caesar salad sat untouched in a large wooden bowl in the center of the black dining table. He wanted to be on his own, he told her. But he wanted to stay friends.

"I tried to…" Michael started, pausing to empty the last drops of Chianti into his wine glass and down them in one fast draught. "I tried to make it work between us. I just can't explain why, but it isn't."

At first, Angela was silent, just staring at him, tears pouring out of her eyes again. Then she felt anger building up inside her, anger that he had let their relationship go on for so long. Betrayal, that he let her love for him grow and mature and how it was all a lie.

"I'm sorry," Michael said.

"I don't get how you could love someone like Liza, but despite all we've been through together, all you've asked me to do for you, allowed me to do for you, you don't love me," Angela said, then she threw his own words back at him. "You don't know what love is."

"Yes, I do," Michael said. "You just want me to love you, and I'm sorry I can't."

"Then, you were wrong," Angela said. "Love is not about commitment; it is irrational."

"No," Michael said, shaking his head, seemingly unable to explain any further and becoming even more defensive.

Michael looked Angela straight in her eyes. Then his head lowered, and he lowered to his knees, and finally, he was facing the window.

"Have you gotten over Liza?" Angela asked, point-blank, not sure if she was pointing a metaphorical Beretta 9 mm at him or at herself.

Michael's eyes now were locked upon the window.

"No, and yeah, it's fucking unfair to both of us."

Then Angela saw him seeing Liza and the longing in his eyes. His lips opened and shut like the mouth of a poet searching for the verse, the words that spoke desire…no, *the need.*

Liza thrust her hand out through the glass, her fingers beckoning. His hand reached to meet hers. Michael crawled on his knees towards the window, his arm outstretched and grasping.

Then as his fingers almost touched hers, Liza pulled her arm back into the glass, sparks flying where her hand slipped back, gray smoke lingering in a cloud in front of the window. Her mouth expressed laughter, silent laughter in the loft, but loud beyond the glass.

"Liza!" Michael cried out. "I love you."

Liza laughed harder, rocking back and forth on her knees, her breasts like stone gargoyles, tits pointed like spears.

Michael's face fell to the ground. Tears erupted from his eyes, and then nothing. His body collapsed still as a corpse, his face in his hands, sleeping, the weight of either the wine or the vision of Liza knocking him unconscious. His chest moved gently, the only indication he was alive.

Angela ran her fingers through his hair and wondered what the woman in the window was thinking. Did she think? Was she a fantasy created by Michael or by Angela or by both of them together? She raised her eyes to look at Liza, who was still now, smiling and extending her fingers again through the glass. And suddenly, Angela saw something different—how beautiful Liza was, how tantalizing her body, how sweet her eyes.

"I am so sorry," Liza whispered, her voice like a little girl. "I never meant to hurt him. I never meant for him to love me so much."

The woman in the window was transformed to a little girl with a pixie haircut, flat chest, innocent eyes, a tiny crooked smile.

Then she was Liza again, darkly tanned, pure sex and yet still innocent, a child-woman, her fingers dangling from the window, the arm pushing out further.

"Help me," Liza said. "I tried to leave him, but he wouldn't let me go. I need your help, Angela. Help me break free of the window."

Angela realized that she had never heard Liza's voice before.

"Why are you speaking to me now?" she asked.

"I can only be heard through the glass if someone wants to listen," Lisa answered. "He wanted to listen every day. He didn't want to lose me and that's why he put me here."

Angela hesitated as her mind tried to rationalize Liza's words.

Michael had told her the story about the day he found Liza at the door with all her suitcases packed. He described the quarrel and the broken glass shattered on the floor after she hurled herself out the window. She should have died or at least broken her back from the fall, but no body was ever found. Somehow she had just picked herself up and never returned, even for her suitcases. Another window, another apartment, but could he have taken the window with him somehow?

"Did he push you?" Angela asked, frightened that the man she loved could be so cruel.

"No," Liza answered. "But he wouldn't let me go. He held me in a window of his memory."

Liza was silent for a moment, seemingly pensive.

"And now I have been watching your life and I envy you for it," she said. "I envy the way you sit and create your pots, the way you unload your groceries, friends who come over and watch movies. I want to go back out there and learn to live again, but not with him, not with someone who always wants more than he can have. Will you help me? Will you help me escape the window?"

Angela reached for Liza's fingers, letting them wrap around hers and lift her from Michael's side. Liza's arm was strong enough to gently pull Angela upwards until she was standing. Then the arm pulled back into the window and took her with it. The glass parted like water, like a shower of waves caressing each part of Angela as she passed through, refreshing and remaking her. The water washed back and Liza's body met hers, hands flattening, arms to arms, breast to breast, feet to feet, legs to legs, lips to lips, both lips. As bodies, they formed a perfect match. Only Liza's was firmer, Angela's softer.

Liza kissed Angela, wet and long. She then slipped two fingers along her thigh, massaged her clit and passed them inside her. Angela felt a flood of moisture, shaking almost immediately with orgasm, and sensed another building as Liza trailed her tongue down her neck, fingers still caressing.

Teeth nibbled gently along her collarbone and onto the curve of her breasts, sucking each nipple. Liza's tongue drifted lower, onto her stomach now, in her bellybutton, her lower abdomen, her groin; one hand on her breast, the other inside her, massaging in and out. Tongue curling, tracing, sucking, coming, curling, tracing, sucking, coming, curling, tracing, sucking, coming.

Angela floated, her body in perfect balance, perfect release, her sensations merging through repetition into pure pleasure and understanding and finally drifting into sleep.

She didn't know how long she slept, but when she awoke, Liza was no longer touching her.

"Liza," Angela called, wanting to hold her lover, kiss her, touch her everywhere Liza had touched Angela.

"Liza," she called again.

Silence. Darkness. Liza was away perhaps, but she would return. Angela let herself fall back to sleep, wrapped in the memory of Liza's body heat.

Icy glass awakened her. Icy glass and light. Sunlight flashed all around Angela, warming her body as she lifted it from the glass floor. The sun was blinding, forcing her to turn the other way into her own reflection. Her hazel eyes, her auburn hair, her pale lips, lipstick smeared across her cheek. It took her a moment to realize she was staring into glass on all sides, the glass of a rectangular window, divided into panes. And inside the window was the loft, her potter's wheel, the leather sofa, the kitchen, Michael's naked body still passed out on the wooden floor.

Angela stared down at Michael and did not care for him, saw why Liza rejected him, why he was not equal to her passion. She remembered how Liza touched her, how Liza made her feel whole in a way that no lover ever had. No wonder Michael had loved her so much.

But where was Liza?

She wanted to feel Liza's lips upon her breast, between her legs.

She turned to look behind, but the sun again blinded her and compelled her vision back through the window into the loft. If the window was so small, where could Liza have gone?

Then she knew the answer.

Angela saw Liza, draped in Angela's own red oriental robe, kneeling beside Michael. She saw the trick, the same scam this woman had played on Michael played on herself. Michael mumbled something, but it was like watching a silent movie and Angela could not hear a word. She saw only the hunger in his eyes as Liza took him into her arms and kissed him. Then Liza made love to him with all the skill and tenderness that she gave to Angela. As he fell back into slumber, Liza packed Angela's clothes into a suitcase, rifled cash from Michael's pockets, took Angela's jewelry box, her credit cards, her purse, and her car keys. She pasted a note on the TV and walked out the door.

Angela watched as Michael awakened with the smile of a man who had just experienced the dream of a lifetime. He stumbled over to the TV and took the note into the sunlight of the window. All she could read was that it was signed with her name. She beat her hands against the window and yelled.

"Michael!"

He turned and headed for the kitchen.

"Michael!"

He started coffee, foraged in the refrigerator,

"Michael!"

He spread cream on a bagel,

"Michael!"

He left the kitchen, opened the door to take in the newspaper,

"Michael!"

He poured coffee into a mug, sat down on the couch, took a bite from the bagel, began to read the paper, sipped some coffee.

"Michael, I love you."

The words slipped out as Liza's own statement rang in her ears.

"I can only be heard through the glass if someone wants to listen."

Michael didn't want to hear Angela. He didn't want to see Angela. Angela made him feel guilty, reminded him of what he couldn't have, of what he didn't realize he had imprisoned, of what he didn't know was now free—that Liza was in the world again the way she wanted to be and not with Michael. He didn't care that Angela was the one he believed had left him. He understood why she would leave and felt no urge to follow.

But Michael did feel something missing. Angela could sense that. He looked up into the window and knew Liza was gone.

Michael drank more and more scotch every night and he fucked women and he tried to paint and he was never happy.

And Angela watched it all from the window.

Setting: Nuremberg Prison, West Germany, 1947.

Cast of Characters

Lana Davis, a young American woman, 27, attractive.
General Franz Schiller, a German man, 51.
Colonel Ralph Stephenson, an American officer.
Private Chambers, an American soldier.

Scene One

Colonel Stephenson's office. The main furnishing is the Colonel's desk, which is scattered with various papers, photos, etc. The Colonel is on the phone. Enter Lana Davis escorted by a Private. The Private stops and stands at attention. Lana is dressed in a fairly conservative but fashionable black dress and hat, circa mid-1940s, and black wedge-heel pumps. She looks uncomfortable.

Colonel: *(into phone)* Listen Hal, I've gotta go. She's here. *(pause)* Yeah, I'll ask her. Uh-huh, it's most, *(he glances at* **Lana***)* most interesting. *(pause)* Right. Good-bye. *(hangs up phone and stands to greet* **Lana***)* Miss Davis, I presume. *(extends hand)* I'm Colonel Ralph Stephenson. Have a seat. *(to* **Private***)* Thanks, Chambers. You're dismissed. *(***Private** *salutes and exits)*

Lana: Thank you.

Colonel: How about a Hershey? *(extends a bar split into sections)* Got a sister in Dallas, mails me a couple of bars every week.

Lana: No, thanks. My little boy likes it, but I've never had much of a taste for sweets.

Colonel: No? Well, everybody's got their secret vices, I reckon. Mine are these little lumps of chocolate. *(stuffs a section in his mouth)* Never can eat just one. You agree, Miss Davis? About the vices, I mean.

Lana: Yes, sir. I mean, I suppose so.

Colonel: You're from Indianapolis, aren't you?

Lana: Well, Danville actually.

Colonel: Been through Indianapolis once. Had an Aunt Sue Ellen who lived there for a while, in a big ol' white house. She had green shutters, bright green shutters—like Christmas. And that little boy, his name is Franz?

Lana: Yes. He's three.

Colonel: Mighty odd name for a boy from Indianapolis.

(Long pause. **Lana** *does not respond.)*

Colonel: I've considered your request, Miss Davis. Frankly, ma'am, it does seem rather unusual. You give no solid reason for wishing to see General Schiller. And obviously, my dear, you aren't a relative. However, I have made some inquiries, and it seems as if the general is equally interested in seeing you. *(he pauses expectantly, but* **Lana** *remains silent)* You're an American, but you lived in Paris from 1938 to 1944? You were a performer of some sort.

Lana: I was a singer in a night club.

Colonel: And you met General Schiller during the Occupation?

Lana: Yes.

Colonel: Is your boy named after Franz Schiller?

Lana: Yes.

Colonel: You loved the man, yet you knew who he was and what he did?

Lana: He was an artist.

Colonel: *(chuckles)* An artist? Well, that's an interesting way of putting it. So I hear was his *Führer*. Listen, let me be frank with you. This is highly irregular, but I've decided to let you see him.

Lana: Thank you. I had hoped you would be understanding.

Colonel: No, Miss Davis. I *don't* understand, as you put it. I said merely that I've decided to let you see him. I don't think many folks would understand, Miss Davis. They might just call you a traitor to the United States of America.

Lana: A traitor because I loved?

Colonel: It's not the love, Miss Davis. It's the lover. Surely you've read the transcripts of his trial.

Lana: Every word. Seven times.

Colonel: Then you know what your lover did.

Lana: I read it, Colonel Stephenson. But I also know the man. He's no devil with horns, Colonel.

Colonel: Sure, none that can be seen with the naked eye. You'll pardon me if I question your judgment, Miss Davis. Your passion is quite clear, however. *(picks up receiver on phone)* Donna, could you send Private Chambers back in here?

Lana: Thank you, Colonel.

(Enter **Private.***)*

Colonel: Private Chambers, take Miss Davis to see General Schiller. *(***Lana** *rises)* And Miss Davis?

Lana: Yes?

Colonel: Don't thank me.

(Private leads Lana out of Colonel Stephenson's office.)

Scene Two

General Franz Schiller*'s private cell. The cell is reasonably well-furnished, suggesting that this prisoner is of a higher status. It should include a small bed with covering, perhaps a blanket, a small desk, and a vase of flowers on the windowsill. The small window itself is barred.* **Franz** *is seated at the desk, drawing on a piece of paper. Also on the desk should be a glass of water and a set of watercolors.* **Franz** *is dressed in the gray shirt and pants of a prisoner. He has black gloves on his hands. He turns in his chair as he hears the sound of the bolt being removed from the cell door and the sound of the door opening. The* **Private** *enters, followed by* **Lana. Franz** *rises.*

The **Private** *exits. The audience hears him bolt the door behind him.*

Franz: Lana. I did not dare dream that I would see you again.

(he approaches and starts to take her into his arms, but she pulls away.)

Lana: Franz, I'm sorry. I had to see you, but I'm not sure that I…

Franz: Should love me? (long pause; Lana does not reply) I understand. Lana, I have been lonely.

Lana: The flowers. They're lovely. Who sent them?

Franz: *Meine Mutter.* I suppose she imagines that pretty things should keep me company. She is a funny woman. She thinks about things. Like those flowers.

Lana: She sounds nice.

Franz: Yes, she thinks of others. She even gave Him flowers once. She used to say that it was the most wonderful moment of her life. He kissed her on the cheek. She could not talk of anything else for weeks. Nothing else. I do not think she understands how things could change so quickly. Poor woman.

Lana: My mother doesn't understand, Franz. I went home…

Franz: Yes, where was it? Danville, Indiana.

Lana: Yeah, good ol' Danville. They know there was a war, but they only saw the corn ripen. Some of our boys went, and some of them didn't come back. Just us, good ol' Americans—red, white and blue, in God's name—we won again. Amen.

Franz: But you believe that, too, Lana Davis. Don't you?

Lana: I don't know. I never knew even in Danville. All I knew was that I didn't belong there. So I left, like the prodigal son. Only I was the prodigal daughter, so I wasn't supposed to want to go out and seek my fortune. I saved all my money, hopped a train to New York, a boat to France. I was so young. So…so idealistic.

Franz: But not very innocent. Not when you met me.

Lana: No, Franz. Not anymore.

Franz: I never thought of you as Danville, Indiana. You were always the American woman. Strong. Vivacious. And very passionate. About life. About me.

Lana: Oh, Franz. Let's forget. Oh, I want so much to forget. To wipe away the words of the world, the walls of this prison. Why can't we just be man and woman, alone but together. Have you missed me like that?

Franz: Oh, I *have* missed you.

Lana: Hold me. I wanted you to when I first walked in. Kiss me, Franz. I want to remember. *(they kiss)*

Franz: The first night in the club.

Lana: Out in the audience.

Franz: Standing by the piano, the single burst of light. I saw only your eyes.

Lana: A handsome man at a table in the front, his eyes on me every moment I was on stage. And after the show, I came back to my dressing room and found a single red tulip.

Franz: It was spring.

Lana: He invited me to his table. He was dressed in a black tux, like any other man. He said he was an artist. So I asked him what it felt like to be an artist.

Franz: Well, it cascades me. It pours over me like rain, but not water. Wine. And I am drenched until I'm drunk.

Lana: Do I cascade you?

Franz: You cascade me. I want to drown in you.

Lana: Then I will be your lifeboat. And you'll ride me.

Franz: Yes, I'll ride. Both top. *(pause)* And tail.

Lana: You were very naughty for a *Deutscher* officer.

Franz: You were a very naughty girl, no virgin from Danville, Indiana. You flirted with a German.

Lana: I thought I was flirting with an artist. I didn't put together the images of marching soldiers and martial law with the portrait of a handsome German artist in a nightclub.

Franz: And if I had been dressed as a soldier?

Lana: I don't know.

Franz: Lana, there was something I wondered, though.

Lana: What's that, you mischievous man?

Franz: If you accepted all your propositions, Lana?

Lana: Oh, you know better than that.

Franz: But Lana, you were…

Lana: Were what?

Franz: *Eine Hure.*

Lana: Your personal temptress perhaps, but don't call me a whore.

Franz: But Lana, you were. There is no reason to delude ourselves, just for an excuse to look back fondly on a past affair.

Lana: Franz, the tone of your voice. You're serious. What's wrong?

Franz: Only the entire world. Tell me, my lady Lana, were you *eine hochpreisigen Hure*? Did this chevalier apprehend *eine Schnäppchen*?

Lana: Franz, why are you suddenly so cruel?

Franz: You have read the papers. You have read the transcripts of my trial, I am certain. I am a cruel man. Have not all the good folks in Danville told you that? Have they not told you that only a whore could love a man like me?

Lana: I asked you not to call me that.

Franz: You asked me to ride you.

Lana: I don't understand you, Franz. One moment we're embracing each other and talking about love, and now you're reducing our love to just another bawdy romp in the hay.

Franz: What is there to understand? For a moment, I gave into a lovely dream. But my life is over, Lana. I was on the wrong side of the war that the world has decided was between good and evil. I have been sentenced to life imprisonment. All my friends are dead, or in prison like me. It does not matter anymore if we loved or if we fucked.

Lana: Franz, a moment ago, you weren't like this. You were so happy.

Franz: A moment ago? A lifetime ago? I remember once I was happy. One spring afternoon walking with Him at *Berchtesgaden*. Eva Braun was there, too. And others. Albert Speer. We were talking about building a new museum in Berlin. The *Führer* wanted it to be the largest art gallery in the world. The plans were incredible. Speer was to design it. I can remember His words. The pride of the German people. He wanted to build a huge park around it with a thousand trees and flowers, lots of flowers. And a long avenue. Three times as grand as the Louvre with golden ceilings that would have made Louis the Fourteenth shed tears with envy. It was to be a symbol of the strength of the Fatherland that had never before been so great. We were building a new world. A world of learning and art and beauty. A new Atlantis. And I was naïve enough then to think it could really be done. (long pause, looks down at the artwork on the desk, and then back at Lana) Have you ever read about the natives in Australia, Lana?

Lana: No.

Franz: They have this idea about something they call "Dreamtime." A world that is perhaps tangential to what we think of as the world, the place in which we live out our pathetic day-to-day existence. But it's more than just a longing. The Dreamtime represents another level of consciousness on which they feel how close they are to the land, to nature, to the animals, to the plants they eat, to their Gods. I fought a war, Lana. But I was living in the Dreamtime. And I *sketched* and I *painted* and I *killed* to make the Dreamtime real.

Lana: No, Franz. Our love wasn't in any Dreamtime. It was flesh touching flesh, feeling with our skin, with our souls. You said you missed me. We touched. We felt. And yes, we made love. Even if our time together was limited, our love is the one thing that isn't. You may not have created a new world, but you have created new life. Franz, you have a son.

Franz: A son?

Lana: Yes, and he's a swell boy. Three years old. Wavy blond hair. Blue eyes. Takes after his father. See, I brought photos.

(Lana opens her purse and pulls out a handful of snapshots.)

Franz: A son. What have you named him?

Lana: His father's name.

Franz: Franz. *(looking at the photos)* I never had any idea you were with child. Oh, Lana, I wish I could be a real father. I always wanted that. What do children call their fathers in America? Dad, isn't it? Or Daddy?

Lana: Dad, or Daddy.

Franz: And American dads, they teach their sons to play baseball and that American football, and they take them fishing. It's really not so different in Germany, you know. When I was a boy, I played ball games with my father. And he would take me to camp out in the forest. He was a forest man, what you call a ranger. In the *Schwarzwald*. We took long walks in the woods, and he taught me the names of every bush, every tree, every plant on the ground, every mushroom and which one could eat and which was deadly poison. He taught me to care for the animals, not to kill just for sport. He was a gentle man, a simple man, proud in a very quiet way. Like my mother. But what am I going on about? I cannot ever be any daddy to the boy. This is foolish.

Lana: Why, Franz? I thought maybe I could stay here, in the village. Then at least you could see him.

Franz: No.

Lana: But why? A son should know his father.

Franz: No. Absolutely, no. I do not want him to see me as a shell of a man, rotting away behind the brick walls of this prison. What pride could he have then? And the village boys, they would know. American soldiers everywhere telling him that his father is a monster. Never. I will not have him suffer for my deeds. Every man should have the right to choose his own way. Maybe he should know nothing at all. You must just take him away, as far away as you can, back to Danville.

Lana: But Franz, what about me? I need to…to be near you. I've come so far.

Franz: We cannot think of ourselves before our son. Besides, you will change your mind about me.

Lana: When I was home in Danville, all I wanted to do was forget you. But no matter how hard I tried, no matter everything that I was told the German army did, I couldn't forget you. And now, seeing you, that's the last thing I want to do. I can't see that it wouldn't be easier on our son if he grew up knowing his father and knowing his sins, rather than finding out later like a slap in the face. Then he would at least have a chance to love you.

Franz: No, Lana, think. Think about having to live your entire life knowing that your father stood for, that your father did… The world condemns me, Lana, and even a son who loves his father cannot remain deaf to the world. Better he be an orphan.

Lana: You don't ever want your son to know who his father is.

Franz: You know that is not what I want, just what must be. Damn. If only I was not trapped behind these bars. Then we could be a real family. I could be a real father. But I do not want him to know me this way. Is that why you came? To plan a life for us together? You knew that could never be, didn't you, Lana?

Lana: Yes, I suppose. But I had fantasies on the ship coming over of you escaping and us running away with little Franz to Brazil or Bali or some other faraway exotic place on the edge of the world. Outlaws, but free. Free and together.

Franz: Escape?

Lana: Yes, maybe if you were very alert and watched for just the right moment. It might take a year or two, but…

Franz: Oh, Lana. You have spent far too many Saturdays at the cinema.

Lana: I suppose I was just dreaming.

Franz: Dreaming. I know dreaming. Yes, we could go to Australia. Build a little cottage in the outback. Can you see me as a shepherd or a cattle rancher? With little Franz helping with the chores, growing up all innocent of his heritage. It is a lovely dream, Lana.

Lana: But surely, at least someday. You'll have parole, won't you?

Franz: Parole? Lana, can it be you have not read the transcripts of my trial? Do you know what I did?

Lana: Seven times. Every word. Over and over. But Franz, that's not you. You said something about the killing. But I can see it in your eyes. You now know you were wrong.

Franz: Do I? You say you came for the sake of our son, but that's not the real reason you came, was it?

Lana: Why didn't you come back to Paris like you promised?

Franz: You know I couldn't. Within two months after I was called back, Paris was liberated by your army. I had to fight a war. I had sworn my allegiance.

Lana: To your damned *Führer*.

Franz: Do not ever call him that. He was my...*meine Lehrer, mein Vater, mein Freund*. He took a special interest in me. Perhaps because I was young for my rank—not yet a general. But perhaps because I told him that I was an artist.

Lana: In the papers, I read he was insane.

Franz: Didn't you read that I was insane, too? Why did you come back? Why now? Why did you wait until after the trial? Where were you?

Lana: I thought about trying to find you, but with the fighting so heavy, and I was pregnant. So I went home, and Franz was born. When the war was over, I read that you had been arrested. I was so glad just to hear you were alive. Then I read about the trials. And when you were convicted, I struggled about whether to come see you or to stay home and forget. But I knew I had to come. It took me a while, but I had to get so many answers. I had to know if there was something wrong with me.

Everyone in Danville sure thought there was. I should never have told them, and I admit it took me a while. But there was little Franz and no one could understand why I gave him such a German name. I think they guessed that I must've had an affair with a German, but when I finally confessed it was you to my parents, their mouths fell open and they tried to make me feel ashamed. Told me that I just hadn't realized who you were and that I must now be horrified. Sure, they tried to be sympathetic. And we must keep the whole thing so quiet, change little Franz's name quick to something more respectable like Frank. Some good American name. That's when I left. We lived in Chicago for a while, until I saved the money for the ship.

Franz: Then you came to find out about me. The truth. You could not trust your own memories. You had to confirm them and confirm the world was wrong, that my crimes were perhaps just a, a dream. Well, Lana, perhaps it is good you came. Because now I can show you who I really am. We played a sweet charade back in Paris, but it was only a corner of the Dreamtime.

Lana: Franz, I found out what I needed to know. You don't need to go on with that nonsense about the Dreamtime. I can feel that you love me, that you are a man, not the foul beast they told me you were. You didn't run any death camp. I wasn't crazy.

Franz: Weren't you? Death camp? No, not a death camp but… Do not deny the Dreamtime, Lana. It is far from nonsense.

Lana: How can it be anything but? Yes, we all have dreams and often we realize they can't come true. But we're flesh and blood, breathing human beings, and we live on solid, firm earth. When we touch, our love becomes real.

Franz: Our brains register the feeling. But real?

Lana: It was they who said I was crazy, that you were crazy. Don't prove them right, Franz. I don't want that. I want you…things as they were before. If I can't have that, I just want the memory, whole and beautiful.

Franz: Only the Dreamtime is beautiful, Lana. Reality is crisp, dark, ugly. Full of dirt and dust and blood. Black and white and red. All the other colors are dreams.

Lana: Nonsense. Philosophy. If you're trying to show me the soldier, all I see is the artist in you, Franz.

Franz: But the two are one, Lana. How can you say you love me without loving the total man?

Lana: All I need to love is your soul. In the way you talk, I can sense the weight of your sadness, that you realize the dream was flawed.

Franz: Did I ever tell you a story, Lana—a story about how in the forest camped under the stars as a boy, I discovered the Dreamtime? Then, there, I felt so close to it. Yet I could not quite grasp it, hold it in my palm, did not know its name yet. I just knew I was a part of the nature around me, one with *Wodan, Donar, die Götter von meine Vorfahren*, but I did not know exactly which piece of the puzzle was my own. That is when I started to draw.

Lana: Yes, you told me. You told me in the country outside Paris. We had a picnic in the tall grasses by a brook. We made love in an ocean of reeds until it grew dark. Then, when we were under the stars and the moon—a sliver that night so the sky was dark enough to see constellations—you talked about staring at the stars when you were a boy. But you never said anything about a Dreamtime.

Franz: I still did not know what to call it then. I found a book in the library here at the prison. Travels of some Englishman in Australia. He talked with the natives. Aborigines, he called them. They were really very creative for savages. They say the Australians are not really *Schwarze* but another race all together. Not that it matters. I never did really believe in the *Führer*'s racial theories anyway.

Lana: But if you didn't believe, why did you follow him?

Franz: Living in the Dreamtime, Lana. The *Führer* gave me...opportunities. He appreciated my vision. He encouraged me almost like a son. And he reminded me of my father...Except that my father did not have the temper, that wild rage that sometimes erupted in speeches so passionate that they moved crowds to tears, but other times grew into a terrible anger in which rational thought gave way to revenge without mercy. Sometimes he frightened me, but then I looked inwards and saw the same fury in myself. The energy that could burst forth in both wild creation and hideous destruction. I would hear the Dreamtime calling and feel this terrible, urgent craving to let it take me. To pull it closer as quickly as possible, no matter what the cost. Even if it meant the deaths of innocent civilian men, women, children for no reason except that they were not German. You were right. I did not supervise a death camp. No, I ordered them burned in their barns, at home, in the little French villages where they lived, broiled alive like sides of beef. All for my Dreamtime. Did you ever hear me doubt, Lana? Not by the little brook under the stars. Not in the loft of the Hotel Valois. Think, Lana.

Lana: No, Franz, but we never talked about the war. The subject was like an unspoken taboo. I wondered. I mean, sometimes I yearned to ask you. I think I even tried. But you never replied. You'd brush it off with a kiss, and in your arms, it was so easy to forget. So I never knew if you did anything but sit in an office and assign marching orders. I never pushed it because I was scared that I might find out...

Franz: What you still want to deny?

Lana: Maybe I should just leave now. Franz, don't go on. I don't want you to try to prove to me that...

Franz: Stop now? Really, Lana, you don't mean that. If you walk out that door right now, you will walk out with the same doubts with which you walked in it. In a week or two, they will creep back in like tiny serpents and nip at you. And you will come back. Cannot you see that it is important for me that you know the real man, the real Franz Schiller. General Franz Schiller. I think you should know, that you need to know. To know that I never sweated about what I did. I felt them sweating around me. When I walked into the club, voices would drop to a whisper. Only German voices laughed into the night. The French were silent, silent as the stones. All but the French *putes* laughing loudly until dawn with German soldiers under their bed sheets. And you and I. Were we really so different?

Lana: Yes, Franz. I have to believe that we were. Please let me go. Don't destroy this moment, too.

Franz: Maybe it is just that I do not understand how you can still love me knowing what I have done. Why not reject me now to my face and get it over with? You are not German. You are not, cannot be part of the same Dream. All that you have been taught is against who I am.

Lana: Yes, they pounded it into my brain day after day, night after night. How? Why? Could? I? They called you names, filthy names, and degraded my son. My son plays with fingerpaints, but he doesn't own any guns or toy soldiers like every other little boy in Danville. He hasn't even asked for them.

Franz: And what are you going to tell little Franz when he asks about his father?

Lana: You know what I'll tell him. That Daddy was an artist, a man with tremendous creative spirit, with great dreams.

Franz: Words. Just words. Lovely but empty. What when little Franz asks you what were Daddy's dreams. What then, Lana? Will you tell him of the flames, the screams of terror, the excruciating agony of being burned alive. I still can see so clearly the little boy with his stuffed monkey clinging to his mother's skirt. Staring at me with eyes wide as tea saucers, trembling with a fear so great even *Maman*'s hands could not soothe it away. I turned my back on those little eyes and ordered my soldiers to shoot down every man, woman, and child without mercy. I would be hanged for that except the order came down from above. But it was me who executed it, who did not refuse. If you had been there that day, Lana. That boy had blond hair just like little Franz. What will you tell him, Lana? Will you tell him this fairy story so that he can really know his father?

Lana: But you were forced to do those things. You would have been executed by your *Führer* had you said no. That's not you. Not the real you.

Franz: Why, Lana? Why is it any less the real me? Why do you shut your eyes and look away when I speak of the charred corpses, the boiling blood bubbling in tiny puddles like fresh soup, the savory aroma of a herd of human flesh cooking on an open flame. Pass the Béarnaise sauce, my darling. These sights, these smells, these screams, these eyes, they are always with me, you see. But Lana, I do not turn away.

Lana: What do you mean, that you don't turn away?

Franz: Will you tell our son that his dad even in prison after confessing his sins still is not able to feel the pain he has wrought on so many people? That what really haunts him is that he is not certain if he is truly sorry?

Lana: But you just said…

Franz: I say, Lana, but what do I feel? Emptiness, only emptiness. As if I am encased in the shell of a giant turtle. I do not feel guilt. I don't even feel sad except that I may never leave here, never walk in a field on a sunny day, never camp in the *Schwarzwald* underneath a starry sky again, never do things I have just dreamed of like pilot a plane over the lush, green jungles of Africa. I feel sad only for myself. And even then, I feel mostly the bars, the boredom, the frustration that I cannot do or undo or have a choice. This is my entire future. Pain is solitary. And my soul aches with the injustice of it all.

Lana: Injustice? But you said that you know you are guilty. You confessed in court and before me. By the laws, by any human conscience, how can you use that word? Injustice.

Franz: See, Lana, you *do* condemn me. Like all the good folk in Danville, Indiana.

Lana: No. I mean…

Franz: What, Lana? What do you mean?

Lana: I mean, that you did all those things under orders. You had no choice.

Franz: But I am an officer. I do not understand you, Lana. One moment, you say I am guilty. Then you change your mind and say I had no choice. Does it really matter?

Lana: Oh, dammit, Franz. Dammit. Why then did you do all those things? You aren't evil. I know you're not. All you've ever wanted to do was to create beauty. You're right. I don't understand. Just answer me one question. How could you love me with such a beautiful, tender love and yet do all those horrible things if you had a choice?

Franz: If I had a choice? Didn't I tell you that I chose? Do you still love me, Lana? It's important.

Lana: Damn you. A few minutes ago I would have said yes without thinking.

Franz: Then go ahead, Lana. Think. Take all the time you need. I will make it easier by reciting my sins to you. I burnt a village to the ground and locked every man, woman, and child in a barn and then ordered it, too, burned to the ground. I will never forget the smell. Like one million steaks roasting on spits. But that is not all. No, far from it. I placed thousands of Jews on trains going east. Just east. I told them, you are being resettled, new homes, new farms. I hear many of them were baked, too. An easier method, much cleaner. But I am still not done. I ordered a boy with a stuffed monkey named Zéphir shot without mercy in the shadow of his mother's limp skirts. Funny, I remember the monkey's name and not the boy's. Make a note to buy little Franz a monkey. Say it is from his daddy and it is named Zéphir. Maybe you should douse it in ketchup. Shall I continue? I can. I can list hundreds, hundreds of individual deaths. A man named Flambord, a painter, of houses not canvasses, shot between the eyes. A woman named Josette, someone's grandmother, lovely embroidery on her blouse, the stomach, six bullets, resilient. Marie, a woman in a blue dress, milk splattered on her white apron, just done with the cows, I think, two shots, the heart.

Lana: Stop!

Franz: Why? I am just describing a catalog of portraits. Yes, I drew, Lana. I drew death with a pistol, painted it with a blowtorch. Images of pale faces with terror in their eyes, teeth clenched in expectation of the end or mouths hanging open like avenues for the soul to fly out of the body and up to heaven. Images in art, Lana. I have drawers and drawers full of sketches, paintings.

(He pulls open the drawers of his desk, pulling out piles of sketches and throwing them madly in the air so that they scatter across the stage; it should be apparent that he is deriving great pleasure from this action.)

Lana: *(picking up the pictures, glancing at them, sifting through them)* I don't remember you like that, Franz. I'm sorry. I just don't. I remember a tender man. Not shy or quiet, but inspiration flowed through your veins. *(holding a bright, impressionistic piece that stands out even at a distance from the other pieces by its vivid colors)* You spoke about light colors and bright colors. Green trees, blue sky, yellow sun. Landscapes vibrant with hyacinths and tulips and tall, tall irises. You spoke pictures like these. You spoke of *liebe* and called me "*Liebling*" and "*Honigbienchen*," your little honey bee.

Franz: *(snatching the picture from her and tossing it aside)* A spritey Aphroditey. We bounced in the hay. Fiddle-dee-dee-di-dough. And a ho-diddle-oh.

Lana: If I've sinned in loving you, Franz, then God forgive me.

Franz: And not me?

Lana: Forgive him, God. He knows not what he says.

Franz: Or knows too well that I am already condemned to damnation in the fiery pit below. It is futile, Lana. Save your prayers. As I have burned, so shall I yet burn.

Lana: Why are you laughing, Franz? This prison has made you mad.

FRANZ: Mad? Mad?

There was a mad old man from Nantucket
Who thought he would live in a bucket
But when he looked in, he could
See nothing but blood *(pronounced "bloud")*
So he bent over and started to suck it.

I'll suck you, too, Lana! *(grabs* **LANA** *and starts to kiss her)*

LANA: *(pulls away)* Stop it, Franz. I came only to see if I still loved you. If you loved me. To find out the man whom I…I…

FRANZ: Fucked, Lana. Fucked.

LANA: Loved. Why is it so God-damned important for you to shatter that totally? What will I tell little Franz now?

FRANZ: Go ahead. Tell him I was a painter. Is that not what you were going to tell him? Look at my fingers. (pulls off his gloves. He has bandages wrapped around the tips of all his fingers)

LANA: What have you done to your hands?

FRANZ: Why, Lana, don't you know that blood is the most vivid color to paint with? Such a deep rich red. It changes to brown as it dries, but when you mix it with other colors. See here, my own finger painting. Red with yellow. I call it "blood red sun over Indiana cornfields." Of course, I've never been there. What do you think? Have I got the colors right? *(pause)* Lana, have you seen Vincent van Gogh's self-portrait?

LANA: He didn't paint with real blood, Franz.

FRANZ: No, but he was mad. He cut off his ear and mailed it to the woman he loved as a gift. He was one of the greatest artists of all time. Have you got a knife, Lana?

LANA: A knife? Is that what you would have me show little Franz, the token by which we should remember you. Dreamtime? Sounds more like a nightmare.

FRANZ: Now, Lana. Now, do you see, see the forces of decay? How the Dreamtime betrays. It betrayed me. It betrayed you. It betrayed us together. Now as an artist, I am blind. I can create only from blood. These hands, Lana. These hands are stained. And no matter how I wash, I scrub, like Lady Macbeth, I can still see the red.

LANA: Franz, the Dreamtime. Do you feel it now?

FRANZ: I feel it always. Beckoning. Reckoning.

LANA: What do you see?

FRANZ: *(as if in trance)* Wide open land stretching to a horizon far, far away. Sand red as blood. Wild grasses. Black sky. Full of stars, but the constellations are strange. A round red moon. And music. Soft chanting. Dark figures dancing around a bonfire, under the moon.

Lana: *(eyes closed)* I'm trying to see, Franz, but the glare of the sun is so bright.

Franz: Chanting. Chanting. Louder. Louder. Calling. Calling. Calling.

Lana: I feel cool, a cool breeze. The smell of azaleas, freshly bloomed. So, so quiet, but I can hear voices, faint voices whispering. Almost over. Over. Over. A few weeks, months at most. Almost over.

Franz: On the horizon. Coming. Closer. Closer. In the wind. All red and transparent and electric. Full of wide-eyed children and vibrating with the clatter of machine guns. Screaming. Screaming. Huge red glowing eyes. And horns. Horns all over.

Lana: Stop it! Stop! The knocking. Go away. Leave us alone! No. No. No. Not the Man in Black. But it's almost over. How? Why? Not Jimmy. Mom! Smelling salts! Hot tea! Fast! Fast! The azaleas, they smell so sour.

Franz: It's too big. Too big! Too horrible. I'm frightened. Lana! Lana!

Lana: *(pulling close to him, hugging him close to her)* Franz, I'm here. Here. So warm. The sweat. Smell. Touch. Feel. Ride. In. In. I. I. Love. Love… *(pulls away suddenly, but not too far)* Jimmy! Not my…not my brother!

Franz: Too big! Too big!

Lana: *(calmer)* Mom, look at it. Look at it. They sent it. For him. It glistens. The ribbon. Red like…like blood. What he did. He did. While I. Mom, don't look at me like that! Not little Franz's fault!

Franz: I feel…it wants to devour me. Eat me alive. Ever so slowly, nibble, taste, gnaw on my bones.

Lana: Pack. Pack. Must leave. Got to get out. Get away from the eyes. The voices. Over. Over. No, still can't tell. Won't understand. Mom, I'm so. So sorry.

Franz: Dark faces. They have no expression. Just spin me around and around and around. Shaking. Twitching.

Lana: The eyes. All over. Everywhere. Following me, always one step behind. Staring, Was not. Not he. Not you. Not like that. Her eyes. Red. Wet. Weeping. Black lines down, down her cheeks. Shut up. Shut up! How can you be so cruel? So sorry about Jimmy. Jimmy? Franz, where are you?

Franz: They're laughing now. Laughing. Laughing. Louder. Louder. Their eyes glowing red.

Lana: Don't. Don't look at me. Don't push me. Not to brown wood. Sweet mahogany. Keep it down. Keep it down. No, no. Can't look. Won't. Don't make me. Please. *(sigh of relief)* The black like a pile of peat with dried leaves. No dark-haired boy with gray eyes, used to ride a hobbyhorse in the backyard, giddy-up Charlemagne. *(cries)* Turned to ashes and dried blood. Don't make me…touch.

Franz: They're pulling my arms. They're taking me, taking me to the waterhole. Again. Again.

Lana: My hand. Don't pull it down.

Franz: When, when, I put my hands in the water—so cool, so dark—all the water turns red.

Lana: Black. Black. Where are the blues? Greens? Yellows? Must go. Find. Know. But I forgot when I went. Do I know? Time. Time. Running out. Franz. Franz! Where? I hear you…Dammit, Franz! Take them out! Are your…are your hands…are they clean?

Franz: No, they're redder than before. And the laughter. They are all laughing. It, too, with its gaping, colossal maw!

Lana: I hear them. All around me. They echo.

Franz: Come live with us, they say. Come live with it. That's the only way to save your soul.

Lana: Can you hear me, Franz?

Franz: Lana, where are you?

Lana: Lost, lost in the blackness. Near you. Here. Here. For better or worse. I'm here. Though I be damned.

Franz: Then we are damned together.

Lana: Come back, Franz. Back to me. Time to come. Feel me. You don't see anything but me, Franz. Just me. Just Lana.

Franz: Mmmmmmmmmmmmmmm… What happened? I heard you talking as if in the distance. As if you were talking from across the world.

Lana: I was. Don't you remember?

Franz: What?

Lana: The Dreamtime.

Franz: Was I there? I remember only your voice. But you were not speaking to me. Not at first. You said, eyes, voices, Mom, Jimmy?

Lana: Jimmy? He was my brother. I was talking about Jimmy? But Jimmy's dead, blown to bits defending me against you.

Franz: Lana, did I slay it?

Lana: You do remember.

Franz: When a man has the same dream for a thousand nights, he cannot forget it. Did I?

Lana: Only you know that.

Franz: Then I did not. But soon. It must be soon.

(Sounds of door being unbolted and opened. Enter **Private.***)*

Private: Miss Davis, your time is up.

Lana: Please. Private Chambers, isn't it? Just one more minute?

Private: All right. One.

Lana: I just wanted one long moment to look at you.

Franz: And what do you see now—the lover or the monster?

Lana: Both.

Franz: Will you take little Franz to see *meine Mutter*? She would be so proud.

Lana: Yes, Franz. I will do that.

Franz: When you see her, thank her for the flowers. Tell her that they really brighten up the room. She speaks a little English.

Lana: Uh-huh.

Franz: I am very glad you came, Lana.

Lana: Yes.

Franz: Can I hold you?

Lana: Yes.

Franz: Come back and see me, Lana. Tomorrow. Please.

Lana: Good-bye, Franz.

Franz: Lana. One last thing. If our son asks, tell him his father was an artist.

Lana: Yes, Franz. What else could I tell him? Good-bye.

Franz: Tomorrow, *meine liebling* Lana. *Auf Wiedersehen.*

Lana: *Auf Wiedersehen. (she adds softly and nods, not to Franz) Auf Wiedersehen.*

Lana *and* **Private** *exit.* **Franz** *watches her leave, then stands in place staring at the door for a long moment. Finally, he sits down at his desk. The lighting dims until the only light is provided by a spotlight on* **Franz.** *He sketches a few lines with his pencil. He opens up the box of watercolors. He takes a brush out of the box and dips it in the glass of water. He dips it in the yellow paint and applies a few strokes to the paper. He pauses, then puts the brush down. He removes the bandages on his right index finger. He takes the pencil and stabs the tip into the finger. He dips the brush into his finger and starts to paint. Finally, he dips his fingertip directly into the painting and smudges it across the paper. He removes another bandage, and prepares to puncture that finger, as the spotlight dims.*

Another spotlight fades in on the opposite side of the stage to reveal **Colonel Stephenson,** *talking on the phone.*

Colonel: Yeah, Hal, General Franz Schiller was found dead this morning. Though the cause of death was diagnosed as lead poisoning in his blood, it was unclear whether his death was a calculated suicide or merely the unintentional result of lead-based paint being mixed into his bloodstream. Seems like the bastard's been pricking his fingers with a pencil for months and smearing them in yellow paint, which is like a double-dose of lead. The only color in the box that's lethal. May even have been drinking the stuff, too, the doc says. Weird, huh? In any case, his death must have been gradual and real painful. His final words, scribbled on a scrap of paper on his desk were to "Lana." Obviously Lana Davis. "Lana. Tell little Franz that his father is safe in the Dreamtime." Next to the note was a small painting of what seems to be some black African native playing a little pipe. Miss Davis was sent for immediately, but it seems as if she has checked out of her hotel and left no forwarding address. Quite frankly, Hal, I pity the boy.

Curtain

The Prince of Lyghes

Jenny didn't go looking for it. Todd didn't mean for her to find it.

She felt an odd sensation after dusting a book or maybe wiping a shelf, like a spider slipping onto her arm, scuttering rapidly up her sleeve and wriggling into her ear. She slapped her hand up quickly, wondering if perhaps a mosquito had bitten her or maybe the itchy burn of built-up wax. Then she sensed something squishy behind her eyes for just a moment. Perhaps a speck of dust that could be washed away with a stray tear? Finally a squeeze around the nape of her spine like something grabbing hold with tiny pin-like claws.

Later a vague pain developed that a pair of aspirin did nothing to relieve. That evening she planned to go to bed early, thinking that sleep would cure her headache, but somehow she stayed up late washing the dishes and then the laundry while Todd locked himself up again in his office.

Business, he said. Always business: emails to Hollywood executives about the latest potential deal that never happened, self-consciously clever social networking updates that generated fawning responses from a few of his four thousand acquaintances, messaging sessions so crucial that dinner had to be postponed for an hour or two, and then he would complain about it being cold or overcooked or just plain shit. Everything was shit when the side dish was Scotch or 1.5-liter bottles of cheap white wine. Not that she ever saw the bottle until the dead soldiers lined up behind a door. Nor did he ever admit he was drinking.

As Jenny headed downstairs to unload the clothes from the dryer, she noticed the door to Todd's office was now ajar. Through the crack, she could see his body collapsed and akimbo over the cluttered paperwork on the forest-green carpet. A snort from his nose trumpeted, made her head twinge again. Or maybe it was a light pressure as if something behind her temples were expanding?

Basket full in hands, she headed back up to their bedroom, emptied its contents into the dresser drawers and changed into pajamas. For most of the twelve years of their marriage, Todd had come to bed and held her, at least for part of the night. She'd taken those embraces—hugs that joined the two into a comma—as proof of his love for her even when they'd had arguments the day before. But now he rarely came to bed, and if he did, he barely held her at all.

When Jenny woke alone the next morning, cigarette smoke wafted in through the heating vent. The heavy aroma of tobacco intensified her headache, and a slight pain now welled in her mid-back and curved around to her stomach. This time, she took three aspirin. Maybe later she'd try four ibuprofen.

Was her heartbeat a bit quicker, too? Surely that was just because she was so angry at Todd not only for starting to smoke again after seven years of kicking the habit but also for breaking the inside house no-smoking rule. She thought about confronting him, but didn't want to hear his derisive denial again, or worse, risk him striking her. So she lay in bed and fumed quietly, waiting for the pain in her head to ebb enough for her to crawl downstairs and start a pot of coffee.

Jenny could usually concentrate herself into a machine and grind through even the most mundane and boring of design assignments. But today, even after two cups of coffee, the odd tactile aches and sensitivities made it difficult for her to focus. She had to email one of her clients for a deadline extension—something she hated to do in this unstable economy. She met Todd briefly in the kitchen, making himself bacon and eggs and baked beans. All she could stomach was one slice of toast with honey. They exchanged a few vague words about weekend plans and who might go grocery shopping, though she doubted he'd be sober enough to drive to the store. If he insisted, she'd have to choose between letting him and risking one more DUI or triggering another fight, another blow to her head. She watched him carry the plate downstairs, suspecting he'd eat no more than a few bites. She wondered if he'd remember to return the dish or abandon it on his desk until the leftovers attracted roaches.

Jenny's only other contact with Todd today was when a delivery man rang the doorbell with another box. As always, she noted the same return address—Kolonia, Pohnpei, FSM. When she looked it up, she found the abbreviation stood for Federated States of Micronesia, until 1986 a U.S. territory and still closely tied. She carried it downstairs to his office and knocked gently on the door.

"Todd, you've got another package."

Todd cracked open the door, eyes glazed, thinning hair disheveled, chin peppered with brown and gray stubble, wearing a faded black Led Zeppelin T-shirt and sweat pants so gnarly with holes that they belonged nowhere but the trash.

The customs labels always simply read "books," and Jenny assumed they contained books. After all, Todd was a writer and owned lots of books, so why shouldn't they be books? She sometimes asked him what books they were, worrying about the high cost of ordering books from so far away. They'd already taken out an equity line to reduce the interest rate on his credit card debts. He told her that books in English weren't popular in Asia and the cost of living was cheap, so Micronesian book dealers were willing to sell whatever was left from the libraries of Americans from territorial days, which often could be extensive, for surprisingly inexpensive prices. And the sellers gave good deals on shipping, too.

If Jenny pushed Todd a little further, he'd get increasingly edgy. He'd say that he was researching entomology or otolaryngology or the archaeology of some ancient city—what was it called? Yes, Nan Madol—or some other obscure topic that she would have no interest in, and remind her he didn't ask questions about her packages. Not that she received many, for she was very frugal with her meager earnings which barely supported both of them. Todd rarely made much money anymore and seemed to spend all of it paying off an unknown amount of credit card debt, which Jenny assumed was spent mostly on booze, cigarettes, and the contents of the packages. She knew she ought to demand that he tell her his card balances, but he'd get so angry when she asked. One time when she suggested he take out a new card with a zero percent balance transfer offer, he punched her so hard that he broke one of her ribs.

Jenny preferred to hunt for her bargains in person at thrift shops or discount stores—"treasure-hunting," she called it. She excelled at finding that unique vintage dress or perfect-fitting pair of tight jeans at a great price. Today she was wearing a Bettie Page-label pencil skirt and a tight-fitting red shirt with white polka-dots and ball sleeves.

But Todd didn't notice how cute she looked in her pin-up ensemble when she told him she was lunching with a friend. His eyelids fluttered as if he could barely focus. He just coughed and spat a gelatinous ball of brown tobacco phlegm on the rug. Then he took the package from her hands and closed the door. She could hear him shuffle his feet over the papers on the floor, the loud rustling of unpacking, then what sounded like a tiny chirp. She turned away and headed back upstairs to fetch a paper towel and carpet cleaner before the gooey stain set in the fabric.

Halfway up, a pang of nausea assaulted her, and she grasped her stomach. But the pain passed swiftly, and after the clean-up, she stumbled back to her computer screen. An hour later she had canceled lunch and curled up in a ball on the bed, trying to nap away throbbing pain that began between her temples and descended deep into her abdomen.

By the second morning, the disconcerting sensation had spread to Jenny's arms and legs, making them mysteriously tingly. The last few times this happened, Todd hadn't been as drunk and stirred up an antidote, which he said included Alka-Seltzer, pickle juice, ginger beer, and a secret ingredient he wouldn't divulge. The concoction tasted terrible but it always did the trick. She'd thrown up about ten minutes later and then feel rejuvenated, normal. In those times, he'd tell her he'd given up drinking and collecting. She'd believe him, her being an optimist—both a blessing and a curse. They'd go out to movies, watch television together snuggling close on the couch in the den, and he'd fix her a few lovely dinners—lamb with mint sauce and roast potatoes or chicken Tikka Masala. These idyllic "staycations" sometimes lasted just a couple of days but occasionally endured for weeks or even months, further filling her with an inexplicable and reckless sensation of hope.

But this time Todd was spending more and more hours locked in his office, so many that he didn't notice that Jenny was sicker than on the other occasions. When she made even the slightest pain complaint, he told her to "shut the fuck up" because he didn't have time to listen to her whining. She was "interfering," trying to "control" him, and he needed to get back to work. Every time he spoke cruelly to her, she felt a slight heave inside her head or her stomach or her arm as if whichever body part was expanding. But that was ridiculous. Perhaps she had the flu.

The cramps resonated so severely the next morning that Jenny stayed in bed. She was drifting back to sleep when she heard a high-pitched wail rise up through the vent—the cry faint at first and then growing steadily in volume until she almost had to clamp her ears. It stopped as suddenly as it started, and then silence for about five minutes. The next screech grated against her ears so violently that she pulled a pillow over her head. As it dissipated, she unburied her face, and a chorus of chitters followed, like an army of cicadas accompanied by metal spoons banging against pans.

Jenny crawled out of bed and crept into the hallway, alternately massaging her temples and holding her stomach, her aches almost overwhelming her with each step. Leaning over the landing, she could see that Todd's office door again was half-open, the cacophonous sounds drifting out from behind it and now including the frenzied chatter of what sounded like mewling cats, croaking frogs, and other animal noises she couldn't identify. Her head throbbed even more urgently at the sharp sounds that spiked again in volume as she slowly descended the two short flights of stairs. Once she reached the door, she paused to listen in case Todd might be shuffling behind it or rummaging in the closet. With all the paper scattered on the messy floor, he couldn't move around without making noise, though she couldn't be sure with all the other ruckus.

Peeking inside, Jenny saw no sign of Todd. Maybe he was smoking outside, or more likely he'd slipped out the patio door to sneak to the neighborhood liquor store or make a cellphone call. He always insisted the signal wasn't good in the house, though she never had any trouble with her own phone.

Still, not knowing if he could return at any moment, she entered carefully, tiptoeing through the paperwork. To the right, the cabinet doors in his bookcases vibrated in and out, the source of the animal chatter behind them.

Unexpectedly, she thought she heard Todd's voice, making her spin around to see just the empty hallway.

"I love you. The one thing I fear most in the world is you leaving me," the voice repeated three times like a broken record.

Then other words…accusatory words…

"Why is it you just lie there? Why is it you shrug me off when I touch you in the middle of the night?"

"That's because I'm asleep. I don't remember…" her own voice protested.

"You should be ready to make love whenever I'm ready to make love to you," he countered.

"You just want to control me.

"You don't know what love is.

"Rancid cunt."

Now the cabinet doors rattled like a rapid heartbeat. The palpitations frightened her but also beckoned Jenny's curiosity until she could do nothing else but fling them open. The action felt strangely freeing, even electrifying. She was finally going to see the books that came in the packages. But inside were no books—just cages and terrariums of various sizes filled with strange creatures.

Some beasts twitched their clusters of long gelatinous appendages, beating them like thumping cats' tails. Others leered with gaping eyes oversized for their bodies and their vaguely amphibian heads. Some spread razor-blade teeth and sashayed left to right on scaly chicken-like legs that weren't quite in the right places. But most didn't resemble anything she had ever seen—lacerated red flesh with spiderwebs of purple veins on translucent pale skin interspersed with dreadlocked fur and bulbous sacs that looked stretched almost to bursting with yellow pus. Things with too many ears, too many eyes, ears but no eyes, eyes but no ears, lips with teeth on the outside, others that puckered and occasionally extended long blue and green cyst-covered tongues.

Then their voices lowered and those that had appendages lifted them up and beckoned as if welcoming her, inviting her closer and still chittering, chittering, chittering.

Jenny's head pounded with every scratch-on-a-chalkboard sound the creatures emitted. Her back stiffened as if the slightest movement would break it in two, her stomach churning painfully and melting into oscillating gelatin. The creatures' chattering escalated, flesh glowing effervescently like cameras flashing, photographing not just her most intimate parts but x-raying beneath her skin to her brain and internal organs.

Then the shimmer faded like lights dimming in the cinema, replaced by fuzzy images that gradually cleared until she could see Todd in every one—a wall of monitors, each broadcasting him having sex with another woman. At first, the sex was just sex, warm and sweaty. A black woman in missionary position. A tiny Asian body with long dark hair writhing in sixty-nine—perfect toned buttocks pointed in her direction. A redhead doggy-style.

Those images dissolved and were replaced with more deviant ones. A threesome with two women, one sucking his penis, another perched over Todd's face, his tongue eagerly licking. Him rolling a nerve wheel over the nipples of a laughing brunette. Todd in black leather furiously beating another Asian girl with a riding crop as he roughly penetrates her ass.

The pictures then dissolved into multiple views of one petite woman with long straight blonde hair. Todd spooned against her like he used to do with Jenny, fondling a nipple, kissing her neck. She giggles. He whispers in her ear, "I love you. I love you unconditionally."

The blonde turns, fixes her icy blue eyes on Jenny, and hisses, the "s" holding long and snakelike on her tongue.

"What are you doing in my office, cunt?!" Todd's real voice shattered the spectral woman's venomous face into broken shards of glass. The vision readjusted back to the creatures, now shaking furiously in their enclosures.

"This is *my* office and *you* don't belong in here."

Jenny's head jerked towards the doorway and took in his angry visage and arms wrapped around a big brown paper bag. He chugged a hefty swig from the value-sized wine bottle wrapped within and placed it on top of a filing cabinet. And before she could even process her lack of an escape route, his fist pounded down on the top of her head.

Jenny crumpled to the floor, and Todd's fist descended again. Her skull rang with its impact, her head immediately heavier, swelling, and the beak of his sharp silver raven's head ring cut into her skin. The third time, his fist fell on the side of her temple, and as the pain registered, she also sensed scratching inside, as if something was moving, repositioning. Jenny heard herself screaming, "Help!" Or was it the victim of some other crime far away in the distance?

Jenny wanted to fight back, but Todd had her pinned so she couldn't move. Again and again, his fist throttled her head. Then the pointed toe of his cowboy boot kicked her side, triggering a loud crack and a sudden burning pain. Had he broken another rib? She tried to curl up into a ball on the floor so he couldn't reach her stomach or her breasts, and she felt the next impact beat into her lower back. She was just screaming now. At the top of her lungs, surprised at how loud she could scream, her head expanding from the inside—big and airy and burning.

This was how it felt to die, the part of Jenny's brain that wasn't in full shock thought as she continued to scream, the windows shut so no one was likely to hear, call the police. Was there even time for her to be rescued? The blows came down again and again. Todd twisted her arm, pushed her face to the floor to better position his fist to target the rear of her head. Her insides churned and bile rushed up into her throat, the first spasm of vomit. But as orange chunks exited her mouth, something else did as well. The pressure stretched her esophagus, neck and head, excruciating as each expanded to its limit, and Jenny felt like she was choking, hemorrhaging, coming to an end.

Then a rush of fresh air flushed through her lungs as something inside shot from her open lips onto the floor. The chittering around her mounted, became deafening. Stringy appendages draped across the carpet, a mass of discoid flesh using them to pivot and leap across her head.

Todd's blows stopped as suddenly as they had begun. Glass shattered, bars broke, a thousand scurrying, scampering, slithering sounds. Then Todd began to scream, a prolonged screech of agony. Aching, throbbing tension overwhelmed Jenny's head as she forced herself to roll over onto her back and see what was happening.

Through blurred vision, she barely made out Todd's body covered in the creatures, nibbling, gnawing, sucking, bits of his flesh crunching in the mouths of those that had mouths, bright red blood showering them en masse, dyeing their amorphous shapes in his guts and gore. The protruding appendages of the thing that had been inside her stuffed Todd's mouth, as if he'd swallowed something much too big to chew and the rest was trying to force its way in, pushing, curling back and pushing again. He could no longer scream, barely groan, his cheeks bulging. His eyes expanded out of their sockets. His nose exploded in a giant sneeze, blowing off his face into myriad tiny pieces.

Todd's blood and snot soaked her, but other than clamping her own mouth shut, her hands and arms were too injured to reach up and wipe her face. Though basted in slime, she found herself silently smiling. Each bite or suction served as a release to her, a sign that he was feeling the physical manifestation of the beatings and emotional pain she had lived with for so many years. The old Todd that she had loved so deeply had dissolved into a distant memory, and this stranger who drank, smoked, and fucked everyone but her—that one blonde woman especially—held no resemblance.

His suit of skin was completely ripped off now, remnants of tattered red muscles all that lingered. As the creatures parted slightly, she could see Todd's heart still pulsating—purpling with the pressure of pumping blood through severed veins. She looked up into his eyes to search for any sorrow or regret, but she could not identify either emotion. And then Todd's eyes were gone, bursting from their sockets, shooting past her face like soft torpedoes and squishing into the wall behind her.

Todd's heart was slowing now, the red meat almost completely devoured, inner organs bitten through, bones sparkling pearly white thanks to licking tongues and fleshy, suctioning pressure. The monster that had been inside her was visible again, a pale amoeboid entity fluctuating between solid and transparent, widening and narrowing as it navigated organs, thinning as it slipped inside Todd's esophagus, expanding into a hammer shape as it battered against his stomach. Its spidery tendrils had fully looped themselves inside his skull mouth, curling into what was left of his arms and twisting around his spine like nerves in an anatomy model. The thing had completely avoided his brain, however, concentrating first on the destruction of the rest of his body. If the loss of blood had not been enough to make him comatose, might his mind not still be functioning, feeling every bite, every thrust, every squeeze?

The monster's head penetrated Todd's stomach with a loud splat, undigested food and fluids suddenly flying outward. But it didn't linger long, its appendages pushing down to grasp his intestines, unfurling them like jump-ropes, ripping into his colon and pushing out of his buttocks like a cat of nine tails.

Jenny felt sad that Todd's heart finally stopped before the monster reached his penis, inhaling it in a motion so quick that she could not tell if it was a gulp or simply an absorption. The devouring process was satisfying to watch but far too fast. She had suffered the bites Todd had taken verbally from her self-esteem, her creativity, her dignity, and the more overt pushes and punches for years, and especially the lies that twisted into her like slow-growing cancers. The denials of his drinking had been impossible to hide thanks to the sometimes subtle, sometimes blatant changes in his personality from kind to cruel. And worse, the secret liaisons.

She'd realized neither that he had committed so many transgressions nor the extent of their deviance and the relish with which he enjoyed inflicting pain on other women, women who enjoyed it. And worst of all, that he'd given his heart to another. At one time Jenny'd even had the naïve thought he'd never cheat on her, that her battle was only with the sweet lure of alcohol. If she was safe from anything, for so long she had been so sure it was from him fucking another woman. Then she found out about one—maybe the blonde; she never saw a picture—and he begged her back, promised to cut it off right away, even quit drinking for a while, made her believe. And

she did, even though she was a smart, educated woman. He was sober for six months, and then the packages began to arrive again.

A sharp crack woke Jenny out of her reverie. The beasts were now down to consuming Todd's skeleton, a chorus of sharp crunches, chewing and squishy ingestion. The big thing hadn't forgotten his brain, just saved it for last, tendrils and fleshy mass cracking the skull like a nutcracker, then allowing the little ones to slide in and slurp on it like a fine delicacy. The last body parts to disappear were his feet, ironic perhaps because Jenny had thought so many times that if he'd broken a foot or leg, Todd wouldn't have been able to walk to the liquor store, push the gas pedal on the car, or make it across the room to hit her.

Finished with their meal, the creatures fell into a deep hum. Was it a song of satisfaction, satiation? They spread all around her on the floor. The larger monster, the one that had gestated inside Jenny, was now fully revealed—a bulbous thing with no discernible shape, fluctuating from spherical as a fat spider, then stretching long and flat with hunched sores and bubbles. At first, its many eyes seemed glazed and unfocused, but as if becoming conscious of the intensity with which she was watching it, they shot open wide and engaged her. And in that moment, all the creatures that had eyes did the same, turning in her direction in one sudden wave.

Jenny felt her terror return. Their food source fully devoured with Todd, would they now eat her for dessert? Those creatures that had nostrils seemed to be sniffing the air, considering.

The beasts crawled slightly in her direction in one great oozing wave, but then they turned towards the outer wall, climbing or slithering or simply spreading up the legs of Todd's desk and onto its surface. Shattered glass and a few quick gnaws—or was that a burst of acidic spit shot from one thing's mouth?—and the window and screen now bore a large hole. Tiny behinds, gelatinous masses and jittering tails disappeared into the darkness of the night. Were they looking for more people with damaged souls to feed on their twisted dreams, their desire to cause pain? Or were they simply returning to the soil until someone else placed the next order in the mail?

Soon Jenny's only companion in the blood-splattered office was the monster that had gestated inside her. Was it the queen bee, the mother alien? Or was it just the catalyst, the leader, the top chef that the others needed when the time came for the final devouring, when the human being was fully prepared, seasoned with negative thoughts and marinated with pain inflicted on others?

Jenny waited and it waited. Then it lifted one of its tendrils and gestured in a wavelike motion, slowly, gracefully easing towards her—not a threatening movement, more a question. Its body didn't move, just this arm-like appendage, until it stopped right in front of her face, still undulating as if it wanted to touch her forehead but wasn't sure if she would recoil or slap it back.

She knew she should be scared. Shouldn't she? She should pull back and not risk that it would change its mind, hurt her. But the creature had been inside her and had not killed her, and she had already faced death tonight from her husband. What did she have to be afraid of? Instead she felt a mutual curiosity. What did it want from her?

Jenny leaned in, let the tendril touch her brow. A tingling surged through her head and into her arms, down her spine and legs and toes. Not an unpleasant feeling, almost healing though her rib bone was not re-aligning nor did the dull ache in her head from the repeated pounding dissipate. She felt an activity in her mind, and realization came to her. It wanted to understand. What exactly she wasn't sure—probably why she had stayed with Todd so long and put up with all the pain he unleashed on her. That made sense, didn't it? But she didn't understand it herself. She wondered if she ever would.

After what seemed a long time but was probably less than five minutes, it pulled back its limb, stared at her for one more long moment. And then it, too, climbed onto Todd's desk and out the window.

Once it had fully disappeared into the night, Jenny crawled to the desk herself, pulled down the cordless phone and dialed 911.

Sensoria

"Not only is it the last show, but it is the last show I will ever do."
—David Bowie as Ziggy Stardust,
Hammersmith Odeon, London, 1973

The smoky hole of church-turned-club pulsates—vibrating sweat-drenched bodies getting off on themselves and each other packed among the pews of a gigantic granite womb. Sasha fanned her chest with a show flyer, the heat of tightly packed bodies tempered only mildly by her rain-soaked but quickly drying hair and the removal of her lightweight white shawl, which she had wound around her purse strap so as not to lose it. Sober unlike most of the throng, she imagined the audience a great gyrating beast, arms rising up like tentacles, legs scurrying side to side like centipedes to the throbbing industrial drone that the DJ was spinning until the band came on. The "pit" crowd pushed into her and she shifted with it, reactivating her punk-rock instincts to navigate her way towards the chancel-turned-stage. She staked her territory, leaned her chest onto its lip. Wasn't she too old to be hanging with the horror hipsters, Goth groupies, and neo-punks who had bought their way in to use him as their dildo? Why did she come out in a pouring thunderstorm, pay for an expensive taxi so as not to be late? And yet here she was waiting to experience Dorian Cain *LIVE* for the first time.

The music halted, and the crowd applauded. Mist tinted scarlet by spotlights spewed onto the stage and out into the audience. The crowd quieted, the pounding rain outside momentarily audible on the stained-glass windows above the pulpit. The keyboardist took his place first, a tall purple-Mohawked black man in a fringed leopard print jacket. His fingers initiated a jangly lullaby-like melody. The rest of the band came on stage, one by one, the volume building as each instrument joined in. A red-haired female cellist in a netty purple gown seated herself. A shaved-head guitarist in shiny silver shirt, red pants, and cowboy boots took his station by a standing mic. The Iggy-skinny, spiky hair and goatee, bass player in a Wolf Man T-shirt and tight jeans slouched towards another mic stand. A pudgy guy with teased big white hair slipped in last, behind the drums at the rear. From above the stained-glass windows, a large screen descended, on it a flickering image of a dark-haired woman with big eyes lined in black. She closed her eyelids, reopened them and had no eyes, blood dripping down her deeply chiseled cheeks like tears.

Stretch Limo to the Dimension of Darkness.

Sasha looked up to see Dorian Cain towering above her, all black leather, licorice tongue lapping tense circles within his lips—curving in, breaking out.

Better Hide Your Soul.

He swung his long dark hair in a wide loop, then his eyes exploded open gazing down at her, black onyx rimmed with a corona of sea-green.

Guard Your Passion.

His pointy black shoes literally grazed her nipples through her stretch velvet sleeveless white mini-dress. She felt a wet dribble of Dorian's sweat fall on her cheek.

Thieves everywhere.

Then he danced away, all thunder and tease.

A granite ripple of bass guitar wove down, down.

Crash.

Pale and Salty.

Dorian sang now from the other end of the stage.

Salt Milk.

He swiveled his pelvis like Jim Morrison…no, Nick Cave.

Be Your Daddy. Teach You.

The music softened back to a cello tingle, followed by frenzied strumming.

Rose up again, drums pounding, the chancel vibrating and her body shaking with it.

A shatter of cymbal.

Now center stage, Dorian leaned into his crotch, his jeans ripping across his knees. He dropped his black leather jacket onto one shoulder, flashing black T-shirt, sleeves ripped off, and the tattoo she'd seen in photos—the horned skull, the black rose.

Rock 'n' roll stays the same. Rock changes.

Dorian was more dynamic musically and exuding more goddamned sexuality and stage presence than Sasha had heard—and she had heard all of that. She reminded herself she was supposed to be a rock journalist, here just to watch and document.

As Dorian thrashed at the far left end of the stage, Sasha's view of him was blocked by the bouncing heads of a gaggle of big-haired groupies. Left-right, left-right they swayed, the old in-out played out in the rhythmic throttle of teased manes—the kind sprayed with so much Ultra-Hold Aqua Net that not even a follicle strayed from place. One blonde like lemon meringue pie filling in a sleeveless zebra print mini-dress. Another strawberry redhead with brushstrokes of metallic gold in neon purple. But mostly Goth chicks in spidery black.

Behind them Sasha noticed a man with short-cropped dark hair and black sunglasses. His trench coat made sense for the rain outside, but considering how hot it was inside, she couldn't imagine anyone keeping it on. Was he a flasher? She couldn't tell if he had pants on, his legs lost in the throng of the crowd. Mr. Trench Coat was staring intently at the blonde, then his gaze wandered to other women in the crowd, lingering on each for several seconds and then moving to the next. Mechanical. She forgot the concert for a moment, caught up in the weirdness of his ritual.

As if he sensed someone was watching, he shifted—a stiff jerk compared to what had been a slow ritual—towards her. He lifted a black-gloved hand to adjust his sunglasses and grinned, full and toothy—gray heavy metal braces.

Sasha averted her eyes back to the stage. A new song had started and the volume spiked abruptly. The big screen now projected a woman with shortly cropped white hair, dressed in a long black gown, running through a cemetery, hands reaching up from the graves and grabbing at her ankles.

An ornate crypt loomed ahead with a weeping angel at its door. The angel's eyes moved.

Angels and devils call to her.

On the screen a black-gloved hand brandished a large hunting knife. Slashed into the woman's back. Blood spewed like a fountain from her wounds. Every horror movie cliché and yet the cinematography was stunning, Sasha thought.

She won't give them her number.

"Slip it in, baby," a male voice said next to her—Sid Vicious clone, pale with black spiky hair, white ripped T reassembled with safety-pins, and Levi's.

The Sid twisted his tongue in spiral eights around the lobe of his Nancy, lapping along the edges of her mass of blonde perm curls up the rim of her ear. With his other hand, he pulled a black box out of his pocket, opened it delicately and removed a red and black beetle. It scrambled in his fingers, legs flailing, wings fluttering, eager for escape. What the fuck?!

But the Sid gripped it firmly, the creature exuding a loud squeaky objection that reverberated above the music which had now eased back to cello and keyboards.

Nancy opened her mouth, he popped the insect into it, and she closed, crunched down and swallowed. Sasha could see in the chick's eyes how quickly it kicked in. Her pupils went from tipsy and glazed to dilated, irises rolling up.

Eyes flicked onscreen. Blinking.

Eyes of the ages…

Sid pulled out another box. This beetle didn't struggle as much, allowed him to gently stroke its back, a low hum more like a cat's purr before he popped it in his own mouth and his eyes now glazed over into white empty ovals. Empty to the outside anyway. The two were still grooving to the music but at a slower pace.

Watching her, touching her…

A masculine hand traced the curve of a nude female body above the band as reverb rose, the beat quickened to near hardcore speed.

A conga line of thrashers bumped into the center, feeling their way blind to all but the music, hopping in their combat boots, feet together. They smashed into the Sid, but he was gone—lost in the beetle's whatever effect.

Beyond.

Sasha felt a tap on her shoulder. Behind her stood an albino man with red contact lenses and cat-eye pupils beneath a mane of dreads, smiling perfect white teeth. He curled a hand under her arm and opened his palm in front of her face to reveal a black box similar to Sid and Nancy's.

"Try?" he whispered in her ear, accent Island via Queens. "Only fifty, madam."

Sasha shook her head. She hadn't even had a drink in two years, no drugs in a decade—and then just the most mundane—marijuana, cocaine, one dance with LSD.

"Milady, I saw the way you watched the others experience the wonders of the sensor-scarab, how you are transfixed on Dorian Cain," the man said in caramel tones, his other arm now caressing her waist. Why didn't she brush him away? He could be a rapist, for all she knew.

"I'm a journalist, just here to watch," Sasha protested.

Another cascade of cello. Dorian Cain towered above her again, swinging his hair. The images on the screen now all blood. Dripping like curtains. Pulling back to reveal a giant beetle, red and black like the one she saw the Sid and Nancy consume.

Hide and seek, till death is all.

"I don't drink, don't do drugs," she said, wondering how they could even hear each other in the loud music.

The scarab dealer lifted up Sasha's left hand with his own left, then flipped open the box with his right. The beetle inside was on its back, legs fidgeting as he lifted it out. He turned it over to reveal the same red markings.

"What is it?" Sasha says. She had to admit she was curious. After all, a journalist always should observe every detail. That is, if she had an assignment. If this concert wasn't an attempt to resurrect a career that had fallen away as she missed deadline after deadline to care for a guy who when he could walk again after being hit by a speeding van made it clear he didn't care for her. A memory flashed of coming home to find all his stuff packed up and gone, no note.

"Sensor-scarab, milady, they call her."

"Scarab, like ancient Egyptian?"

"This lady hails from Guatemala. She will not kill you, just make you reborn."

Sasha imagined his tongue was snakelike.

She glanced up from the insect to the screen to see on it a giant version of the same creature, its shiny crimson back resembling a more rounded version of the black widow hourglass, its legs twitching, its elytra flexing and spreading as it took flight.

She thought back to the little girl who collected cicada skins. How she liked to listen to them sing. How she watched a praying mantis once for an hour. How even spiders always fascinated her, and she would catch one in a jar and take it outside rather than kill it.

Why not try it? While she didn't like the idea of killing an insect, she'd eaten grasshoppers before in China with her parents, and she ate meat. What was different? Sid and Nancy were clearly having a good time. They were holding each other close, their eyes blind but fingers pawing, lightly scratching. She wouldn't have anyone to share the experience with, but right now was all about reclaiming her life, making her own decisions, finding some pleasure. Who knew if she could sell an article anyway, if she had burnt every bridge?

Sasha dug into her purse and pulled out two twenties and two fives. The dealer slipped his right hand off her waist, took the bills from her with the deftness of a magician. Then he placed the scarab in her mouth.

"Bite down, princess, as I let go."

Sasha ground her teeth down on the insect, feeling the crunch of its exoskeleton as a creamy liquid spread into her mouth, swishing in her teeth, under her tongue. The insect must be dead from her bite, but its juice, its lifeblood? Can liquid be alive? She chewed and swallowed, felt the hands of the dealer withdraw from her.

"Salut, darling."

She knows he is gone, dissolved into the throng which presses against her again. Pushing, pulling, vibrating. A low hum, a buzzing drone, like a symphony of cicadas. Are they singing along with Dorian? Has everyone consumed the scarab? She feels herself being carried up like the crowd might take flight. The screen wriggles, full of scarabs, tightly packed, hive-like, crawling over each other in all directions. Their red backs pulsate, flashing bright to dark, bright to dark.

Smoke and mirrors.

Above her, Dorian leans, singing, singing into her mouth.

Your love like a velvet blanket.

His tongue lapping in and out of his own like kisses.

In the rain.

No, like something else, a guitar in his hands, playing the length of the strings, the center hole—her G-spot—like a keyboard, snakelike and amplified.

Down, down, down, down…

Orgasm starts high, shudders, descends into her thighs, her brain condenses to happy jelly. Is this what the beetle-juice does, not a joke like the Tim Burton movie?

She can get used to this. The scarab isn't a black widow but a love bug. You don't have to really fuck the star; even the ugliest wallflower in the crowd gets off now.

Her euphoria dissolves into rain, her dress soaked and sticky to her body. She's climbing a ladder against a stone wall towards a row of tall arched stained-glass windows. Colored lights sparkle against the panes inside. The rungs are slippery so she shakes off her shoes, hears them bounce on the pavement below. She reaches the base of the window and climbs onto the ledge, meets the glass in an embrace. Throbbing amped rumble vibrates through the panes. Enthralled by the light's beauty and the beat, she begins to dance, well, more sway, the space too narrow for anything else. Her hair is wet and heavy. The light, the sound through the window comforts, calls. She can see shadows of movement inside.

She glances back to see if he is still watching her from below—the man in the trench coat. He is, expressionless, still wearing dark glasses, clutching a wide black umbrella. He pulls the blade from his pocket with his black-gloved left hand, brandishes it with a single slash and nods.

Sasha turns back to the window. She looks down, her dress is zebra-striped. She wants to escape from the rain. She shivers at the cold drenching drops and inside looks so warm. She slams her head into the glass.

Sharp pain in her forehead, through her eye, down her cheek. She propels her body forward, leaps—no, flies. Hundreds of tiny stabs impact her flesh, so sudden, so many.

Like freedom.

Slow-motion and then a heavy slam as her body ricochets. Flash of drums, tuneless brr-ng of cymbal hit too hard. Tumbling, down steps and landing hard on her back onto stone.

Music stops, leaning towards her, a man in black leather with long dark hair—Dorian Cain. Other hazy faces. Screams surround her. Lights bright now—flying buttresses above her. She feels energized, a thousand pinpricks like electric shocks lying in a puddle of warm water. Drowsiness overwhelms, seduces her to sleep, sleep. She thinks of poppies and Dorothy, the Emerald City so close and their deep red color, their scent so sweet.

She turns her head to her left side. The man in the trench coat grins his metal mouth under a stone arch. He steps towards her, kneels beside her, next to Dorian—does Dorian even see him? Does anyone else see him?

Her arm is weak, but she's able to reach up and pull the glasses off his face. Where his eyes should be are empty sockets—out of them crawl sensor-scarabs. The scarabs spread their elytra and fly to the left, to the right, each transforming into a poppy—clouds of floating poppies. Then one scarab zooms straight from eye socket towards her. She scrunches her lids to prepare for the impact. None happens so she cracks her left eye and finds herself staring straight into flower.

She shuts it again as sleep comes down.

A scream, shattering of glass.

Sasha snapped her eyes open. No poppies. The music had stopped, house lights on. Dorian was bending down towards the supine form of the blonde chick in the zebra-striped mini-dress, one of the groupies who'd blocked her view earlier, in the center of the chancel. The stained-glass windows were broken, the girl's body stabbed and blanketed in shards of glass, a large frame jabbed right through the center of her face, blood seeping from her many wounds.

"Don't panic," Dorian urged the audience.

Sasha was surprised to hear how Midwestern-ordinary his non-singing voice was. He sounded nervous, vulnerable, a hint of a stutter.

Groupies were screaming now, though to Sasha, their shrieks sounded garbled as if underwater. A residual effect of the sensor-scarab-juice on her hearing? More onlookers just stared, some mumbled to each other, and others made for the doors, including the dreadlocked sensor dealer slipping out to the side. The Sid and Nancy and other random dazed crowd members didn't move except to sway—other users, though whether from the scarab or another drug she could not be sure. The man in the trench coat had vanished.

The rest of the band had put away their instruments and encircled the body. Two uniformed security guards were climbing on stage. Bouncers in their usual uniform of black T-shirts and jeans appeared in the pit.

"You need to leave now," said a heavy-set balding man wearing a Blue Öyster Cult T-shirt in a booming voice. When Sasha didn't budge, he glared at her.

"I'm press," she said drowsily, holding up her media hangtag. There was no way she was leaving now. The concert review wasn't just a review, a feature any more. It was a news story, an exclusive.

"Ma'am, everybody has to leave," the bouncer said, stepping forward to push her towards the rear. Despite her hallucinogenic funk, Sasha outmaneuvered his grasp. She headed stage right in a warbly conflation of side steps and collided directly with Dorian himself as he descended the bottom step from the chancel. They stumbled into a clumsy embrace, their eyes meeting in an uncomfortable lock. Oh fuck, she'd just had a drug-infused sexual fantasy with this guy. And now she was sure she'd just get tossed out, no hope of finding out what happened to the girl, much less a quote from Dorian. No story, and she wasn't in any state to call a cab.

Sasha felt the bouncer's hand on her arm. Sirens blared outside.

"I'm sorry, Mr. Cain," he said. "I'll escort her out."

"No," Dorian said, not letting go of her. "Don't worry about it. I'll take care of her."

"But, sir."

"No buts, Hank," Dorian said more firmly.

Hank let go, grumbled. Dorian shifted, putting an arm around her.

"Are you okay?" he asked. He pulled up her hangtag and read her name. "Sasha Alexander."

"Yeah, that's me," Sasha nodded, confused at her sudden rescue by the rock star himself.

"Follow me," he said, leading her into the transept and through the arched side door. He nodded at the security guards who'd taken up posts at that exit. She saw the crowd being herded toward the front, just-arrived police officers maneuvering through their throng.

The rain had slowed to a light drizzle but a tent canopy protected them on the short distance to the tour bus. Dorian adjusted his hold, guiding her up the steps in front of him but signaling he could catch her if she fell back. Through her blurry vision, she saw two of the other band members in the front cabin. The drummer by the bar poured what looked to be scotch into a tumbler, throwing a questioning glance towards Dorian. The cellist sat cross-legged, her head in her hands, crying. But Dorian guided Sasha past them into the back towards shadowy bunk beds. He pulled the duvet back on the bottom bed on the right, then lowered her onto the mattress—gently seating her, taking her purse from her hand and placing it behind her, helping her remove her white go-go boots, lifting up her legs. She curled on her side, laid her head on the pillow, and fell asleep instantly.

When Sasha's eyes opened again, the room was only dimly lit by fluorescent striping along the center aisle. It took a moment for her to remember why she wasn't in her own bed, where she was. Fully clothed, her underwear on, she noted. No one had taken advantage of her sedated state, but then she was sure Dorian and the band would have no trouble finding willing groupies. A snore. In the bunk across from her, the drummer sprawled belly-down, shirtless, jeans and bare feet on top of the duvet. The upper bunk was empty, looked like it hadn't been touched. Soft breathing told her that the cellist was likely right above her.

Sasha reached for her purse, unwound the white shawl and wrapped it across her shoulders, stood up. She scanned and quickly found the bathroom. In the mirror, the eyeliner on her upper lids amazingly had not run. She splashed some water on her face, did a quick touch-up, and then ventured back into the hall, opening the door into the front cabin.

The shades were lowered so she couldn't tell if it was morning or still night. Dorian was sitting alone.

"Come in, sit down, Sasha," he said. "I don't bite. Well, not on first meeting." He chuckled softly, adding, "I suppose we could get some light in here."

He stood up, headed for the bar. She expected him to flip a switch, but instead he struck a match and started lighting tall white candles in a brass menorah. How did it stay standing when the bus was moving? Was it nailed to the bar? Or did he just put it away?

"Do you want some Kombucha?" he asked.

"Sure," Sasha said. Weren't rock stars supposed to drink booze? Well, it was late. Or more likely early.

"If you're wondering what time it is, it's about six a.m., almost dawn," Dorian said, as he dipped under the bar and opened a small refrigerator. He pulled out a bottle, poured the green liquid into a glass, and handed it to her.

"As you can imagine, what happened is already across the Internet, the cable news, crews camped outside the bus waiting for my statement," he added as he poured himself a glass. "Woman hurls herself through stained glass at Dorian Cain concert at church—apparent suicide. Or was it murder? Or was she under the influence of a dangerous new street drug?"

"Why am I here, Dorian?" Sasha asked.

"Call me James," he said, motioning for her to sit. "You used to go to Mars back when it was still called Masquerade," he continued once she was seated.

"Yeah," Sasha said. Why was he bringing up an old Atlanta night club?

"The good old days," he nodded, breaking into a sardonic swagger. "When synth and hip-hop ruled the Top 40, there was a rock that still shook in the guts and the groin and the guitar. Before MTV and the record execs killed it all with that alternative crap and then synthetic masturbation gave birth to rave counter culture. So sayeth wankers like *Rolling Stone*."

"That's almost a direct quote. Good little local music rag, that *Stomp and Stammer*. Luckily *Rolling Stone* didn't take it personally and gave me a job for a while. I'd forgotten you were from Atlanta."

"I was that scruffy kid in the corner, sneaking in underage," James said. "Imagine me—shy?!"

"Your first band was Sasquatch, I remember. I never saw them, but early articles talked about your stage presence even then. And then you moved to New York, spent some time in London, ended up in San Francisco."

"You've followed my itinerary."

"What makes you different is that you don't just want to use the crowd. You want to bring back old-school performance, flesh and feeling, like Mick Jagger, Roger Daltrey, Jim Morrison, Lou Reed?"

He laughed, rocking on his feet.

"In the words of Jeff Park: 'Cain drains the brain…has the audacity to conceive that fans both want to watch him and to pay attention to his music. This is the O-Teens, baby. Like a kick in the soul *live to the World Wide Web*.'

"Sometimes I dream I'm no one," he continued, serious. "I compose notes and words, let them touch the ears of millions of idiots seeking some sort of fleeting gratification they can't pull out of their pitiful jobs or their lovers or from the asshole who happens to be president or the clouds of clear waste that clog their lungs with invisible cancers."

"That's why you played in a small church. All your locations on this tour are small, intimate compared to where you could book. You want to be a performer in a ratty old club in the sixties or the seventies."

James swigged the rest of his Kombucha as if it was whiskey. Then he glanced down, stroked the thin stubble on his chin, looked up again and into her eyes—somewhere in between the stage Dorian Cain and shy scruffy kid from the Atlanta suburbs.

"I thought I had finally made it to where I could do what I wanted—that rock star arrogance, I suppose. Rock is dead, punk is dead, Goth is dead, grunge is dead, Kraut-rock, even funk, all dead. But I had made enough money I could bring it back, take it to the next level. Back to Bowie. Beyond sound. To all five senses."

"The sensor-scarab. Sold at a price not too cheap as to be suspicious as a handout, but affordable enough for free-spirited audience members with, let's say, a sense of adventure."

James raised an eyebrow. "You're quite observant, Miss Alexander."

"You're talking to a journalist."

"A journalist who just took an illegal substance and who hasn't had an article in a major publication beyond her blog in three years."

"Are you blackmailing me?"

"No, you can write anything you want. I'm not a pusher. I don't have anything to do with distribution, so there's no story there. But I have been, let's say, writing songs with the effect of the sensor-scarab in mind."

"Where did it come from? I mean, how did people even figure out to eat a beetle?"

"Central American tribes figured it out first, who knows when. Anthropologists classify it as an 'entheogen'—generating the divine within—a ritualistic substance used by shamans. They used it to create a communal effect—shared hallucinations like group mythology. That's why the CIA took an interest back in the eighties as a way to calm down mass hysteria. Like the street battles in Ferguson between the cops and locals. Rumor has it that the riots only simmered down after sensor-serum was added to the water supply. Rumor also has it also that it could be weaponized to create unrest, but there's not been a single documented case of anyone dying under the influence."

"Nice. You've done your research. And you want to use something that the CIA is playing around with to create a multisensory experience that ties into a specific song? From what you've just told me and what I experienced, it sounds like it's not that easy to control, and it could have triggered that girl to go kill herself. Or was I the only one on sensor-juice, or whatever you want to call it, who was in that chick's head when she jumped through that window?"

"Umm…what?!"

"I had a vivid vision of being that girl before she crashed through that window."

"Really? What did you see?"

"I was her climbing the ladder, dancing on the ledge. No one pushed her, but on the ground, a man in a trench coat with dark glasses was watching her. He had a knife but he didn't stab her, just like he was using it to signal her to jump. I saw him earlier in the crowd, surveying all the groupies, one by one, as if carefully choosing which one was to die."

"Weird. Reporters have been interviewing people who saw the show, but no one has said anything like that on the news. Police didn't mention it

either when they interviewed me. Not that they'd necessarily give much credence to a drug trip, but if it was so close to what actually happened...

"Anyway, the long and short is I could use a journalist on my side," he said. "And a reporter who sampled a dangerous new drug might not hurt. I'm also interested in hearing more about that vision of yours."

"But you don't want me to admit any of that in print," Sasha said.

"Probably not."

"Hmmm. What do you have in mind?"

"Exclusive on my reaction to what happened last night. Then you can have whatever you want, an in-depth interview, backstage pass, lodging and transport to the rest of my tour."

"Why do you trust me?"

"Just call it an instinct, and you need a ticket back to the music media. I can hook you up with other musicians, bands—whoever you want."

Sasha didn't need a lot of time to think. Was she compromising her journalistic ethics? If some proof surfaced that tied the sensor-scarab or James/Dorian directly to the girl's death, she could always reassess. But for now, his offer was exactly what she needed to reboot her career.

"Okay."

She opened her purse and pulled out a small digital recorder.

"Are you ready to start talking?"

James nodded.

"Testing 1-2-3. This is Sasha Alexander interviewing Dorian Cain."

That was the first time she met Dorian Cain. When Dorian Cain was just beginning.

Six months later she and Dorian traveled back to Atlanta so she could trace his roots for the book she was now writing. They'd been spending almost every day together doing interviews but also just talking, discovering they shared interests in art and literature, cooking, gardening. At Mars, he asked her to dance when the DJ started spinning nostalgia disks—Velvet Underground, Joy Division, Bowie—"Ziggy Stardust." They swayed like old-timers, moving apart and close, him hard at her lower lips. She'd driven in her decrepit 1989 Camaro, and in the parking lot, he pushed her ass up against the door, grating his fingernails across the chipping red paint, shards crumbling loose onto the pavement, as he deep-kissed her and ground against her. They had rough sex in the backseat before heading back to her apartment and making love again in her bed.

~

Prowling the borders of Oblivion
Reach your hand in
Reach your hard-on in
But the Devil has a stake…

The last time Sasha met Dorian Cain, James did it for her—wore a black suit, pulled his hair back in a ponytail. Her mother served Chicken Kiev, and later they made love in her little girl's room on the canopy bed with its lacy comforter. He teased her stuffed lion with his nose. Two years more famous, two years more determined, two years more loving.

Sasha could feel the frustration draining down his spine. James took reviews personally. He could feel his creative power over his audiences. It made him feel guilty and humble and chosen. He pressed his lips softly on Sasha's and sucked her tongue.

"I wish I could be there in Miami, baby," Sasha whispered.

"Wish you could, too, but you've seen almost every show I've done over the past two years," James said. "And you're giving me a pretty nice warm-up. See me, hear me, feel me, taste me."

"Warm me," Sasha said.

Curled with her back to his chest, she looked out the window at the big red full moon. He cupped her nipple with his left palm, and she closed her eyes.

In the morning, Sasha drove him to the Atlanta airport. She was on deadline for the authorized memoir of the life of Dorian Cain.

She was sitting, her laptop on her knees, on the leopard-print sleeping sofa in the living room of her two-story blue Craftsman cottage in Grant Park, when the call came around midnight. In the middle of the Miami show, Dorian had collapsed. He was dead before the medics even arrived.

In the next eight hours, Sasha went from car to airport to plane to taxi to hospital morgue to just staring at his ice-cold body, numb and nauseous. The official cause of death was heart failure. Dorian/James, the most passionate man she had ever known, his heart had just stopped. She stroked his tattoo, the memory of her lover's tongue inside her lips, his arms holding her from behind. She broke into tears.

He'd promised her not to experiment any more with the sensor-scarab, but she knew. And if she doubted, it was in the footage. In the pre-concert interview, he told another reporter what he would never say to her.

"Tonight I won't give them any choice about what they see, what they smell, what they touch. They'll get sex all right, but on my terms. Just one song, and I take it back for the artist. And Jeff Park can suck my dick."

The camera surveyed the crowd and revealed a familiar figure—a man in a trench coat with dark hair, dark glasses, dark gloves.

Sasha flew home to Atlanta, stopped at the package store on the way home from the airport, bought three bottles of Tullamore Dew. Then she sat on the window seat in her bedroom staring out at the big sprawling oak whose leaves were starting to turn with autumn's embrace, drinking whiskey after whiskey after whiskey, lining up the dead soldiers on the hardwood floor next to the red marble urn that contained the ashes of Dorian Cain. She left her perch only to pour the occasional glass of water, use the bathroom, sleep, turned off her phone after the beeps of condolence texts and messages became too much. The air was turning chilly at night, but she kept the window open to listen to the melody of the crickets, the rumble of the train down the end of the street.

On the fourth day, after the third bottle was empty, she opened James' satchel, the one he always traveled with but had forgotten on his way to Miami. She found his iPod in the side pocket where he always kept it, the one on which he saved his own recordings. She scrolled through the contents—songs he'd never played for her, promised he'd play when he returned. Titles like "The Maze of Her Own Dreaming." "Man Ray Awakens." "The Devil's Matchbook." "Forever and a Day." The song he'd been playing when he collapsed.

Sasha brewed a pot of coffee. Drank it all day until she felt the alcohol's effects purged fully from her body. Showered and washed her hair. Pulled on jeans and a Dorian Cain T-shirt. She made the call and waited.

About an hour later, three stiff pounds on the knocker. She hadn't made an order in nearly a year, but the code hadn't changed. She glanced out from the bathroom window and saw a purple Volkswagen Beetle parked in the driveway. She opened the door to find a girl in a knit cap and red braids, fringed brown jacket.

"Where's Lucio?"

"He's busy," she said. "But I have what you ordered."

"Busy, uh-huh, doesn't want to show his face after what happened to Dorian," Sasha said. "So, honey, what's your name?"

"Susie." She fumbled in her backpack and pulled out a black box.

Sasha picked up her purse from a table by the door.

"You don't need to get any money," Susie said, looking down. "It's on the house."

"Really?" Sasha said, putting her purse back down. "And why is that? Is that Lucio's way of saying he's sorry?"

"I don't know, ma'am. That's what he said," the girl answered, still no eye contact.

"Anything I should know about this batch?"

"It's what you asked for, the same as Dorian Cain."

"So Lucio is admitting that Dorian was on sensor when he died?"

Susie handed the box to Sasha, gave a half-smile.

"Can I go now?"

"Sure, but tell Lucio if anything happens that gives me concern, I might pay him a visit…down at the lab."

"Okay," Susie stepped back. "Night."

The girl gave a jittery wave and headed back to the VW.

Sasha closed the door, sat on the fainting couch. She leaned back, raised her legs and cradled the box in her hand. In the beginning, she and James had consumed the scarabs together. Their juices enhanced his music, and later their lovemaking. But then things changed. She started seeing odd things at the corners of her vision—curtains blowing, beetles scampering or fluttering, blinking eyes watching, a gloved hand with a knife. She asked James but he denied any similar anomalies. And yet she detected a shakiness in his voice, saw a twitch in his hand after sessions. Still, she didn't push. What was it when a woman got close to a man that sometimes made her not speak up even when she was worried? Was it because with her last lover she did speak and warn and then he left her? She hated the thought of being that woman, even though James gave no sign of even thinking of leaving her. And yet now he had left her. If she had pushed him more, even gently, instead of giving into her own fears of being abandoned again, would he still be here?

She had suspected that James had continued to partake in the scarab. He would disappear for hours, telling her he was at the studio. She hadn't minded. More time for her to write his bio, and she valued her time alone, too, knew from past experience that too much time together can be strangling. She thought of that moment when her last lover had left and how "I Wanna Be Free" by Davy Jones came on the radio, and she realized she was happy he was gone, remembered that the only child in her could entertain herself quite well. But oh, it was nice to be held at night.

Sasha opened the box. The scarab inside began to buzz softly, flutter. She couldn't let it fly away so she grabbed it quickly and firmly. It twitched, but then fell still as if zen with its fate. The creature was big, four inches long, and almost all red, not just the smudge on the back of the ones she had before. The jewel-toned scarlet shimmered in the light from the Peter Pan lamp beside her, a bit of 1940s kitsch with an Erté-esque femme fatale in green tunic and cap holding up the bulb.

She hesitated, considered letting the scarab fly away instead. But she needed to figure out what Dorian had seen, even if she had to admit she was scared of what she might discover.

"Sorry, little guy."

Sasha popped the scarab in her mouth, crunched down, felt the entheogen spew into her cheeks as she chewed, then swim down her throat. She picked up the iPod from the coffee table and selected the first song in the sequence.

A rough wiry bass line slashed across her eardrum, like hot lava coursing down the ear canal. Then the music curved, reconfigured.

The splash of water, foamy waves flowing onto an empty beach. Sand sea-green. Palm trees curved like archways. Walking through the sand in her bare toes. Shells sparkle in the twilight, setting sun on the pink horizon. A monkey with white-framed features scampers out from the trees, pauses, startled to see a companion on the beach, then runs along.

Do angels believe in ghosts?

Dorian's voice, like a pendulum's swing muffled by water. Ambient rather than hard.

Do angels, do angels, do angels believe in ghosts?

Dorian's voice mysterious over the tide.

An army of mermen, sensuous with long, thick green seaweed hair and piercing blue eyes—pure sex—their fins flip up and down in the waves. They tease her, testing her celibacy after Dorian's death. She walks to the water's edge, feels clammy sea-stained sand against the soles of her feet.

Follow me to the other side.

A slippery fall of cello. The mermen are gone.

Sky now periwinkle darkens into blackness, starless night. Out in the ocean, the waves rage rough as a drum solo gathers force, strike the shore, splashing her until she is soaked.

Follow the tide.

Theremin edge.

She feels a tickling, scratching on her toes, looks down to see sensor-scarabs scampering across them. The water isn't water, but an army of insects. They flood across her feet and onto the beach until there is no beach, just a seething horde and more coming, an incoming tide of bugs.

Forever and a day, we'll be together forever and a day.

The music recedes again into chittering as the scarab wave reaches the line of palm trees and up the creatures climb until they reach the leaves and the coconuts. Only the coconuts aren't coconuts. They are giant eyes and they are watching her.

Never tear us apart.

Guitar riffs cut like a chainsaw. Sasha opens her eyes. How time passes when under the influence of the sensor. She stretches, yawning loudly. She curls into a ball—content, secure, inexplicably filled with happiness. The chittering is gone, and Dorian's voice sings deep in her head like a lullaby.

Even love won't tear us apart again.

"It's true you know, baby."

Sasha rolls over and sees Dorian on his knees by the bedside. Only it's her bed from her house—the black wrought-iron canopy bed with red-velvet curtains—but not her floor. Instead a checkerboard of granite tiles and behind a row of tall arched stained-glass windows. Scarlet concert smoke swirls around them, its smell cloying. They're in the church where she first heard him play.

A ripple of keyboards.

She is lost in the maze of her own dreaming.

"I loved you, James," Sasha whispers, knowing she's found what she was looking for. "I loved you."

His hair folds around his cheekbones like a rock barbarian, his chest bare like a romance novel cover. He reaches out a hand and strokes her cheek. She expects his touch to be cool but finds it unexpectedly warm.

"You think I'm a dream, pussycat. Don't you?"

"Of course you are, some fuckin' dream I'll regret in the morning."

Sasha sighs and reaches her head up to kiss his cheek.

"Do I feel like a dream?"

"No, but that's the nature of dreams. They feel real, inexplicably real."

Sasha can't resist his lips, the opportunity to kiss him again long and full in the illusion.

The bass cuts in again like a razor.

Screaming, fuck you. I'll fuck you baby, too.

"I've been waiting for you to play the music, Sasha," Dorian says, running his tongue up her neck.

Fuck me.

In the dreamtime.

And don't let me wake up until I've come.

Sasha gives in to his hands, his lips, lets him touch her and lick her all over. Run his fingers across her chest, pinch her nipples, suck them, probe her insides.

Any moment it'll be over.

Dorian rolls onto his side, caresses her cheek, smiles into her eyes. She turns over and he wraps himself around her back.

"You've got to get me back into my real body, so we can be together," he continues.

"What do you mean?" Sasha asks, fighting the urge just to relax, remain safe in her lover's arms. Does she need answers or would it be okay just to give in? Except she knows it isn't really safe—that safety is part of the illusion.

Sasha rolls back over to look at him.

"Don't you see what's happened?"

His eyes twitch, his hands twitch.

"When I played in Miami, Sasha, it was just too much. Something went wrong. Went bad. One moment I'm on stage, the next I'm part of the songs. I can't escape by myself. The scarabs won't let me."

"What?"

"I'm sorry I didn't tell you but I know you know I'd been experimenting with the sensor-scarabs. Just think of the concept artistically—if we could transmit the same message, transport them to the same place. Like acid, baby, a shared acid trip without getting fucked up."

"That's crazy, James," Sasha says. "The sensor-scarab is just an insect that has some kind of life-blood that taps into the brain and plays with our subconscious."

"No, you don't get it. When I play for the scarabs, they listen, and if I concentrate on the senses I want to express, they absorb what's in my head, memorize it, recreate it. But something went wrong, and my mind became severed from my body, melded into the music. I don't fuckin' understand it myself. You've got to go see Lucio. He knows what I was doing. He can bring me back."

"I saw your dead body. Then I had you cremated, just like you wanted. Your ashes are in an urn at my house."

James's eyes stare at Sasha blankly. He loosens his grip and slips out from their embrace, spreads his arms wide.

"No. That's not right. There's been some mistake. Can't you fuckin' see, Sasha? I'm alive."

James rolls away from her, turns his head towards the window, his hair hiding his face. Sasha reaches her hand up to stroke his shoulder. Can Dorian Cain—the late great, her lover—be alive, trapped by insects inside the song he composed? The whole experience—see, hear, touch, smell, taste—does seem far too vivid to be merely a dream. Can this be James?

Drums build in the periphery of her hearing. Behind him, through the window, a shadow and then as if walking out from the wall, a familiar figure with dark glasses raising a knife. The glass shatters inward behind the man in the trench coat, curving around him, not affecting his pace—slow, deliberate. The wind of the impact knocks her and James off the bed onto the floor into a pool of blood.

The red liquid ripples outward, thousands of tiny bumps scurrying, swimming—sensor-scarabs everywhere. Sasha reaches to grab James' hand, but it's icy cold, limp. The man in the trench coat is turning to come around the bed, knife in his black-gloved hand ready to strike. He opens his mouth—the metal grin.

Sasha closes her eyes, wills herself awake.

When she reopened them, she was back on the fainting couch, her heart beating rapidly, the crickets humming outside.

For the first time since James was gone, she shut the windows, room to room, all through the house. She crawled into bed, not sure if she could sleep but knowing she needed time to think, time before she went to see Lucio.

The following night, Sasha put on the white dress and shawl she wore when she first met James/Dorian, emptied his satchel and repacked it with his urn. In the bag, she'd found a notebook, a map, and a postcard—Atlanta Undead Apocalypse. The AUA was an annual homegrown Halloween attraction "labor of blood" created by local horror SFX artists and staffed by the city's hordes of horror fans. Every October, the Southern metropolis transformed into Halloween-Town, not that anyone would know it from any of the official tourist brochures. It was all very grassroots, word of mouth. Lucio was the AUA's benign benefactor, its executive producer. The old motel complex with its woods out back not only was big enough for an expansive paintball zombie war zone, but also a perfect front to hide a breeding laboratory for entire hives of sensor-scarabs and launder all that hard cash.

The AUA was south of the Starlight Drive-in, its vintage neon sign and the line of cars outside a vestige of a past the city mostly had neglected to preserve. Beyond the Starlight, Moreland Avenue faded into a dark industrial wasteland. Sasha passed one other oasis of light, a mega-pump gas station as she came up on I-285, the perimeter highway that looped around Atlanta. On the other side, the shadow of a giant landfill loomed to the left like an ancient burial mound. A block later she eased the old Camaro onto a right-fork ramp which merged into a streetlight-less stretch of road, turned the bend, and pulled into the AUA's chain-link gates. Spotlights illuminated the camouflage-painted façade of the former two-story motel, a design which made sense when one considered that most of the year the place was a paintball weaponry course, popular with the Second Amendment and survivalist crowd.

A shaggy-haired kid in a Metallica shirt waved her down. She rolled down her window.

"Parking's five bucks."

"I'm here to see Lucio."

The kid threw her a squinty look.

"The word?"

"Osiris."

He shrugged, backed away, waved her along. Heavy metal music blasted in her windows as she drove past the motel's front, a long loud line of haunt-goers, mostly in T-shirts and jeans, trailing along its edifice. She parked at the less-lit far end. A lone zombie, face airbrushed green with latex scarring, terry-cloth white bathrobe slathered in blood, sat in a lawn chair before a door covered in black paper. As she stepped out of the car, the satchel slung over one shoulder, he looked up from his iPhone.

"Tell Lucio it's Sasha," she said.

"The word?" he asked.

"Anubis."

The zombie texted into his phone.

A few seconds later, it rumbled back that a return message had been received.

The zombie rose, beckoned for her to follow him through a glass door that had been taped over with rows of black electric tape. Once inside he pulled out a pin-flashlight. In its far-from-sufficient light, she could see a stairwell, but he quickly guided her through another glass door into a hallway. The rank smell of moldy carpet assailed her. She pinched her nose as he led her past a row of doors, some shut with rusty numbers, others cracked open and dark inside. With that tiny light, she couldn't see much. Screams and bursts of paintball AK-47 rounds drifted up from the far end of the hall.

About halfway down, the zombie turned again, the flashlight's thin beam flashing briefly against a dark cracked Coke machine and an ice maker. The sticky floor caught at her boot soles momentarily, and then they were outside again, emerging onto the cracked concrete patio of a tarp-covered swimming pool, its only visible feature a gray paint-chipped diving board on this end. She heard a faint insect hum as they circled past decrepit metal chairs and round tables with posts in the center but no umbrellas. Groaning, gunfire, and screaming erupted on the far side of the adjoining courtyard as a pack of faux-zombies converged on about a dozen AUA patrons being herded by a couple of full-geared commandos.

The bath house couldn't look more deserted, more derelict, even though it was clearly the only part of the motel complex that had ever had any real style. Some owner must've thought they could cash in on *Gone with the Wind* fans if they gave it a plantation theme with white columns and green double doors. The paint was badly peeling like everywhere at the AUA that hadn't been rehabbed with faux graffiti and horror-themed murals, but Sasha guessed that Lucio had adopted it as his HQ since the antebellum look didn't really fit with the modern zombie world-coming-to-an-end theme.

Her zombie escort did the triple knock. A few minutes passed before one of the doors opened wide and a giggling Susie popped out.

The zombie kid hesitated, but she quickly shooed him away with her hand, shutting the door as soon as Sasha was inside.

The foyer was round with an about ten-foot circumference, two narrow sofas, a few metal chairs. At the far end was a window where an attendant once would have sat, handing out towels and selling snacks and sodas. A small table lamp was lit in the booth, a magazine spread open. But what Sasha noticed first was not the sight but the sound. The humming, chittering, the music of the scarabs. They weren't here but they were near.

She didn't see Lucio enter, but he must have come in through the black curtain from the left. He looked the same as when she first met him—his long yellow dreads, vampire-pale skin, red contact lenses, long fingers with manicured nails. He was dressed in a silver smoking jacket with black pants, tall biker boots. He clearly fancied himself a rock star of his own ilk.

"Bonjour, dearest Sasha," Lucio said, stretching out a hand.

She lifted hers, but he didn't shake. Instead he turned it over and kissed it.

"My deepest condolences. Dorian was an exceptional man, you know he was dear to me, too."

"Dear to you because he was your meal ticket," Sasha said.

"Now, now, Sasha, that isn't very polite when you haven't seen someone in a long time and I have provided you with so much..." He paused, stretching wide open his mouth, smiling with his perfect straight teeth. "...pleasure."

"What happened to Dorian? What were the two of you up to? What did he attempt in Miami? Some super-sensor-scarab? He went on about the five senses. And then last night he told me to come see you. That you could bring him back."

"Last night? But Dorian Cain is dead, my love. Oh, sweet girl, did he speak to you from beyond the grave?"

Lucio threw his head back and laughed. Susie twittered again, too.

"Can you?"

"I am not God," Lucio said, his face turning somber. Susie stopped laughing as well. "The elders in Guatemala, they say they cannot say what the scarab can do and not do, so how can I?

He stretched out his palms towards her, revealing on each a sensor scarab, the largest she had seen, bright red like the one she had consumed last night. They fluttered their elytra but did not fly away.

"But there is a legend they tell that if a man—or a woman—takes last breath with the sensor serum inside then he—or she—lives forever. Are you here to find out if it is more than legend?"

Smooth Lucio, she knew he would never answer questions in any kind of straight fashion. From the notebook in Dorian's satchel, she'd learned that he was a retired SEAL, then CIA. Hard to imagine him in a crew cut and fatigues, harder in a suit. He'd discovered the sensor-scarab on a mission. He'd brought the first batch back, headed the experiments. How did someone retire after all that? Then he took what he learned and used it to set up a booming business as a drug lord.

James believed Lucio was a friend, that he could be trusted, that they were collaborating in a grand experiment that would change the face of rock music. Among his notes were references to the FDA and a big pharma company called NECO. Just think of the net profits if sensor were legal, by prescription. But the resurrection part, was it more than ironic that she was talking about life after death at a zombie Halloween attraction?! Or was it just part of the sensor-fantasy, the seduction to lure her back? Make her forget the bad sides of her trips?

The scarabs in Lucio's palms had ceased fluttering, but they hummed loudly like lead vocalists over the general orchestra of buzzing, the chitterers and occasional squealers providing the equivalent of bass, drums, and intermittent Nina Hagen shrieks.

"I assure you, princess, we would never let anyone, much less the great Dorian Cain, consume the sensor-scarab if it had not been tested thoroughly," Lucio said, shifting his tone as if trying another tactic. "Are you sure, lovely Sasha, that you weren't experiencing the combined effect of it and some other hallucinogenic substance? Raza, jetsam, old-fashioned LSD perhaps? We don't recommend that you use the sensor while under the effects of any other drug, you know, except perhaps common alcoholic beverages."

Susie chirped again.

"Cut the bullshit, Lucio, and you know I don't even drink," Sasha said, impatient.

"Bullshit, that isn't kind, precious," Lucio said. "But I know what you want. You want to know what James and I were doing together during all those days when he left you home alone."

Was it some instinct honed in his intelligence training to cut right to her deepest vulnerability? Sasha forced herself not to give him the satisfaction of showing he'd touched a deep wound.

"Yes, show me."

"Then follow me, my dear," he said closing his hands again around the scarabs. They both squealed, objecting to the sudden pressure of his fingers. Then he swept his left fist towards the black curtain. "Ladies first."

Susie reached down under the shelf in the service booth and pulled out a large stocky flashlight. She snapped it on, revealing a beam considerably wider and brighter than the one the zombie kid had brandished. Sasha stepped through the doorway and into a changing room. Lucio and Susie followed behind her, letting the curtain fall back after they had passed.

In the room's center was a wooden trapdoor. Lucio stepped forward and grasped the metal handle, pulled it up to reveal a ladder. The insect hum rose from below, louder, closer. The three descended and Lucio pushed open a metal door that took them into a large tiled chamber, the symphony of the scarabs now so loud and shrill that Sasha almost stuck her fingers in her ears. Lucio and Susie flanked her, the beam revealing what she had suspected. They were in the pool, and they were not alone. Sensor-scarabs everywhere—crawling on the floors, the walls, buzzing through the air all around them. Not like the ones she had first sampled with James but like the one Susie brought her last night, the ones in Lucio's fists—bigger, redder, shinier.

"My dear, I should not have teased you upstairs," Lucio said. "You've had a highly vivid dream. Believe me, it would be quite fascinating if our little scarab could resurrect the dead. We know that it has an ability to remember images, scents, even touch sensations. What James and I discovered was that if you play a specific piece of music to the scarab, it memorizes it. But not just that, they have a hive mind. So if you play a song and you partake of the sensor at the same time, whatever is in your subconscious gets transmitted to all the scarabs within the hive. James was right, for at least one generation of scarab, anyone who listened to his new album would have a shared, similar if not exact sensor-fantasy. So in a way, yes, your lover is still alive—at least as long as these scarabs are."

Susie giggled again, or was it more of a chitter?

Then she lunged at Sasha, her arms surprisingly strong for a girl that size. Lucio raised his right fist and then the other to Sasha's mouth, prying it open and stuffing first one, then the other scarab inside. She tried to struggle but could already feel the entheogen kicking in. With Lucio's hand over her mouth, chewing became a reflex to prevent her from choking, suffocating, the liquid flowing out with each bite, the taste sweet and bitter on her tongue like eating dreams.

Sasha felt Lucio's hand pull away, her mouth fall open, oxygen flow in. Through blurry vision, she saw him reach to the side and flip some kind of switch. The music began. First softly, then faster, faster, louder, louder, the scarabs more and more frenzied, the room itself shaking. Sasha couldn't make out individual beetles any more. Just swirling clouds of scarlet.

The last drop of sensor slid down her throat, rushed to her head. The satchel slipped from her shoulder, a thud as the urn hit the floor. Then she followed it.

She feels a hand on her pulse.

"She's very cold." Susie's voice tingles faintly, from faraway.

"Bring up her body heat," Lucio replies. "I want to see what happens."

Sasha feels her shawl being removed, pokes across her chest, around her heart and on her forehead as if buttons are being attached.

Then scarabs stream across her, no, a blanket. She wraps herself tightly, curling fetal into a sand-pocket, and stares out into a jet-black ocean. The waves glide gently against the shore, calm with the lack of wind. The air almost unearthly still.

Do demons believe in ghosts?

Dorian's voice quivers in the breeze. If he was trying to create a consistent experience that would run through every play of the same song, this is remarkably close. Though different. No mermen this time. Different enough.

Do the devils, do the devils believe in ghosts?

Sasha turns away from the sea towards the sparkling green sand, sees her blue two-story Craftsman cottage behind a wrought-iron fence. The sand is soft, not grainy, and moist under her step as she walks towards the door. She opens it and steps inside.

How relaxing to be home. She can't remember how she got there.

And then he's standing in front of her—James naked and smiling.

"I knew you'd come back," he says. "Now, darling, just tell me how I can get back into my body. Have you got it ready?"

"I dropped the urn," Sasha says, looking around her feet on the floor. "When Lucio fed me the scarabs."

She has never seen him cry, but tears well up in his eyes and run down his face. His skin seems to be falling with them, slipping down and gliding back in place.

"There's been a mistake," he says, shaking his head again and again, faster and faster, grabbing her by the shoulders. "Sasha, I'm alive. Can't you fucking see I'm alive?"

Sasha pulls him close to her and runs her fingers lightly through his hair.

"I'm sorry, baby," she whispers. "I'm so sorry."

James pulls back. His eyes upon hers, with one hand he reaches up and caresses her cheek.

"We can be together, baby. Don't you see? You can stay here with me. We might even live forever. Who knows? I mean, hell, how could we die? We're in some other dimension. We'll be immortal—no bullshit, no fuckers."

"What are you talking about? Stay where? I don't even know where I am. Inside the sensor-scarabs' hive psyche? Lucio said that when the herd dies, so will the memory."

"No, Sasha," he shakes his head, his hair falling across his left eye. "*Not in the scarab, inside the song.* Playing my songs opens the door; come through, and your mind accesses me. Like you type in the password and the contents spill onto the screen. Except they're spilling into your brain, baby. Just the right combination of notes to recreate all the happiness I feel with you, here in your house. The problem was, I fucked up, baby. I felt too strongly. I got so involved as I played the music that my mind couldn't pull out. So here I am, all alone, here, in the place where I loved you with no you."

He kisses her forehead.

"But you're here now," he says. "The music brought you here. And you can stay forever."

"Forever," she repeats. "Forever and a day."

Forever and a day alone with Dorian. Forever and a day, Dorian alone.

"Please say yes, Sasha, yes, Dorian, I'll stay. Sasha, I love you."

He kisses her on the cheek, on the mouth, curling his tongue into a thick snaky loop down her throat and out again. He licks down her neck, traces her breasts slowly in a figure-eight, her stomach, bellybutton, abdomen, pulls up her skirt, touches her beneath. She feels a sharp tinge of pleasure, of memory, of how he knows every inch of her body, every nook, every crevice.

Then he is just licking and she is standing still, her eyes locked on the whiteness of the ceiling, the familiar—the fainting couch, the Peter Pan lamp, the photo of them together in the little red and green Italian frame.

The words echo in her head now on permanent repeat like a scratched record.

Forever. Forever and a day. Forever. Forever and a day. Forever. Forever and a day.

She pulls away. She stares into his eyes and sees something she has missed or hasn't wanted to see so clearly.

A simple child's game—a pinball shot and a roll. The pupils are dilated, the whites wide and hungry—as if at any moment they can open like a white hole and suck, a gaping mouth not with a hunger but with an inevitability that extends like a tunnel into infinity. Into nothing.

She walks over to the small bookcase. The books still sit there on the shelves. The covers are even colored, but they have no titles. She pulls a green one off the shelf and cracks it open. The pages shine white, no words, just blank. She turns back. James is watching her every move.

"James, what do you do when I'm not here?"

He stares at her.

"I mean, what do you do? How do you pass the time? Do you watch TV? Surf the Net? Listen to music?"

But he says nothing, just looks at her—just marbles. He walks over to her, takes the book from her hands, and lays it down on the shelf.

"I've been waiting for you, Sasha. Isn't that enough? Isn't forever enough?"

Dorian Cain was larger than life, but neither Dorian nor James would have been content to be shut inside an illusion with her. He would go ape-shit in one day. She'd never wanted to be trapped in a cage either. She needed to have two lives—one to share, one to keep. He did, too. He *did.*

"Tell me, James, that book you really loved, the one about the two brothers. What was it called?"

"Who gives a fuck. Come to bed, baby."

"Your sister? What's her name?"

"Come, baby, come."

"Your father? What's his name?"

"I missed you so much."

Sasha pulls her hands from his grasp and slaps him hard across his cheek.

Dorian looks back at her as if staring through a haze. He squints his eyes. Then he reaches his head forward as if to kiss her again.

"No, James," Sasha pulls back further. "You don't know, James. Do you?"

"Kiss me, Sasha," he begs. "Why won't you kiss me?"

"No, James."

Sasha says it even louder, almost shouting it. He keeps groping for her.

"Sasha, I love you. I love you. I'll love you forever, forever and a day."

She trips backwards towards the door. His voice is a dull whine, and then behind him she sees a familiar figure in dark glasses approaching from the kitchen.

"I'll love you, Sasha, forever, forever and a day."

A black-gloved hand lifts a butcher knife.

An old warped LP spins round and round and round and round. James is moving towards her like a slow motion video-blip, arms outstretched, a visual to an easy-listening love song, droning on:

"*Forever, forever and a day. I love you.*"

Sasha tries to reach out and save him, but invisible hands pull her back, yank her into the front door. The man in the trench coat plunges the knife into James' back. Blood explodes everywhere as the knife descends again and again, and James crumples to the floor.

Dying forever for the third time.

The man in the trench coat is now stepping across the body towards her. Sasha scratches at the pressure on her chest, on her forehead, feels small weights fall away. No longer tethered, she swings around and pulls the door open, leaps into darkness.

The beach is gone, replaced by pitch black, pouring rain, a flash of lightning? The deafening hum. The rain isn't rain. Scarabs. Everywhere. Falling from the sky.

The scarabs land on her dress, circling it in wide bands, a tingling sensation as they crawl on her body, dripping thick black liquid icy cold through the fabric to her skin.

A hand grabs at her arm as she starts up the steps, but she shakes it off. Or maybe the clouds of scarabs around her protect her. She keeps running until she is outside, throwing open the doors, a wave of scarabs flooding out behind her flying up into the night sky.

She circles the covered pool and dashes into the courtyard, scarabs trailing her, swarming everywhere and away. On the other side of the lawn, she hears heavy music, a band playing somewhere ahead, remembers vaguely from the flyer about concerts after the AUA's closing. She's not sure where she's going, just keep moving, get away, get to the music, find people. Most of the scarabs have left her now, flying to wherever, free. But a few linger, buzz. Her dress is striped with their inky residue.

As she rounds the side of the motel, the music is louder and she sees its source, the back side of a curved stone building with tall stained-glass windows, colored lights reflecting against the panes from inside. If she can just get to it, get inside. A ladder leans against the wall. She climbs it. The rungs are slippery so she shakes off her shoes, hears them bounce on the pavement below. She reaches the base of the window and climbs onto the ledge, meets the glass in an embrace. Throbbing amped rumble vibrates through the pane. Enthralled by the light's beauty and the beat, she begins to dance, well, more sway, the space too narrow for anything else. Her hair is wet and heavy. The light, the sound through the window comforts, calls. She can see shadows of movement inside.

She glances back to see if he is still watching her from below—the man in the trench coat. He is, expressionless, still wearing dark glasses, clutching a wide black umbrella. He pulls the blade from his pocket with his gloved left hand, brandishes it with a single slash and nods.

Sasha turns back to the window. She looks down, her dress is zebra-striped from the inky stains of insect trespass. She wants to get out of the rain. She shivers at the cold drenching drops and inside looks so warm. She slams her head into the glass.

Sharp pain in her forehead, through her eye, down her cheek. She propels her body forward, leaps—no, flies. Hundreds of tiny stabs impact her flesh, so sudden, so many.

Like freedom.

Old Tsah-Hov

Lights flash on, a door slams, I jerk awake. Footsteps approach, and through the bars, I see bent bodies, faces staring. She says the word enough that I know it to be his name—Archer. The adam shakes his head, adjusts his glasses. He wears a pricker-prodder white coat and on it a pin the color of the sun with six points like the one she used to wear.

I jump up and yell, lunge for the bars. I cannot help it. The pin makes me angry because it reminds me of her and how I am trapped in this place with no sun, but blinding white lights that hurt my eyes and how I am not with her, and most of all not in the city where I yearn to be with that longing so deep it aches inside my heart.

Archer and the woman, who has short red hair and a similar coat but no pin, pull back, stand up. They are not afraid of me which makes me yell louder.

"Let me out, you fuckers!"

The other prisoners start shouting now, too. Whenever one of us yells or screams or even whines, we all do. They cannot silence us.

The couple turns and walks away, out the first door, the one through which I was brought. The prisoners nearest to it talk loudly and happily when they leave and when they return. They think they won't be here for long, that their families will be coming to pick them up soon. Sometimes they don't come back and I assume their offenses were less than mine and that they have homes to go to.

The door at the other end, the one that slammed, is different—thicker, colder. No one ever returns.

Once Archer and the woman are gone, we all begin to quiet, one by one. Saliva churns thickly in my mouth, but spitting does not help. I feel myself shaking not with cold but with a simmering rage that I cannot release. I glance at the full dish of food but am too angry to eat. The water, I cannot even look at, for in its reflection I see the King's eyes slitted and mocking.

I lie down again on the hard floor, curl into a ball and squeeze my eyes shut. I concentrate with all my might on the memory of her scent and her singing and imagine myself back in the city where the buildings and streets bore the same color as the sun, the city of yellow, the City of Gold.

I remembered the days when I ran with my brother and sister through the streets like they were just yesterday or a long, long time ago—never anything in-between. No one was faster than us. Our Ima had bade us be careful and avoid strangers. Sooner or later some thug would challenge us for a piece of food or pick a fight just because he did not like the way we smelled. Ima lectured us sternly that we were too young to win in a brawl, and every day she taught us a little more about how to disappear into a crowd of adams or fade into a shadow in a wall. She also warned us that most dangerous were the adams who were tall and could surprise you from behind with big thick sticks and stones. But we were young and like all the young, we believed ourselves indestructible.

Because I loved Ima and knew no other way, I listened and studied, but then one day I saw a fight between two adults, a rough-and-tumble ball of punches, kicks, and bites. I was surprised at the victory of the smaller combatant—whose color was the same as mine, somewhere between the sun and the sand and the city. The only difference was that he had a short stump instead of a curled tail like my own—its absence likely a scar from some previous battle. His bigger foe, dark fur like the night, limped away, flesh torn and bloodied, while the winner feasted on the slab of smoked meat that must have inspired the struggle. My mouth watered at its delicious aroma, and I thought to myself if only I could learn how to punch and where to bite and claw, I would never have to worry about eating well again. That, and fighting looked like pure pleasure.

I stepped slowly towards the victor. At first, he raised his head and growled, but when I explained I had no interest in his spoils and complimented him on his combat skills, he calmed. He clearly enjoyed my admiration and began to consider my proposition that I would bring him food if he would teach me to fight. He told me his name was King of the Streets, and it suited him. He was the most impressive of my kind I ever met. Most of us just called each other by the way we looked and recognized each other for how we smelled. My brother was Big Eye, because one of his brown eyes was larger than the other. My sister was Straight Tail because her tail didn't curl like Ima's, mine, and my brother's. And I was Lop Ear, because my left ear was crooked. But King, he earned his title in battle and the rest would either bow to him or give him a wide berth.

So my arrangement with King began. Every day while my brother and sister would siesta in an alley, I would sneak away and meet him. He taught me how to pick a fight, and soon I was not just scrapping with others my age but some even older. From the beginning I was winning. King told me I had a natural talent. That he thought so made me happy.

The day that my life changed started like every other. While darkness still cloaked the city, the adams called from the sky in all directions. My sister would try to sing with them when she was younger, but Ima always hushed her—afraid to draw attention. We were just squatters among the big burlap sacks of rice, couscous and fava beans—so much more comfortable to lie among these than the cold hard stones of the alley where we were born. Ima had discovered the broken window on one of her explorations—the opening just wide enough for her to squeeze through. Then one day she never returned. Her scent ended by a wall of trash cans. We imagined an adam found her while foraging for food for us, and for once, she was not able to disappear. We searched all the streets we knew and even streets we had never wandered before, but we never found a trace of her.

Once we heard the call, the three of us moved quickly. We needed to be outside before the adams who lived above the sacks were done spreading soft cloths on the ground and extending their forearms like we did when we wanted to communicate our desire to play.

We slipped out the window and into the alley. The first rays of the sun accented the yellow hue of the stones beneath our feet, like the first embers of a fire. We sniffed for signs of others who might have come in the night, and as soon as we caught even the faintest whiff, my brother and I lifted our legs and released our spray to declare this place was ours. After eight full moons, we were old enough that we could do that as adult males, not squat like our sister.

When we reached the market street, the scent of fresh bread baking tempted our noses. My brother and sister and I danced at the wonder of it, our stomachs yearning for its soft texture. After tasting the bread of the City of the Sun, no other food could ever fully satisfy—even raw meat, much less the bland hard dry pebbles in the bowl of my prison cell.

Shop doors opened, shutters lifted, canopies unfurled, and carts wheeled out onto the street. Soon adams would be everywhere, for this is how they hunted. They looked, then pointed, then exchanged wispy slips and metal pellets and took away their rewards. We needed to act quickly if we wanted to procure breakfast when eyes were still distracted with preparing for the day. Today, I didn't even have to snatch a loaf of bread from the cart. The adam let his son carry it out, but the boy's arms were not big enough to balance his haul and he dropped one. I grabbed it in my teeth before he could yell "*Kelev Ra!*" Then I ran back to the alley. I let my brother and sister each tear off a piece, but hid my own for King. My stomach ached with emptiness, but I couldn't arrive without payment and I'd found what he said to be true—one fights harder and better when hungry.

We wandered the streets, looking for other opportunities to scavenge and scored a few apples. As usual, I became restless for when the heat would become too much and my brother and sister would want to disappear back into the alleys to siesta in the shade. My brother stretched himself against the wall, and my sister curled her back against mine. Once she was asleep, I gently eased away—not knowing it would be the last time we would sleep beside each other.

I found King waiting in the usual place on the edge of the square outside one of the adams' great houses of gathering. They had many such buildings in the yellow city, some with half-suns nestled egg-like in their roofs. I once tried to creep inside, but an adam quickly shooed me away, and one of the rocks he threw at me came close enough to convince me it wasn't worth the risk. King told me inside there wasn't any food—only crowds of adams shuffling for position in front of sparkly bright objects. I was impressed that he was able to get inside—but if there wasn't any food, what was the point?

I placed the bread at King's feet. He sniffed and ate it so fast I wondered if he even tasted the flavors. Then he announced it was time for me to advance my training. Today he was going to teach me how to steal from an adam. I told him I was already good at watching for when one dropped something or was distracted setting up his wares in the morning.

"You tasted the bread I brought you, wasn't it delicious? The best baker in the old town."

King turned up his nose and snarled. I jumped back, startled at the magnitude of his derision.

"Do you like meat?"

"Of course," I said.

"The adam never drops his best meat, does he?"

"No."

"And if he leaves it unattended, it's only for a moment and you have to move as fast as a cat."

I raised my jowl to reveal my teeth. I didn't like cats.

"Well, then, are you brave and are you hungry?"

"Yes."

"You don't have to be afraid of the adam if you strike faster than he can pick up a rock to throw at you."

King led me within sight of a butcher shop. In front was an adam dressed all in black and with a long mane of black fur hanging in front of his face. I stiffened, recognizing him as one who had yelled at me when I was simply standing across the street minding my own. But oh, the wonder of the meats that always hung outside his shop—some raw and others that had been smoked and seasoned! For me, raw was always the tastiest, but I would settle for either.

"I will run fast and bite his ankle," King said. "While he is distracted, you jump up and grab some meat. I'll let go, and you and I will run like the wind. By the time he has a chance to grab a rock, we'll be long disappeared up there."

King motioned with his nose towards an alley that led to another of the great gathering homes. I wasn't scared of fighting other dogs—I enjoyed that—but my mother's stories of how much the adams hated us dug deep into me, not to mention the times when I had narrowly escaped being hit by a rock. King was a formidable champion among our kind, but was even he taking on more than he could chew? Still, I was afraid of seeming a coward in front of King.

I stole another glance at the adam, who was now engaged with a customer—a female with long black hair in a light-colored dress that clung tightly to her body. The adam leaned in close to her, gesturing to various of the hanging meats. I assume he was describing them so she could select the one she wanted to eat, but his body language indicated he also enjoyed the way she looked.

"Are you ready?" King asked, not giving me a chance to object.

I wasn't but I scratched my paw on the stone to signal yes.

King shot forward. I charged after him.

When I reached the cart, King's teeth were embedded in the man's leg and the adam was screaming in pain. The woman had backed away, her hand over her mouth. I leaped up and sank my teeth into a juicy raw slab. It gave way easily, but as my paws touched back to the ground, King let go, spun towards me and butted his head into my groin. The surprise assault from my teacher startled me, and I dropped the meat. King seized it up quickly from the ground and took off. The shock of his betrayal made me hesitate just long enough for the adam to pick up a rock.

I barely made it a few steps when it grazed the side of my hip and my legs slipped from beneath me, sliding me sideways onto hard stone. Several other adams shifted quickly out of my way as I hit the ground.

I scrambled to get back on my feet, but my leg hurt and my hip wouldn't cooperate so I had to just roll back down. I saw the adam bend to grab another rock. I growled but knew the adam had the advantage. Soon I would be gone to the place Ima went.

"Thief!!" shouted the adam, his cheeks flushed underneath his black beard.

But before he could hurl another weapon, I heard a loud shout.

"Isaac, no! Don't hurt the dog!"

The female with the long dark hair grabbed the adam's arm.

"But you saw what he did!" the adam protested. "He and his buddy stole one of my best beef shanks. Jerusalem would be better if all these mongrels were struck from our streets."

"Please," she said and waved him back. She turned towards me and then she crouched and stretched out her hand. I continued to growl. Again Ima's words came to me—never trust an adam.

"Sweet, sweet," she called to me.

The adam had backed away and was muttering irritably. Then she began to hum, her voice soft and soothing—the most beautiful sound I had ever heard. I stopped growling. Soon I was whimpering softly. She stroked my side. No adam had ever touched me, but her hand felt surprisingly nice. She scratched around my loppy ear. That felt especially good. I curled my front legs and rolled on my back. I don't know why I did that but I wanted her to rub my chest. She did, and it felt better than anything else I ever remembered.

She pointed to herself and said "Cassilda," repeating it three times slowly, lingering on every syllable. The pain in my leg had almost subsided, and with her help, I was able to stand. She took my head in her hands, placed her face close to mine, smiled and gazed in my eyes. If it had been anyone but her, I would have bitten, but I felt safe. I never wanted her to let go, to remove her face from mine.

Then she said: "Tsah-Hov." Again she said it three times, her eyes locked on my own. And I knew that was her name for me.

Isaac yelled again, and I suppose he was warning Cassilda about me—how our kind can't be trusted, how I would bite her. But I knew that I could never bite her.

She beckoned and I hesitated. I thought of my brother and my sister, and what they would think when they awoke, when like Ima, I just disappeared. I wondered if she had met her own Cassilda, but I knew that an Ima would never desert her children even for a Cassilda. Beyond the crowd in the entry to the alley, I saw King, glaring, the meat still in his mouth. I wondered if he was disappointed that I had found a savior.

I turned away from King and followed Cassilda. Sometimes she would pause and pet my head. I trailed her down the familiar market streets to the great wall, where I sat and waited while she did as the other adams did—slipped a leaf inside it, touched it, bowed her head, spoke.

When she returned to me, she said, "Good Tsah-Hov."

We continued out the giant gate—I had never traveled so far nor along such a wide street. In its center, giant mifletzets rushed by us at speeds I could never run. I had seen such creatures before but never in such numbers. Finally we came to a building as tall as the gathering homes but so high that I could not see if its roof had a sun on top.

Cassilda held open the door then led me to a strange box. Inside it made a funny noise and shook slightly. The box opened and we emerged in a different place with many doors. She went to one of them and grabbed what looked like a paw. She twisted it and it opened into her home, my new home.

So that's how the adams used all the cloths that hung outside the shops, I thought. They spread them on the floor to make it soft and warm, not like the cold hard stone of the streets. She led me into a small room that smelled of food and placed a bowl of water on the floor. I drank it eagerly. Before then I never had so much water in one serving except perhaps when it collected in a pot after a rain.

Cassilda coaxed me into another room and lifted me into a pond of bubbly warm water. At first, I didn't like it, but she massaged me until I could almost faint with pleasure. Even Ima with her tongue had never washed all the street smells away from me. Cassilda rubbed me with more soft cloths, then blew hot wind from a paw she held in her hand.

When I was completely dry, she led me to where she slept and patted her hand on her bed. I leapt up onto a place softer than the cloths on the floor, soft beyond all imagining, so soft I jumped back down. But she tapped her hand again and I returned. She lay down beside me and I snuggled my back within her arms. Again she began to sing.

I had never understood what the adam had spoken before now, but I knew her words. Cassilda sang of the city, the city of the setting sun, the city of Gold, the city of Tsah-Hov. She sang of it as if it were my city, hers and mine, and how we shared it with our tribes. Here it all began and here it would all end. The old city was lost but the lost has been found, and while we have our enemies, the city gives us strength and shall endure until a great King descends from the sky.

I saw a tear trail down her cheek. My eyes were full of tears, too. Until then I never knew that dogs could cry.

From then on I lived with Cassilda in her home above the streets, sleeping with her in her bed. During the day she would leave me, and sometimes I feared she would not return. But she always did, bringing bread and scraps of meat I did not have to steal. Before sleep, she sang to me the same song.

In the morning and evening, Cassilda took me for walks around her building. I marked my new kingdom zealously, but the only others of my kind I saw were clean like me, walking with adams. I had seen dogs with adams in the market before, but my brother, sister, and I had laughed at them. She also took me to see the pricker-prodder for the first time. His house was full of many dogs and cats, some I saw and some I could just smell. Two adams had to hold me tightly when he pricked several sharp claws into my back. I wanted to bite him, and I wondered why Cassilda brought me here. But as soon as I saw her again, I forgave her.

Once a week she took me along when she shopped in the market. Sometimes I would see one like me who lived on the streets or a small pack. I sensed they were jealous of Cassilda and me. They knew I had found something special and different, even if they had no idea how it felt to lie on a soft cloth instead of cold stone or a bag of rice. I scanned the shadows for my brother and sister, but I never saw them. I only glimpsed King one time and he just turned away as if he pitied me. I dreamt of King nightly though, only now he wasn't giving me lessons. Instead we fought. Each time he appeared more bloody and scarred, but he still always won, admonishing me that my fighting skills had become soft from living with an adam.

Then came the day Cassilda brought Shmuel home. He had no fur on his head at all. When he visited, he would always pet me quickly on the head, and then he would ignore me for the rest of the evening. She laughed when he spoke, they'd sit and eat together, and after that they touched lips. Sometimes he stayed all night and I no longer fit on the bed. They made groans of pleasure and emanated mating smells. On those nights, I slept on the sofa in the living room. The cushions were softer than the bed, but I missed Cassilda. I wished Shmuel would stop coming.

Shmuel visited more and more often until one day he just stayed. Cassilda grew bigger in her belly, and I could smell the little adam growing inside. Shmuel started taking me on my morning and twilight walks, sometimes after dark if he came home late. He didn't talk or sing to me like Cassilda did. He just took me far enough to empty myself and then we returned home. I slept on the sofa every night now, King taunting me as we dream-battled about how I was afraid to challenge an adam.

The little male was born, and Cassilda called him Chanan. She seemed happy but always stressed. Though she no longer left every day, she had even less time for me, having to prepare his food and tend to him. Still, during the day she sang to both of us about the city, and while she sang, I did not feel replaced or alone.

Other days were not so nice. Chanan would cry and Shmuel would get a growl to his voice. One day he struck Cassilda. King's voice shouted in my head, and I yelled at Shmuel, started to lunge. I barely got close before he hit me hard on my head. I yelped and jumped back, growled more. I wanted to tear him apart, but I remembered what Ima said about adams being bigger and stronger, even if I had teeth and claws and despite King goading me in my head. I also knew Cassilda loved Shmuel like she loved me, so instead I retreated to a corner, where I lay down to stare at him. She cried and Chanan cried louder, and now Shmuel was soothing her, stroking her hair, putting his lips to her cheek. Later she crept out of bed to check on me, placed her hand on my brow. She couldn't sing because it would wake everyone in the house, but I could hear her voice.

Cassilda started taking Chanan for walks in a cart that she pushed. I danced when she indicated that I could come along. She gently calmed me, I suppose afraid I'd jump on the fragile baby, though she should know I would never harm him. She hummed to us as we walked down the old familiar path to the market, where she filled a bag with food from sundry vendors, and I filled my nose with all the old smells. I even thought I caught a whiff of King near the gathering house where we used to meet.

On the way back, a large clap seared into my ears and the ground shook with such anger that both Cassilda and I almost fell over. Adams screamed all around us and a cloud of dust enveloped us. Cassilda began to cough and run pushing the cart, Chanan crying at the top of his lungs. I sprinted after her. Everyone was running and yelling. When we finally got home, she locked the door quickly behind us, took Chanan in her arms and sang more loudly than I had ever heard her sing. I could hear both love and fear in her voice as she lamented that the city had enemies jealous of its beauty, enemies who also thought it holy. Even I knew that some adams didn't like others in the same way we didn't like the scent of all of our kind—and what had happened was rooted in an enmity so ancient that it might as well have always been.

Shmuel came home early. He held her like the old Shmuel had courted her. They talked for a long time in great seriousness. In the days that followed, I only walked with Shmuel and I saw the first signs that my life was about to change. Objects disappeared from shelves and closets, boxes, and crates piled up in the living room. King and I no longer fought in my dreams—he just raised his jowls and made a sound that I had never heard any of us make—laughter. Then one day adams came and took everything away.

Shmuel brought a large crate with bars like the cell I am in now. He placed a big beef-bone in my bowl, pushed it inside, and called to me. The savory aroma enticed, but I didn't trust to enter a place so dark and narrow. Shmuel yelled at me, but Cassilda shushed him. When she stroked me and coaxed me, I couldn't deny her. Once I was inside, I heard a snapping noise behind me and began to whine.

Cassilda spoke to me through the bars, repeating my name "Tsah-Hov," and from the gentle tone in her voice, I knew she did not want me to be afraid. I stopped calling out and lay down. I was more afraid than even when the adam was stoning me, but for her I would do anything.

The crate was shoved into one of the great street beasts, and then unloaded at a place full of terrible rattling noises and people yelling all around me. Next I was moved to a dark place with many cases reeking with the odor of adams. I felt a sensation like being lifted—as if the very ground was rising. I cried loudly in the near-dark but no one even shouted to silence me.

I finally fell asleep, and all I remembered of my dreams was Ima's stern warnings, and King opening his mouth to reveal too many sharp, pointy teeth. A heavy thud shook me awake, and I sensed I was on the ground again. Adams pulled the case out into the sunlight, but I knew I was no longer in the Gold City. Even the adams smelled different. They lifted me onto another mifletzet. Then finally the creature stopped, its canopy lifted, and I heard Cassilda excitedly calling my name.

"Tsah-Hov!"

She opened the bars and I jumped all over her in joy. She didn't scold me but hugged me. I could see Shmuel behind her holding Chanan, his sneer revealing he would have preferred to have left me. As Cassilda quieted me, I realized the ground felt like soft cloth under my paws.

And so I arrived at my new home, not a building with many homes but one place for just us with many rooms and stairs and what Cassilda called a "yard"—covered with the soft rugs in the back. I knew we must be far away from the City because the only thing I recognized was the sun. This place was not the color of the sun, but different colors, colors that resembled shadows to me and for which I had no names.

At first I admit I was a little excited by my new home. Cassilda would take me and Chanan on long walks in his cart. The streets were smooth like a single stone, and I did not have to step carefully to protect my feet. The city of Gold had few trees, but trees were everywhere here, towering above. And the houses were big and separated from each other by yards. An adam family lived in each house and there was no market street. Cassilda and Shmuel would ride instead inside a mifletzet and return with food. Sometimes they took me, and we would emerge to walk in different places, places even softer and filled with more trees. Or they took me to see another pricker-prodder, a female who tried to soothe me with a gentle voice and crunchy food, then stabbed me just the same. At night, though, Cassilda still sang the boy to sleep with the song of the City of Gold, and I would listen. She put on a mask of contentment, but I could sense we both were lost now. I still dreamed of King, but we did not fight and he was silent.

Many like me lived here, but unlike in the City, they came in more sizes, shapes, and colors. Their smells didn't tell many stories because they spent their nights in the houses with adams. Some would yell at me from their yards behind fences—and others would strain their leashes. I now had to wear a collar around my neck and walk on a rope like them. I hated both, but the others seemed not to mind, as if they accepted whatever the adams bade them do. Sometimes when Shmuel walked me, I would shout back and once when he took off my lead on a dirt path with lots of trees I even attacked a big prissy one of my kind whose long fur resembled a horse's mane and tale. When I walked with Cassilda however, I mastered an innocent stare that only seemed to infuriate my foes and make them shout louder at me.

At first the new soft place seemed to calm Shmuel's anger. But then he and Cassilda began to fight as never before—shouting and shouting. I swore to myself if he ever hit her again, I would rip him apart. One day he left and then he would only come sometimes to take the boy away for short periods of time. Those times when I was alone with Cassilda, I would crawl close to her and she would stroke my head. We both shut our eyes and were back in the City, the sun's rays painting all the buildings the color of my fur.

I was dreaming not of King but a happy memory of the streets and the scent of baking bread when a heavy knock jolted me awake. Cassilda rose and opened the door. Shmuel quivered with anger and wobbled unsteadily on his feet, and even Chanan trembled in fear of his father. Cassilda shouted at him, yanking the boy away. He wiggled even out of her grasp and ran towards the stairs, grabbing onto the railing and lingering as if torn between watching his parents and escaping to his bedroom.

I yelled at Shmuel to stay away from Cassilda, but she was consumed with the rage of an Ima afraid for her child and moved closer instead. His hand came up quickly and swatted her across the face. She fell back as he lunged again towards her, but tripped on one of my bones on the floor. I heard King's shouting now loudly in my head, "Coward! Coward!" I pulled myself into position to leap while my foe's legs were still teetering.

Just as my paws left the ground, Chanan ran in front of Shmuel, shouting, "No, Tsah-Hov! No!"

It was too late for me to pull back my teeth which bit down hard now not on Shmuel's leg but on Chanan's cheek. The taste of his blood filled my mouth—both similar and different from the blood of my kind. The boy screamed, and something hard and wood descended on my head. I yelped and let go, my instincts cutting. But as I spun around to attack and grabbed the arm of my combatant, I saw it was Cassilda. I yelped again, let go and ran for the window, hurling myself against and out it. As it shattered, sharp

blades cut my flesh like a thousand pricker-prodders. I dashed into the black night and to the back corner of the yard, scrambled into a hole under the fence through which I sometimes escaped to explore the neighborhood by myself. I had no place to go without Cassilda, so I crept to the front of the house and waited.

A giant mifletzet covered in spinning lights charged into the driveway. It made a screeching noise which hurt my ears. Another smaller one followed with more lights and noise, and then another. Adams emptied out of them into the house, and soon they brought out Cassilda and Chanan. Her head was bowed and she clutched her arm. I called to her even though I knew she would grant no absolution. I had bitten her child. Ima would never have forgiven anyone who did that.

Cassilda lifted her head and looked at me. I could see tears flowing down her cheeks. Shmuel exited the house behind her. I shouted and raced towards him. At that moment I felt a tight noose lasso around my neck and a rough jerk backwards. Soon I was caged in the back of one of the mifletzet and then I was here.

"Tsah-Hov," says Archer.

My eyes blink open when I hear my name, angry to hear anyone utter it but Cassilda. I growl and raise my lips to show my teeth.

Archer signals to another adam—a heavyset one who opens the cage. Then he lassoes the metal noose around my neck again. I lunge to attack but he wields his weapon with a skill I cannot evade and jumps back before I can snap my teeth. Oh, Ima, the adams have their ways to hurt. They have been doing it since the beginning of time.

The door to the Chamber stands open, and I enter, knowing I will never leave, never see Cassilda again. I wonder if she thinks of me, if she understands that I did what I did for her.

I no longer struggle, just allow the burly adam to lift me onto the cold smooth table.

I see Archer, the pricker-prodder, lift his claw and close my eyes. As its juice flows into me, I see the Yellow City. Cassilda stands before the great doors to the gathering home. She sings and opens her arms and I run to her, but when I reach the entrance, King awaits instead. His yellow fur is no longer drenched in blood but glows so bright and luminous I have to avert my eyes to avoid being blinded.

I turn to flee. But King springs and sinks his teeth into my neck, drags me in through the doors. Inside everything is shiny, just as King told me, with no roof, just open blue sky and not just one sun but two. Cassilda sings but I cannot see her. Adams are everywhere. King hurls me towards them. They yell "*Kelev Ra!*" in chorus and raise their arms so I can see the many, many rocks.

Jehessimin

A crack rips open the fast lane blacktop of Interstate 91, blacker than the newly night sky. An enormous narrow head, pale as bleached bone with pulsating red eyes, shoots outwards from the tenebrous void. Tangled branches, like antlers or the crown of a tall tree, tower from its crest, billowing wildly into dark clouds.

Angie slams the Nissan's brakes. No time to swerve and avoid a direct hit into whatever the fuck—

Her seatbelt straps her tightly in place, surreal slow motion kicking in as she surrenders herself to the aftermath of impact. Her glasses don't so much fly off as dematerialize. In a dreamlike haze, she senses the car spin slightly to the right, watches the hood buckle and the airbag simultaneously inflate from the center of the steering wheel.

The monstrous tree-like thing reaches out a knotted branch and peels away the hood and half the front bumper. Gnarled lips open, a barbed brown tongue extends like a drawbridge, and a blurry herd of green creatures slithers across it onto the shredded engine compartment's innards and up the cracked windshield.

A fractured strip of glass gives way on the passenger side.

One of the things snakes in and onto the dislodged glove compartment which is bent forwards and down towards the floor. A sulfurous odor overwhelms the car's interior. It rears up and spreads, flattens, puffs its neck, and unfurls leafy frills around its bulging pustulent face. Clumps of eyes in the wrong places leer as if sizing up the young woman trapped by the seatbelt.

It opens a mouth, lower than a mouth should be, full of teeth like needles.

Angie jerks back reflexively, a hot pain as her hip hits the door. No time for flight, but she doesn't scream, quietly freaks out and wonders if she has any chance of fighting off what she expects to be an imminent attack.

It hisses at her:

"*Jehessimin.*"

But it doesn't strike, instead disappears into the crack between glove compartment and passenger door.

The car rattles as the remaining creatures pass across the roof, rear windshield, and trunk, then ooze out from under the front. A screeching wind sucks them into the orifice, which now resembles a hole in a gigantic tree. One emerges a moment later and turns towards her—the one that was in the car. It must have slipped out via whatever hole was left by the disconnected glove compartment.

The beast twists and shakes tiny arms from its serpentine body. She catches a shaky glimpse of a different shade of green in its grasp.

Jehessimin, it hisses again.

Then it, too, spirals backwards into the aperture.

Gigantic jaws snap shut and the monstrous visage shrinks until sucked entirely back into the fissure, which ripples and vanishes.

[A flash of the bulky rear end of a white welding truck, its taillights like red eyes. A cloud of smoky exhaust.]

What the hell just happened?

Gazing out through the mostly missing windshield, her eyes snap into focus on a severed hose sticking up from the exposed engine.

I'm not dead.

Beyond, the Nissan's lone remaining headlight illuminates a blurry, unblemished stretch of empty road.

Jehessimin.

Angie has heard that word before somewhere, some time. It didn't make sense then, but she now recognizes it.

It's my name.

Time stopped.

Knocking.

A hazy shape in a pink sweater.

I should open the window.

While the rental car was unfamiliar, the button should be on the door. Angie reached over with her left hand.

Yes, there it is.

The window slid down, letting in a waft of chilly November air. In that motion, Angie noticed an oval scrape of exposed pink dermis at the base of her thumb.

"Are you all right? Are you hurt?" asked the woman.

"I scraped my thumb," Angie said, holding it up.

"That looks like an air-bag burn," the woman said, a concerned look on her face. "Does it sting?"

"A little, not much," Angie said. "I think I'm in some kind of shock. Did you see the accident?"

"Sorry, no, I didn't," said the woman. "It'd already happened when I drove up behind you."

"Something in front of me…something big," Angie said. "I tried to brake but I couldn't stop fast enough…"

If she said she thought she'd hit a monster, this nice woman would think she was crazy, maybe on drugs. That wouldn't go over well with the police when they came.

Officer, I think I hit a giant monster. It suddenly came up from the pavement.

The pavement looked completely intact in front of her.

[A flash of the bulky rear end of a white welding truck, its taillights like red eyes. A cloud of smoky exhaust.]

If they tested her, all they would find would be caffeine from the take-out coffee that she purchased before leaving the airport, if that even showed up on tests. Maybe they would wrap her in a straitjacket and cart her off to a mental ward.

Did they do still do straitjackets?

She wasn't even in North Leeds yet. When she was little, her dad, Albert, had told her scary bedtime stories about North Leeds State Hospital, also known as Old Leeds, her hometown's second claim to fame after Plath College, one of the nation's top women's higher educational institutions. Rumored to be the site of all sorts of atrocities and also haunted, it had closed in that 1980s wave when some policy by President Reagan shut down so many mental institutions across the country. Her mom, Julia, told her that the reason North Leeds had so many homeless begging along Main Street was that they were Old Leeds patients with no place to go. Angie's mind meandered to a skinny woman with ratty long hair who screamed every time she walked by and scared the shit out of her as a little girl.

What did she say again?

"*Jesse James.*"

No, it couldn't have been.

Jehessimin.

"I think I hit a truck," Angie said.

"Sometimes when you hit a truck, the driver doesn't even feel it," her good Samaritan said, shaking her back to the present.

The woman had kind eyes, Angie thought, even not seeing clearly without her glasses.

"I guess I should get out of the car," Angie said, still trying to rationalize and not eager to move at all.

"Yeah, I think it'd be safer for you on the shoulder," the woman said.

Angie thought about rubberneckers causing a secondary accident when they slowed down to leer at a wreck.

A better reason kicked in.

What if whatever I hit returns.

[The red taillights of a white welding truck.]

"I need to find my glasses," Angie said, reaching down to skim her hand around the base of her seat.

Thankfully she felt them right away. More amazing, they weren't broken. She slipped them on and unsnapped the seatbelt. She reached down to lift her overturned tote bag back onto the passenger seat. She pulled out her wallet, checked for her driver's license and insurance info.

The nagging questions of modernity replacing the impossible weirdness of what had just transpired.

Will my insurance cover this? That consumer advocate guy always said that buying the loss-damage waiver was a waste of time. But she just totaled a new car and her insurance covered a ten-year-old Honda Accord.

The accident would be her fault since she rear-ended whatever was in front of her.

There was nothing in front of me.

I shouldn't be keeping this kind woman waiting.

Standing in the emergency lane, Angie finally saw the full extent of the damage—the curled and crushed front, the peeled-away hood on the passenger side. A long line of creeping traffic in the middle lane.

"If you're okay with me leaving you for a moment, I've got a mobile phone in the car so I can call the police."

"Where am I?"

"You're almost at the Longmeadow exit, right across the Massachusetts border."

Angie saw a neon gas station sign some ways down the highway to the right. At least that meant a pay phone and a place for Curt to pick her up. She'd been thinking of getting a mobile but they were so expensive.

"Oh, okay, that's good. It's less than thirty minutes from North Leeds, where I'm going."

Her rescuer nodded and then walked back to her car which was parked behind the Nissan.

Angie wanted Curt right now. Even if he was barely her boyfriend, she wanted him to hold her, to kiss her, to make love to her, to make her forget whatever she saw, whatever had happened. He had expected her to arrive soon. Now he was going to have to drive and pick her up. At least it wasn't all the way to Bradley Field, the Hartford/Springfield airport.

She'd rented the car so she wouldn't have to wait until he got off work at the video store to pick her up. Plus she had been wanting to do some exploring on her own in North Leeds, her birthplace. She hadn't been back since she was six. The "Un-Happy Valley" was the first place of many where she didn't feel like she fit in. Until she suddenly had a boyfriend there.

Could I?

Maybe going back to my beginning could be the first step to finally finding my way.

Her thoughts were interrupted by her rescuer's return.

"I called the police. They're on their way, but they said I should go because I wasn't a witness. Are you going to be okay on your own?"

"Yeah, I guess," Angie said, not wanting her to leave. "What's your name?"

"It's Judy," she said.

"I'm Angie. Can I give you a hug?"

"Sure."

Angie threw her arms around Judy and almost shouted.

"I'm alive! I'm alive!"

She realized she was smiling.

"I'm sorry," Judy said, as Angie stepped back.

"Thank you," Angie said.

"I'm just glad you're not hurt," Judy said.

Angie watched Judy walk back to her car, then blink her right turn signal, merge, and disappear into the night traffic. She shivered and wished the police would get there soon.

An eternity but per her watch only five minutes later, a state patrol car arrived, siren whirring and blue lights flashing, tailed by a fire engine.

Two firemen approached her first. In a thick Massachusetts accent, one asked her if she was injured, wanted to go to a hospital. She said no, answered a few questions. No, she hadn't hit her head, didn't think she had a concussion. No whiplash, her back and neck didn't hurt. Just the mild airbag burn at the base of her thumb.

Then they let the police officer take over.

"What's your name, miss?"

"Angie Templeton."

"Do you have your license and registration?"

"Yes, I have my license. But it's a rental car. I have the paperwork."

She pulled her license from her wallet and handed it to the officer.

"What happened?"

"I think I hit a truck. It suddenly stopped dead ahead of me."

"Are you sure it was a truck, miss?"

"No, it happened so fast."

"How fast were you driving?"

"I don't know. I didn't look."

With it being at the tail-end of rush hour, traffic was heavy enough that she couldn't have been speeding, could she? But there'd been *nothing* in front of her, nothing to gauge her following distance.

More standing alone, the air growing progressively colder. The temperatures had been uncharacteristically high for November—fifties—when Angie left the airport, so a sweater had been enough.

The officer returned and reported that he had called a tow truck that operated out of West Hartford.

"Are you going to give me a ticket?" she asked

"No, but I can if you want one," he replied without emotion.

Just like a cop.

"I was only asking because I've never been in an accident where I've been the driver before," she answered, as politely as she could given her stress level.

The officer turned and walked back to his patrol car. The tow truck arrived about five minutes later, just as Angie felt she couldn't last any longer without her leather jacket. The cop and the driver, who introduced himself as Joe, exchanged a few words. Joe then attached the hook on the end of the tow chain to the front of the Nissan and loaded it onto the flatbed.

When the procedure was complete, Angie joined him in the cab and asked him to drive her to the gas station at the next exit. She pulled her tote bag from the front passenger seat and gathered from the floor what she thought was everything that had fallen out of it—toiletry pouch, a granola bar, a hair clip, two books, a *Newsweek* magazine, and her laptop.

Joe couldn't pop open the trunk because the battery was disconnected, so she suggested pulling down the backseat, asked if she could try. She quickly found the release, pulled out her suitcase and jacket which she slipped on immediately.

She thanked him, then hoisted the tote bag onto her shoulder and dragged her suitcase to the phone booth in front of the gas station.

The first time she tried Curt, he didn't answer. She called again.

"Hello."

"Hi, Curt, I've been in an accident. I'm okay but the rental car is totaled."

"Christ, Angie, what happened?"

"I don't know. I was driving, and it's like nothing was in front of me, and then I smashed into the back of a truck. Only then the truck was gone."

"Baby, that doesn't make any sense."

"I know. Can you just come and get me? I'm at the Shell station at the Longmeadow exit."

"Sure, I was just about to leave work. I'll be there as fast I can."

"Thanks."

"Okay, see you soon. Stay safe."

"I'll try."

Curt hung up, and she lugged her bags into the gas station to buy a can of Coca-Cola. As she pulled open the tab, she realized her left hand was shaking and a dull ache was forming on her left hip.

Curt drove up about forty minutes later. Angie collapsed into a long hug.

"You got a haircut," she said as they separated, running her fingers through his spiky short blond hair and down the satin lapels of his vintage black suit jacket, playing with his narrow red tie.

"Yeah, yesterday," he replied.

"Looks good. You look good all over."

Curt half-smiled, then stashed her luggage in the trunk of his old Mustang. When she was safely tucked into the passenger seat, and he was pulling out, she realized he hadn't kissed her.

They didn't say much during the drive. She was still processing what happened, and she sensed he preferred the silence. Maybe she'd weirded him out. What a shitty start to a date weekend.

On the phone over the three weeks since they met at that horror film festival in New York, he had talked a mile a minute. A graduate student in the film program at Hurst State University, Curt always was keen to discuss his favorite movies or his own concepts he wanted to write and direct. Her own movie obsession had led her to a publicist job at Turner Classic Movies in Atlanta, long hours for little pay, although it had nice perks, like that trip to New York where TCM sponsored a retro revival night including Val Lewton's *Cat People* and Universal's *Creature from the Black Lagoon* in 3-D. But then she didn't want to write movies. She had a gig on the side writing CD reviews for a local music tabloid and dreams of travel-writing, something that would allow her to visit new places until she figured out where she belonged.

Maybe Curt was quiet because she worried him. Or like a typical guy, did he just not know what to say faced with a real-life situation?

I hoped he wasn't another typical guy.

Also, stop over-thinking everything.

Traffic flowed surprisingly quickly through Springfield, but by now, almost eight p.m., rush hour was over. By Holyoke, the cars had really thinned out. Curt took the first North Leeds exit and curved onto the state highway, which became Parris Street when it drifted into a typical college town downtown. On Main Street, the shops were dark, but clusters of students and townies ambled on the sidewalks, perhaps just finished with a restaurant dinner or getting an early start on bar hopping.

A few more turns, and Curt pulled into a parking spot in front of the old North Leeds jailhouse, three stories of brick with a bell-tower in the center converted into condos. As they pulled in and parked, Curt broke silence with one of his anecdotes.

"Josh Westfield used to rent a bachelor pad up top," he said, pointing to the top-center of the building. "He was one of the two creators of the Alien Jujitsu Otters. You know, they made millions? Josh used all the money to start his own comics company and even a museum that used to be based here in North Leeds. Lots of famous comics artists stayed at that flat, but Sam who lived here since it opened told me that Josh also used it for hook-ups and parties where the coke flowed like candy.

"You'll like this part more," he continued. "Sam says there's a creepy stain in the ceiling in Josh's penthouse right under the bell-tower which is sealed up. And flies gather there. No matter how many times it was cleaned up, the stain and the flies come back.

"*Spoooooooky!!!*"

Curt shook his hands as if to mock the scary vibe and then dove into a kiss on her lips. She responded eagerly.

"Don't move," he said.

He jumped out of the driver's side and zipped around to open the door for her.

"Milady!" he said. "Welcome to the Jailhouse Rrrrrock!"

As Angie stepped out, he started to air-guitar. She laughed, thinking how all through college she cringed at guys who air-guitar, thought how nerdy. His Ramones-rapid strokes, however, instead endeared him to her.

He grinned, seemingly pleased at her response, and pulled her suitcase out of the trunk. He motioned for her to follow him to the end of the building, the furthest to the right of three front doors.

To her side, she noticed a black wrought-iron gate and beyond it, barely illuminated by the streetlight, gravestones. She was aware that North Leeds Cemetery, which dated back to Colonial days, fronted on state highway Nine. But she didn't remember her parents ever taking her down these back streets. They had lived on the other side of downtown, the other side of campus.

"I didn't know you were next to the cemetery," she said. "That's kind of cool."

"What, do you want to take a walk among the tombstones at night, you creepy girl?" Curt teased as they reached the doorstep, took her hand, leaned in, and rubbed his nose against hers.

"Ha-ha, not tonight, I'm starting to ache a bit now," Angie said. "Honestly I hate to be a party pooper, but I kind of want to go straight to bed."

"I bet you ache, but I'm down with going straight to bed."

He released her hand and put his key in the lock. Once in the hallway, his apartment was up one flight of stairs and the first on the right on the second floor.

"Do you want some water? A beer? A glass of wine?" Curt asked as they entered the living room.

The layout was pretty much what she expected—basic futon couch with a dark red cover, glass coffee table full of movie books, media center with a TV and VCR, and movie posters on the walls. Russian classics: Tarkovsky's *Stalker*, Eisenstein's *Potemkin* and *October: Ten Days That Shook the World*, a trio of framed stills from *Aelita, Queen of Mars*.

"Some water would be nice," Angie said. Her throat was parched after at least four hours since she'd even had coffee.

She followed him into the kitchen, watched him pour a tall glass from the filtered tap in the refrigerator.

"In case you go out without me, the spare keys to the front and apartment doors are on a nail in the kitchen," he said, back to unemotional. "I'll take your bags to the bedroom."

Angie watched as he disappeared down the hallway, wishing he'd kissed her again. She didn't want to seem needy even if her mental balance was seriously wobbly after the accident. Their relationship was new, and she feared any vulnerability would frighten him away. In New York a month ago, they hadn't even gone all the way to sex, but then she was sharing a hotel room with a co-worker and he was crashing on a friend's couch.

Did it qualify yet as a "relationship"?

She finished the water, put down the glass in the sink, and almost collided with Curt in the bedroom doorway.

Whether excited or simply surprised, they fell into a rough embrace, followed by rapid removal of each others' clothes. She hadn't been sure she wanted to have sex immediately upon her arrival, but here she was, letting him bite her nipples, thrust his fingers inside her.

If the accident hadn't happened, Angie might have protested, asked to wait. Or would she? She hadn't other times and only later thought she should have when the sex didn't lead to anything more. But right now she really wanted to feel cared for or at least desired, as if her life meant something to someone else.

She let Curt lower her onto the futon, and they made fast moves despite aches in her back and hip. He came quickly. Then he held her, wound around her back like a comma.

After a while he let go, and soon after, Angie fell asleep, deeply enough that she didn't sense him crawl out of the futon, nor hear him get dressed and open and shut the front door.

The Tiger Girl sat perched on a bar stool, face-out towards the crowd, legs crossed. Her ivory-blonde hair so silky, teased like the mane of a Persian cat. Visage pale as porcelain, red lips, arched eyebrows, azure eyes, winged jet-black eyeliner—not Goth, but Sixties Mod, Factory Girl. Her shimmering sleek spandex bodysuit yellow with black stripes, spike-heeled white go-go boots made for walking right over. A tigress hunting prey in a throbbing club scene. Relaxed but ready, the Tiger Girl flexed her fingernails.

Pearl Bar was almost empty, maybe thirty people, clothed in black leather and lace and combat boots and T-shirts and jeans. But everyone's eyes were watching her—men and women.

How could they not be? Even though they'd never met her before, they were certain they knew her and greeted her as they passed so as not to be embarrassed. They exchanged pleasantries. She made small talk. They told lame jokes. She laughed. They wanted her in their beds. They left knowing that she was a potential lover. They all had a chance with her.

Curt scribbled on a narrow reporter's notepad.

Fuck, she makes me write like a poet, words I didn't know I had in me.

The Tiger Girl stretched, as if to confirm her feline nature. She extended one arm straight upwards and the other to her side. Then she accepted a cigarette and a light from a balding man with a goatee and a ponytail, in a black turtleneck. A match, not a lighter. She watched it burn almost to his fingers before leaning in. Beatnik Mephistopheles rubbed the flame out with his fingers, seeming not to mind any pain she induced.

Is that her type?

The Tiger Girl smiled in the direction of the earnest young blond man in a black suit jacket, narrow red tie, and jeans. She turned to watch him, her blue eyes and enticing lips telling him how easy it would be for her to fulfill all his wishes and be the girl of his illicit dreams. He was impatient, but she wouldn't make him wait much longer.

The Tiger Girl sensed how she ignited him, fired the rapid boil of his angry young writer bravado. He had a fantasy about her that he had been nurturing since she first appeared a dozen days ago. She was the forgotten heroine of some lost black and white silent film. Her eyeliner was not as thick as Theda Bara's.

He imagined Lillian Gish briefly, but no, of course, she was a Russian beauty, fired by the heat of revolution.

Siberian tigress.

Pure Eisenstein.

Not impossible. Some of her kind wandered in winter. Some of her kind liked to stoke revolutions.

The Tiger Girl finished her cocktail, stubbed out her cigarette in a nearby ashtray. She shooed away Hipster Mephistopheles.

Once alone, she made herself available to Curt. Too soon to catch, but time to make the next move, to reel him closer.

Curt had waited for such a moment. She watched him observe her finish the cigarette and then pick up the blue pack again. She let him see the brand clearly—Gauloises, French, unfiltered.

She raised a cigarette to her lips. He was there in that instant, flicking his Bic.

The Tiger Girl inhaled deeply, then blew out smoke in rings. She smiled at him and stifled her amusement when he almost melted in place, forced down her excitement at the thought of him actually melting.

"Your hand is shaking," she said.

Curt self-consciously tucked lighter and hand into a jacket pocket.

"I'm Curt," he said with newfound confidence. "What's your name?"

"Erla," the Tiger Girl said, placing the emphasis on the "ahhhh." She spoke with an accent that Curt could not identify but could swear sounded Slavic.

"That's an unusual name," Curt said.

"All the first-born in my 'family' are Erla, my mother and my grandmother before her," she replied, rolling the "r" as if purring.

"Where are you from?"

"You ask a lot of questions," Erla said.

Her cigarette still lit in her right hand, she placed her left in his and guided him to the edge of the stage. The small crowd parted until they stood directly in front of the lead singer, some critically celebrated up-and-comer with long dark hair named Dorian.

Erla released his hand and gave him a cigarette. He had been trying to quit, but she didn't want him to quit.

Curt stifled a cough with the first unfiltered puff.

"Sorry, out of practice," he said into her ear so she could hear him over the band. "But gotta admit, the burn feels so good."

How did she smoke them, one after another?

Unnatural girl. Supernatural girl.

The Tiger Girl began to sway.

The crowd separated around her, creating an island.

Curt imagined holding a camera to film her dance, him not asking permission, her not objecting.

She needed no direction. The slightest hand motion, bend of a leg, toss of her hair would be the most meaningful footage he had ever captured on film.

A long white frock coat and a round ivory fur hat. A white horse to ride. She whips its loins as she drives the beast relentlessly through fields and forests of snow. Belladonna of Bolsheviks, leading the peasants out of their farms and factories and into the cobblestone streets of Petrograd, across the curved canal bridges of the Venice of the North.

"Erla Petrova" lifts a white-gloved hand and strokes the cheek of a marble angel brandishing a stone sword at the edge of the square, a final moment of reflection before compelling the mob in front of the Winter Palace. Then she charges, fighting Cossack after Cossack with a curved scimitar.

Finally there are just too many. The Cossacks push her and the mob back. She falls from the steed at the base of the Angel.

The snow so soft cushions her body, curled to one side as blood—black because no color—stains first her coat and then the snow.

"Long live Lenin," she whispers.

Erla Petrova closes her eyes. The Cossacks remove their hats and bow their heads to honor their enemy. She is the martyr of the Revolution—its Joan of Arc.

At that moment, the Angel bends. The statue touches the cheek of the heroine who awakes, accepts her sword which transforms from stone to blade. The battle recommences until every Cossack lies dead in the square. The peasants cheer.

The Tiger Girl hands the Angel back her sword before lying again on the ground. She rose from the dead, but her good work is done. The people are free.

Papa Lenin walks through the crowd until he reaches her and bends to kiss the cheek of the goddess to the godless.

The scene melted like a burning reel of film as Dorian wrapped his final song.

The bar lights went up.

"It's true that I've fought men with swords," Erla said.

"What?"

He hadn't said a word out loud.

Had he?

Erla leaned so close that her eyes overwhelmed his.

Her blue irises opened like curtains, enveloping her sclerae, and her pupils narrowed to catlike slits.

Her gaze was so intense, attracting and weirding him out at the same time, that his eyes blinked reflexively as he waited for the kiss.

In the second it took for them to reopen, Erla was gone. Onstage, the band was breaking down their equipment.

Confused, he spun and saw Erla heading towards the door with Beatnik Mephistopheles' hand cupped on her behind.

The Tiger Girl turned back and winked her left cat-eye. Curt's anxiety relaxed into anticipation.

She'd be back and his pleasure would come.

Soon.

~

Red cat-eyes pulsate in blackest black. Laughter like the on-off gusts of a howling wind. Crown of a tree or is it antlers?

Angie slams the Nissan's brakes again.

Seatbelt jerks her back, car spins, white blob in the center of the steering wheel, hood scraping away like amplified fingernails across a blackboard.

Sulfurous odor. Serpentine green creature rears up, a slithering twine of vine, leafy frills flaring around its bulging pustulent face. Clumps of eyes. Needle-like teeth.

Reverse jerk, hip pain.

Hiss:

"*Jehessimin.*"

The giant gaping mouth opens and sucks the worm-thing in like it's swallowing spaghetti.

The red eyes dissolve.

[Taillights of a white welding truck.]

The image abruptly cut off as a stainless steel refrigerator door slams shut.

A familiar apartment. A familiar man in black T-shirt and black jeans unscrews the cap on a bottle, tilts the neck, clear liquid fizzes loudly as he pours into a tall transparent glass. He picks up a white lime from the fruit bowl on the counter, cuts it into wedges.

The lime juice burns her cuticles, but she isn't him.

She's watching him.

She doesn't know his name.

The man of her dreams?

The man in her dreams.

The action plays as it always does—black and white, mundane, intricate details of a life. He squeezes the lime wedges into his drink, leaves the kitchen, places the glass on a white coaster on a black coffee table, presses "play" on a black CD player... he's putting on the Trane again. She recognizes the piece but cannot name it. She can name old punk songs, but she's not so good at jazz titles.

He takes a white book from a black bookcase, The Bloody Chamber and Other Stories *by Angela Carter, sits down on the black leather couch. He holds the book as if he is starting to read, except he has no eyes. He has no mouth to drink the sparkling water.*

His face is pale and flat, completely featureless.

Angie woke on her left side, heart pounding. The clock radio by the futon read two a.m.

The dream again. A total stranger and yet strangely familiar.

Not a friend.

More, but no sexual desire.

In each of the dreams, she watched the man perform ordinary tasks in the same black and white apartment. But whenever he finally faced her dream self, he had no face.

Before that, car, monster, accident, green, slither, hiss, truck.

Did it happen in real or dream life?

Both.

Disorientation from the nightmare and being in an unfamiliar location delayed her realization that Curt was missing.

Curt, my boyfriend.

Is he my boyfriend? Or is it just a second date with sex?

She crawled out of the futon, feeling the knot in her left hip tighten.

The bathroom was empty, light off. A sliver of streetlight from the window confirmed the middle "office" room empty, too.

Shadows danced on the living room carpet. Outside the bay window, heavy knotted limbs thrashed in a fierce wind. She jerked back.

No, not. Just an oak tree.

She re-approached the window. The trees inside the cemetery were blowing wildly, too. Farther beyond, streetlights illuminated the stretch of State Road Nine that passed it.

For a moment, she thought she saw something more. Two people hand-in-hand zigzagging among the graves, coming together as if embracing. Sparks flew around them, a flash of gossamer, and then they moved on, disappearing down the path between two mausoleums.

Must be her eyes and mind playing tricks, the accident still dislocating her. As a little girl, she'd imagined ghosts in that cemetery. Her mind shifted back in time to swinging round the bend in the backseat of her parents' Volvo on another cold, windy night.

A strange-looking blonde woman frolicking among the tombstones, similar sparkling bursts.

Her mother, Julia, didn't see anything, but her eyes were on the wheel.

"Must have been your imagination, my little witch girl," Julia had teased. "Always seeing things."

No ghosts.

Ghosts everywhere.

But after her family moved away from North Leeds, Angie didn't see ghosts or strange fires or weirder things. That is, not until tonight when she'd already seen more than her share, including weird things that almost killed her.

She noticed that her right hand was faintly glowing. She lifted it, flexed and twitched her fingers, examined the faint green luminosity. Then it flickered and her hand returned to normal.

A trick of the eye?

Her hand felt warm despite the apartment being cool, especially by the window.

She looked out the window again. A gust rattled the oak's branches. Down in the cemetery, the light was gone.

She remembered what she was missing.

No, it couldn't be missing. Not that.

She'd gathered everything out of the car, hadn't she? She examined the floor around the passenger seat carefully to make sure nothing had fallen out of her toppled tote bag. She'd packed this precious item where she couldn't possibly lose it.

Angie ran back to Curt's bedroom and pulled out the tote, turned it over, emptied it onto the carpet by the closet.

No, it wasn't there—a small green silk drawstring bag.

Even her parents couldn't remember where the tiny pouch came from. They guessed it had been a gift from her Grand Aunt Helen maybe, but Grand Aunt Helen died when she was small so she could never verify. As a baby, she cried when it wasn't near her, so they kept it by her crib. Julia, "*Mom,*" was worried that she would chew on it, that the yellow powder inside could be poisonous, but she never did.

Angie kept it under her pillow at night. Wherever she went, she kept it in a pocket. She tried not to wear clothes without pockets for that reason, and if she had a breast pocket, as in her leather jacket, she stashed it there, near her heart. Once she was old enough to wear a bra, she sometimes slipped it inside that, too—a strategy which a few times had caused some embarrassment and frantic excuses when she made out with a guy.

The pouch, the powder was *my magic, my luck.*

She'd always had strange backwards luck. Like when the motorcycle *almost* hit her when she was ten years old, or the guy in the green sedan who asked if she wanted to see his "rubber thumb" *didn't* linger, drove on. Tracy, another little girl in the neighborhood, disappeared and was found dead by the creek soon after. Later, when she was in college, a thief opened the passenger door of her friend Laura's car at a stoplight and stole her purse off the dashboard. It was the first of two robberies where she *didn't* lose any money. She didn't have any cash, only make-up and a checkbook. The thief abandoned the purse a few blocks away in the mud and the police returned it, including the unused checkbook.

The bag originally only contained the yellow powder which glittered in the dark. Maybe that was all it was, dime-store glitter, enough to make a little girl think of magic. But starting when Angie was a toddler, she'd added little things—fortune cookie messages, a few ruby-red beads from a broken bracelet she bought at a Halloween white elephant sale at her elementary school, a tuft of fur from her collie Rory who crossed the Rainbow Bridge when she was twelve, wax from her sixteenth birthday candles, a plastic monkey's paw from a barrel of monkeys, the stone from the mood ring she had in fifth grade after the glue failed and it came loose. She wasn't sure how all those things even fit inside.

Yesterday before leaving for the airport, Angie stashed it in her tote bag to avoid the possibility of an embarrassing search at airport security. She had meant to put it back in her jacket pocket after the checkpoint.

How could I forget to do that?

How could it have taken me so long to realize it was lost?

A sunken feeling overwhelmed her.

I lost my magic.

Stress turned to anger with herself.

She'd call the tow yard in the morning.

It won't be in the car.

Green and shiny.

The creature didn't fall into her car by accident.

The accident wasn't meant to hurt me.

It was about my magic.

Separating me from my magic.

But the bag didn't have any real magic.

Did it?

Angie crawled back into bed, not even thinking any more about Curt's abandonment. She didn't watch the clock, but it took her a long time to fall back to sleep.

She might not have realized she finally was asleep except the faceless man was making his black-and-white breakfast and then unloading a silver-gray washing machine.

She woke again to a creak of door hinges and soon after Curt's body lowering onto the futon. Cracking open an eye, she saw four a.m. on the clock radio. He lay on his side, facing away from her, his hair and skin reeking of tobacco.

He told me he was quitting.

Curt rose a little after nine, and Angie lingered in bed for another half-hour. She should be elated after surviving the accident, but her hip still had a receding but dull ache. Mostly she was feeling anxious and depressed.

I lost my magic or whatever that bag represents—a piece of me.

He left me alone.

Even if he wasn't going to be her boyfriend, how could he leave me alone the night after I had a car accident?

She silently cursed her decision to return to North Leeds, crawled stiffly up from the futon, and forced herself into the shower.

By the time she was done, the scent of eggs cooking wafted down the hallway. She pulled jeans from her suitcase and a black angora sweater, tight-fitting, with a V-neck. She'd packed the top because she thought it looked sexy on her.

Did it even matter?

Outside the bay window, the day didn't look inviting—gray sky and light rain. The TV murmured low in the background. She was surprised to see Curt had the channel turned to *The People's Court* rather than a movie.

Breakfast conversation started quietly—no apology, no explanation. Angie complimented Curt on the omelet of bell pepper, mushrooms, and gruyere cheese. His coffee, too. And felt stupid afterwards.

Who compliments coffee?

Am I trying to impress him still?

He left me alone the night after I had a car accident.

Angie tried to engage Curt on the radical feminist message of *Now, Voyager*, and how it inspired her to want to travel.

He hadn't seen it. Okay, she didn't see it herself until after she started working for Turner Classic Movies, but he was a film studies major and it starred Bette Davis.

Curt shifted the conversation to his dream project about a Russian heroine of the Revolution. Most of it seemed focused on showing off the protagonist's beautiful looks. He'd discovered the perfect actress locally, some "Tiger Girl." Apparently she had blonde hair and wore stripes. Angie found herself zoning out. The premise sounded self-consciously arty and pretentious, and he didn't show any sign of breaking off his monologue for her opinion.

"I can do the dishes," she finally interrupted when their plates had been empty for a half hour.

As Angie rose to clear the table, a "Breaking News" segment appeared on the TV, the local reporter announcing the discovery of a man's charred body by the banks of the North Leeds River, the fourth in or near the town in two weeks. A driver's license was found in a coat close to the corpse. Cut to a police detective stating that the easy ID was consistent with previous cases in which pieces of clothing, or in one case a satchel, was found near the burnt remains.

A photo went up of a guy with a goatee.

Curt stood and moved close to the screen.

"Do you know him?" Angie asked, while the reporter brought up a series of unsolved burn cases from seventeen years previously.

"No, not personally," he said, visibly shaken. "I just saw him..."

From the way he stopped himself, she finished his sentence.

"Last night?" she asked.

Curt glared at her.

"Are you accusing me of something?" he said, his tone suddenly hostile.

"Umm, no, but you went out last night after I went to bed," she said.

"And you want to know where I went," Curt said. "Well, it's none of your fucking business, but yeah, he was at Pearl Club last night. He left with some gal."

On the screen, a doctor discussed the phenomenon of "spontaneous combustion."

"I'm sorry, Angie, I just need to be alone for a while," Curt said, grabbing the remote and abruptly switching off the TV. "Listen, I like you, but maybe this was a bad idea."

He walked back to his office and shut the door.

Angie guessed how it would go down. The actual break-up wouldn't be until after she was back in Atlanta, but he'd spend the entire weekend lowering her expectations. If they had sex again, it'd be going through the motions. She'd always be on her own.

Except the man in her dreams.

But he wasn't a lover.

If only to stop thinking about everything else, Angie did the dishes. Then when she was done, she called the rental car and insurance company. Both customer service reps were surprisingly kind as they took her information, told her not to worry, that they'd take care of everything.

"*The important thing is that you are okay.*"

The pain in her hip had almost disappeared, and her back and neck weren't especially stiff.

But I did lose something.

A bag.

Possibly my mind.

Angie sat down on the couch and hugged her knees.

Here I am in North Leeds not even starting a new beginning.

An hour later, Curt emerged from his office. No apology, but he asked if she wanted to take a drive to Hurst, about a half-hour down the state road. He showed her where he had class, the film department office, student center which contained the university cinema. All of the campus buildings were generic mid-century modern high-rises since Hurst State hadn't opened until the late sixties. Nothing like Plath College where her mom Julia had taught with its arched Gothic gate, nineteenth-century ivy-covered brick façades, and romantic lake with a wooded island. On the way back, they stopped at the dying Mountain Crest shopping mall, caught a mediocre action movie at an almost empty multiplex. Then they picked up Thai takeout and got back to the apartment just after sunset.

Over curry and beer, they talked about forties noir films. While the discussion was spirited, Angie noticed Curt checking his watch.

"Listen, Angie, I need to go out," Curt interrupted before she could finish her thoughts. "I'm sorry. I promised I'd meet a…friend. Um…*he* needs to talk."

"Okay," Angie said.

What can I say to that?

That she wanted him to stay and hold her, even if things were weird. Had the accident made them weird, even if she hadn't told him how weird the accident actually was? Or was him going out without her two nights in a row a sign things would have been weird anyway?

I don't really know him. Guys can make you believe anything on the phone.

Curt put on his coat. He kissed her on the cheek again.

"If you're still aching after the accident, there's some ibuprofen in the medicine cabinet in the bathroom."

He opened the door but hesitated, turned back for a moment.

"Sorry, Angie. I like talking to you."

Then he left.

Angie knew she couldn't sleep. Not because of Curt. He was just a symptom. She needed to work things out in her head. She needed to walk.

I need to figure out what is happening to me.

I need to see what I remember, if anything, about North Leeds.

Angie thought momentarily about the murdered men, but they were all men. She'd just walk up Main Street maybe as far as campus, her parents' house. It was only ten p.m. She'd keep to well-lit streets, be careful, and be back by midnight. The backwards luck would protect her.

And if my luck was dependent on my "magic," well, I don't want to think about that.

She put on her leather jacket and grabbed the ring of spare keys and headed out.

Last night's wind had returned, though not as strong as what thrashed the sinister oak tree in the wee hours of the morning. The cold cut into her jeans, but her jacket shielded her from the worst, and in a way the chill felt exhilarating.

She walked briskly down the length of the jailhouse, past a tight row of wooden houses across the street. Another turn past more homes, a closed florist and a few other shops, and she was on Main. She almost bumped into a trio of bar-hoppers stumbling out of the dive on the corner.

By the time Angie crossed Parris Street, the number of pedestrians picked up—townies, young women from Plath, and panhandlers. Downtown North Leeds seemed like a typical college town with a Main Street lined with restaurants, several coffee shops, two churches, two banks, Parris Street Video where Curt worked, used and new bookstores, vintage clothing shop Josie's Place, and Spin, which she could tell from the window display was that kind of mandatory student store with posters, cards, kites, mugs, and plastic storage units.

Still she strained to match any of the darkened storefronts with a specific toddler memory. The drugstore newsstand with comics was definitely gone. Coolidge Cinema—was that where her parents took her to see *The Wizard of Oz* and Disney animation "revivals" such as *Sleeping Beauty*? She thought maybe her dad had taken her to the record store a few times. Now, of course, it would sell CDs. The only place that definitely resonated was the green awning of Crown Market. She lamented that Reece's Ice Cream in the basement must be closed. Maybe tomorrow she could stop by and order her little girl favorite, chocolate "smushed" with Heath Bar bits and raspberries.

Angie continued up the hill where Main cut through the campus of Plath College, passed the shadowy fronts of classroom buildings and student residences. In daylight, she might have explored the campus, found the hillside overlooking the lake where her dad Albert took her for picnics, and sometimes Rory and her stuffed best friend Nanny Big-Dog came along. They'd sit on a blanket, feast on peanut-butter-and-jelly sandwiches, and drink Cokes in glass bottles while watching the all-women crew teams practice. Her mother, Julia, would take her to the greenhouse full of flowers and bizarrely beautiful tropical plants. Sometimes after dark, the frogs would sing in the nearby pond. Maybe she did have some pleasant memories of North Leeds after all.

After she passed the last two student houses, connected and curved in a crescent, Angie counted the streets on the left from memory: one, two, three, then four houses down on the left. Number 210, a two-story wooden frame house that dated to the 1920s. Her parents had rented the bottom floor, and Ben and Lucy, another couple who didn't have children, let the upstairs. Lucy read her fairy stories and made her fairy paper dolls with wings which still flitted, hung with silver thread, on a shelf above her childhood fairy tale books.

The house was white now, but it had been green. She wanted to walk up the steps onto the porch—which still had the swing!—and knock on the door. But it must be eleven and only one second-floor light was on.

Angie turned back up the street and retraced her steps. She'd made the pilgrimage. Maybe it was better not to see the changes made by later residents. She didn't want to know if they'd removed the glass doors to her bedroom. Her mom, Julia, had pasted Angie's crayon drawings in the panes with red construction paper backing so she wouldn't be kept up by adults using the living room lights. There would be no cardboard playhouse, no boxes of blocks and little animals, and most of all, no Rory, no dog.

Yes, better not to see, Angie thought as she walked down the hill into town.

Fewer people now. Several small groups of students headed back to campus after bar-hopping. Hurst men, done with scouting Plath women, waited in front of the marble-columned Odeon at the stop for the free public bus that made a circuit between the campuses.

As Angie passed under the green Crown Market awning and turned to cross the street, a wrinkled woman in a ratty coat and a knit cap hobbled towards her with a cane.

"Have you got a dollar, missy, a dollar to buy a lady some breakfast," the crone asked, her other hand outstretched.

"Jesse James! Jesse James!" she screamed suddenly and drew back from Angie before she could even rummage for change in her pockets.

No, she said, "Jehessimin!"

"Wait! Why did you call me that?" Angie yelled after her. But the woman was now huddled face-down on the ground a few storefronts down.

Unnerved by a memory she didn't expect to relive, she crossed the street and sped up her pace, ready to get back to the jailhouse, crawl into bed. Maybe she'd try to change her plane ticket and fly out tomorrow, one day early, if it wasn't too expensive.

As she reached Parris Street, she saw them.

Curt and a woman with long blonde hair. His arm around her back.

What was she wearing?

A striped bodysuit. Curt's "Tiger Girl," who he wanted to cast in his epic Russian movie.

The pair turned left at the railroad bridge that passed over Main.

Where were they going? Surely he wasn't taking her to his apartment.

Not with me staying.

But they did turn two blocks down, towards the jailhouse. Angie followed, keeping her distance.

Curt and the Tiger Girl passed the jailhouse and went on through the cemetery gate.

I should go back to Curt's apartment. Who cares if he's with another woman. I've given up on him anyway.

Angie was almost at the sinister oak when the wind picked up. The tree seemed taller as a torrent of dried leaves swirled to the ground around her. She almost jumped at the sight of red eyes glowing in the billowing branches.

Something large took flight.

Maybe an owl. Definitely a bird.

Angie sighed with some relief and glanced back through the cemetery fence.

Inside among the tombstones, the Tiger Girl wrapped her arms around Curt.

Caressed.

Humped.

A female voice whispered in the wind:

"*Jehessimin.*"

That voice didn't care about Curt.

It was calling *her*.

"*Jehessimin.*"

Angie was walking to the cemetery.

Entering under the arch.

A short distance ahead, the Tiger Girl had let go of Curt.

Her sclerae vanished and blue cat-eyes bulged as if stepping forward from their sockets. Her arms bent and stretched like elastic, knotted inside each other. She twitched and spun, jumped and fluttered, her bodysuit shredded as she landed on branches where there had been legs, branches with paws. With claws.

The sphinxlike creature purred as twigs sprouted in a ridge along her back and tail.

Sparks flew wildly in the circle of tombstones, and Curt watched the Tiger Girl like a movie.

The Tiger Girl was no longer beautiful.

Yet she was strangely beautiful, perhaps even more so than in her human form.

What happened next happened fast.

The Tiger Girl twisted back to Curt and once more entwined herself around him, guiding him in an accelerated waltz-like dance.

The sparks ignited into flames. Extreme heat wafted in Angie's direction, halting her approach.

The missing men.

Anger. Rescue. Escape. All options vanished except watching the scene play out.

The fire emanated from the Tiger Girl. Not from her mouth but from her pores. She was immune to its burn.

Curt was not.

His clothes ignited, his face flushed, eyes widened, mouth opened as if to scream but emitted no sound.

His detached tongue was lodged in the teeth of whatever the Tiger Girl had become. She spat it onto the ground, then continued to lead the macabre dance of incineration.

The blaze turned to blue.

Enveloped in the cobalt flames, Curt's body toasted into a charred husk as rapidly as an untended marshmallow on a campfire.

The blue fire dissipated, and Curt's dark charred remains, still maintaining the rough shape of a human body, fell hard to the ground in a cloud of ash.

Holy fuck.

The Tiger Girl reared up on her hind paws and laughed, only her laugh was something shrill that didn't emerge naturally from a human mouth. Like a cat's meow crossed with fingernails scraping across the bark of a tree.

She swayed and weaved in Angie's direction, opened her right hand and revealed a small green silk bag.

Angie felt the urge to lunge forward and take back what was hers. But whatever thing that was the Tiger Girl had just burned a man alive with blue fire right in front of her.

"Who are you? What are you? Why are you calling me?"

"Don't you know by now?" the Tiger Girl replied. "I am *Erla*. But you are asking all the wrong questions. You should be asking who you are.

"*Jehessimin.*"

Familiar green creatures slithered out from among the tombstones, bobbed their heads, puffed their throats, and tangled their long, leafy bodies at Erla's feet, wheezing and hissing.

Memories flooded back.

They were *Wyrm*.

The Other Place where Angie was born, where she was Jehessimin, when she had wings, a beak, more eyes and legs than two.

"My father, the Erl-King, showed you the door to take you home but you stopped too soon," Erla said. "Don't you want to return? You're not happy here.

"*You never belonged.*

"*You never belonged here or there.*

"*You don't belong anywhere.*"

Erla held the green bag up to her mouth and whispered:

"*Erda-aski-hebennum-ginkanna-phedorum-keski.*"

She kissed the pouch, her red lips sucking on its base. It was Angie's magic, and Angie could feel it hesitate. But it strained and gave under the pressure of Erla's teeth.

The Wyrm oozed forward in one undulating throng.

The ground opened beneath her feet.

Jehessimin fell deep into the darkness for what seemed like a very long time.

The monstrous bleached head reached forward a branch-like appendage and ripped the hood off the car.

A broken hose in the engine compartment.

Dissolves into a welding truck with red taillights.

Dark, empty tarmac.

Something broke her plummet, wrapping her in its muculent membrane. As she seeped through, she felt her body reshaping, arms stretching, wings pushing out from her shoulder blades, extra legs unfolding, and a beak pushing out from her face. She could not see in the darkness, but she sensed more eyes than two.

And then she dropped again, more gently as if carried on the wind rather than falling, floating to the bottom. She landed facedown, her breasts, stomach, and legs pressed into a pelt of soft wet groundcover over stone.

Her eyes cracked open to green moss and yellow lichen. She rolled her head sideways and saw a purple sky, the perpetual twilight of the Other Place. She felt no pain from the fall, and whatever aches remained from the accident had vanished, too. Her wings must have opened, instinctually protecting her. The smell was familiar and at first cloying, like rancid human body odor broiled by humidity. As her nostrils readjusted to their true form, the scent became less pungent and even pleasant.

She was not alone for long. She heard the slushy stampede of approaching Wyrm before she saw them advancing in the fetid pools surrounding her. Wingless, they must have traveled a longer way, through the earth. If the cemetery was an ingress, cavernous passageways also led beneath the graves.

She knew this because Fae infants remembered from the moment they left the wombs of their mothers and sometimes even before. And that was how her Fae Mother Castinelle had crept up one moonless night with baby Jehessimin. Castinelle pushed back the tombstone and carried her daughter down dark streets till she heard a baby crying through the open window of the green house rented to Albert and Julia. The screen was loose and easily pried off with her Fae Mother's hawk-like talons.

Castinelle was adept in the glamour and the human infant in the crib did not cry. A quick glare at the dog silenced a nascent bark into a whispery whiny resignation followed by a cowering retreat behind the couch. Later Rory the collie would become her protector and keep the secret of that night from his master and mistress for a decade until he passed, her first experience with earthly death.

Her Fae Mother took the real baby Angie in her arms and placed Jehessimin in the crib. She touched her own child's forehead and pulled the green bag from her belt, loosened the string, poured a pinch of sparkling yellow powder into a clawed hand. She sprinkled the powder on the child's bare chest and placed the bag under her pillow. The change happened so fast that Jehessimin/Angie remembered nothing of it—no stretching or shrinking or pain. Only a lilting song sung by a shrill voice, rattling and comforting her little body.

From then, she was a human baby so she didn't remember her Fae Mother departing with another human baby, identical to her.

Jehessimin's reawakened recollection was halted abruptly by the flapping of frills, loud hissing, and a rotten-egg smell as the slimy servants of the Erl slithered onto the granite outcrop.

Jehessimin tried to stand, to fly away. But she wasn't used to her wings, to the new muscles in her back. The Wyrm milked her clumsiness, hastily ringing her, twining their stringy bodies around her arms and legs to drag her back down.

Even if she could escape their gluey grasp, Erla had her magic. Resigned to whatever fate awaited and eager for answers, she lay back.

Other Wyrm slipped beneath her and flattened, lifted her body. They oozed and thickened as if fusing into one larger organism whose purpose was to carry her.

Low to the ground, they began to glide, simultaneously slipping and sliding over her skin, sometimes sinking her into the shallow muck and then hoisting her back up again over moist mossy rocks.

The stench of stagnant water weakened and the ground grew firmer as she saw massive trunks of ancient trees rising ahead.

Thick forest replaced fetid bog. The Wyrm slid roughly with their load across exposed knotted roots.

Followed the old path betwixt and between white birches and red-leafed maples and mighty oaks and regal pines. The tops of trees of northern woods streamed by her, cracks of purple light peeking between their leafy canopies. The forest smelled of sap, pine resin, and warm, dry earth, an occasional whiff of honeysuckle, but something was missing.

Except for the sliding of the Wyrm, the vegetation was still. No wind blew swaying leaves and branches. And soundless. No chitter of crickets. No buzz of bees. No birdsong.

The tree cover thickened and clasped, grew heavier and gloomier until all her eyes had to squint in the shadows and her glutinous litter had to condense and squeeze between tightly packed trunks.

This was a forest that would eat you.

Finally they arrived at a tree that reached higher and spread wider that all its brethren. Its first leaves were too lofty to guess its species, but the bark at its base was coal black and coated with yellow lichen and brown fungus. Old beyond old, this great tree was for keeping secrets, not for cheery postcards with a two-lane road passing through. It could devour a fleet of cars.

Her captors carried her to a place where the roots spread from its bottom. They slipped her inside a hole and let her go. Her back, slick from their ooze, slid swiftly down the steep spiral, down until she landed on her bottom in a rough bed of what felt like dried leaves, dirt, and something prickly.

In the pitch black, she heard the Wyrm pop out of the chute, felt them wriggle onto her back, slip and slide underneath her. Grotesque players in a revised game that had snakes and chutes, but no ladders.

Erla's high-pitched voice in her head: "You never belonged here or there. You don't belong anywhere."

The creatures lifted her again, this time chest and stomach down, their moist, gelatinous shapes molding and sticking to her curves. Underground, their touch felt even more clammy and cold, easing themselves inside more intimate places. She sensed no sexual intention, just firming and adhering their grasp. Like worker ants or termites, they methodically completed their task.

Still, at the violation, she reflexively pecked her beak at an undulating coil. The point merely sank into its squirming body. A pasty taste permeated her mouth, and she had to pull back vigorously to avoid getting further stuck.

Clammy and cold upon her skin, their slithering mass carried her again. This time she sensed a succession of tunnels, felt an occasional scrape of bark or tickle from what she assumed might be the roots of the great tree.

If the forest had swallowed her, she was now deep in its intestines.

Faint chirping, peeping, tweeting, chirring breached the subterranean silence as they went deeper. At first, the unexpected sounds seemed random, punctuated by shrill bursts and periods of quiet, like birds in the afternoon. Not that it made any sense that birds would be so deep underground.

Closer and closer, trills and warbles joined lilts and purls. The different chords steadily amplified, taking on a mournful tone as if weighted down by an unbearable sadness. Simultaneously, a cloying sweetness seeped into the musty air.

Abruptly darkness and tight burrows gave way to glistening light and a large open space, the birdsong spiking and shifting from peripheral to above. Her captors began to loosen, even to detach, narrow and stretch back into their original winding shapes.

The very air sparkled, swaths of light strobing and spinning. The last of the slithering glob that carried her advanced towards a cluster of paws and twitching wings. New voices emerged, high-pitched and muttering. Word of her capture had spread rapidly and all the Erl had ceased whatever task to congregate in anticipation.

The last of the Wyrm slid out from under, leaving Jehessimin face-down on rough dry ground, pitted with roots and rocks. She lifted her head, rose as far as her knees.

How many Erl were there? Dozens? Hundreds?

Above, pale scraggly roots dangled like ropey stalagmites, and among them dozens of bell-shaped cages. Through their bent branch bottoms, she could see that each held a single bird. Sparrow and robin. Canary and cardinal. Titmouse and kingfisher. Crow and mockingbird. Dove and woodcock. Hummingbird and oriole. She didn't know the names of all the species but most looked like typical northern forest birds—no parrot or macaw or ibis or penguin—and small, except for a single hawk, owl, and eagle in larger cages on the far side.

She had no time to count or contemplate their variety. The Erl approached her in a hurried mass of arboreal, feline, and moth. Tails swung, back ridges like sticks still covered with dead leaves rustled. Jagged bark-covered arms bent, knotted paws with long, sharp claws caressed and scratched her body and then withdrew, replaced by new paws and claws.

She swatted at her inspectors, but they continued to cluster, to circle, to graze and blow, to pinch and poke. She tried to spread her wings, but the Erl only pressed closer.

A loud roar echoed through the cavern.

The birdsong instantly ceased and the Erl swept away from her. Her view cleared, Jehessimin saw now where the Wyrm had retreated, squirming within a wide crevice below a slab of buried rock.

She raised herself to stand, still unused to wings and additional legs and feeling vulnerable in the nudity of her altered body.

On the slab, a familiar figure loomed, towering still but no longer so colossal as to be able to devour a car.

Jehessimin saw the Erl-King's face more clearly than on the night of the accident. Impossibly narrow, the elongated bone-pale, pocked, and stained visage hung or swung, rather than lifted, from a neck the texture of bark. Tangled branches and antlers crowned long silver straight hair, the consistency of twisted rope tangled with dead vines of blackened leaves. He wore a long robe of black, brown, and gray feathers, long twig-like fingers twitching at the end of loose sleeves. Every aspect suggested age and pestilence beyond reckoning.

Behind the Erl-King to the left, Erla emerged, dancing in a reverie solely her own, emitting blue sparks, flexing the green pouch in her left paw-hand, twig-like spikes billowing with each undulation of her back and tail. Etched with black stripes, her ivory countenance accentuated her Tiger nature. Over her white-blonde hair, she wore an antlered headdress with bangs of tiny bones. More bones and human ears were strung into a layered necklace.

What have I done to inspire so much hate?

To the right of the Erl-King crawled out a clue. Despite tousled hair, unwashed and caked with mud, a face greased with dirt, a shapeless shift, Jehessimin recognized…

…herself.

Or rather Angie.

The real Angie.

The woman with the face she knew as her own for twenty-two years bent forward and wheezed, rocked back on her bare heels and snickered. The Erl-

King reached down and stroked the tangled hair, and her sound softened. He groped deep into a feathery pocket and pulled out a tiny yellow bird.

Angie's eyes lit like a toddler offered surprise chocolate.

She grabbed it roughly from his hand, twisted its neck and gnawed gleefully.

Jehessimin stifled an urge to heave.

So much now made sense. Albert and Julia weren't her real parents. They'd denied she was adopted. Julia broke down in tears at the suggestion. Albert scolded her for upsetting her "mother" and banished her to her room. Did they suspect that she wasn't their real daughter?

Their real daughter just killed and ate an innocent canary.

Who was the changeling?

A flash in her head of switching on the TV one Sunday morning in the green house in North Leeds and happening accidentally on the 1935 black and white movie of *A Midsummer's Night Dream.* Oberon and Titania, glittering and unbelievably gorgeous. Her young self had been captivated by a desire to step into that enchanted world, Lucy helping her make the fairy paper dolls and also coat-hanger and tulle wings for a fairy Halloween costume. Albert snapping a Polaroid photo of her wearing it and attaching it to the refrigerator with a magnet.

Be careful what you wish for.

She noticed that she wasn't the only one upset by what had just transpired.

The Erl-King's daughter abruptly ceased her dancing. Her cobalt eyes grew icy, her gleeful smile hardened into a sharp frown.

Angie slurped down the feathers, spittle dripping down her chin, and hurled the bones over her shoulder. The Erl-King rewarded her with neck scratches.

Jehessimin remembered now from Shakespeare's script that Oberon wasn't pleased when Titania did "beg a little changeling boy. To be my henchman." He wanted the child as his own attendant. Maybe some Titania did cross this Oberon and that's why she, or her surrogate, was absent.

But who knew if this foul freakish court was the one that inspired Shakespeare? Shakespeare lived centuries ago and could neither help her comprehend nor escape.

She tried to give in not to fear but to the notion that she'd be dead soon and none of it would matter. She felt sorry for Mom and Dad, Julia and Albert, because if the Erl-King was fond of the real Angie, they would be left with a complete lack of closure—a missing daughter who was never the daughter they were actually missing, their actual daughter weird and wild and altogether inhuman.

She felt an inextricable longing for the above world, the only place she'd ever known beyond the recent retrieved memory of her infancy. She wished that she had never had any magic, that she was boring and human after all, that she had never seen or known of her not-twin. She should have followed her instinct, should never have come back to North Leeds.

Would Erla have found me anyway?

Surely if one gateway reached up from North Leeds Cemetery, there might be others. And if not, planes and trains and automobiles?

Her Fae Mother had stolen a human baby to keep her safe. And she had given Jehessimin a bag full of special powder, *her magic*, for protection.

I was careless and allowed it to be stolen.

She had failed both her Fae Mother and her Earth Mother.

Angie crept towards Jehessimin on all fours, her eyes inquisitive, sniffing the air with her nose like a curious puppy. She reached out a hand but before she could touch her "sister," Erla leapt forward and swatted her arm away.

Angie fell back, buried her face in her hands, and cried hysterically. The birds erupted in a chaotic blast of chirps and squawks, trills, and screeches.

The Erl-King let loose a harrowing shriek. Erla's blue eyes glowed angrily, but she backed away and retreated behind a tangle of roots.

He extended his massive head towards Jehessimin, his crown blowing back behind him—the same posture as on the highway. He pounded heavily onto the stage floor with all his black stumpy toes.

The Wyrm re-emerged from beneath like a swarm of snakes. The birds amplified their cacophony.

Jehessimin dropped to the dirt floor and covered her eyes, anticipating her end.

She felt a sharp blow to the back of her head.

"Unlike the book, *The Wizard of Oz* is strongly suggested to be a dream in Dorothy's head, or is it?" Angie said.

"Terry Gilliam's *The Adventures of Baron Munchausen*, a theater production or the Baron is the world's greatest liar?" Curt countered, his responses hurried, perhaps a tad impatient.

"Shakespeare did it with *A Midsummer Night's Dream*—a play within a play. I love the 1930s version. The cinematography, set design, costumes so alluringly beautiful. As if the black and white only enhances the magic."

"I could never get into it, something about fairies turns me off right away," Curt said dismissively. "However, you have it wrong. A black and white film isn't just black and white. A great director, like Eisenstein, understands that it's all in the gray, capturing the subtle gradation. It's why film noir literally works better in black and white."

As he continued, Curt's voice rose in pitch until it was more of a chirp. She caught stray words, names, Lang, Lorre, M, Welles, Touch, Power, Alley…

The colors of Curt's North Leeds apartment faded, dissolved, bubbled and spread like a film negative burning in black and white with shades of brown and yellow.

The projector sputtered to a stop, fade to black.

Clattered on again, a different apartment flickering on the screen, black, white, and more shades of gray than she'd noticed on past visits. A man in a black bathrobe and black slippers stands at the window.

Turns and has no face.

The first thing Jehessimin noticed when she woke was the same foul, dank odor as before her last awakening. Her skin felt damp, though she wasn't exactly cold. Not warm either. Her new or reacquired form seemed more resilient to temperature changes than her human body. Lying on what felt like moss and wood and crumbled dirt, her head throbbed, swollen, tissue pushed against bone from the punch. She opened her eyes to darkness, but she sensed she must still be beneath the gigantic tree.

Her eyes gradually adjusted. Or rather she realized that, like Erla, she had the ability to will light. Her light, however, didn't flash and spark, strobe or burn, but was rather like draping a shimmering cloak. She was surrounded by walls of tangled tree roots and soil. Above she sensed emptiness, air descending, but she couldn't tell from how far up. Perhaps the Erl or their Wyrm servants had emptied this pit, or they'd just taken advantage of a space under the tree that suited their need for a cage to hold a bigger bird.

As her eyes adjusted, the glimmer revealed more.

She wasn't alone.

A hand twitched among the roots, pale with nails so long and curled that they mustn't have been clipped since a forgotten time. She directed the glitter along the length of an arm overgrown with moss. Tatters. Broken, torn wings. A leg and a foot wrapped in a vine rooted deep within the tree. Up again, she finally found the face.

Pale, streaked with swirling green lines.

Jehessimin touched the beak's tip.

Eyes snapped open.

As green as Erla's were blue, with round pupils instead of jagged slits.

As green as her own.

So overgrown that she was almost one with the roots, Castinelle must have passed a long time since she last opened her eyes.

Her Fae Mother moaned.

The cry of a mother who had given up her only child for her own safety. A mother resigned never to see her daughter ever again, hoping never to see her daughter again, seeing her daughter.

What passed as laughter among the Erl rippled down. Erla had been watching and waiting for mother and daughter to know that she had achieved her revenge.

What horrible thing had Castinelle, her Fae Mother, done to Erla?

Me.

And because of me, Angie is in the Other place, vying with Erla for the Erl-King's favor. She hates us both, but she can't strike back at Angie because her father has taken her not-twin as his little "henchman."

The laughter receded, Castinelle's mournful call enough to sate Erla. At least for now.

Was this her fate then, to fester with her Fae Mother in this musty pit beneath the Erl Tree? Never to see natural light or earth. Would she even die? Had her Fae Mother been imprisoned here for all of her twenty-two years? Or did time pass differently in this Other Place?

And yet she also was happy to see her Fae Mother.

Tell me the truth of who I am.

Castinelle's tears dried or rather absorbed into molting brown feathers that furled from her cheeks.

Jehessimin helped her untangle the vine that bound her four-fingered hand. Her Fae Mother was clearly weak from inactivity and lack of food, though maybe not water, since the moisture—and her tears—suggested that some water, maybe rainwater, did seep into the space. Perhaps her kind didn't need much sustenance.

Castinelle touched Jehessimin's forehead. Her talons were dull, broken, her fingers rough and muddy. She was reaching in as if through skin and bone, all the way to brain. Until Jehessimin saw nothing but memory as vivid as if it was happening again right now. As if a dream.

Beak down, foraging for mushrooms, eyes on the trail.

The farsnips croak. Their foul procession passes nearby, tail to snout. But as soon as they sense Castinelle's presence, they scatter into the low blue hortleberry and orange cloudberry plants that blanket the ground between the trees.

A little further, an ant path parallels. Red wood ants, each the length of a finger, carrying branches, even pine cones, until they veer to the right towards their hill built of forest debris at least three feet tall.

A living forest—wrapped with birdsong.

Her Fae Mother, not yet a mother, with green feathers, bright and carefree.

Castinelle has guessed right, doesn't go far before coming upon a patch of morels, which she plucks and scoops into her basket. And then chanterelles and enoki. Though their names are different in the Other language, Jehessimin recognizes them, has always adored mushrooms, made a point to learn their varieties. Every kind of mushroom that grows in the forest is within a few steps of the trail, including mushrooms she has never seen before. Castinelle skips with all her legs, spreads her wings, flits and spins.

Her Fae Mother's body oozes with the pleasure of her harvest, creamy moisture secreting down her legs. The ground twitches beneath her clawed feet, stimulated by her juices, hungrily imbibing their savory taste.

The Fae fertilize the forest, she trills to her daughter. The Erl excrete fire and silence song.

Soon more berries will ripen, mushrooms sprout. Even the farsnips cautiously creep back to lick the dirt on which Castinelle has frolicked, engage in a tug of war with the ground as to which can consume the most of her essence.

And so Castinelle dances into the meadow where among the wildflowers she plunges right into the son of Ole-Luk-Oie and drops her basket, the mushrooms spilling out among the tall grasses. The dark-haired progeny of the Lord of Dreams absorbs her motion and moisture into his own. They move together furiously, relentlessly, his skin against her feathers. He lifts and swings her lithe body, spinning nimbly on his two legs and she kicks back her own four. Her wings flutter with elation. His face is flatter than hers, more human though not human, his eyes as bronze-brown as hers are green, she with a beak and he a nose, but their tongues find each other's for they are other. The grasses vibrate and flowers bloom as their juices intermingle and spray and seep down into the soil.

Later they recline together and Lukoje gifts Castinelle dreams of many colors.

She still has those dreams in this dark place, she says. Except they are in black and white.

So do I, Mother.

"Your father is in the world above," Castinelle said. "He goes by Lukas and lives in a place called San Francisco. He does not remember who he is nor me nor you, my daughter. The two fathers, the Erl-King and the Dream-Lord, agreed on a peace between the Erl and the Realm of Dreams through the union of Lukoje with Erla. Only he met me in the forest on his way to the Erl Tree. The Erl-King was so enraged that he emptied Lukoje's mind and banished him to the world above. He had barely time to send me a dream to warn me that they were coming for me next.

"For as long as we have been Fae, we've sometimes swapped our babes to protect them from the Erl. Ours wonder why they are different but never know. Most of those from where you were reared don't survive beyond the Veil. The Erl burn what breathes, steal what sings. Fae dwell in the trees and Erl dwell in the roots. Thus has it always been, as long as we and they remember.

"The Erl-King wanted to join Erla with a Dreamer, one of those who inhabit another place. You have to pass through to get there, but it is a different way than that to where I dropped you, a way that Fae do not ken. A child begot of such a union, who knows what such a child could do. And if more than one child…

"I did not know how to care for a human baby, how to keep her from always crying and hide her stench. And so their Wyrm found me. They read her memories and knew which path I took, which way to the other world. Fortunately, when they first looked, you must have been gone."

"My family moved when I was six," Jehessimin said. "You gave me your magic to protect me."

She hesitated.

"I lost it. I'm sorry."

"Yes, I hoped they wouldn't be able to take you. I crafted it with the most powerful spells and the help of your grandmother who has much knowledge of enchantment."

The Erl-King caused an accident and sent the Wyrm. I didn't realize it was taken until too late.

Jehessimin leaned into her Fae Mother. Her mother strained against the vines until she freed herself enough to hug back.

Was it human to hug? Did the Fae hug?

She felt certain that the Erl did not.

At that moment, however, she realized something.

She didn't really know how to use them, but her wings weren't shredded like her Fae Mother's.

"The space above is not empty," Castinelle said, reading her mind. "It was the first thing I tried. It's filled with Nurl that will devour your wings, my daughter."

The Erl wanted Erla to mate with Lukoje to beget a hybrid child. She was half-Fae but she was also half-Dream. She didn't have her mother's magic, but what abilities did her father have?

Maybe escape was possible after all if she could only puzzle it out.

"You won't have a chance if you carry me, and the roots have grown around me," Castinelle said. "Soon I will be part of the Erl Tree."

"If I make it out, I will return for you," Jehessimin said.

"Oh, my daughter, you are a dreamer," Castinelle said. "Like your father."

She let go of Jehessimin, and Jehessimin slept.

With jazz playing as always, the faceless man in black rummages through the refrigerator. This time he pulls out a package of grocery store sushi. He pours soy sauce into a saucer and blends in the provided lump of wasabi with chopsticks. He dips the pieces one by one.

Except it's not just jazz in the background. The scene pans to something new in the apartment, something in color, living color. A cage holds an olive-green bird with a bright yellow crest and underparts.

Lukas opens the door to the cage and the golden-crowned warbler flies out into the apartment. She lands on his hand first, lingers, while he mimics her chirps and slurs and they sing in unison for a few bars. She hesitates, wants to get to know him but now is not the time. She flutters and glides to the crest of the sofa, trills a few more bars. The shiny granite kitchen island. A bowl of white apples. A bookcase shelf. The narrow edge of a painting under glass, of a wispy man with a flower for a face. The top of a lampshade.

The windowsill.

Jehessimin sees her father's face for the first time. She can't look long enough to see if he recognizes her or she knows she won't be able to leave.

The bird flies out the window.

With her eyes shut, Jehessimin never saw her attackers, only heard their whirrs and their buzzes, steeled herself against the barrage of pin stings on her arms, legs, chest, stomach, even cheeks. Mercifully the swarm of Nurl quickly fell away and into somnolence, but she waited until the pricks abated completely before she opened her own eyes and willed a trickle of the shimmer.

She hovered above the pit, and fortunately the trail up led in only one direction. She threw one last glance down to where Castinelle remained imprisoned. She would return somehow and free her Fae Mother, but for now, hesitation was perilous. Sleep-flying straight up was one thing, but she needed her glitter to see the trails which led up to the surface. And who knew what sentinels and traps lay ahead.

Bear left and take care, my daughter.

Jehessimin slowly crept up the winding first leg, keeping to the barest glow, enough not to trip on a root or stone. The constant dirt and mud felt yucky in her toes. She never had liked being barefoot except on grass or a sandy beach, and now she had four feet and no shoes. At least the soles of her Fae/Dream feet were thick and resilient against bumps and hopefully also splinters.

She hadn't gone far before she arrived at the first fork. Remembering her Fae Mother's advice, she went left, even though that passage seemed to slope down. But after she rounded a bend, the trail climbed steeply, to the point that someone—*or some thing?*—had laid flat stones as steps. She recalled the long slide down, but was relieved that she was at least making upward progress. Having been carried unconscious to the pit where she and her Fae Mother had been imprisoned, she had no idea whether she was closer to the surface than the length she slid down or further below. The journey could be hours or days. How did time even operate here?

The "staircase," if one could call it that, had no railings, but like the rest of the Erl underworld, the walls were thick with roots for grasping. More legs and feet, however, meant more shins and thighs to ache as the climb pressed on with no end in sight. She also had to remember to keep her wings pressed in and down so as not to damage them.

Her hope that the steps led all the way up was dashed when they abruptly culminated in a circular chamber propped up by a tangle of heavy roots whose angles reminded her of Gothic cathedral arches. Under each arch was an opening, six in total. She opted for the one immediately to her left, hoping that she'd interpreted correctly since her mother hadn't specified what to do in case of multiple options.

She found herself again in a tunnel? A corridor? She was still insufficiently experienced in the Other Place to understand whether the Erl slept and carried out their daily business in the space under the great tree or just used it to keep their avian and Fae prisoners. She was relieved not to have run into any Erl, Wyrm, Nurl, or other yet unimagined enemies thus far. As on any city street, she needed to stay vigilant. Occasionally she would hear faint whispers and taps, scuttering and fluttering. And echoing, hopelessly sad birdsong.

She slowed as she approached the next bend, again forked left and started up another set of steps. As she climbed, the noises seemed to multiply. Some she recognized as the Erl speech. At least those sounds weren't ahead but to her right. They suggested the "walls," despite the massive roots, weren't so thick. The birdsong subtly amplified, still above but closer.

At the next landing, Jehessimin cautiously threw a faint glimmer, barely enough to see the ground, and again pivoted to the immediate left of another circle of arched openings. In the dim sparkle, however, she heard a plaintive chirp and saw a shadowy shape twitch in the dark to her right.

She froze.

In the center sat a figure with ratty tangled hair, cross-legged and only two-legged, head down and focused on a wriggling thing in its two hands.

She extended a bit more of her shimmer.

The sudden glow startled her not-twin. Her head spun in Jehessimin's direction.

The unexpected interruption caused her to loosen her grip on something struggling in her grasp. The blue bird wriggled free and flew up into the darkness.

Angie leapt to her feet and reached for it, but the little creature was too quick. She pivoted back towards Jehessimin, her mouth in a snarl, cheeks twitching with irritation.

Petrified that her not-twin would summon the Erl, Jehessimin placed a finger to her lips, whispered "Shhhhhh."

Did Angie even know what this human signal for hush meant?

Her not-twin's frown softened and she tilted her head. Like Rory, her dog, used to do when he was trying to understand. At least the Erl-King gave her some independence, so maybe there was hope that no one would come looking for his "pet" right away?

Still, she was stuck in a quandary. If she ducked into a tunnel and ran for it, Angie surely would sound an alarm and bring the Erl and their servants down upon her. Her not-twin's allegiance must be to the only world she knew. Her only hope was to gain her trust somehow.

She eased towards Angie, maintaining eye contact with every move.

Angie shifted back down into a crouch as if to pounce.

"Angie," Jehessimin said. "That's your real name. Do you remember anything of the world above? Of my...your parents? Albert and Julia?"

Angie twitched and tilted her head even further to the right until it was virtually horizontal. Jehessimin sensed a battle between uncertainty and curiosity. At least she hadn't made a sound. *Yet.*

"Of course, you don't. You were so little, and human babies don't remember."

She stretched out a hand. Angie straightened her head, bent forward and sniffed it.

"I never meant to steal your life. I never understood why I felt so different."

As she would do with a nervous cat, Jehessimin reached her hand slowly towards Angie's knotted hair and gave it a light stroke.

Angie jerked her head away and let loose a low squeak.

Jehessimin pulled her hand back and snapped her finger again to her lips.

"Shhhh, so sorry, I don't want to hurt you. In a way, I'm happy to meet you."

Angie leaned back and bowed her head towards Jehessimin. She took the gesture as a cue it was all right to stroke after all. Like the cat that changes its mind, but you still have to be careful it won't bite a moment later. In addition, the texture of the hair was so rough and matted that she was afraid she'd pull it and hurt her not-twin if she wasn't careful.

Angie pushed in further and grunted lightly, then reached a hand to Jehessimin's beak. She didn't clamp or pull, seemed to be inspecting it like an inquisitive child. Whether her not-twin comprehended the two's complementary relationship was unclear, but she appeared at least to sense that Jehessimin's intent was non-threatening. Perhaps Erla's antipathy to both of them had created a basis for trust, however tenuous.

Angie pulled back her fingers and laid her head in Jehessimin's lap. She curled herself into a ball, breathing through her mouth—*putt...pause...putt.*

Just like Jehessimin had done while asleep when she was Angie.

She realized that all the other sounds had dissipated. No faint Erl murmurs, no birds calling. In the heavy silence punctuated only by her not-twin's breathing, she felt a bond growing for this motley dirty young woman. She'd been raised as an only child. Albert and Julia never had another baby. She'd made up imaginary sisters, sometimes a mischievous one named Angelica who brought sticks inside the house and stashed them in her cardboard playhouse. Weren't Fae supposed to be mischief-makers? Was she imagining her true self, instead of that good little girl Julia wanted her to be?

Did she bear some responsibility for the woman whose childhood she had usurped, or at least a responsibility to her "adoptive" parents, *this woman's actual parents*?

A crazy idea brewed inside her. She could bring Angie back with her, back to Albert and Julia. They'd finally understand why their daughter didn't belong. They'd have their real daughter. Obviously Angie would need extreme cleaning up and education. Could she even learn to speak English at age twenty-two? She remembered reading about wolf boys in India who after a certain age couldn't learn human speech.

Yeah, the whole idea was insane and possibly disastrous, but now she couldn't leave Angie either. She'd have to save worrying about that until later. For the time being, she had to concentrate on building Angie's trust, getting them out of the Erl Tree and "home."

There's no place like home.

Her shimmer fading, she willed a new cloak and gazed up to assess her surroundings. On a ledge above at the base of a narrow chute, the freed blue bird perched silently, watching. It gestured its beak upwards and to the left. She aimed her glow higher and spied a prick of purple light. The bird took wing and flew straight up. The lavender glow flashed as its shape passed through and out.

What did the song say? "Happy little bluebirds fly…"

I've lived my whole life on earth, not in Oz. No matter who or what I am, Fae or Dream, it's the only home I know and right now it looks a whole better than it ever did before.

But she had no ruby slippers. Her wings could fly her up and out of the tree. But how would she get all the way back, especially no longer traveling by herself?

The light in the hole flickered again, and the bluebird flew back down the chute. It hovered momentarily above Jehessimin and then to her right and up. Silly thing had been free, escaped. Why had it returned where it could be recaptured? She directed more shimmer behind and above the bird who seemed like it wanted to show her something.

First, the bird flew by a bell-shaped cage with an open door, low enough that Angie could have reached it just barely on tiptoes. Then it soared a little higher.

One by one, the rest of the cages illuminated. Her care with the glimmer had kept her from realizing where she was—the chamber where she'd been brought to the Erl-King.

With no Erl or Wyrm present to distract her, the sheer number of imprisoned birds overwhelmed her, their eyes staring stoically in the silvery misty glow. They had to have sensed her enter, heard her as she spoke to Angie, but they held their song. The blue one she saved from Angie flitted from cage to cage, from robin to hummingbird, from canary to crow, finally to the farthest away in the largest cages, the hawk, owl and eagle, and then curved back to Jehessimin.

Without making a sound, she knew what it, they asked her, implored her. The emotionless gazes of its avian comrades bore into her, battling with her drive to simply survive.

She already was poised to deepen the Erl-King's anger at her by abducting Angie, but if she freed his birds, his rage would be…

Jehessimin thought of her wings, her beak. Were the Fae not like the birds? Did the Erl-King keep other Fae than her mother in cages? Was he imprisoning or collecting? Did it matter in the end? She felt like Castinelle might have been less sympathetic, but "Mom," Julia, had always kept a pair of binoculars and a bird guide book by the kitchen window which looked out onto the backyard.

She glanced down at her not-twin, still asleep in her lap. Angie's eyelids twitched rapidly.

Dreaming.

Beyond the walls, a whisper of Erl-speak, a flush of wet slithers broke the silence.

The brown barn owl blinked, flipped its head around and then back at her. The hawk shuffled his feet. The eagle flexed its wings. The bluebird fluttered urgently.

Jehessimin lowered her head sideways to the dirt floor. Angie stirred but didn't wake as she gently repositioned her arms and curled around her not-twin.

She closed her eyes and concentrated on her father. She didn't sense he was directing her. Under the Erl curse, he couldn't even remember his coupling and love—*was it love? Did love even exist here?*—for her Fae Mother. He didn't know he had a daughter. But the last dream about him had helped her escape the pit and she was still figuring out exactly how to wield her dream abilities.

Her eyes hadn't been shut long when the black-and-white apartment materialized in her head. No opportunity to see her father's face this time. He was seated with his back to her in a black leather armchair. She heard purring. Her dream-self tiptoed behind him and saw a sleeping calico cat in his lap.

Through the thin dream wall, the cat and Angie wheezed softly.

Her dream-self melded with her father, lifting the cat with his right arm as she eased her not-twin to a standing position in front of her, locked her right arm tightly around her. She spread her wings and flew.

One by one with her left hand, she loosened the latches on the cages.

When all the birds were freed, Jehessimin ascended behind the flock and gently pushed Angie out through the hole.

....

Angie teetered like a rag doll and then plopped face-down in a clump of undergrowth. The perpetual twilight lent a slight purple hue to her shadowy surroundings. A narrow clearing circled the immediate periphery of the Erl Tree, rimmed by densely packed white birch trunks. Low leafy plants sprouted orange berries interspersed with clumps of mushrooms, mossy rocks, and lichen.

Jehessimin struggled to get some kind of bearing. Had she emerged in the same spot where the Wyrm carried her down or was there more than one egress? How would she know which way to go now?

As if in answer, a long melodious chirp sounded next to her. The blue bird landed and pecked at a berry, swallowing it whole.

"Hush, little bird," Jehessimin whispered. "The Erl will hear you."

The bird ignored her and tweeted again, holding the final note high and long.

Jehessimin started to scoop Angie back up, duck into the woods, any direction, when she heard a response from above.

A warble.

A coo.

A caw.

A hoot.

The reciprocal bird sounds gained in volume, more like a song. They hadn't scattered after their newfound freedom. They had waited for her.

Angie tossed and stretched.

A slippery sound emanated from the tree, and a familiar snakelike head poked out of the hole.

All the birds took flight.

No time to worry about whether Angie would wake. The Erl would not be far behind.

Jehessimin scooped up her non-twin and followed the birds. The blue bird lagged behind the rest, only taking paths wide enough among the tightly-packed trunks and branches for her larger rescuer to squeeze through.

As Jehessimin approached the treetops, she glanced down and saw a column of Wyrm sliding rapidly along the forest floor, their twitching leaflike appendages making them resemble an oozing hedge. They were headed in the same direction the birds were flying.

No time to lose, she pushed up through the leaves and into the amethyst sky. For the first time, she clearly saw the purple round "sun," wispy periwinkle clouds, and stars. Either this other Sun wasn't bright enough to outshine the stars in what passed as perpetual day, or this place had its own cosmological rules. Was it really beneath the earth's surface or was it somewhere else altogether?

There's no place like home.

Jehessimin continued to follow the birds. Beneath her the immense forest stretched as far as her eye could see in three directions to horizons of shimmery mountains, literal purple mountains' majesties. The Erl Tree towered behind, looming high above the rest of the woods. It should have been steadily receding but instead while behind, it seemed no further or closer than when she'd first taken flight.

Ahead though she was relieved to see the marshlands where she'd entered the Other Place, or rather fallen into it.

Almost home.

....

As the procession reached the edge of the woods, the attack began.

It happened so fast that Jehessimin couldn't tell at first what had engulfed her rescuers. Just a rising ambient buzz and then a tangle of winged creatures in battle. The Nurls' heads were narrow and their bodies a burnished red. If this was some conventional fantasy world, they'd be tiny dragons, but from what she could see, they had stingers rather than teeth, more like hornets or wasps.

The lower-flying birds were now dropping at the mercy of their stingers. Those that were higher in the sky had some warning and started to flee, their chirps and trills and warbles turning to frantic shrieks as they passed her.

Perhaps to allow some of their comrades to escape and to protect her, the eagle, hawk, and owl engaged the attackers, nimbly dodging the stingers

and going for their tail-ends, ripping their wings with talons and beaks. Some of the monstrous pests fell to the ground.

Jehessimin flew back sharply to follow the retreat. The rapid jerk of her about-face woke up Angie, who screamed and struggled. If she didn't land quickly, her not-twin would work her way loose and she'd drop her, plummet to certain death. She spun around the frenzied battle and angled herself to land in the marsh.

As soon as Jehessimin's feet hit the water, Angie bit hard into her arm, breaking her hold and tumbling knees down into the water. Jehessimin plunged after her not-twin but realized that her descent hadn't escaped the notice of her enemies. The Nurl abandoned the birds of prey and swarmed around her instead. Angie crawled away, repeating a two-toned mix of guttural groan and shrill scream and lifted herself onto a moss-covered boulder where she crouched like the closest human approximation of a frog.

Jehessimin shielded her head and body with her wings, expecting stings and shreds like those that had disabled her Fae Mother. But instead the creatures hovered a foot away. Were they waiting for a command to attack, or simply creating another living cage?

Horns sounded in the distance. And repeated, closer.

Angie giggled like a small child, legs bent, rocking back and forth on top of the rock.

A dozen Erl in dark bark armor emerged from the edge of the woods on the bare backs of giant stags. Or at least stags were the closest animal that Jehessimin could compare them to—at least twice the height of a tall man with horns that stretched up significantly higher and many, many more legs than four. Everything here in the Other Place seemed to have more eyes and legs. They separated into two groups of six and halted just in front of the tree line, leaving a space between.

Then the Erl raised horns, issuing another eerie high-pitched burst.

From their center, out of the woods emerged an even larger goldenrod creature with a massive cat-like head and long pointed canine teeth like a prehistoric saber-toothed tiger. On its back sat Erla, also armored in a mossy breast plate that enhanced her figure and what appeared to be a "chain-mail" tunic made of intertwined vines beneath it.

Further behind in the forest, heavy footsteps thundered and the ground shook as if in the throes of small quakes.

The Erl-King was coming.

Erla didn't wait for her father's arrival. Through a cloud of hovering pests, Jehessimin watched her guide the ferocious mount through the shallow water and tall marsh grasses, whipping its haunches with a staff. It growled in mild complaint, its many paws splashing with each step. As the beast neared her, Erla screeched a command, and it bent its legs. She swung her own legs, bare from mid-thighs to paws, to one side, with a rush of rattling chain, and sprang off. Knee-deep in the wet weeds and wildflowers, she approached. She lifted her arms and stretched her fingers above her head, then twisted them back down and threw them open to each side.

The swarm of Nurl peeled away like curtains opening. Jehessimin's eyes followed them up where they hovered in a red cloud. She noticed a band of birds, including the hawk, owl, and eagle, had lingered to watch high in the clouds.

She lowered her eyes back towards the approaching Erla. Angie's seeming amusement had devolved into heavy breathing and nervous sputters. Her not-twin lifted an arm across her eyes and curled into a ball like a frightened roly-poly.

The thumping steps of the Erl-King approached, not close but not far.

Erla turned and gestured to the Erl behind her. They reversed their mounts and disappeared back into the woods.

Whatever Erla had in mind, she intended to do alone. She circled around Jehessimin towards Angie. She seized the young woman by the hair and yanked her down from her perch, so fast that she literally unraveled. Angie banged her fists on the front of Erla's chest and shrieked and spat until her adopted sister forced her head down until she was neck deep in murky water.

"At first I was angry that you had escaped, Jehessimin," Erla said, speaking in English with that strange Slavic accent perhaps to be certain her every word was understood. "But then I felt joy when I learned the Changeling had taken this wretch. When my father learns that you killed his pet, he will wreak his most horrible punishment upon you. You will feel every instant of pain and it will last a long, long time before you die. If unlike Castinelle, he even lets you die."

Jehessimin looked at Angie, saw the terrified look of a mouse under the claw of a cat. Curt wasn't off in calling her the Tiger Girl. Killing wasn't enough. She toyed with her prey. That was what fed her hunger.

"Don't think too hard about saving her either," Erla continued. "You got lucky with the Dream magic, but you don't know it well enough to truly wield it. Neither did Lukoje, which is why my father could subdue and banish him. The one talisman that protected you from me was your mother's. But you were careless. You lost it. You betrayed your mother."

Erla pulled the green silk bag from a belt at her waist with her right hand. Then with her left, she pushed Angie's head hard under the water.

Her usual fire would have been faster, but of course, she couldn't burn Angie because then the Erl-King would guess he had been tricked. She had to kill her not-twin by "human" means.

The Erl-King's footsteps shook the water. He must be getting close.

What the fuck, I've got nothing to lose.

Jehessimin inhaled and dove into the water, too shallow to swim, holding her breath and trying to ignore its pungent odor. She grabbed Angie's legs and pushed her struggling not-twin straight up.

Angie's head emerged above the water, and the Erl-King's daughter screamed. Jehessimin surfaced to see Angie's teeth digging deep into Erla's wrist. The green pouch flew from her hand.

Whether the angle was accidental or her Fae Mother's magic potent enough to attract back to her, Jehessimin caught the bag. Castinelle's voice echoed in her head.

Open it.

She undid the drawstring and poured some of the yellow powder into her hand.

Angie's teeth were still lodged as if she was holding on for dear life, and she was. Erla regained her grip on Angie's hair and pried her mouth loose. She was poised to plunge her back into the water as Jehessimin hurled the powder.

When it hit her face, Erla shrieked. She released Angie and clamped both her hands over her eyes. Through gaps between her fingers, Jehessimin saw Erla's skin turn first pink and then red. Smoke flowed from her fingers as the heat spread like acid, her fingers crusted brown.

Erla dove into the water, resurfacing a few moments later to reveal a charred black visage with cold angry blue eyes.

Jehessimin grabbed Angie and shot skyward so fast that she jetted by the Nurl before they could organize an attack.

On her way up, the remaining birds gleefully chirped and squawked and sang and pointed up with their beaks and wings.

My instinct has to be right.

I fell into the marsh. The Veil must be above.

The only question is how high.

Booming steps reverberated beneath, so loud as to almost shake the sky. The Erl-King erupted from the forest, his head towering above the treetops in the giant monstrous form he held when she first saw him on the night of the car accident. Around his roots squirmed a mass of undulating, slithering green. Behind, one hundred Erl or more mounted on the stag-like creatures seemed to fold literally out from the trees.

The Erl-King paused, bent his mammoth trunk slightly towards his daughter, them snapped straight again and reached up all his branch-like arms, unfurled his twiggy fingers.

Jehessimin was relieved to see that even if he was a giant, he was far beneath her.

The Veil must be close now.

The Erl-King emitted a deafening roar. His body shook and stretched.

Branches hurtled up towards her and Angie.

Her not-twin grinned and squirmed, extended a hand downwards.

If she struggled too much, she'd have to let her drop.

Don't let go. Don't let him trick you.

The purple air bristled and glittered.

The Erl-King vanished.

....

Jehessimin felt her extra set of legs retract into her body, her wings fold into her back, her beak reshape itself into a nose and lips, her extra eyelids close and eyeballs shrink back around. None of it hurt.

Her not-twin looked confused by the sudden transition from flight to dark passage and the physical transformation of her companion. Did she realize how much they looked alike? Had she ever seen her own reflection?

"Welcome, Angie," Jehessimin said, brushing her not-twin's hair away from her face with her fingers. "Welcome home."

A dank odor suggested they were again underground but not in a cave. The floor was paved with concrete. Perhaps a dried-up sewer or the kind of tunnel that people built beneath towns for commercial or secret purposes.

Angie's fingers twitched nervously as they walked hand-in-hand. It occurred to Jehessimin that perhaps this had never happened before—Changeling and Offspring both in the World at the same time.

One day she would re-embrace her real form. She'd given her word to return for her Fae Mother. Not that she had any illusions that would be easy. The Erl-King would only hate her more for disfiguring one daughter, stealing another, and freeing his menagerie of birds.

But I can't think about any of that now.

The passage halted abruptly at a short set of steps that led up to a loose stone. Jehessimin pushed it aside and climbed out into the cemetery. She was relieved that it was still night, though she saw a faint purple hue of morning twilight in the distance.

Shivering in the icy air, she dove for her black leather jacket which thankfully was still on the ground at the top of a pile of her clothes. An odor like burnt barbecue permeated her nose and she cast around for its source. She'd completely forgotten about Curt. Was she that callous? Yeah, he had been a self-absorbed jerk and she hadn't really known him long, but did he deserve to die because of her fucked-up heritage?

At least she hadn't returned to an active crime scene. Nevertheless no time again to think about anything but moving fast before the sun rose and someone discovered the body and called the police.

Recalling the news report, she scanned the area for any discarded clothing that could have a wallet in a pocket, then remembered that he was wearing his coat when he combusted. That meant hopefully the police wouldn't ID the body immediately, that she would have time to go to his apartment and collect her things. Of course, her fingerprints and DNA would be all over everything, and she had no alibi. But she wasn't in town for the other combustions, except the last one. Even if she wasn't a suspect, they'd want her for questioning. Another reason, beyond its spatial connection to the Erl, to get the fuck out of North Leeds.

Angie squatted and sniffed at Curt's scarred body. She was about to poke a finger into his blackened flakey remains, when Jehessimin yanked her up. Her not-twin let out a whiney protest and grabbed at her jacket. She let her have it, trying to ignore her own cold and the wafts of foul unbathed body odor as she maneuvered Angie's arms into the sleeves. Did her not-twin smell worse in this world or did her Fae-self just not mind the stink? At least the stench and raggedy under-dress might make an early riser mistake her for one of North Leeds's homeless.

Angie pawed at the jacket, caressed the sleeves as if their texture felt entirely new to her, while Jehessimin made sense of the rest of her clothes. Her underwear was seriously shredded from her transformation, but fortunately her sweater and jeans were mostly intact. She hastily slipped them on while clutching the green bag of her "magic." No way was she going to trust a pocket.

She scanned the area and found her boots a few feet to the side under a flower arrangement, then quickly collected what was left of her socks, panties, and bra so as not to leave any trace.

Thankfully they made it to the jailhouse door without encountering anyone. She reached into the breast pocket of the jacket Angie was wearing for the keys.

Angie hesitated in the doorway.

"It's okay, Angie," Jehessimin said, trying to suppress her own tension and sound as calm as she could. "It's safe here."

Once inside the front door, she took Angie's hand again and led her upstairs to Curt's apartment. She wiped her feet on the mat outside the door, and guided Angie to do the same. The last thing that they needed was muddy carpet stains to alert the police that she'd returned to collect her belongings after a barefoot romp in a cemetery where a murder just happened.

Once inside, Jehessimin had to keep Angie from touching everything. This level of comfortable living must be completely new and utterly alien to her.

She guided Angie, grunting with protest, into the bathroom and helped her through her first "shower." Her not-twin displayed curiosity at how the water could be controlled with the faucet. She wondered how she had bathed. In a pond or a waterfall? Surely she had bathed some time in twenty-two years. All creatures had some way to keep themselves clean.

Jehessimin squirted shampoo into Angie's hair and helped her rinse it out. Then showed her not-twin how to rub soap into a washcloth and scrub her body. Once Angie was done, she showered herself quickly.

Running a brush through Angie's more-than-tangled hair elicited cries of pain and protestation. She glanced at the blow dryer but decided even using it on her own hair might distress Angie. She'd have to leave their hair to air-drying no matter if it was chilly. She let go of when-she-was-Angie worries that hers would be flat and frizzy.

Jehessimin slipped into a black turtleneck, jeans, and chucks, and helped Angie into a T-shirt, pull-over, skirt, and boots. An attempt to get her into a bra and wool tights wasn't fruitful. All of Jehessimin's clothes basically fit, although loosely as Angie was thinner. She scanned Curt's closet for a hat to hide her not-twin's messy hair. Of course, a guy like him would only have a fedora. After a few minutes of protestation, she was able to get Angie to leave it on and let her stuff the wad of messy matted hair up under it. At least now she looked eccentric rather than completely unkempt. Later when they were safe in a motel room, maybe she'd attempt to cut it.

Fortunately she'd pretty much been repacking her clothes into her suitcase already so it only took a few minutes to gather all her things, remembering to stuff her filthy, torn cemetery clothes into a plastic trash bag to be disposed later, far away. As she replaced the spare keys on the kitchen nail, a police siren sounded on the street outside. She let herself and Angie out and guided her not-twin to the building's back door.

As the sun rose, the two walked briskly down an alley which let them out a few doors down from the rental car office next to Carefree's Restaurant to finally pick up a replacement car.

Just after eight a.m. Jehessimin drove a black Toyota Corolla up to Carefree's take-out window. In the passenger seat, Angie immediately gobbled up her first chocolate-glazed doughnut, her—*whose?*—favorite as a little girl, and then another, powdered and filled with strawberry jam. Jehessimin also bought a big to-go cup of coffee, but thought caffeine might be a bit much on one's first day on earth.

As Jehessimin merged from the ramp onto the southbound freeway, she flinched when she saw a white welding truck in the slow lane. She pumped the gas pedal, merged into the center lane and passed.

The sun shone brightly on the tarmac, as the truck receded in her rearview mirror.

Angie slurped a large Sprite loudly through a straw. Jehessimin switched on the radio.

"California Dreamin'" by the Mamas and the Papas.

Twenty minutes later, she switched highways and headed west.

Black Stone Roses and Granite Gazanias

Waves of moonlight descend from the heavens and illuminate gargoyles. Their tongues glisten when glimpsed in the lenses of binoculars focused skyward. Delicious green and blue and yellow.

Beware women who dream and transform the spotlights of Bateau Mouche tour boats shining on the gray walls of Notre-Dame de Paris into eerie rainbows of the Damned and speak in riddles rather than fair modern sentences. Is she self-consciously post-modern, endowing the text of her life with excess meaning and a strained consciousness all her own? Or is she a throwback to an over-intellectual, mooning past age of Romanticism—women like Mary Shelley who could be brought down to domesticity only by Byronesque scoundrels (dashing assholes) who composed odes in their honor and idolized the Devil as the ultimate revolutionary? Women who would otherwise choose to remain alone or at least say so.

The power of language—the red-haired woman continued to scribble on her pad—can be a curse. There are ways to write which are applauded and others to be entered into only with the utmost caution. For if words are combined experimentally they must be obnoxiously avant garde to attract accolades (and never romantic).

I heard her writings quoted on the best authority by a crotchety old French street bum who claimed he saw this woman cross a forbidden line. He claimed he saw her talking to a demon who once was a gargoyle, who said he was carved with a chisel by the hands of a young apprentice sculptor from Flanders who had ended up in Florence. An artisan with long, thick dark hair.

If you look carefully up at the far right corner of Notre-Dame, you can spy an empty perch where this demon gargoyle once sat, a gnarled corpse of a warthog dripping from his fangs.

This gargoyle dreamed nightmares and under the weight of his passion, they came true. A man passing the cathedral felt the urge to steal his neighbor's horse, and the next day found himself suspended from the gallows. A young noblewoman was filled with such enthrallment for the Almighty that she would beg a brick mason to wall her into a tiny cubicle so that she could, without distraction, devote her entire life to God. A mob gathered and headed towards the Bastille, transforming a revolution instigated by intellectuals with the best of intentions into a bath of blood.

As for our heroine, she was just a student of English Literature at Plath College. They often are—aspiring wordsmiths fed heavy doses of Dickens (like medicine) and Shakespeare (which teaches you everything) and Eliot (poetry takes a lot of work, but mostly suffering) and Nin (she cheated for pleasure). Either writers or artists or musicians or dancers or actors or—occasionally—just dreamers.

Her name was Ivy. Well, not her real name. It was Lois, but her soul name was Ivy, after Poison Ivy of the Cramps, and that was what her friends called her. Or was it that she was captivated by the green vines that she pretended transformed the walls of her parents' otherwise unremarkable suburban brick ranch house to make it look more like a castle. Or drawn to the poison ivy which her mother warned her against as a child—the pink rash which was a sensation she had never experienced—like the excitement and pain of true love which she only had read about in books.

Now the child who had waded unscathed through those fields of poison ivy had grown to a woman, a woman on the verge of graduation, a woman who craved to be more than a reader and a teacher and a voyeur of lovers' trysts. She played with her pen diligently, trying to fulfill some uncertain peak of literary perfection—somewhere above bodice-ripper paranormal romance novels and below critically-acclaimed learned and glib pretentiousness. She was always thinking she'd just know it when she reached it and thus constantly revising texts that she had written in staggered bursts between term papers and exams and frivolous journeys pursued simply for the sake of knowledge.

Like this trip to Paris. Ivy was on day nine and slated to return to New Jersey tomorrow. The stay had proved disappointing, maybe because of two days lost due to an annoying stomach bug contracted after eating a very oily pizza napolitana in a grubby Italian restaurant. But more likely because she had been on a tight budget, feeling unmercifully shy and alone while wandering the streets of Paris.

Ivy had spent most of this final evening bemoaning the pointlessness of this foolish trip while taking an obligatory stroll up her least favorite street in Paris, Les Champs-Elysées. Paris's most famous boulevard was way too commercial for her and packed with tourists. Still, it was necessary to see the Arc all lit up at night at least once on any trip to Paris.

She grabbed the Métro back to Hôtel de Ville station and was in the midst of that last walk, across the Ile de la Cité to her favorite street in Paris, Boulevard Saint-Michel, and back to Le Home Latin, the tiny Left Bank hotel where she always stayed and her parents had stayed before her—though back then it had cost only a dollar a night—nestled a block from the Musée de Cluny.

On the way, she made her favorite stop of the evening, a luxuriously long pause to sit on a ledge on the edge of the square in front of the towering Gothic façade of Notre-Dame de Paris.

Notre-Dame at night was, for Ivy, the most magical place she had ever been on earth. She could sense the cathedral's age and power resonating from the stone itself. Its history extended back centuries before the cars that skirted periodically before its base, long before the tourists who so enthusiastically scurried to pose before the heavy wooden doors of the central west portal, its arches carved with scenes that chronicled the Last Judgment. In that age of great spiritualistic wonder when the figures were sculpted, people fervently believed in God, and He was a living aspect of every part of one's daily existence. But the Devil also played an integral part in everyone's daily life, an omnipresent threat to every man's ascent to eternal happiness in Heaven.

Everything reaches up to Heaven in the Gothic cathedral, every arch, every buttress, every saint carved in the walls. But the great arched doorways with their parades of apostles include devils in their citizens. And the gargoyles loom above and spit God's water down onto the streets to drain into the famous sewers of Victor Hugo where Inspector Javert chased Jean Valjean, dripping even into the depths of the soil below the concrete shell of modern Paris, into the Catacombs, stacked with bones, and Hell beneath.

Some things never change from century to century.

Ivy was writing all this down, whispering as she wrote, the fever of creativity propelling the words from her mind onto her tiny notepad. She forced two sentences between every line to ensure she had room for all the thoughts that urgently poured from what she was sure was some deep pocket of her soul. She gazed up occasionally, fascinated by the periodic explosions of headlights pouring past the ancient cathedral in sudden, rhythmic intervals, each time the traffic light on the left bank of the bridge changed from red to green.

According to the gargoyle, the sheer volume of her passion was what awakened him while his comrades stayed still in the slumber of the centuries. Or maybe it was that pesky memory buried in his granite soul that he had once been human, a man with long dark hair who drank a toast in a black goblet to Mephistopheles and agreed to sculpt the most terrifying beast ever hewn from stone. That foolish man, younger in mind than his years should have made him, craved compliment and fame from the pursuit of ugliness through his scalpel. He also once loved a simple peasant girl just for the way the sun shone on her auburn hair, but he now was doomed never to love anyone for so simple and pure a reason ever again. Or was he?

He says her whisper crested on an accidental wind, a breeze that blew up from the square right to the crevice where he sat perched with the boar's head clamped between his fangs. His ear twitched first, the stone melting gently into flesh. Then his eyes blinked open and he found that he could see a young woman in a denim jacket with long, wildly teased scarlet hair scrawling madly on a tiny pad of paper way below. He let the boar fall from his fangs for the first time in five centuries and leapt joyfully into the black sky.

For several minutes the foul monster just hovered, supported by his bat-like wings, glorying in his newfound freedom. Then he flew to each of the monstrous companions with whom he had believed himself doomed to spend eternity. He taunted them and laughed in his most bestial expression of glee. But they sat as always, unmoving, blind to everything including any hypothetical demons from which they were supposed to be protecting God's House.

"Pitiful watchmen," the Devil had sneered—a smelly gentleman with a long matted goatee and yellow slime dripping from his nostrils back in the fifteenth century. Of course, today he dresses much better, neater, looks a lot like Brad Pitt. Last century he resembled Mick Jagger, before that Lord Byron, and Alexander Hamilton, Oliver Cromwell, and Sir Walter Raleigh—each in his own time.

Lucifer had gotten in a good snicker about transforming a dreamer of darkness into a true demon and then forcing him into the body of his own grotesque creation. Not to mention, imprisoning him on the peak of God's most beautiful house, the only gargoyle with a true consciousness. Another sip from the black chalice, and young Hans felt his body hardening into a denizen of the damned—precisely the type of creature whom gargoyles, despite their monstrous appearance, were supposed to frighten away.

Hans felt the center of his heart congeal and harden, picturing the red organ darkening to black as any remaining stray goodness seeped out of his brain and body. He became evil made flesh. Therefore now he could not help but gloat that he was awake and free while his fellow gargoyles stared with rock-hewn eyes into the night at nothing like they had for centuries, creatures of lifeless stone. He whizzed by each one, sniffing it. No scent, only the pungent odor of gasoline exhaust fumes rising from the street below. He'd grown not to mind that stench, it being less noxious than the multitude of aromas of earlier centuries, the eras before baths and sanitation.

Hans was glorying in his new awakening up above, when the flood of language in Ivy's head suddenly dried up. When the words no longer flowed, she happened to look up and see his beastly form hovering from gargoyle to gargoyle, heavy black batwings flapping above a dark shadow of a body and thrashing a long, thick tail crested by pointed spikes.

Ivy didn't scream. She just stood, her notebook dropping from her hand onto the ground. (Where it was found the next day by an American editor in desperate need of something provocative to add fresh juice to his very New York literary horror anthology of great renown. He told an editor-friend about her and they tried to track her down to commission her to pen a novel. But that was later, and much too late.)

For now, Ivy stared so hard at Hans that he whirled around, throwing his bulbous jaws downwards in her direction and narrowing his large yellow eyeballs to slits in order to appear especially ferocious.

Needless to say, it was love at first sight.

Hans motioned for her to follow him around the side of the cathedral, and she advanced in his direction into the shadowy side street. After all, he didn't want dopey, camera-toting tourists from Nebraska or Tokyo spying on the heartfelt lovers' tryst to which he was luring her. She walked around the corner, past an empty café and dark shop windows. He flew for several blocks just to make certain that no one would observe their clandestine meeting, no one interrupt his feasting on her flesh. Finally, he led her into an ancient narrow alley and touched down onto his haunches in front of a row of thin metal garbage cans spilling over with paper and banana peels and wine bottles.

Being a demon, of course, he frothed at the mouth and raised his lips to reveal the long line of pointed fangs. Ivy turned to run, suddenly overcome with fear, but he grabbed her with a clawed paw and was surprised to find himself apologizing profusely.

"It's just that I am unused to this new freedom," he said.

"Et tu es très belle," he added, "et très mal."

"Mal" means Evil," Ivy mused to herself, still a little frightened. She thought of Cocteau's *La Belle et la Bête*, one of her favorite films of all time. But that Beast was attracted to the goodness in Beauty. She then briefly recalled her own fancy that she was born a dark fairy in a land of the night, exiled to the dull monotony of mortal existence because her mother had dared to love the dark prince of dreams who was betrothed to the Erl-King's daughter. This nymph of the night within her made her turn cold towards nice guys who had crushes on her, questing ever for that ideal elfin lord of darkness who loved her, too. Relationship problems were easy to explain away when they were the consequence of a curse.

But Ivy had made up this metaphor on a lonely night in Des Moines and confessed it only to her journal. Now she stared at the beast and wondered suddenly if her tale might have some veracity.

"It's not true," Hans said, for demons can read minds. "Not true that you are anything but human."

She felt a sudden urge to cry.

"I was human, too," Hans continued.

He paused to spit.

"I was once a Flemish sculptor named Hans Bogaert."

Then the gargoyle told her his story, and she did cry, drawn as much to her imagination of the handsome man he once must have been as to the tormented evil that dominated his being today. She stroked the dark green scales that coated his back and laid her lips upon the side of his snout. In one long moment, he transformed into a slender naked man with deep cheekbones, a long mane of dark hair, and delicate long fingers.

"Would you like to live forever?" Hans asked. "Would you like to see the centuries endlessly pass before your eyes? Men and women make the same mistakes over and over again?"

"Would you like to live your life without purpose?" Ivy queried back. "To read, to write, to create for no one but yourself?"

How could she, a woman with such a romantic nature bursting from her giant heart, love a man so attractive if he was such a vile monster in his soul? She posed the question to herself, and then remembered she was a romantic. A romantic hears the call of love in a quick heartbeat. She inspected his face closely because she desperately yearned to understand how such a volume of violence could ascend from any living creature. She ignored the answer and instead replaced logic with pity and a sense of mission. She herself would bring this poor tortured and yet beautiful man back to perfection through the sheer power of her love.

But then what is evil? Ivy searched her mind and thought of world leaders and politicians and businessmen and women. Whatever the demon had done with his mind control, she had seen far worse on the twenty-four-hour news. Tiny pranks in comparison.

She gazed into Hans' eyes and nodded.

The naked man gathered her into his arms and became the beast again. He spread his wings and carried her up into the night, cool air blowing against her cheeks as they flew up the edge of the cathedral. She grazed her fingers against the row of flying buttresses. She asked to touch the stained glass of the great rose window and he swung around to let her. They flew up then and she reached her hand to the stars.

Hans glided over the Seine, and for a moment a blue light from a Bateau Mouche boat sparkled against the tip of his right wing. He pulled it in quickly and for a moment lost his balance. They fell right into the spotlights, and Ivy waved. But the boat was almost empty, the last run of the evening. Only a small boy gazed up in wonder and waved back, the handful of other tourists all fixated on the cathedral.

Hans extended his wings again, and the couple were flying above the lights of the tourist boat, over the crowded traffic and cafés of Boul Miche, and circling towards the needle-tip of Tour Eiffel, its metal spire illuminated tonight in golden yellow. Over the roofs of Paris they flew, over Arc de Triomphe and down the wide avenue of Champs-Elysées. Hans dipped down close to the crest of the L'Obélisque du Luxor and the mad traffic of Concorde. Then he curved towards the Corinthian columns of La Madeleine and whisked her east past the white dome of Sacré-Coeur atop the hill of Montmartre, the highest point in Paris. He headed north above streams of apartments, shops, houses, train stations. Then once the city limits had finally faded into black countryside, he spun west under a clear starry sky.

An hour or two later, she felt the wind quicken as he flew out over the sea somewhere south of Mont Saint-Michel.

Maybe another half hour passed, her body wafted with colder and colder air, when over the Atlantic, he dove.

Ivy died almost immediately, icy liquid filling her lungs with the impact, and she, startled by the frigid water's embrace, gave herself over to death's passion without any struggle. Holding her in his arms, he watched her green eyes close, her red hair expand like a corona of fire in the water—she looked like a mermaid in the moonlight, he thought. In some other lifetime, she might have been dangerous. In any lifetime, she would have been left behind.

Hans the monster opened his own mouth now to let the water flood his throat, halt the pumping of his own lungs. He tasted what he imagined would be death, final and total escape from the monotony of the centuries and the curse played upon him by his own folly.

As the ocean entered, he felt his skin swell, his flesh harden and drag him down beneath the water. He waited for consciousness to slip away but just felt himself sinking, Ivy's limp body still entwined in his arms. At that moment, he realized that it wasn't the heaviness of death but the weight of his body returned to granite that was pulling him leagues and leagues deep into the black sandy bottom of the Atlantic. Then as if the Devil's final joke was to return him as approximately as possible to his former self, a small shark swam in his path and got caught in his jaw. It flapped its tail fins in panic, trying to break from the grip of the stone teeth to no avail.

The demon gargoyle who once was a man no longer gazes down from the high pinnacle of God's Castle but instead stares forever up from a Hell of pitch black water. Ivy's body is now decaying, her hair completely gone, her face withered and pockmarked as the water slowly eats away at her flesh locked in his rocky embrace. At some point soon he knows he will just hold bones and even those the water will whittle away until he is finally fully alone, his night vision allowing him only the shadowy sight of the constant stream of fluttering seaweed, slow-moving crustaceans, and schools of fish that might be plain or exotic.

Grass

Can a body be a forest? A deep dank overgrown woods? A tangled jungle of viscous vegetation that requires a machete to slash a pathway to its dark, dark heart?

Sheila would never have thought so until she saw Dave's corpse stretched out on the steel embalming table, metamorphosed into marsh. Thin blades of tall green and drying yellow grasses sprouted amongst blackened scabs, tatters of black T-shirt, dark clots of jet fuel and thick chest hair. The jagged point of a trimmed gray branch poked through the left side of his stomach, another spiked at an angle through his right arm just above the elbow. More branches impaled his legs through his torn tan mud- and oil-stained khakis. One foot was laced up in a brown hiking shoe, the other detached and sockless, placed just below the empty cuff of a tattered pants leg. Bones poked out at jagged angles, cartilage dangling, the severed appendage stained a faded green and coated with dark bruises and cuts, toes gooey and gelatinous as if a mere touch might melt them away.

A ripple of yellow green light caught the corner of Sheila's eye, shifted her gaze back to his chest. Matted tufts mingled with swollen slashes on a floor of gray-olive flesh, hair and grass twitched slowly as if tickled by a light breeze, his skin glowing momentarily underneath. She closed her eyes, reopened them, found the movement ceased, the luminescence vanished.

A trick of the fluorescent lighting? Or a hallucination from stress caused by the unexpected jolt to her equilibrium preceding her arrival at the Maddox and Sons Funeral Home, which doubled as the morgue in south Georgia's Camden County. Seven a.m. call after barely three hours of sleep. Voice laced with Southern gentleman drawl informing her that a Cessna Skyline JT-A licensed to Dave Thompson had crashed in a marsh on the banks of St. Mary's River, and someone needed to ID the body to ensure it was him. She asked why they didn't call Monica, his current wife, how they found her name. A female body discovered near the wreckage was assumed to be Monica, explained Mr. Maddox, the funeral director who doubled as coroner. Sheila Baxter had come up as an emergency contact in electronic medical records Dave must have never updated.

Maybe Sheila should have tried to get a bit more sleep, but her adrenaline was pumping—the same way it did during their marriage when she'd lie in bed, mind and heartbeat racing. Until anger and frustration would force her up, and she'd wash dishes, dust shelves, write in her journal, anything to exhaust that energy churning within. She threw on a long-sleeved shirt and black skirt, grabbed a sweater because it was bound to be cold in a morgue, right? She checked that her ensemble wasn't too wrinkled and looked somewhat businesslike—working from home meant an eclectic wardrobe and being slack about ironing. June in Georgia, but she'd run the AC in the car. What the hell does one wear to ID a body anyway? Quick pack-up of toiletries and spare underwear just in case she had to spend the night in a motel. She got into her Toyota Corolla and drove the four hours from Atlanta to Woodbine.

Sheila felt a compulsive need to see every detail of Dave's corpse, to memorize it in a documentary film she could rerun in her mind. Not an alien autopsy, but an ex-husband autopsy. That was why she insisted on inspecting the entire body even though Maddox, stereotype of a small town funeral director—early sixties with thinning gray hair, a mustache, and a jiggly gut in a loose-fitting black suit—said he only needed to lift the sheet enough for her to see Dave's face. The coroner warned her in the foyer that viewing Dave's corpse could be traumatic. With the physics of impact, the body falling at high speed from the Cessna's cockpit, the sharp blades of sawgrass that grew in the swamp had cut like a razor through the flesh, he explained. She'd only seen a few actual corpses, and those had been embalmed and dressed up, but even as a child, she had been fascinated with crime-scene and morgue photos after finding a copy of Weegee's *Naked City* in one of her dad's many bookcases. Later she was both repulsed and fascinated that graphic police photos existed of Jack the Ripper's victims. Yeah, she was pretty sure she had seen much worse inflicted by human hands. And she definitely didn't want to start with Dave's face.

Besides, Sheila rationalized, seeing his whole body would help her be sure, absolutely sure, beyond the shadow of a rat's ass, that the bastard was dead. Though she wouldn't know the answer to the question she'd really like to ask him—did he slam his fist into the side of Monica's head as the plane began to dive? When they were still married, Dave had told Sheila that if ever they were heading for a plane crash, he'd knock her unconscious before they hit the ground, spare her the agony of dying from the impact or worse—burning alive if the jet fuel ignited.

Except he didn't wait for a plane crash to hit Sheila. And he did it many more times than once.

Sheila had been in the embalming chamber only a few minutes, but even through the surgical mask, the strangely sweet smell of decomposition seeped and hung in her nostrils. She had expected the odor to be repulsive, rotten eggs or formaldehyde maybe. However, despite a pungent undertone, the scent more resembled rotting fruit. Before she entered the chamber, Maddox had offered her a little Vick's rub to dab under her nose to ameliorate the odor. She refused it, too—stuff gave her the jeebies after Dave once rubbed too much on her lower back and she ended up fetal-curled on the bathroom floor with cramps throttling her abdomen. An Internet search later verified menthol poisoning, but the excruciating pain passed within an hour and she never went to the ER. She never called an ambulance nor drove herself to the ER no matter how much anything hurt or even when she feared internal bleeding that could hemorrhage if she had a concussion. But in the case of the menthol poisoning, the harm inflicted by her ex was accidental, not intentional. Happier times? Were there any?

Like she needed to see, Sheila told herself, she also needed to breathe in the aroma of Dave's dead body. Every sensory experience reassured that he was never coming back.

Uncertain how long she could take that smell, Sheila finally looked at Dave's face. Like the rest of his body, the skin she remembered as olive and copper-tanned was stained a smoky green. The coroner had warned her that part of his right cheek would be missing, but like so much else about the body, the geometrically perfect impact hole was a surprise. When he was thrown from the Cessna, a thick shaft of bamboo had ripped right through it, Maddox said. To make that accurate a circle, she would have needed a compass. She found herself momentarily transfixed on the shape.

Other than the piney tint, the rest of his face looked relatively normal—his heavy brows, lids shut so she didn't have to see the chestnut eyes that charmed so many women including her in the beginning. His nose was wider than she remembered—rosacea from years of alcoholism finally taking its toll—but his thick lips curved, frozen in a slight sardonic smile. His dark wavy hair, that he had always styled so perfectly yet effortlessly, shone slick with fuel and looked like someone had combed it back from his forehead. The mechanics of the fall had planted a jungle across the rest of his body, but alas, hole aside, had preserved most of his face, the part she least desired to see.

The yellow-greenish glow pulsed again, this time inside his thick hair. The light shimmied and seemed to shake, maybe even slither, curl down his cheek and then snake into the tangle of his chest foliage, in and out of slashes of shirt fabric. A burst of heat burnt her forehead.

The biggest surprise was a sudden emotion of loss, sadness—*no, not love!* Should she be crying? Did Dave deserve her tears? She never thought she'd ever cry if he died. He deserved to die, didn't he, for what he had done to her? No, she didn't have any reason to cry. She didn't love Dave, couldn't even remember loving him, though she did remember saying she did. The emotion churned, intensified into hate, the back of her head burning as it used to after he slammed his fist into it. She closed her eyes and grasped above her forehead, wincing at the pain.

A finger tapped her on her shoulder.

"Are you okay, ma'am?" Maddox asked.

Sheila heard a momentary oozing sound like paste squirting from a tube followed by a splatter onto the floor. Intense feelings disappeared as suddenly as they had begun.

"Yeah," she nodded, opening her eyes and dropping her hand. Again the glow had vanished, the body back to the brambled chaos caused by the crash. What was that? Her emotions must be more mixed up than she realized.

"Take your time," Maddox said. "We ain't in no rush."

"It's him," she said, turning towards the coroner. "It's Dave."

"I need you to state his full name, ma'am," said Deputy Hank Jones. The African-American officer spoke with sensitivity as he stepped closer with his clipboard and placed a hand on her shoulder.

"David Charles Thompson."

"Thank you, ma'am," Deputy Jones said. "I know this can't be easy. You can step outside now."

"Is the body under the other sheet Monica?" she asked, motioning to the neighboring embalming table. "Could I see it?"

Maddox and the officer exchanged glances.

"We've got to stick to procedure, ma'am," Deputy Jones said. "You're not her next of kin, and her sister is flying in from Denver tomorrow. Besides, she's not in the same condition as Mr. Thompson here. Let's just say, ma'am, where and how she landed was not kind to her…er… complexion."

Sheila nodded. Did she really want to see Monica dead anyway? Or was it more morbid curiosity because she'd never actually met the woman for whom her husband left her? Friends had forwarded happy couple photos from Facebook and curiosity drove her to look, fighting back mixed feelings about whether she really wanted to see. Still the affair was not the nail that broke her marriage; it was merely a symptom of the Gordian knot Dave was locked into—addiction to booze, cigarettes, and eventually Monica. Textbook. The alcoholic has an affair with an enabler, either someone close by with whom he drinks or someone faraway with whom he can orchestrate an emotional affair fantasy that his problems are really with his wicked wife, and once he's free of that bitch, everything will be different.

In the case of Dave and Monica, an online emotional affair grew into clandestine weekend trysts and marriage after the divorce. After all, with Sheila no longer picking up his pieces, he needed someone else, and pronto! They'd barely been divorced six months. She might pity Monica, but for better or worse, like her own wedding vow, she didn't. Monica had never shown any concern for Sheila so why should she care what happened to Monica? Still, if Monica was alive, she wouldn't have to be here, taking responsibility for the body of a man she'd spent two years trying to forget.

Sensing that the coroner and the officer were growing impatient, Sheila shut off her memories and scanned Dave's overgrown corpse one more time, toes to head.

"Okay, I've seen enough."

The officer headed for the door and opened it while the coroner replaced the sheet over the body. As she rounded the table on her way to the door, she felt something wet and gooey splash against the back of her ankle.

"Mr. Maddox, I think I stepped in something," Sheila said. When she looked down, though, she saw only the slightest hint of moisture on the white linoleum.

"Sorry, ma'am, looks like somebody spilled some water," Maddox said, and then yelled "Eric!"

The young assistant who had initially greeted Sheila shuffled in. Grandson? Thinner but she could see a family resemblance, trying out his first thin mustache.

"I don't think it's water," Sheila said. "It feels thicker."

"Grab a mop, get that cleaned up," Maddox ordered. "I'm sure it's just water, Ms. Parker. Just water."

Sheila wanted to believe him, but whatever she had stepped in had felt slimy, lotion-like. Maybe water with some cleanser in it? Or a bit of jet fuel—uck if that were the case. In any event, the liquid had drenched her sock, making her bare foot inside damp and squishy in her shoe as she followed Maddox, who had taken the lead up the corridor to the arrangement room.

A waft of powdery air freshener greeted her nostrils as she stepped in the doorway. Maybe she should have been taken the Vick's after all. The room itself was decorated with all the creativity of a stereotype of a country funeral home—ugly blue and gold floral wallpaper, maroon drapes, faux-antique furniture. Paintings included still lifes of fruit baskets, a pastoral scene with rolling hills, and a blond Jesus, lantern in one hand and knocking at a door, in colors so neon-bright he looked almost 3-D.

"Take a seat," Maddox said, motioning towards a long shiny wooden table lined with high-backed cushioned chairs. He sat on the opposite side, facing her, and Deputy Jones at the end.

"In all my years of seeing victims of planes crashed into the marsh, I have never seen anything like this one," Deputy Jones said. "He's a regular Swamp Thing."

"Hank, I'm sure the lady doesn't want to hear that kind of talk," Maddox said, shifting to a practiced slow and saccharine tone as his role switched from coroner back to funeral director.

"It's okay," Sheila said. "My ex-husband owned a comic book store for a while. Used to have some copies signed by one of the artists."

She swallowed a chuckle. Dave, as a child, wanted nothing more than to be a comics artist. He had told her how he showed off his portfolio to every artist and every editor at every comics con he could find, his work only to be belittled as not good enough. So when his dad died, he splurged his inheritance on opening a comic book store instead, one so successful that it expanded into a chain. Made a ton of money during the comics boom of the early nineties, the rise of the graphic novel with *Watchmen*, *Dark*

Knight, Eastman and Laird's Teenage Mutant Ninja Turtles. All those hyped-up first issues from flyboy superhero artists brought in fanboy speculator bucks. Dave lost his shirt later when Marvel came tumbling down thanks to the stock manipulation by Revlon tycoon Ronald Perelman and its aftermath, though the business might have pulled through if he hadn't blown all his savings on booze and cigarettes and coke and strippers. He had to close all but the flagship store. By then he hated comics, hated everything about them including his customers. So yeah, it was a bit funny that now he looked kind of like Swamp Thing.

"Ma'am, we'll be happy to take care of the arrangements for Mr. Thompson here at Maddox and Son, but I need to verify some information from you first," Maddox continued. "Ma'am, you seem to be the only living relative of Mr. Thompson."

"I'm not a relative," Sheila said. "I'm his ex-wife."

"Yes, ma'am," Maddox said. "Does he have any other kin?"

"No, his parents are dead and his brother Luke never married and committed suicide after serving in the Iraq War," Sheila said. "Dave did have an Aunt Penny in assisted living, but she had some pretty severe Alzheimer's last thing I heard. I don't know if she's still alive. Dave wouldn't go see her because, well, he didn't like her too much when she was *compos mentis*."

"Then looks like it'd be you as can best handle his final arrangements," Maddox said, throwing her a well-rehearsed sympathetic smile. "I'm assuming you want to take the body back to Atlanta. We can work with any funeral home up there. You just need to provide a name and a number."

"What about Monica's sister?" Sheila asked. "Doesn't it fall to her responsibility?" Damn, her foot felt totally soaked now, and yet she hadn't stepped in any more water.

"Mrs. Caroline Shelley has already said she will not handle the arrangements for Mr. Thompson," Maddox said, smooth as molasses. He was working her for sure. "To put it delicately, she didn't seem too happy to be coming out here at all to take care of her sister's body. She didn't seem too fond of Mr. Thompson."

"What if I say no?" Sheila said. "What happens to his body?"

"If you don't do it, ma'am, there's some county ground but there'd be no marker, no funeral," Maddox said. "That don't sit right with most people."

When Sheila didn't answer right away, he kept talking as if reciting an oft-repeated script.

"Does he have friends, ma'am? Friends who'd want to come to a memorial service, who deserve a chance to say their final farewells."

Dave didn't deserve them, in her opinion, but probably a lot of people would come out to pay their final respects, Sheila thought. He was well-liked, even if most of his friends abandoned him in recent years due to his drinking—and some because of the way he treated her. Crap. Could she just abandon his body to a county burial, or did she need to do the right thing? She always did the right thing, even when she hated herself for it. Her foot felt like it was soaking in a pool of water, yet when she reached a finger down to touch her sock, it was completely dry.

"Okay, so I assume the costs would be covered by his estate?" Sheila asked. "At the very least there's his store, Fantastic Comics, that'll be sold."

"I apologize but we don't have any way of accessing any estate money," Maddox said. "That'd be something for the lawyers. The estate has to be opened in probate, have to see if he has a will and designated an executor—since his wife is dead and he has no next of kin, the court would likely assign an administrator. But yes, usually under these circumstances, as long as he doesn't have a long line of creditors, you'll be able to file expenses and get back any money you spend on arrangements from the estate. Do you know if he had a will?"

"He probably does, probably left whatever there is to Monica, and now it'll go to her sister," Sheila thought aloud. "That's probably why she's coming. Because she wants to get whatever she can get. And I get nothing as usual. Do I have to pay upfront?"

"Sorry, ma'am, but yeah, that's the way it works," Maddox nodded.

All through the last few years of their marriage, Sheila's freelance PR-consulting income had paid the mortgage and other household expenses. Thanks to Dave somehow affording a kickass divorce attorney, she'd only gotten a pittance back in the settlement, barely enough to pay her own expenses. Now she had to fund his burial and funeral, too?

"So what's cheapest? Cremation, and I can carry the urn back up to Atlanta for the memorial."

Maddox paused, put on his most doe-eyed expression. Man, that guy was slick. And probably after as much money as he could get out of her, too, Sheila thought.

"Ma'am, I am afraid we can't do a cremation when jet fuel is on the body," he said. "It has to be a burial."

"Burial, that means a coffin, right, and a plot?" Sheila said. "What's a ballpark figure?"

"Our minimum for our least expensive casket that might be suitable for a service will run you about $1,725, then another few thousand for plot, headstone and carving, internment, obituary, and service," Maddox said.

"Delightful," Sheila could hear the snap in her voice. "So what happens next?"

"You need to pick a funeral home in Atlanta and then we can walk you through a call with them to make the transport arrangements," Maddox said. "You'll probably want to meet the director in person to set up the obituary, plan the memorial service. Don't worry, ma'am, you won't need to take out your checkbook down here, they'll pay us and I'm sure they take credit cards."

"Wonderful, just perfect," Sheila said. "Okay, how about A.S. Clement and Sons. It's on Clairmont Road."

And the only funeral home in Atlanta she knew by name. Both her parents had their final rest orchestrated by A.S. Clement, a respectable middle-class establishment that so far hadn't charged top prices.

"Okay, we'll give 'em a call," Maddox said.

"I think I'll get along since it seems like you got things handled," Deputy Jones said rising. "You all right, Ms. Baxter?"

"Yes, sir, thank you," Sheila said politely, shaking his hand.

"Bye then, and don't hesitate to call if you do need anything," he said, handing her his card and tilting his hat. Maddox followed him out, and they exchanged a few more words in the hallway, but Sheila couldn't hear what they were saying.

While waiting, Sheila remembered how in the early days of her divorce, a divorced male friend had said to her, "They come back, they always come back."

Dave was back in a sense because here she was making funeral arrangements and spending her own money. Suddenly he was her responsibility again. Death had given him back to her.

She didn't want him back.

And dammit, why was her foot so fucking wet and slimy?!

Making the necessary arrangements only took another hour. Sheila waited while Maddox called A.S. Clement, put her on the phone with a director long enough to set up an appointment for tomorrow. She could negotiate the basics, see the available caskets although she'd already decided that whatever was cheapest would have to do. No way was she spending one penny more than she had to even if in theory she might get the money back. That is, if Dave had any money left in his estate. At least funeral expenses would be reimbursed ahead of creditors and any disbursement to heirs, Maddox assured her.

As Sheila left the building, she heard voices to her right. On the far end of the white columned porch, backs turned, Eric and a skinny blonde girl with a blue medical smock over black pants were taking a smoke break.

"Crash impact must've catapulted her straight into that alligator paddy—smack!" Eric's voice rose and dissipated into laughing. "That crap turns rock hard, not to mention pfew!!!"

The girl twittered as she took a puff.

Sheila chuckled under her breath despite herself. So that's why Monica looked worse than Dave.

As soon as she was in the car, she grabbed a towel she kept for wiping condensation off the inner windshield and slipped off her shoe. But as she removed her sock and started to dry her foot, she realized that it wasn't wet any more. Even the sock was bone dry.

The drive home seemed long and mind-numbingly boring as clouds moved in amid sporadic downpours of gray rain. Even music did not help, so she finally turned off her car stereo, listening only to the rhythmic drone of the drops on the roof and windshield. At this point, some tears fell, too, but not for Dave. She wasn't sure what they were for.

By the time Sheila pulled into her driveway, the sun was out again, but the grass remained wet from the recent rain. She walked back to the mailbox, pulled out the power bill, junk mail, and a solicitation from the Sierra Club begging for a donation. Glancing at the flowers in her front bed, she was relieved at not having to water them tonight. She was tired and had enough to do inside. She paused back at the car to scoop up her purse, the unused toiletry bag, the navy blue folder containing the funeral home paperwork. Then she headed for the front door, turned the key, switched on the lamp just inside, laid her stuff down on a chair, slipped off her shoes.

Emptiness overwhelmed her. Her dog Sam had died two months ago, Spook the crazy cat that had loved Dave gone more than three years. The house so quiet that she could almost hear its silence if it were not for the hum of the refrigerator. The living room too tidy because there was only one person to mess it up. Four orderly stacks of books and magazines on the coffee table; photos, figurines, and a candelabrum with red candles positioned with symmetry on the desk to the side; the sofa bare and generously cushioned; a small pile of unsorted mail under her purse on the chair.

When Dave had lived here, he'd left clutter everywhere—comics from the store, mail, lists he never looked at again, sundry paperwork that he insisted he was sorting but never filed away. A chaos that she had finally given up on asking him to clean because the drink always had him teetering on the edge of anger. At least with her. Was he the same way with Monica? How could he not be, she thought, if he was still drinking at that same pace? Or was he drinking less? Did he achieve some peace with this mysterious other woman? Some balance he couldn't have around Sheila? Was there something about Sheila that triggered his depression, his cheating, his hitting? Before the alcohol took hold, they barely fought at all. Except that time he tried to strangle her in the car and then swore off tequila for two years. Or the time he told her that everyone, friend by friend, despised her, and then apologized profusely and proclaimed his love for her in the morning on his knees by the bedside—that the biggest fear he had was that she would leave him. Those incidents were so far between that every time they happened they caught her totally by surprise. All those times had been fueled by an extra big binge of alcohol. Should she have given them more credence as portents of what was to come once the switch fully broke and he drank all the time? Did she remember everything all wrong?

Sheila shook herself, walked into the kitchen to pick up the watering can and twisted the faucet to fill it. Once it was full, she switched off the water, wishing she could switch off her thoughts. She felt simultaneously exhausted and wired. At least watering gave her something to do while her mind raced. She started with the row of herbs on the window sill above the sink—basil, dill, chives, thyme, and parsley. Their savory aromas blended and permeated the air as she aimed the narrow elephantine spout into the soil at their base. For the past two years, she had consciously tried to drown Dave out of her head and had been doing a pretty good job of it. In some ways, it was like they had never ever been married. Sure, she remembered things that happened over the course of two decades, half of her life, that she dated and was wed to Dave. She just didn't remember doing them with him, which was a strange feeling.

She moved over to the low cherrywood case in front of the dining room window—golden pothos, red angel wing begonia for a touch of color, philodendron close to outgrowing its ceramic pot, skipped the aloe and a small cactus which didn't need daily watering. The bad memories were more deeply rooted, but if she didn't think too hard about them, she could almost pretend they'd happened to someone else. Like she was outside her body when his fist pounded down upon her head. It wasn't that often, right? She would never have stayed if it was, would she?

And why did it happen? Was she just a pathetic victim? How could she have allowed it? Why didn't she leave? It wasn't like they had kids for whose sake to preserve the marriage—just a dog and a cat. These questions went round and round in a loop in her head, worse when she imagined other people asking her, which was she told so few—and never her parents—that Dave hit her.

Seeing Dave's corpse should make her, yeah maybe it was disturbing to think it but…happy, especially in such a condition. Instead it was bringing back all the memories she had suppressed that had made all her friends admire her renewed sense of life and energy. "You've lost ten years in a day." "Nice to see you smile in photos again." "Men will be lining up to date you." "You'll be a prize to the right guy who will treat you the way you deserve." The voices echoed in her head.

Sheila inspected the tall waxy leaves of a snake plant, judged it didn't need water today, instead nourished the staghorn fern next to it. She should be talking to them, not to herself. She wondered if they could sense her tension? After Tommy Shore teased her mercilessly in first grade, she'd found refuge hugging her stuffed snake Fresca under a hanging maindenhair fern in her parents' sun room—or as she called it, the Jungle Room, because her mom literally had filled it with leafy green plants. Her mother had been a consummate gardener, but because Sheila never felt she had inherited her mom's innate talents, she just watered obsessively daily. That ritual might even have been what kept her sanity in the later years of her marriage, she thought. Instead of thinking about anything that happened with Dave, she watered, inspected, whispered to each plant, gradually buying more and more so the daily ritual stretched longer and longer. When Dave was still living in the house, some of the plants seemed unresponsive, died, but as soon as he moved out, they began to grow like never before.

The can now empty, she returned to the kitchen and refilled it, then headed to the living room. Enough time for another memory to intrude. Usually the precursor to an assault was her standing up to Dave about something. She listed them off in her head—asking him if he still planned to make dinner, refusing to divulge where she hid the car keys, approaching the computer and him rising to block the screen so she couldn't see that he was messaging Monica, and of course telling him to stop drinking. By that point she reached the ming aralia tree in the big terra-cotta pot by the sofa.

She hummed, "you can't always," as she watered, then she pivoted towards the line of orchids on the long windowsill at the front of the room, gonzo healthy and growing like weeds. She was proud of that accomplishment, never thought she could nurture something as complex as orchids. But before she could tip the can into the first pot, she felt the disgusting sensation of wet sock again as she stepped into a puddle. How could the floor be wet? She hadn't been here yet with the can, and the house had been empty all day. If she'd spilled water yesterday, surely it would be dry by now.

As quickly as she lifted her foot and tested the ground again, bending down slightly, the moisture had vanished. Okay, the stress of the day was clearly taking its toll—the sense-memory of that earlier wetness haunting her if that even was real and not her imagination. She should finish up the orchids, duck down to the den and nourish the rest of her plants, then go to bed. She started to hum again, this time "Moonage Daydream," tipped the nozzle to the first orchid, and then the second. Yellowish-green light flashed in the corner of her right eye. She lifted her head and saw a faint shimmer not just on the orchid leaves but also on their hairy roots which hung down from some of the pots and over the sill. The plants were glowing, or rather something was glowing inside them, like the glow at the funeral parlor. But like the puddle, that didn't make any sense. Didn't make any sense at the funeral parlor. She closed her eyes tight and when she opened them, the glimmer also was gone.

Mystery solved. Her stressed-out imagination again. She finished up the orchids, took the can downstairs where she refilled it in the bathroom, and watered black velvet plant, philodendron, corn plant, dragon tree, succulents, cacti, bromeliads, curly Crotons, a bird nest fern, a rabbit foot fern, and a *Pachypodium lamerei*, AKA Madagascar Palm. This process took several refills but revealed no more mysterious wet spots, no strange glows and no unwelcome memories. The ritual seemed to have worked its therapy, mercifully cleared her head.

Sheila mounted the steps, paused in the kitchen to stash the can back under the sink. Next she headed upstairs to the bathroom to brush her teeth and then to her bedroom. She switched on the bedroom light and lit the pillar candle in the little shrine she kept atop her dresser which included random sundry items of meaning to her: Sam's ashes and lock of fur in two separate boxes, his collar with tags, a porcelain collie made in Russia, a fossil trilobite, a tin full of fortune-cookie fortunes, a pearl spider pendant that had belonged to her grandmother, paper flowers, plastic dinosaurs, a photo of her parents, a growing collection of programs from the funerals of friends and relatives and other talismans that empowered or comforted her in one way or another.

She slipped out of her clothes and climbed into bed. Too hot to even put on a T-shirt. Then she switched the bedside light off. She tossed and turned for less time than expected and fell into a dreamless sleep. Once during the night she awoke to what sounded like a faint cicada-like hum.

In the morning, Sheila kept her appointment with A.S. Clement, scheduling the memorial for two days later—Saturday. Without the possibility of cremation and the inability to embalm, everything had to happen fast. She filled in the information for the funeral notice—apparently it could still get into tomorrow's paper if they rushed. The cheapest casket was $1575, the total bill a little less than she feared after speaking to Maddox. Dave's body would be on its way to Atlanta.

"It's the right thing to do," she whispered to herself. "The right thing to do."

She lunched later with her friend Felecia at the new Indian street-food place in her neighborhood. Confided some, but not the full state of Dave's corpse nor the weird glows of last night. She wasn't ready to talk about those things with anyone. Maybe she never would be.

"Sheila, I get that they called you and you feel some responsibility, but why don't you just let the state take care of it?" Felecia asked, twisting a strand of her dark hair with her finger like she always did.

"I don't know," Sheila said, breaking off a chunk of paratha bread and forcing herself to eat despite not really feeling hungry. "Maybe it's because I do remember his mom and that aunt with Alzheimer's. His family were so kind to me. Not their fault. And his estate'll reimburse it all."

"That is, if he doesn't have some big debt you don't know about," Felecia said. "Honey, all you ever did near the end was complain about how he couldn't handle money and you had to bail him out. If it was Jeff, I'd…"

"I know but Jeff wouldn't ever do anything like that," Sheila said, cutting her off. She didn't want to think about people who had happy marriages or at least ones that had reached that certain comfort level of a couple who knows that living together is better than living apart. Had Sheila's marriage once been like that? Dave used to tell other people how much he loved her—every person he could find, when he was drinking and not angry. He even told Felecia. Until later he only told everyone how Sheila was a controlling bitch. In any case, Felecia couldn't really understand. How could she unless she went through it? Even Sheila wasn't sure she understood her own actions or how she felt—like walking in fog.

"Did you bring it?" she asked, changing the subject. Really it was the main reason why she'd agreed to meet her friend for lunch even if Felecia was gung-ho about checking on her.

"Hell, lady, of course I did," Felecia said, slipping the baggie into Sheila's hand under the table.

"What do I owe you?"

"Nada, sister," Felecia said, shaking her head. "You know I'll always take care of you and after what you've been through, ain't no one who needs it more than you. Just don't overdo it, okay?"

"Thanks. This means a lot. Your friendship means a lot." Sheila said, slipping the weed into her purse discreetly under the table.

"So when's the service?" Felecia asked.

"Saturday, two p.m."

"That's the day after tomorrow. They can set it up that fast?"

"Had to be because there couldn't be cremation or any kind of embalming since the corpse was such a mess."

"Who do you think is going to show up? You know I'll be there only to support you, and afterwards crack open the champagne."

"Felecia!!!"

"Okay, sister, I gotcha, don't disrespect the dead, even the abusive jackasses." Felecia held her hands up.

"A lot of people still liked him, had no idea what he'd turned into, what he did to me."

"Yeah, honey, you know I ain't got no love for that asshole, but let me help you get the word out, okay?"

"Okay," Sheila nodded. "There'll be an announcement in tomorrow's paper and I've already started a mass email using our old Christmas party list."

"I'd laugh if that wasn't…"

"Yeah, it is. Listen, Felecia, I need to go home now."

"But you've barely touched your food. Don't make me worry about you."

"I'll be all right. I just need to process this all. My head feels like there's a cloud inside."

"There'll be a real cloud when you smoke that weed. You need to chill, Sheila."

"I know. You can take the leftovers."

Sheila forced a fragile smile as she rose, let Felecia wrap her stiff body in a huge hug, insisted she wait while the waiter boxed it up, thrust the handle on the plastic bag into her hand.

"Ain't no way I am taking the leftovers. You're going to want something to nibble on once the pot kicks in."

When Sheila got home, she put the food in the refrigerator. Since no rain was forecast, she commenced watering her outdoor garden. She started with the flowers in front—the daylilies had already bloomed out, but she had marigolds, geraniums, snapdragons. She worked her way around to the small rose garden against the side of the house, also pruning the buds that had already bloomed. Then she replaced the front yard hose and headed around the back to switch on the other hose. The vegetable garden by the fence contained tomato plants, banana peppers, red peppers, leeks, kale. Alas, the raspberry bushes had caught some malady and all died. That often happened after a number of years, she'd been told. She'd tried replanting but the new bushes also died. Needed to start anew in another part of the garden, she supposed though she never formally asked anyone for advice. She was the kind of gardener who mostly winged it and accepted that sometimes things didn't turn out as she hoped.

On the other side, she watered the outdoor herb garden, which also included some phlox, black-eyed susans, and an outbreak of four o'clocks which she constantly had to cut back from her blueberry bush. She needed to dig them out, but it was hard to convince herself to do it while they were in bloom, and they'd been her mom's idea. The mint was also spreading more than it should, but the leaves tasted nice in tea and sparkling water with lime. At the end, she did a little weeding. While she thought she had kept up fairly well this year, it seemed like a never-ending task—always two steps forward, one step back.

Indoors again she tried to catch up with some work—a press release due next week—found herself able to pound out the outline if not craft it completely. Good, keeping busy was helping. Turn yourself into a machine, Sheila. She thought of the replicants in *Blade Runner*. When she was younger, she empathized with Rachel, but was she now Pris? Yes, she would enjoy shattering Dave's skull with her thighs. But Dave didn't need any head-shattering any more. Did the rain yesterday camouflage the tears she actually did shed? Not for Dave. For the loss of something she could not explain. Maybe the growing old together she was supposed to have. Maybe the children she would never have. Or maybe nothing to do with

Dave at all but just how much she missed Sam's wet nose waking her up in the morning.

Sheila heated herself a light dinner of the lunch leftovers she earlier thought she wouldn't be able to eat. Then as dusk began to fall, she took the baggie out of her purse, retrieved the rolling papers from the far back of the shelf where she kept medicine and vitamin bottles. She poured out a small pile from the bag onto the cutting board, separating the lumpy or woody bits. With her fingers, she carefully measured out the right amount onto the paper, added the roach, picked up the paper and started rolling it out from the center. Once the mix felt firm and tight in the paper, she pressed down the edges and rolled the excess around the joint, wet it, and sealed it.

She pulled a box of matches out of the odds and ends drawer, lit, grasped the joint between her thumb and index finger, lifted it to her mouth and inhaled deep, held it as long as she could. She exhaled, a waft of misty smoke hovering in the kitchen. She watched it spread, dissipate, though the familiar aroma hung heavy, calling her to spin for a moment, arms out, free. Yes, the weed was exactly what she needed. Been way too long. In college, she'd been a total pothead. Why had she ever stopped? She inhaled another puff, then filled the watering can with the joint still in her fingers, and headed downstairs first. She worked her way steadily back upstairs to the kitchen and dining room, her head light and airy, her eyelids heavy and warm.

By the time she reached the orchids, only a quarter of the joint remained. She'd need to get a roach clip soon if she was going to finish. The sky outside the front window had darkened to pitch black. As the water began to moisten the soil of the first flower, the white petals seemed to brighten. And so up the row, as she watered each bloom, it switched on like a string of lights or perhaps Japanese lanterns. She'd never had a hallucination like this while smoking weed. Acid, yes. Or rather a hypersensitivity which revealed every color to be more vibrant, heightened. Could this batch be somehow enhanced? If so, Felecia hadn't mentioned anything, but it would be like her friend to decide she needed a little extra when she was under such emotional duress.

The glow spread into the leaves and tendrils, gliding in a wavelike motion back and forth, down and up, tinting the orchid plants first a more vibrant shade of their own colors and then ever more yellow-green. Sheila found herself smiling. She inhaled another hit from the joint.

The orchids began to hum.

Sheila hummed along, at first only semi-aware of the source of the melody because she hadn't heard it in years. Then she realized and jerked back.

"Time After Time." Cahn & Styne. Etta James' powerful voice belting out "so lucky." Her wedding song that she had listened to maybe only once since her first anniversary.

"No, it can't be," she whispered to herself. "Plants can't sing."

The hum grew louder, the glow intensified. "The passing years…"

She closed her eyes.

"Time…lucky…"

Screamed: "STOP!"

The sound ceased as if on her command.

She opened her eyes and the glow was gone, too, the orchids draped in shadow.

Or maybe she never really saw, heard…

Okay, clearly time for bed, let the weed gracefully float out of her system as she drifted to sleep. She started humming the Monkees theme—something funny and innocuous in an effort to expunge the ear worm.

Sheila left the can on the kitchen counter. Feeling only a little lightheaded, she headed up to the bathroom. After the weed-induced orchid light show, she couldn't face bright lights, so she left the overhead off and splashed water on her face to the muted glow of the mermaid nightlight in the socket on the counter next to the sink. Then she squeezed out some foamy cleanser, massaged it into her cheeks and forehead, rinsed it off, and lifted her head back up towards the mirror.

Someone was standing behind her

Not someone. Not a burglar or other assailant from an improperly locked door.

Dave.

Dave with a face that glowed green and that perfect round hole from his plummet onto a shaft of bamboo.

Dave with grass growing from his pores.

Dave still vaguely handsome with that smile that once made her melt.

Sheila girded herself for the attack that must be coming, but nothing. Dave just lurked luminously behind her in the glass, toothy smile frozen on his lips. His eyes were closed.

This had to be another hallucination. Yet she was shaking. What if it wasn't a pot illusion. What was it? Dave's ghost? If so, his arm would go right through her and she had nothing to fear, right? Feel weird maybe but he couldn't hurt her. A zombie would be something else. He was close enough to lean in and bite her head for her brains—no way she could dodge and get away. But such creatures were the fantasy horrors of movies and TV shows, even less likely than ghosts, weren't they? Unless you believed in voodoo—Bela Lugosi's hypnotic stare in *White Zombie*. What was Dave-whoever-it-is waiting for? Maybe the figure was just a trick of her eyes in the dark, a shadow in the dim ambiance of the nightlight?

She girded herself to turn around, when the eyelids opened, revealing sea-green irises with yellow-green sclerae, darker lime pupils.

They weren't Dave's eyes.

These eyes were *gentle. Kind. Sad.*

Then as quickly as the apparition appeared, it vanished…

…or rather it melted downwards and was gone.

Sheila waited at least a full minute, counting the seconds in her head like the distance between a lightning burst and a thunder clap. One-one hundred, two-one-hundred, three-one-hundred. The room felt quite hot now, and she was sweating—and also shaking in rapid successive twitches. Sixty-one hundred.

She swung around.

Nothing there, though she stepped again straight into a puddle. Had she splashed water, overshot some of the foam? With her foot she traced the water into the hallway, found it was drying quickly and completely dissipated again by the time she stepped over the threshold.

Which way had the water gone?

Where had the apparition gone?

No, all this was ridiculous. She had seen the corpse of her abusive ex-husband transformed into a jungle of grass and foliage with a hole in his face just yesterday. What she had seen tonight must be a mix of pot and some kind of PTSD. In Freudian or *Forbidden Planet* terms, her id was acting up.

Just go to bed, get some sleep, that's what she needed.

In her bedroom, she fell asleep faster than she expected again.

She didn't have nightmares. She didn't need to.

The next day Sheila didn't leave the house. She spent the morning typing emails and texts about the "Remembrance"—she opted out of calling it a "celebration of life"—the title of choice for memorial gatherings seemingly nowadays. She had to make a few calls, tried to give "just the facts" when she got someone on the line but was grateful for every voicemail she encountered. The funeral home called, too, with questions. No, she didn't want to do a slideshow—no time to get that together. Just a lay minister to say a few words and let people stand up and tell anecdotes if they wanted. Okay, if a song was needed—"Don't Fear the Reaper" by Blue Öyster Cult. Cliché, but Dave would have appreciated that. Fuck, why did she care what Dave would have wanted at all? She should pack earplugs in her purse.

In the afternoon, Sheila weeded some in the backyard—the slow, methodical kind of weeding that didn't cover much ground, yield much visible results, whittling her way through tiny sprouts of chickweed and the occasional resilient violet plant in the herb and vegetable gardens. The Georgia heat seeped into her even in the shade, her hair sweating under her straw garden hat, but she dragged out the lawnmower anyway. She laughed to herself how she once joked the least a man should do for a woman is mow the lawn and take out the trash. Dave did both at first, then let the mowing go so long that she had started hiring kids to do it since the gas mower was hard for her to power up. By the end, he didn't even know what day the garbage truck came.

When she took the mower clippings back to the compost pile in the far corner of the yard, she saw a crack of sun through a pine tree hit something dark green and glassy in a clump of ivy under a bush. She pulled out an empty and grimy two-liter bottle that had held cheap chardonnay. Once the backyard had been the burial ground for dozens of dead soldiers. She thought she'd found them all in past forages but every once in a while a stray body would work its way back to the surface. She wondered when she'd finally find the last one. Or if she ever would.

After tossing the bottle in the trash and tucking the mower back into the garage, she showered and checked her email for replies, answering questions with as few words as possible. For those who wanted to know how he died—three words, "Accident. Plane crash." Ignored the condolences, from both those who thought she might still care and those who knew she didn't. Once the business was done, she ate some cereal and banana—just enough sustenance to satisfy her now growling stomach. Food is medicine.

She rolled a joint, watched some TV, but couldn't concentrate even on the acidic humor of *The Simpsons*, the pot instead making her so drowsy until she gave in and stretched out on the den couch. Her eyes rolled back open around ten, and she commenced her night watering ritual, taking the remains of the joint upstairs with her. Her mind wandered, starting with what she should wear tomorrow, deciding upon a black sleeveless dress and jacket of a vintage style that Jackie Onassis might have worn to JFK's funeral. Despite all the good he did for the country and keeping the Russians at bay, he was a cad, too, for sleeping with Marilyn, right? But Jackie, she kept her integrity, held her head high. No hats at funerals though. She remembered that rule from an old white-haired Southern lady in all-pastel-floral who admonished Dave for wearing a fedora to a casual wake for the owner of their neighborhood favorite Italian restaurant.

The pot was hitting her again, cutting the seriousness into silliness, giggling at Monica's face landing smack in the alligator dung, the whole absurdity of grass growing through Dave's body. Should she have weeded his chest, too?

By this point, Sheila was at the orchids again, continuing to laugh as she lowered the spout into each pot. The pots sparkled like fairy dust, manic pixie dust, haha!

A glow began to brighten in the glass of the window. Sheila's eyes flashed onto it—it reminded her of a Lite-Brite toy from when she was a little girl. The dots formed first into a flower, but then they moved again—a face.

Someone was standing behind to her left.

Sheila stopped laughing abruptly. Okay, pot, this isn't fun anymore. Two nights in a row? No. She needed to escape reality, not be thrust back into it. After last night's incident, perhaps she should have known better than to smoke again. But she needed to relax so desperately.

Sheila turned slowly. What stood there again looked like Dave. The body nude, now grassless and hairless, effervescent green-yellow, abdomen translucent, almost see-through. A monster with tender eyes. Eyes meant to comfort her into a sense of ease now already amplified by the grass? Eyes trying to trick her? Was it a lie? Had the body been brought to her house instead of the funeral home, reanimated by some scientific procedure stipulated by Dave in secretly filed paperwork? Or was it a ghost after all? Weren't ghosts white? Maybe *Ghostbusters* actually had it right with that gooey green ectoplasm.

Okay, she was loaded with the marijuana effects. This could totally be a dream, a hallucination. Maybe she was still lying on the den couch all the while, the pot having relaxed her into a sleep.

The ghost/creature/thing just continued to stand there, stare at her, its body flowing like liquid—olive, sea-green, pine, emerald, lime, chartreuse, pistachio. Tendrils of yellow, perhaps veins or some kind of connective tissue/string, as if his body wasn't settled about what shape it belonged in. Even Dave's face was shifting now, cheeks crawling like they contained insects—would his mouth open and a nest of hornets fly out? Even the hole in his cheek was filling itself in. Then green lips spread into a smile.

Seeing that grin kicked in that crazy adrenaline she used the grass to tame. Maybe she could make a run for it after all. Keeping her gaze on the figure, she thought about the front door, but it was pitch dark and she was high as a kite. No one would believe her, and she'd get arrested for sure. So instead she mentally blocked out a plan to dash for her bedroom and slam the door.

With her eyes on the green Dave, she slowly set the watering can on the coffee table—she couldn't worry about it leaking onto books and magazines right now. She thought about throwing the joint into it, but no, if she survived whatever was happening, she'd need it more than ever. Assuming she wasn't really asleep all the while.

On the count of 1-2-3.

Sheila ran like hell down the hallway. She could feel her legs dragging from the weed's effects, but she made it to her bedroom, slammed the door shut, locked it.

Then she placed her ear to the door, listening for any sound that indicated pursuit. Nothing. Would ghosts make a sound? And couldn't they move through walls? But if it could move through walls, it would move through her, couldn't hurt her, reassured the voice in her head, spinning like a broken record.

That was when she felt moisture on her bare feet. She looked down, saw the shimmery green liquid seeping under the door. She jumped back towards the bed, her eyes now transfixed on the puddle gathering in front of the door. No longer a puddle, the mound of glimmering goo was steadily rising, shaping…legs, torso, arms and head. Eyes. Only a few feet away, no place for her to hide.

Sheila thought about how she'd read that when confronted with a lion or a bear, the best defense was to freeze, not move a muscle.

The stub of the joint was now burning her fingers. She wished she hadn't smoked it, that her head was fully alert, not groggy. And yet part of her was grateful she had. If she was going to die herself, at least she'd be relaxed. Maybe she wouldn't feel so much pain.

Again the creature stared at her, then began to slip closer, closer, until his face almost met hers. Inches away. She hadn't been this close to Dave's face, his cheekbones, his mouth for years. The eyes though. Not Dave's eyes. Dave's eyes were never so kind even when he wasn't yet a total bastard and telling her he loved her.

Were they?

The sclerae were less green now, more a lighter shade of yellow, the irises lemon, the pupils dark goldenrod. They held neither answers nor declarations but were full of questions. She couldn't tell if they bore any malice.

"What do you want with me?" Sheila asked, just above a whisper.

The head pulled back slightly, eyes still pondering. The mouth opened.

From the lips came the same hum as the plants—like cicadas or maybe a theremin, with an underscore of what she could only call the blues. Mournful. The sound sputtered for maybe a minute, then the face dissolved and the body melted down to a puddle, washed itself back under the door.

Sheila breathed deeply, realized she was shaking again. Her fingers no longer hot, her fidgeting must have extinguished the joint. She wasn't sure how long precisely it took for her to be able to move again. When she could, she set the roach on her bedside table, reached over and checked the door to make sure it was locked. She pulled her robe out of the closet and stuffed it across the threshold, the length of the door, anchored it with heavy books from her reading piles by the bed.

Then she went over to her candle shrine, picked up a box of matches on the floor, relit the joint. One deep inhale, stubbed it out again and crawled into bed. She lay a long time on her back, heart beating fast in defiance of the restfulness she ought to feel from the pot. Would it come back? Could it push out the towel and get under the door, or would the towel absorb its moisture and force the creature to ooze back out before it got inside the room? Would it be standing beside her bed in the morning? Or would it wait until night again? Where had it been all day?

Finally she turned onto her stomach and drifted somehow into sleep.

The memorial lasted nearly ninety minutes. An eternity. After a cello interlude during which attendees took their seats in the modern design nondenominational chapel, Deborah, a Unitarian lay minister who was a friend of Sheila's, said a few words and then invited people to come to the podium and share their anecdotes and remembrances about Dave. Her eyes avoiding the coffin—a heavy conundrum of dark brown wood—Sheila stared at her hands in her lap, fidgeted the red coral "freedom" ring she'd bought on the day she filed for divorce. She tried to stop imagining what Dave's corpse must look like inside, but it was hard not to. She assumed much of the plant material had been cleared away, disposed of—no composting possible because of the jet fuel—the body washed but still a dark gray-green. No embalming but did the coroner patch the hole in his face? What would they fill it with? Cotton? Wax? She had wanted to ask, but didn't want the kind folks at A.S. Clement to think her a weirdo. They already clearly felt sorry for her awkward predicament, had given her a discount on the whole shebang. The important thing was that Dave was in that wooden box. Despite the disconcerting visitations of the past two nights, she had to believe she could trust that much.

Sheila scanned to her side and back at the other attendees. She saw tears on some cheeks, some fidgeting with Kleenex, other faces stoic or inscrutable. Some of the eulogies perhaps should have reminded her of happier times, even might have been funny if she could laugh. They might have reminded her of a person Dave used to be, someone she had loved, someone she missed. But they didn't. They were not memories from her own life, but the biography of a stranger. The photos were familiar, but the man in them was no one she knew. Did she?

None mentioned Monica. Had any of them even met her? A few times Sheila heard her own name, like a supporting actress in a play or movie except she didn't remember any of her lines.

At the end, she stood up, thanked everyone for coming, and signaled for the funeral director to start playing Blue Öyster Cult's "Don't Fear the Reaper." Then like a replicant functioning by programmed commands, she walked out the side door to take her place in the foyer to greet the departing mourners.

A long line formed, each person seemingly compelled to embrace her and recite some nicety. She knew she should hug back with the full embrace of hands/arms/chest, but whenever possible, she limply tapped shoulders, grasped a wrist.

"He really loved you," said Vanessa, who was no more than an acquaintance to either her or Dave, thrusting as much emotion into her voice as she seemingly could. And then she repeated twice more: "He really loved you. He really loved you. Everybody knew that."

Vanessa launched into a years-old anecdote about Dave. Because it would have been rude to plug her ears, Sheila smiled weakly and concentrated on transforming the well-meaning voice into a Peanuts adult WAP-WAP-WAP-WAP-WAP. She wanted to run away but at least two dozen more people stretched back in line behind the woman.

Next up was Clark. She had dated him a few times right after her divorce—her rebound maybe, a super-nice guy but they never did click as lovers and ended up friends. He was dating Nancy now, who stood back a little, looking unsure about what to say since Clark had undoubtedly filled her in on the true horror story of Sheila's marriage. He had his own bad first marriage that left him with years of drowning in damage. While he'd softened now with Nancy, and his relationship with his estranged son—now in college—had improved, he still bristled with visible anger when anything reminded him of his ex. He whispered in Sheila's ear that he envied her because her ex was dead, how he wished his own ex were dead. And while she empathized—*his ex was a bitch*—that didn't help either.

Ben, who used to work at Dave's comics shop, offered her a bear hug and a "hang in there." He knew what Dave had turned into and what Sheila had suffered. The quick gesture and then move-along was better.

And so went the pattern—too much sympathy, too much glee, and the occasional relief of someone who showed sensitivity to her discomfort and the peculiarity of her position. The latter seemed to be the most likely to head for the door and not to the reception room.

To her relief, when the line finally ebbed Felecia appeared at her side, took her arm, and said, "Time for you to go home. You've greeted enough people. You need to leave these crocodile tears behind."

"Alligator tears," Sheila said, cracking a smile. "Caked on Monica's face."

"Right on, sista!" Felecia laughed so loudly that one woman headed to the reception room turned and threw a stiff glare their way.

Noticing, Felecia put a hand to her mouth to hide her grin and lowered her voice: "But I'm glad you're keeping your sense of humor. Do you need to say anything to the funeral director before we leave?"

"No, I've signed off on all the paperwork," Sheila said. "They gave me the option of being present for the internment, but once I told them the circumstances, they understood why I'd want to skip it. A part of me kind of wants to see him go into the ground, but most of me just wants to get the hell out of here."

As the two women approached the glass doors, sunlight almost blinding into the foyer, Jeff fell in line behind them, respectfully keeping his distance. When they reached his Honda Accord, he activated the electronic key and Sheila slid into the back seat despite Felecia's protestations that she should sit in front. Jeff started to reach for the radio dial, but Felecia tapped his hand, shook her head. They spent the ten-minute drive back to Sheila's house in dense silence. Felecia was the kind of friend who knew when to step back and give her space. That was why Sheila turned to her instead of one of her older friends. She hoped everyone would understand, but she knew some felt hurt that she didn't lean on them more.

After they pulled into the driveway, Jeff stayed in the car while Felecia walked Sheila to the door and followed her inside. The sun streamed in—a sliver of brightness that flowed from the door across the hardwood floor and the piles of books on the coffee table. When the door closed, the living room seemed more shadowy than she remembered despite the open curtains. Had the orchids and other plants in the front and back windows grown so much? Maybe she needed to move a few pots downstairs. Yet the touch of gloom was also a relief, the sunlight too harsh for her today. She felt a headache straining in her sinuses. And the air inside bore a cloying overhang of humidity that only made it worse.

"Is there anything else I can do for you," Felecia asked. "Jeff could pick me up later, but I'm guessing you don't want me to stay. Do you need any more weed? Food? I know you don't drink any more after Dave, but if you want to make an exception, anyone would understand. Even Benadryl to help you sleep? We can run to the store, whatever you need."

"I don't need anything, still have weed," Sheila said, forcing a smile. "I just need to be alone. I'm sure the old me will kick back in soon, just need to wrap all this crap up back into my head. Once I've done that, I'll be able to move on. He's dead after all. What can he do to me now?"

"Okay," Felecia said with a nod, giving Sheila a long tight hug. Sheila found herself accepting her friend's embrace, clinging to Felecia in a way she couldn't hold anyone else that afternoon. Part of her actually didn't want Felecia to go, was scared to be alone with whatever might be in the house with her though she still wasn't sure that wasn't just a manifestation of her imagination—all the weirdness of the past few days amplified by the pot.

Still, the part of her that wanted to be alone, her own shadow self, was in full force now. Not grief. Yes, anger. Wasn't that the second stage? And something else—a profound sense of loss that had nothing and everything to do with Dave and was inexplicable even to her. All she knew to do was bottle it back up and hope that what was left on her surface was enough to sustain her.

Sheila locked the door after Felecia left. Not time to water the plants yet, and she felt mortally tired. She lowered the temperature on the thermostat and jacked up the air-conditioning, rolled an extra-fat doobie and headed upstairs to her bedroom. She set the joint in the ashtray by her bedside and her cellphone next to it. Next she lit all seven candles on her shrine, whispered a plea for some kind of direction from her dead—Sam and her parents, other friends lost too soon. Then she slipped out of her dress and jacket, hung both carefully on a hanger and placed them back into the

closet. She lay on her back, pulled the pale green leaf-patterned sheets up to her shoulders, picked up the joint and lit it.

Yes, that was better. By the second drag, her eyes began to water and serenity wafted through her head. By the third toke, her head floated heavy as if an undertow was pulling it down. She stubbed out the joint, rolled onto her stomach, closed her eyes, and allowed herself to submerge.

Literal wetness wakes Sheila—from her hair to her toes, like she's lying in a long puddle, or a baby wading pool, or just emerged from swimming so exhausted she's collapsed on her bed without remembering to towel off. Yet she hasn't been swimming and the liquid doesn't feel like pure water, has a viscous, lotion-like sensation. Did she sleepwalk into her tub, run a bath thick with bubbles and gel as a balm to her confusion?

Whatever. So soothing, she closes her eyes.

A little while later, she wakes again, realizes that at some point in the night, she must have slipped off her T-shirt and knocked away the sheet, rather than pulling up the comforter as she usually does when the AC kicks in. But the water isn't cold, it's the just-right warm temperature she can never quite achieve in the shower—a happy memory of the time she indulged in a full-body seaweed wrap, a perk from a spa client. She curls tighter—almost into a ball—the syrupy liquid rising with her movement and shifting to cradle her. A miniature greenish-yellow waterfall crests her elbow and streams down towards her hand. Creamy, warm, alien, not a wet dream in the sexual sense but the best wet dream ever?

Thanks, Felecia, because this is the most crazy awesome pot ever.

She wonders what time it is, glances over at the shrine for a clue. The tall pillar candle is still burning, though the tea lights have expired. Her blue curtains are drawn but pitch dark, so it has to be full night—if the sun was still up, some light would filter through. Finally she thinks to check her cellphone: 10:45 p.m. She's slept a solid five hours.

A humid, floral scent permeates the air, reminding her of the thick sweetness of the Orchid House at the Atlanta Botanical Garden. She notices her hand, curled next to her face, is glowing. Her entire body is glowing—the color and consistency the same as the recent glimmer of her own orchids, the light on Dave's dead body. No, something separate from her, the orchids, Dave—what's shimmering is the gelatinous liquid immersing her. Sheila stretches, repositions herself again, rolls on her side. The substance follows, matching her every move.

Arms wrap around her, legs against her legs, a smooth wet chest against her back—*a man against her buttocks.* Someone is spooning her. At first, tempered by pot drowsiness, the sensation seems pleasant.

Then realization sets in, followed by panic. Her adrenaline shoots up. Her heartbeat races. Is this what it feels like right before a rape? She's been hit but never undergone that ultimate violation. Dave's blows were usually preceded by arguments. She often didn't see the anger escalating until it was too late to dodge a blow but it wasn't as if she didn't have any warning. She doesn't want to turn around and face her assailant, anger him so he hurts her worse. She wants to pull away, but she doesn't have the energy to fight. Maybe if she lies still, whoever he is will just go away. Maybe it's just another bad dream.

But she knows who/what was holding her. She knows it looks like Dave. The sticky moisture gives him/it away. No rapist has crept through a window, broken in via the back door while she was away at the memorial. It has been hiding in the house with her since she returned from Woodbine. It rode in the car with her. It has been biding its time.

Yet despite having scared her, not once has it hurt her—that and its tender eyes her only reassurance that it isn't some manifestation of Dave.

Not yet anyway.

What is it waiting for?

If she's going to escape, she has to move so fast it won't have time to solidify and tighten its adhesive grip. How fast can it move? Will it chase her in human form or melt into a puddle again and glide snakelike across the floor. If the latter, can she outrun it? She pictures it winding itself around her ankle, up her leg, like a python, then squeezing.

And where can she run—the front door? Does she have time to grab her robe from the bathroom or will she have to run outside naked?

The body or whatever lies beside her is growing warmer. It starts to hum the same strange cross between cicadas and a theremin as the night before when she was watering the orchids. Her mind floods with images.

Swimming in a river thick with mud, undulating snakelike, long and slender, propelling forward with webbed limbs that stretch and retract, reshaping with each motion into something different. Slithering around driftwood and roots in the green, murky water, contracting into a thin line to wind through gaps in reeds and vines and lily pads, diving deep beneath to avoid a massive piece of driftwood…the unmistakable shape viewed from beneath—an alligator lounging on the water's surface.

Joy and solitude meld, the knowledge that no other exists like you.

Then a deep weight of sorrow, like an anchor caught in waterbed mud.

Once there were others.

All gone now.

Sheila's feelings of uncertainty and danger melt away, replaced by inexplicable comfort and safety—emotions she's had to relearn after years of living on tenterhooks and never wholly recovered. Her self-education on how to compartmentalize pain both emotional and physical has worn away over the past few days since that unexpected early morning call. Surely trusting whatever is holding her is as reckless as trusting Dave, but she slowly eases herself out of the spoon and turns if only to see:

Dave's countenance, yellow-green, with no wavy hair but gentle sea-green eyes. The creature, the not-Dave, the not-ghost, corporeal but more liquid than solid, pulls back from holding her, slides sideways in a fluid movement resembling a receding tide. She feels her body drying and, within seconds, restored from green glow to natural nude. Is it being respectful of her space? No hint of intended violence shows in the eyes. Aren't the eyes the window into the soul? Not the religious soul, she thinks, but the secular soul—the essence of what a person is.

But this thing isn't a person. Dave's eyes hid lies. How can she trust eyes in a face that looks like Dave's?

The two stare at each other for what seems like a long time to Sheila, but is probably only minutes. The being on the bed resembles naked Dave lying on his side, head propped with crooked arm, only hairless and many shades of green—all fluid, flowing, glowing, translucent. Gradually the face changes and restructures, resembling Dave less and less. The nose thins, the eyes expand, cheekbones become more defined, lips widen—mouth shut and serious. It's sensing her thoughts, her discomfort with Dave's visage.

Does it only mirror Dave because that is all it knows to look like?

Does it/he want to please her?

Sheila stretches a hand out towards a green cheek, her fingers sinking into a moist doughy substance with a consistency that reminds her initially of Play-Doh. No, not that solid. A better comparison is Green Slime, the gooey stuff that came in jars when she was a little girl. As she pulls her fingers out, the slippery substance sticks to them at first like the toy. Then it gradually loosens and melts back into the face.

Sheila laughs softly.

The green slime monster man looks confused, mouth contorting into a frown. Did she hurt him with her laughter?

"It's all right," she says. "I'm not laughing at you. It's just the way you feel—it's so different, like nothing I've ever touched."

Does it understand what she's saying?

Yes, his mouth rapidly spreads into a grin, revealing gummy green teeth. Laughs, too, but the sound is unlike any human laugh. Insect-like maybe. Is it mimicking her? Is it mocking her?

Waves of warmth, relaxation, and happiness wash into Sheila's mind. The emotions feel alien—only dimly remembered. She thinks again of Green Slime and the silliness of it sticking to her fingers, and making a Blob that attacked her little plastic dinosaurs. And having to wash them well to get all the goo off and using Mr. Bubble. Do they still make Mr. Bubble? Do they still make Green Slime? Did other little girls play Green Slime stars as *The Blob Versus the Lost Valley of the Little Dinosaurs*? Or was she just the lone weirdo girl who preferred plastic prehistoric creatures to dolls?

Other little girls had sisters and brothers, but Sheila was an only child. While she had friends, she also spent a lot of time playing by herself. She still liked being alone most of the time, got used to it, could spend her entire day alone. She often supposed that was why she was good at the freelance life. Some people didn't have the discipline to work at home. She liked making and keeping her own schedule, not having to think up small talk by the water-cooler and especially avoiding corrosive office politics. Her first PR stint with a comic book publisher—the job through which she met Dave—had been office toxicity at its worst. A unit publicist/office manager-gig with an independent film company had been much better, but her boss there had suffered from depression and eventually fired everyone to move to Japan and study ninjutsu. Before Dave became a full-blown abusive alcoholic, he'd been gone all day at the shop, sometimes till late at night. They'd watch a little TV on the den couch and then sleep together. Most nights they didn't even snuggle, but not lying alone in bed had been surprisingly nice.

Even after Dave began to hurt her, she was never afraid of him in bed. Later that realization chilled her.

Is that why she isn't worried now? If so, should that worry her more?

Her positive-negative thoughts about Dave yank Sheila out of her little-girl flashback reverie. The strange green man's expression suggests he knows she is thinking of Dave. She's actually remembered what it was like to be with Dave.

That makes it all worse.

She begins to cry.

His face reshapes itself even more, now less and less human. His gelatinous body slides closer to her. She lets him. At that moment, she trusts the slime monster, like she always trusted Godzilla and Gorgo and the Creature from the Black Lagoon and the Beast in Cocteau's movie. Not that she is any Beauty. Though over forty, she still feels like that same geeky punk rock girl with average looks and a brain and imagination so big that the guys she liked when she was young ran away. She grew bored with those who didn't run away because they elevated her on a pedestal and she felt uncomfortable with anyone who would worship her. As glutinous hands wrap around her back, she remembers how she used to wonder if she could even sustain a long-term relationship until Dave. Why were things different with Dave? He wasn't one of the misunderstood monsters of the movies. He really was a monster.

Wet lips press upon hers, teeth like gelatin, no biting but nibbling, serpentine tongue licking, sticking deep, sweet-tasting, refreshing.

Was this what it was like to be kissed by an amphibian? Was he the real frog prince? Would he turn into a human man if she kissed back?

No, no, please no more human men.

Warm, gummy fingers massage her back, slip down to her buttocks to give them a squeeze. Viscoelastic body molds to hers, shakes, stretches, stiffens where it should stiffen. She feels her own juices gushing inside her with arousal. She reaches to guide him, but no need. Like a river, he is surging in and once inside, hardening. His arms release and flail outward as he begins deep rapid thrusts. Her body shudders, her hips now moving in rhythm with his, and she moans with joy.

She's never had sex in water before, much less sex that is…she knows it reminds her of something.

Swimming.

Yes, that's it.

He's *swimming* her.

She can't describe it any better than that, frog-like strokes, legs and arms spread wide and penis pounding inside her.

Driving deeper, deeper, deeper…

And then the body spreads and is no longer body, no face, just yellow-green mucoid matter filled with squiggly floaters like one sees when one closes one's eyes.

Maybe her eyes are shut. All she can think about is the constant pressure between her legs, the constant pleasure, the building orgasm, so close, so close.

Her body shudders, then cries out.

And shudders again.

Again.

Then he shrieks—a shrill birdlike wail!

Is he orgasming?

She feels a gush of warm, wet goo rush inside her as he withdraws, the syrupy substance flushes out onto her thighs and then swims back into him. Hovering above her, she sees the length of the appendage that was inside her—a tendril longer than she ever thought she could sustain and yet there was no pain, only pleasure. She wants to pull him back inside her but it collapses into the gooey puddle of shimmering blob in which she's lying.

The jelly-like mass congeals quickly, reconstituting arms and legs and head, curves beside her, shifts her back into the spoon. It nibbles and laps at her neck, then lays its viscid head against her shoulder.

While a moment ago she reverberated with energy, now her eyes again feel heavy with drowsiness…

The cries of terror—too shrill for human ears but terrible in their urgency. She wants to throw hands to her ears to quiet them but their melancholy compels listening. Above, a vast panorama of stars, so clear that one can see the wispy tendrils of the Milky Way. The big, beautiful sky makes no judgement, feels no remorse, just is, as green and yellow glimmering shapes and fissures surface in the dark water. And then the black substance so thick and viscous and moving too quickly to swim or wade away, their moist biology stuck like glue in the muck. An abyss in incessant, monstrous motion, consuming birds, snakes, turtles, and creatures that pre-date all men. A bubbling stew of glow and pitch black, eyes and mouths and limbs and tendrils. Shrinking small, expanding large, nothing helps, nothing saves. And the chemical stench—the same on Dave's body but one hundred times stronger. She recognizes this black death born of dinosaurs which humans wrenched from far inside the earth, beneath the nearby sea, deeper than they were meant to dig. From the bayou, she knows when it happened, not that long ago. The BP oil spill.

Far enough ahead of the pack, slithering onto the low hanging Spanish moss, shimmying onto the branches, melding with the bark. Cries fade to silence, merging with the muck until they are no more. A sorrow so immense it makes her own calamities seem like mere trifles.

Can't touch the water and have to find other ways, climbing high and where the trees subside, touching only the tallest tips of the grasses until this marsh bayou is a memory. Then crawling along the ground a long, long way, drying almost to nothing.

Like a movie projector shutting off, the images in her head cut as quickly and unexpectedly as they began. The slime monster man still holds her, his body not withered but slick and wet and melded tight to her. Kissing her forehead and her cheeks, mouth on her lips, teeth spongy like marshmallow.

Liquid and light merge. The bedroom shimmers yellow-green, her body tingles as what feels like a tongue but isn't really a tongue explores her breasts, what feels like lips suck on her nipples, lap and nibble down her stomach, kiss her clit. A hand-like appendage slips inside her, strokes her G-spot, triggering waves of orgasm.

A longing for connection as strong as her own. Not a voice, but an emotional and physical conjoining as if this thing has been waiting for her and she has been waiting for it or him. Should she call it love-making? Whatever it wants, she lets it explore until exhausted, she falls into a deep dreamless sleep.

When Sheila wakes, a ray of muted sunlight shines in through a crack in the blue curtains, her body is dry, and the AC is blowing cold air from the vent by the bed. Shivering, she reaches down and pulls up her comforter. Where is the strange being that shared her bed last night? She feels a pang of regret that there will be no morning orgasm, remembers how Dave used to complain that she preferred sex at night when he was ready to sleep after a day of drinking. She used to have so little energy in the morning before coffee. Now she wants to have sex any time, all the time.

She eyes the half-smoked doobie in the ashtray by the bedside, but instead swings her feet out the side of the bed. Rising, she slips on her dressing gown, heads down to the kitchen. Mmmm, she thinks, the scent of the herbs on the windowsill seems stronger, more savory than usual. Still lightheaded from recent waking, she plunges straight into her routine—pours grapefruit juice, pops a birth control pill. Does she need it when she's fucking a being that defies science? Would it even work on preventing a monster baby, assuming their biologies could even allow impregnation? Well, at one time, she had wanted to be a mom, ha-ha!

She makes coffee and toast, spreads two slices with butter and raspberry jam, then takes the mug and plate into the living room and sits down on the couch. Because she went straight to bed after the memorial, she realizes she never watered the plants. She feels guilt for a moment, then thinks surely they could go one day. Yet they don't look neglected. If anything, more orchids have sprouted, their hairy roots multiplied. No wonder the room is so shadowy—even darker than yesterday. She doesn't mind. She likes it.

Glancing over at the cherrywood case in front of the dining room window, she notices the red angel wing begonia and golden pothos look larger than she remembered. The philodendron has definitely outgrown its pot and urgently needs transplanting. The snake plant has shot upwards, and the staghorn fern also seems thicker, its hanging basket inadequate. The aloe hasn't reached that point, but its tendrils hang over the edges of its yellow and green porcelain vessel, even more reminiscent of its namesake Audrey in *Little Shoppe of Horrors*. Except that it was Dave who named it. She regrets remembering that immediately—the second time she's consciously thought of him this morning.

Only the cactus doesn't look well—having turned a dark sickly green as if over-watered, yet she hasn't given it a drop for at least a week. Has she? The last time she watered, she was high. Maybe she did water the cactus and just doesn't remember. So much has happened in the space of a few days.

And yet when she finishes her coffee and walks downstairs to the den, she sees the same with the plants down there. Everything has seemingly grown larger and more verdant than ever before. The black velvet plant required some nursing when she acquired it from a friend, but now its leaves are a deep dark green, almost black. The downstairs philodendron and Madagascar palm look ready for transplanting. She's never seen so many leaves on a dragon tree. Again only the cacti look unhealthy, overwatered like survivors of a flash flood in the desert. If they get any more water, they'll likely die.

Sheila smiles, knowing only one explanation can account for the sudden fertility in her home. She glances down at the DVD player—ten thirty a.m., a long time till nightfall. She can't explain her sudden kinship with the strange slime monster man, but she now eagerly anticipates his return.

She'll have to find some way to keep herself occupied while waiting. She starts with a shower though oddly after all that sex she isn't sweaty. Then she brushes her teeth and dresses in a T-shirt and jeans. Noon now, she switches on her Mac, checks both her main email addresses, Facebook, Twitter, the traffic counts on her blog. Damn, only twelve thirty p.m.

The phone rings—Felecia calling to check on her. She tells her friend she's "all right, doesn't need anything" but a quiet Sunday, that she's going to water her plants and watch movies. From the concerned tone in Felecia's voice, she can tell her friend isn't buying her answers, but she doesn't press when Sheila says goodbye.

What is she going to do? Outdoor gardening could make the hours pass, but even the sunshine coming in through the windows above her desk strains her eyes. She pulls the shades down and heads back to her bedroom, lights up the half-smoked joint, sits on her bed, legs crossed, takes a deep toke. She concentrates on the candlelight from the shrine flickering just beyond its end, meditating on the flames, wills herself not to think about anything, especially not Dave. At some point, she lays the joint, now down to a quarter, in the ashtray by her bed and closes her eyes.

The scene in The Creature from the Black Lagoon *where Julie Adams swims oblivious to the Creature plays out in her mind, a primal memory rather than a scene from a movie. Except the green slime man, not the creature, swims with her.*

Alligators also swim in the warm water, and soon she doesn't see him at all. Only their long toothy snouts next to her, above and beneath, in a dance that surely will result in her death. Dread wells within her, but the alligators fall away, one by one, the green slime man shooing them like cats, swimming beside her again.

New things appear beside, above, below. The Others of its kind. Very old, older than memory. Swimming together—one with the water and also thicker than water, lighter at the surface and heavier when diving deep among the reeds. All different shapes. Some like men, like women. Some like snakes or frogs. Some like things that humans have never seen, with thin tendrils and eyes and mouths in the wrong places. All glowing, green, yellow, and also sometimes blue and pearl white.

They don't seem to see her, but that's because she's one of them. Rising onto liquid limbs to wade through shallow water tall grasses. Some two legs, some four, some six, some more, some not legs at all. The grasses don't sting their appendages but pass right through, mud grasping and giving way. Gnats buzz, mosquitos whine, hot air heavy with humidity, snakes curve and glide in the dark green water. Waiting, waiting, eyes just above the muck.

She wakes, soaked and sticky as if she really has been swimming in a humid swamp. Her companion is not in humanoid form but spread across her like a warm glowing gelatin blanket. Some light bleeds in through the drapes so it's not night yet. She strokes, starting with her arms and then her chest and down to her tummy, rubbing it in like lotion. The substance spreads with her fingers like dough stretching, only it quivers as she kneads it into herself and vibrates against her skin, causing a tingling sensation. Occasional flashes of light pulse and dim. And humming.

When she reaches her groin, she starts to guide it inside her, finds it soon entering on its own like liquid into a drain. At first it feels like her own juices, and then more like wet clay. She finds she can mold it with her fingers, massage it into her G-spot. When she withdraws her hand, her inside continues to tingle as it did outside. She lies back and gives into another cycle of pleasure that begins again as soon as it ebbs. She loses count of the orgasms, the room dark now except for the shrine candle, but eventually the sound and sensation rock her back into sleep.

A big black bear walks on the far end of the bayou. Watching them move as one, merge into one, the chatter of hive brain with one desire in her head—hunger—stream in a V motion across the water towards the bank. So fast the beast only can make a quick moan as the amoeboid mass pulls up onto the shore, devours it, not with teeth but absorbing like/not like a sponge the life-sustaining moisture until the dry carcass of fur and bone falls to the grassy ground.

A light flashes on the frenzy and the mass turns. A wide-beam flashlight held by the shadowy outline of a man in a mud boat on the water. The motor is off, so he must've been rowing. Late to check the shrimp nets but what does she know? Perhaps some other late night business—maybe he'd just dumped a body.

Again in one motion, the creatures dive and glide. This time she swims to join them, reaching the edge of the wooden vessel within seconds. The man doesn't have time to grab the shotgun at his side, fire up the motor.

He drops the light as she, with the others, squeezes his body, spreading into a blob of sentience and mouth, lips but no teeth. Thick saliva, or some viscous excretion, exudes from her form, acidulating flannel shirt and jeans. She tastes and smells salty, sweaty, hairy skin followed by slippery, warm flesh like savory rare steak. Organs dry to crinkled paper, empty like torn water balloons, gulps of coppery blood. Stringy veins harden to rope and then soften to brittle and crumble apart. Her stomach feels full, content, like after a delicious meal, only she is all stomach. Gelatinous and still bonded with the others, she expands, lifts and tosses the remains into the dank water, leaving only confetti-size bits of skin, nails, teeth, dried veins, organ lining scattered in the boat.

Sheila wakes with a jerk to full dark—even the candle has burnt out—and liquid limbs spoon her again. "Fingers" caress her shaking body, stroke her soaked hair and cheek. She senses an intention—to comfort her. Sweet humid air fills her nostrils, more humming. She shifts to her back and sees a face even less human than the night before—a globular head with no nose and round green eyes with saucer-shaped slits in their centers. She wants to let it touch her again, craves that in a way she cannot explain even to herself. But the dream-memory looms fresh, the sensation of breaking

apart and ingesting another human being, and worse, of liking it. The thing next to her has shed all features of Dave, but like Dave, does it hold secrets? How thin is its line between tenderness and violence? Surely it would have already devoured her if it was going to—its kin wasted no time with the bear or the man in the boat. Even if it wants to mend its own loneliness, can it control its own instincts, its hunger? Why does it allow her to see? Is it warning her? Or does it not have complete control over its symbiosis with her mind? Does she just dream what it dreams?

She senses it knows that she now knows about its other side, that she fears it, that it's turning that over in its own brain. Except where is its brain? Its entire being seems raw sentience—something between mind and matter. She wonders if her tenuous hold on reality is simply fraying at the edges. Will Felecia eventually find her huddled in a ball on the floor moaning gibberish, and she'll end up in a straitjacket in a mental institution?

No, the creature is real, as alive, if unlikely, as Dave is dead. Alone and deadly.

She kisses the slime monster man where its mouth should be, lips and tongues forming to meet her own.

"*Where did you learn to kiss?*" she whispers.

"*From you,*" hums a chittering voice in her head.

Is it really talking or just parroting what she wants to hear?

She lets it enter her again. The room pulsates with flashing lights, creating a wild panorama on the ceiling—as if fireworks were flowers but among them things move, squiggly amoeboid things.

Days fall into a new routine. Sheila wakes to a dry bed, her green slime companion gone. She goes down to the kitchen long enough to make coffee and eat toast or cereal or yoghurt. Then she showers and brushes her teeth and crawls back into bed. She carried the baggie of pot up on the first day, along with her rolling papers and a lighter, and a supply of candles to replenish the shrine. She doesn't want to think about them running out—having to leave the house to shop or meet up with Felecia. Maybe Felecia would bring her weed and candles, but she doesn't want anyone else in the house either.

Sometimes she listens to music, mostly jazz, on her laptop, which she keeps on a stool by her bed. On the bed, it could get wet if the slime man shows up sooner than she expects or she forgets to move it and falls asleep. She tries to watch movies, but finds she can't concentrate long enough. She checks email, deletes spam and newsletters. Among the rest some work-related but mostly people offering condolences, "understanding." Some she hasn't heard from in years. She stops reading usually after the first line. Replies can wait. She doesn't have the energy or desire right now. Sometimes the phone rings but she's got voicemail. Calls also can be returned later when she's not so tired.

Later in the day she goes down and forages in the pantry and the fridge for a little more food, maybe a stray apple or orange or she'll boil up macaroni or a can of beans or the rest of the frozen peas. She quickly finishes the chunk of cheddar cheese and the half-jar of homemade salsa from her friend Laura with the last dregs of the blue-corn chips. Just enough not to starve. The pot does make her a little hungry, enough to even eat that can of Pringles she'd bought only in case of unexpected guests, and all the wheat crackers. The food and the weed make her drowsy again and she falls in and out of naps, sometimes remembering her dreams and sometimes not. The worst are the ones where Dave and she are married again and everything's normal, he's acting charming and nice, and everyone else thinks they are the perfect couple. He never hits her, but she knows he might change at any moment.

As the sun fades in the window, she wakes and finds her companion in bed again—sometimes in man-shape curled against her, other times a luminous gelatinous quilt that reflects up onto the ceiling, pulsating with green and yellow flashes and her eyes become entranced in watching the squiggly movements like a looking glass into the late Proterozoic era when Earth was all water and the first life formed in fertile oceans. Was its kind that old—a survivor from earth's earliest birth pangs? Or did it come from elsewhere, from outer space or cross from another dimension? Did it even know?

Sometimes the creature forms the long tendril-like cock and pounds her. Other times it liquefies and oozes inside her, massaging in all her most sensitive places. Or spreads a tingling mass across her, as if a hundred tiny mouths are nibbling on her neck, her nipples, her thighs. Is it exercising self-restraint? How much harder would it have to bite to absorb her? And sometimes it turns her over and enters her that way, rubbing her G-spot from the other side, too.

All punctuated by dreams of swimming and the swamp. The others no longer appear—maybe it senses how their appetite disturbs her. Maybe it no longer misses them as much now that it has her. The other players are now alligators, turtles, otters, sandhill cranes regal on long legs, and water moccasins—scarier than alligators because while smaller they move a hell of a lot faster. Whenever any animal ventures too close, however, it embraces it fast and squid-like, squeezing to the kill.

At first the sensation of absorption is unsettling, but she soon learns to appreciate how it sates her thirst even as the beasts wither and crack in its embrace which also is hers, their flaky debris dissipating in the water.

Is that the doorbell ringing? Faint, she remembers how she meant to replace it with a louder chime.

Knocking.

Pounding.

"Go away, Dave. I don't want you here," she murmurs drowsily, rolls over. "I got a restraining order. The police will arrest you."

Especially while she's trying to rest. She needs her energy when her monster returns at dusk.

More sounds like fumbling with a key in the lock.

A familiar voice calls:

"Sheila! Are you here?"

Female. Felecia. Doesn't her friend know Sheila wants to be left alone, that she needs to sleep. How does Felecia have a key? Oh, yeah, she walked and fed Sam and watered her plants when she was away to take her dad's ashes to be buried.

"You haven't been answering the phone. I got worried," Felecia continues, her voice loud but not shouting. "Jeff's away so I thought I'd come over. I can make dinner, stay the night, even a couple of days. I've got some more grass for you."

The door creaking as someone pushes it shut.

"Go away," Sheila whispers. "I'm fine."

Why can't she speak any louder. She's so tired.

"My God, the orchids," Felecia's voice like a ghost. "It looks like they haven't gotten any water since I saw you a week ago. All the plants. The kitchen! Sheila, this isn't like you. Are you upstairs? I'm coming up! I bet you haven't been eating."

Except she doesn't come upstairs.

From the AC vent, a shrill metallic hum rises up from the den.

Felecia must hear it, too, because the sound of footsteps on stairs go down instead of up.

Followed by rustling, vigorous but quick.

Then squishing.

Then silence.

"Felecia," Sheila calls out now, her voice back.

No answer.

Just another dream.

She rolls over, shuts her eyes again.

When she opens them, her lover seems more luminescent, more dense. He'd seemed a little faded and weaker yesterday, hadn't he? She can't really remember. Maybe there isn't any change at all. What day was yesterday? Was Felecia here? Did she say she brought more weed. She hopes she left it if she did. The bag is almost empty, maybe enough for one more joint.

Her lover is inside her now. She'll call Felecia tomorrow.

The cellphone ring woke Sheila. She answered it, half-asleep.

"Hi, Sheila, it's Jeff."

"Oh, hi, Jeff," she said. Why did she answer? She didn't want to talk to anyone. "Sorry, I was still in bed."

What time was it anyway? Sunlight shone in through the crack in the curtains, and her companion had gone to wherever he went during the day.

"Listen, have you heard from Felecia?"

"No, no, we haven't talked in days," Sheila said.

"I'm in Detroit on business, but I'm worried," Jeff said, his voice shaky. "She didn't call me last night and she's not answering her cellphone this morning either. Yesterday she told me she was going to drop by and check on you."

A fuzzy memory flashed in Sheila's mind—Felecia's voice calling out to her. Was her friend here yesterday? She didn't remember her coming upstairs. She glanced by the bedside—the almost empty bag of pot.

"Sheila, are you there?" Jeff said.

"Uh, yeah, I'm sorry, Jeff, but I haven't seen her. She didn't come here."

"It's just not like her. If we're apart, we always at least text a good night kiss."

"I'm so sorry, Jeff. If I hear from her, I'll call you right away. Maybe her phone died, or you know how cell signals can be."

"Yeah, must be that, but night *and* morning, that's a long time. She would know I'd get worried, get a new phone, call from a neighbor's. You promise you'll ask her to call me right away if you hear from her?"

"Of course, I promise."

"Sheila, are you okay? You sound really…out of it."

"Yeah, Jeff, I'm fine. You just woke me up, that's all."

"Sorry, it's nearly noon. I figured you'd be up."

"Really tired, think I might be coming down with a cold."

"All right, just have her call or text me if you hear from her."

"Yup."

"And I'll let you know if I hear from her. If it's not soon, guess I'll call a neighbor to check on her. And if she doesn't answer, I guess, the police. I don't want to even think about that."

"No, Jeff, don't. I'm sure it's just her phone."

"Yeah, must be, keep telling myself that. Thanks, talk to you later, Sheila."

"Good luck. Bye, Jeff."

Sheila laid the phone down on the bedside table and her head back on a pillow. So strange hearing a human voice. How long had it been? She realized she's lost count of the days since Dave's memorial. Jeff sounded really stressed. Felecia's fine, right? She was always so good at taking care of herself.

The knocking yesterday. Her voice. Was she here?

No, that had to be a dream. Because if she was, she would have come upstairs, and she would have left a new baggie of grass.

Sheila also remembered hearing footsteps going downstairs, that weird rustling noise. How much more vibrant the slime man was last night. The sex especially passionate, vigorous.

No, no, Felecia didn't come.

Did she?

Sheila didn't want to get out of bed. If only someone would bring her coffee so she could get a jump start with caffeine.

Dave used to do that.

She'd knock on the floor to let him know she was awake, and within ten minutes, he'd be up with a hot mug, just the right splash of skim milk.

Then she remembered how he started to get angry at her knocking, tell her what a demanding bitch she was expecting he bring her coffee. Except she never asked in the beginning. It was *his* idea. His snapping at her was just another symptom of drinking first thing in the morning. She used to be able to count on him being nice at least first thing in the morning.

She stopped knocking on the floor, got used to prepping the coffee maker the night before and then sleepily creeping down and switching it on. She hadn't even done that last night—not since her slime companion arrived. She wasn't in any rush to wake up any more.

Still, she forced herself out of bed, threw on bra, T-shirt, panties, jeans—just in case anyone happened by the windows. She paused at the bathroom, took a quick glance at her limp, tousled hair—the result of it getting wet without washing over and over and air-drying in bed. When did she last wash it? Take a shower? Brush her teeth even? Crap, she looked awful.

She really should shower today, but first she had to go look. She had to make sure Felecia wasn't here.

"What the fuck," she said aloud, shielding her eyes as she walked down the steps into the living room. The room was flushed with sunlight. It only took her a moment to see why—the wilted orchids, the leaves brown and shriveled, dried remnants fallen on the floor in front. Only a few days ago, they'd been so thick and vibrant, hadn't they? But when did she last come down and check?

Didn't Dream-Felecia's voice say something about the plants looking bad? She glanced at the front door—shut and locked, but she'd heard Felecia close it so that didn't tell her anything.

Sheila looked down the second set of stairs. Empty steps. Seemingly untouched. She didn't have to go down there, did she? Felecia wasn't here.

Reluctantly Sheila descended. Dried leaves crunched under her bare feet as she entered the room. Dead brown foliage blanketed the carpet like an autumn yard. Ceramic pots stood empty or held only brown stems or trunks. Even the cacti were reduced to shriveled husks.

But no Felecia.

She bent down to examine a leaf, felt it crumble in her fingers from the barest touch. Kneeling now, she scanned the devastation—years of planting withered and dead. Not children, not even dogs, but they'd been friends of a sort, hadn't they? Dependent on her, grateful, gave her some kind of satisfaction, purpose.

To her right, she saw something that filled her with dread—a green plastic case. She reached over, picked it up, and turned it over. Felecia's cellphone. With two quick strokes of her index finger, she lit the screen, unlocked it. Missed message.

"*where r u, baby? pls answer. worried sick.*"

Near it a set of keys and something else unmistakable—a plastic baggie. Sheila picked the latter up, too, stood and held it up. Ziploc quart, three-quarters-full, just what the doctor ordered.

She wanted to roll a joint right then and crawl back into bed, but she instead went up to the kitchen to make coffee. She set the cellphone and baggie on the counter, then filled the carafe with water, washing crumpled dead leaves from the spice pots on the windowsill down the drain after. She emptied three scoops into the filter—enough for four cups. She needed to wake up. She needed to ponder questions, even if she knew she likely wouldn't like the answers.

Oh, Felecia. Why didn't I take the key back from you? Why did you have to come check on me? Why did you have to be such a good friend?

Yet if Felecia hadn't come, would it have devoured Sheila instead? Not because it wanted to, but because it'd already absorbed all the water from every other living thing in the house?

The only substance she knew would destroy it was oil. That was what wiped out all the others, right? She thought about the five-gallon jug of gas for the lawnmower in the garage. It had to be at least half full. Would that be enough? Maybe she could drain whatever was left in the mower, too. What would she use to do that though? The opening wasn't very wide. Maybe a turkey baster? Would the oil eat through the plastic? That would take a long time, too. What if it realized what she was doing before she finished? Where did it go during the day? Did it already know she had gone down to the den? What she saw? It could read her thoughts, right.

Oh, good, coffee's ready.

She poured some into the mug, checked the fridge, discovered she was out of milk. She would have to drink it black. "Caffeine is medicine," she mouthed to herself, adding a dribble of cold water from the tap to chill it to a drinkable heat.

A few sips in, and her thoughts came clearer. No, no, it loved her. It wouldn't kill her. It only absorbed Felecia because it had no choice—it was starving. Why didn't she realize it was sustaining itself from her plants and that they would be a finite source? At first after its arrival, the plants had looked so verdant, healthy. She shouldn't have just lain in bed, taking pleasure from it, not giving back. How selfish of her.

It didn't understand that she could provide it nourishment, just like she gave the plants. All she had to do was fill up the tub, run the shower. Why didn't she think of this earlier? Of course, it didn't comprehend modern plumbing. She had to tell it.

She ran a new plan over in her head. Every morning when she got up, she'd run the bath and leave the tub full.

No, no, before sundown. It rose before her in the morning and might need water right away. She could also fill up all the sinks, keep them stoppered. And buckets. And pots. And bowls. And coolers. They held a lot of water. She could bring the plastic recycle bin inside. Water all the time, all over the house. Wasn't there even an inflatable baby pool left over from a luau party?

Yeah, it'd be just fine. It cared about her. All it needed was water.

The cellphone vibrated and flashed. She picked it up. Another text: "*calling police in hr if don't hear from u.*"

Fuck.

All of Sheila's plans imploded in a second.

If Jeff called the police, how long until they came here to question her? And didn't they even have ways of tracking cellphones now with GPS? That'd lead them right here. She could drive out and ditch the phone somewhere, but Jeff would still tell them how Felecia said she was coming to see Sheila. And she was Felecia's best friend—didn't that automatically mandate a police visit?

She looked around at the dead leaves, the dirty dishes on the kitchen counters, the baggie of pot. Even if she hid it and they didn't have a warrant, the house reeked of pot. In the best-case scenario, they'd just arrest her for use/possession.

The best-case scenario.

Or worse—perhaps her viscous companion would seek to protect her or even simply perceive them as another meal, absorb them, too.

That would bring more police.

Could he absorb them all?

Police had families. They couldn't all be bad cops. She remembered Deputy Jones. He seemed nice.

She gulped down the rest of the cup of coffee, then poured another.

She had only one thing she could do. It wasn't what she wanted to do, but it was for the best. The best for *it* anyway.

Now all she had to do is figure out how to get it to come out during the day.

She finished the second cup, headed upstairs, and ran the bath.

The hum started soft and then gained in volume, the pitch higher as it approached.

Then green slime started to ooze in through the bathroom door. It congealed into a shimmering glob by the tub, then rose up, forming the shape of a man again, the face back to full-on Dave, hole and all. It reached a hand for her arm and touched her.

A thought formed in her head—*gratitude.*

It stepped past her and into the tub, crouching and reclining like any human partaking in a daily cleaning ritual. As soon as the creature came into contact with the water, the liquid began to bubble and change from clear to a psychedelic green and yellow light show.

Liquid fireworks.

The water level started to drop, and with it the creature's hue brightened from yellow-green to olive to vivid sea green. The hole in its face closed up, the visage also again reshaping, less and less like Dave. More and more alien, nose shrinking and flattening, eyes expanding into saucer shapes, mouth widening.

She started the faucet again, but the tub never totally refilled. Finally she left it with the water running, knowing that it read her thoughts, understood what had to happen next.

Sheila packed the car in less than an hour, or rather prepared it for the most unusual passenger she ever transported. True, she had carried "him" once before, but that was fresh from the marsh, fully nourished. She wasn't taking any chances to ensure he'd make it the entire five-hour drive back.

Fortunately her two big coolers, at least one of her three buckets and her rubber boots were easy to find in the garage. She found another bucket stashed under the kitchen sink to catch a leak that since had been repaired and grabbed a plastic tub from the downstairs bathroom. She pulled some old milk jugs from the recycling bin, too, in case she needed refills.

She filled all of these containers with water from the kitchen tap and some of the larger ones using the hose outdoors. Then she placed them on the passenger seats in front and back and the floor beneath. She attached them as well as she could with seatbelts and bungee cords, but she had already reconciled herself to the inevitability of spillage and her car ending up soaking wet. What real harm could mere water cause upholstery anyway?

Periodically she checked on her strange companion in the tub. Each time she found him looking different—the first still in approximate human shape, but later he had let himself spread into an amoeboid blob.

Ready to leave, Sheila checked herself in the mirror again. She never had gotten around to that shower. Wasn't time. But in case she had to stop to pee, she needed to make herself at least mildly presentable. She washed her face, applied some minimal make-up—a little under-eye concealer, powder foundation, mascara. Then she brushed and braided her hair. Nobody'd suspect anything nefarious about a forty-something woman in Anne of Green

Gables braids, would they? Maybe she should change into a plaid shirt, she thought chuckling out loud.

The creature made a metallic coo behind her, as if trying to mimic her amusement. Did it have a sense of humor? How much of her mind could it read? Or was that just its way of bonding with her.

She turned and saw he was back to the green slime monster man again, Dave's bamboo hole disturbingly recreated. By this point, he must have absorbed all the water he needed because the level had stabilized with the tub about half full. She switched off the faucet, thinking how she wished he could just stay here and she could just keep on—what should she call it—watering him?

Even if the police didn't come, how long could he restrain himself from his true nature? She'd already lived with an addict once. They can only suppress their basest desires for so long, and now he'd tasted Felecia. She looked into his sea-green eyes and saw he knew again what she was thinking.

He knew and understood.

Sheila lowered a bucket into the tub. As it filled with water, he stood, body glowing and flowing, and stepped a foot into it. As appendage descended, man-shape dissipated downwards into primordial glimmering green ooze. She paused to slip on rubber boots that she kept by the front door and then carried it out, strapped it into her front passenger seat and drove south.

Five hours later, Sheila pulled off I-95 onto state highway 40 and followed it all the way to St. Mary's. She passed through the modest touristy town center and turned right to where the ferries left for Cumberland Island, Georgia's largest barrier island and a nationally protected untouched wilderness which required advance reservations to visit, usually with a long waiting list. Signage officially declared the coastline "Cumberland Island National Seashore," but it really was the shore of St. Mary's River where it emptied into the sea. Instead of parking at the ferry dock, she turned right, back inland until she reached the railroad tracks, and only then did she head back toward the water.

Sheila settled on a street of modest ranch homes, probably built in the 1950s or 1960s, not the more affluent newer McMansion neighborhoods further south where people might be more likely to notice and call the police on trespassers. At the dead end, cement gave way to dirt, but she kept driving into the tall grasses until she reached the point where the mud looked deep and boggy enough that it would cling to her tires. It'd be dark by the time she left, she was sure, and with no one to guide her or push the car, best not to take the risk.

She checked the car clock. Nearly eight thirty. The sun still skirted the horizon, but the purple-blue of twilight was descending and then dark would soon follow.

She stepped out, her boots squishing in the mud. A vista of two-foot high marsh grass and craggy trees, bark peeled away to light gray trunks, and broken palms extended before her. No tree stood more than five or six feet tall at most, and some looked like they had been sheared off at their tops. She assumed the reason must be a tropical storm or hurricane, not that she remembered one hitting the Georgia coast any time recently. She assumed it could take years for the trees to grow tall again. The river looked at least a quarter mile ahead, a shiny silver ribbon at the edge of the wetland, identifiable only by the higher shoreline on the other side.

She heard a wet splash by her left foot and looked down to see a shimmery band of green. She hadn't been sure which container he occupied by this point, absorbing the water and moving from one to the next throughout their journey. Not sure how much he'd need, she'd only stopped twice—once to pee and once to top off the gas and grab a coffee and a snack of cheddar crackers.

Snakelike, the creature started down what had narrowed now into more trail than road in the direction of the shore. At first, she was unsure whether to follow, even whether she wanted to. Bidding farewell was hard enough. She wasn't sure what she was going home to—a house of dead plants, empty dreams.

She felt a sharp pang in her head.

Ahead the glowing thing had paused. She realized suddenly he never gave her a name. Did he have one? Did his kind even have names? And she hadn't named him either. *Why?* Well, too late now.

Nevertheless he wanted her to come. He wanted to show her something.

He wanted to say goodbye.

The sun dipped below the horizon and the sky dimmed as she walked through the grass and mud. She expected mosquitoes but not the clouds of angry little black gnats and their tiny bites—a hundred pins pricking her at once like a voodoo doll. She plunged her hands into her pockets but could still feel their nips on her bare arms. She should have thought to wear sleeves, but she hadn't been in a swamp for a long, long time.

Halfway to the shore, night had almost fallen, and the glimmering substance shot upwards suddenly and back into the shape of a man. He reached out a spongey appendage and took her hand.

For a moment, she felt tenderness, but then…

A loud crash, the water ripples from its magnitude even though the crash isn't in the water but on its banks nearby.

Swimming, swimming, to see.

Hoisting out of the water, reformed into a creature on two appendages, sinking deep into the mud, but with each step, feet and ground a little more solid. Through green-tinted lenses, the outline of the mangled wreckage of Dave's plane in the near-darkness, smoke rising from its tail. Stepping carefully around the wreckage, avoiding the places where gooey jet fuel has matted into the foliage. Recognizing the smell, recoiling.

The same scent as what had taken the Others.

Monica first, in a strapless red dress face-down into the dried dark brown mound of alligator dung. Were they flying to or from a party? Her feet bare and muddy, one gold slip-on high-heeled sandal nearby, the other nowhere to be seen. Grasses sprout through her back and legs, though not so many as impale Dave's body. He lies about ten feet further inland, the same tangled forested mess or even worse than at Maddox and Sons—his detached bare foot in a mud puddle towards the river about six feet away. If an alligator had been around, the foot would have disappeared.

Curiosity high now—or no, some sort of longing, not nostalgic but angry—bending down next to Dave's cool and hardened body. Sniffing, again disgust at the jet fuel. Stroking one arm, touching Dave's forehead, sticking a long finger into the bamboo hole in his face. Lying down on top of Dave, melting into his chest hair, grass, skin, feeling for any sign of life. Wanting to understand why Dave smells like the black ooze and yet it can touch the dark sticky substance and not be hurt. It wasn't what killed Dave, at least not directly. A desire to devour Dave and yet the smell brings fear that doing so would bring the "black death."

Inside Dave, inside his meat, inside his bones, an intimacy Sheila never imagined or wanted and yet also strangely reassuring if only to hear the deafening silence in his head. She looks not just through its eyes but simultaneously Dave's eyes. "Gary Gilmore's Eyes" by the Adverts runs through her head. "Lying in a hospital…" She silences the lines because her green slime man wouldn't know. The ear-worm is confusing him, breaking his storytelling or whatever she is experiencing—his monster mind-meld. By now she wants the vision to end. She doesn't know whether to continue to trust him or be terrified. She just wants it over.

Sharp sounds which Sheila recognize as sirens break the reverie of hatred. A four-wheel-drive jeep and an SUV-style ambulance/red emergency vehicle with oversized tires charge through the foliage and grind to a stop nearby. Five men and one woman pour out.

Panic. No time to slip out of Dave's body and get back to the water. Have to go with the body, but relishing the thought.

Realizing Dave is a vessel, a vessel to get it to her kind.

Three uniformed people now kneel by the body. The woman touches Dave's wrist, feels for a pulse, is confused for a moment, thinks she hears one, then shakes her head.

"He's dead," she says.

"No one could survive that impact," says one of the men.

They start to lift the body, find it caught in the sawgrass blades that spike up through it. One man pulls a knife from his belt, starts to cut underneath. When it's finally loose, they lift it on a stretcher, carrying it to the ambulance, hoisting it in the back. The other team brings Monica and places her beside. Her body is on its back now and Sheila can clearly see the dark mass of alligator dung caked on her flattened nose, her right eyeball torn loose and hanging out of socket.

A bouncing sensation as the ambulance pulls out and drives roughly on the bumpy marshland, tires sticking momentarily in mud, then breaking free again.

Bump, bump, bump.

Then a smoother ride…the vehicle must have reached a paved road.

The movement stops suddenly, a pause, and a different kind of movement—removal from one place to a cart of some sort, wheels spinning.

Staring at her own face at the mortuary. An overwhelming emotion of hatred against humanity, hatred and hunger not in a belly but in everywhere. An overwhelming desire to absorb, devour.

And then her own emotions interrupt—anger, hurt, tears but not actual sadness. It understands sorrow but not her soupy mixed mess of feelings, ingredients that don't match up, the cacophony of a life of utter pointlessness.

Are her thoughts really so loud? Dissonance and confusion, not fully understanding but sensing that the dead man has done her great wrong. The black ooze killed Dave like it destroyed the Others but he deserved to die. Attraction. Affinity?

Chaos, confusion in his plans. Wanting to comfort her, wanting her to comfort him. Leaving Dave's body, splashing onto the even icier linoleum floor, contract-

ing its being as small as it can and climbing into her shoe. Not knowing why but wanting to go with her wherever she goes even if it's far from water.

Moisture receded from her hand. She watched the back of the slime monster man's luminous green figure as he walked through the tall grass towards the shore. Then down he melted, vanishing into the marsh. By this point the reeds would be growing not in mud, but in water, so she imagined he was swimming already.

Free, alone, but back where he belonged.

Sheila turned and walked to the car, backed it out of the marsh onto the street. She turned right at the tracks and retraced her drive through St. Mary's tiny downtown and back to the interstate. By the time she reached it, night had fallen completely.

She realized she was crying, a flood of emotions colliding in her head. Was she sad to see him go? Or relieved? Did letting him go mean she could let Dave go, too? She'd long ago declared she was over Dave in her head, but in the past few weeks since the plane crash, the memories had intruded again like unwelcome return guests. She'd compartmentalized them, but she hadn't exorcised them. And with the slime creature gone, she had nothing to distract her from remembering.

She wasn't ready to go home yet. She needed some further catharsis.

But what?

Instead of heading north, she took the southbound ramp.

What the hell, she was only an exit away from Florida. She'd seen a river leading to the ocean but not the ocean itself. It was worth a try anyway.

About ten miles down the interstate, the first major Florida exit beckoned with cheap gas, fresh oranges, and tacky souvenirs. Sheila ignored the neon promises for the signs to Amelia Island. She'd never been there and its country-club reputation didn't especially appeal, but it was just eighteen miles due east and the most northern beach in the Panhandle state. She wasn't looking to sightsee and so was only vaguely cognizant in the dark of crossing a long metal suspension bridge into Fernandina and a progression from chain stores and restaurants to historic two-story wooden homes with palm trees in their front yards. Instead she concentrated on not missing any signs to "beach."

Eventually she found condos and hotels, the surest signs a beach was near, and beyond a bar-restaurant that looked straight out of Margaritaville. She pulled into the parking lot, predictable pop songs drifting in her window from the speakers on the crowded deck. She wasn't here for that, not for flip-flops and sunglasses and fruity drinks with umbrellas. No, the gray shadow was what called her, the wide stretch of white sand dissolving into pitch black where ocean met night sky. She thought about removing her rubber boots, and then opted instead for keeping them on. She didn't need to feel sand in her toes nor have the hassle of cleaning the sand off her bare feet afterward in the dark. While she had a car full of water containers, she had forgotten to pack towels—some kind of irony there.

No, she was only at this black beach because she wanted to see the waves at night. At that moment, she also realized that she didn't remember ever being at a beach so dark. Somehow she'd expected some kind of lighting.

All the better.

As she walked onto the sand and closer to the shore, the music faded behind her, replaced by the crash of the waves. She passed a couple holding hands, wondered what they found romantic or were they just happy to be together? Would she ever feel that way again—just happy to be with someone for no reason? She watched them kiss. She had been happy with whatever had been sharing her bed. Or had it just made her forget? Was that all happiness was—forgetting?

A trio of giggling kids ran past her, and she adjusted her route away from where they were headed. At least she understood why kids would like a beach at night—something different, something creepy. Still, when she confronted the Atlantic Ocean, she wanted to be alone. She was used to being alone, maybe too used to it.

The walk to the shore took only a few minutes, the light from a crescent moon and stars just ample enough for her to make her way. She stopped when her boots met the edge of the surf, frothy white high tide washing onto their tips and then withdrawing back out to sea.

Some waves crested higher than others. Some rippled and rumbled, and some thundered as if warning how quickly and unexpectedly a wave can grow to towering tsunami-size. In the dark, the water became shape rather than substance—a pure force of nature that didn't care a lick about any puny human, about her. Nobody cared about what she went through with Dave, that she couldn't seem to move on. They gave lip-service, sure, like Felecia.

Oh, Felecia. Not just dead, but vanished, not even a body for Jeff to identify, another statistic, missing person. How many missing persons were really victims of her lover's kind?

That in itself didn't bother her.

No, Felecia, was dead because Sheila was selfish. She gave in to her own weaknesses, her inability to truly get over what Dave did to her. She should have either forgiven him—"*the Christian way*"—or rejoiced in his demise, heartless as that might seem to some. Either of those and no one else would have been hurt.

Keep walking, Sheila.

Keep walking.

Into the abyss.

Become one behind the curtain of Atlantic the all-powerful.

No one really cares. No one will miss you.

Forget and be forgotten.

The embrace was tantalizing—what did she have to live for, really? No parents, no children, no dog or cat, no best friend, no husband. Not even a monster lover any more.

One foot in front of the other.

She imagined what it would feel like to step into the waves. At what point, would the undertow take over and leave her in the embrace of the cosmos? She was certain it would be black, nebulous and as unforgiving as zero gravity. As the saltwater filled her lungs, would she feel any pain? Would her body be washed back onto the beach to be found in the morning sun?

If she knew she would be swept out to sea, the decision would be simpler.

Fuck, who was she kidding? She wasn't the suicidal type. No matter how she felt, she was the gal who kept going. The Energizer bunny, the watch that keeps on ticking—even if all that was left inside were mechanical gears going through the motions.

She needed to find a way to move on with her life, get to the next stage, clean up the mess in her house and her head, really get over Dave, not just hide him away in a dark corner of her brain. Maybe on the other side, there'd even be another lover—a man, not a monster, who would truly appreciate her for who she was.

If monsters existed, maybe such men did, too.

Sheila turned around and walked back to the restaurant, sat down at a table on the patio. As she picked up the menu, she realized she was ravenously hungry. Maybe she shouldn't be surprised. After all she'd barely eaten anything for days and smoked a hell of a lot of pot. She ordered a seaside comfort drink/food combo of coconut-fried shrimp platter and a side of fried plantains. And a big glass of water, which she asked the waiter to refill twice.

After eating, Sheila headed to the car. She wasn't sure if she'd drive all the way to Atlanta tonight, but at least she'd get started, find a motel along the way. She had a lot of pruning to do inside her house so better get back as early as she could.

She was on the bridge from the island back to the mainland when she started to feel wet. She didn't feel anything much longer after that.

Acknowledgments

Thank you doesn't seem enough to Scott Nicolay, my partner in everything, who believed in my writing whenever I wasn't sure.

My deepest gratitude goes to Lethe Press publisher and editor Steve Berman for bringing this monster into print. And to the editors who first accepted these stories: Sam Cowan, Justin Steele, Ross Lockhart, Joe Pulver, Scott R Jones, Jordan Krall, Tom Monteleone, and Farah Rose Smith. Artists Jeanne D'Angelo and Kim Bo Yung went above and beyond my imagination with covers and illustrations for the chapbooks in which "Grass" and "Passage to the Dreamtime" originally appeared. I'd also like to give a shout-out to Mado Peña, artist for my comics short story "A Stuffed Bunny in Doll-Land," and editor Renae De Liz who accepted it for *Womanthology: Heroic* in 2012. While not in this collection, "Stuffed Bunny" marked a turning point in my life and fiction. And always a big thank you to Roxana Stan who designed my author and ATLRetro blog Websites and keeps them online.

The road to a good story isn't traveled alone. "A Girl and Her Dog" is inspired by and dedicated to my four collies—Rory, Tristan, Duncan, and

Max. "Resonator Superstar!" was sparked by a recreation of the Velvet Underground's EPI shows in Andy Ditzler's Film Love Atlanta series, and Andy's research on the EPI was essential. Without Erik Merkosh's comments on the Soviet aspects of "The Un-Bride," it would never have been alive. Jeanne "Maskmaker" Wesson is the kind of beta reader who always holds my feet to the fire, especially on "Boisea trivittata." "Dr. George" Parlavantzas's "vetting" of veterinary and dog behavior aspects in "Old Tsah-Hov" was crucial, and Eddy Eder and Maura Scherrer shared invaluable insight on Jerusalem. "Jehessimin" would never have been finished without three key comments from Melissa Eisner, as well as countless cups of Joe at her Coffee Bandits in Merced, CA. Selena Chambers has provided years of writerly camaraderie and consolation and ordered me not to take the Devil out of "Black Stone Roses and Granite Gazanias." There wouldn't have been any "Grass" if Terri Carter Kitchen hadn't planted the seeds and Heather Buckley hadn't accompanied me on a road trip to the Georgia and Florida coasts. Mortuary scientist Brittany Godfrey patiently answered all my questions about airplane accident forensics and south Georgia medical examiners and morgues. Thanks to all the friends and colleagues who beta-read these works in progress, often on short or almost no notice including Jamille Christman, my partner-in-ATLRetro-crime Melanie Crew, ATL-Weird sister Kristi DeMeester, Eli Dorsey, Alicia Graves, Mike and Lena Griffin, Robby Hilliard, Paul Jessup, Ian McDowell, Nivedita Ravishankar, Jayaprakash Satyamurthy, Christopher Slatsky, April Stephens, and Damien Angelica Walters.

I am also deeply grateful to so many in the spec-lit, horror, and Weird communities who provided encouragement, inspiration, and friendship through years of crossroads leading to this work's destination, including (but not limited to) Linda Addison, Mike and Anita Allen, sj bagley, Laird Barron, Matthew M. Bartlett, David Bowles, Daniel Braum, Chesya Burke, Michael Bukowski, Nancy Collins, Ellen Datlow, Jetse de Vries, Jeffrey Ford, Neil Gaiman, Sephera Giron, Craig Laurance Gidney, Christopher Golden, John Glover, Orrin Grey, Niels Hobbs, Sandra Kasturi and Brett Savory, Brian Keene, Nicole Kurtz, John Langan, Kelly Laymon, Darren McKeeman, S.P. Miskowski, James A. Moore, Silvia Moreno-Garcia, Yvonne Navarro, Weston Ochse, Rose O'Keefe, Steve Niles, Bob Pastorella and Michael David Wilson, John Pelan, Christopher Ropes, Steve Saffel, Eric Schaller, that zany force of nature known as John Skipp, Anna Tambour, Jeff and Ann VanderMeer, Lawrence Watt-Evans, Michael Wehunt, F. Paul Wilson, Doug and Lynne Winter, and Jane Yolen. I would never have

arrived at this juncture without my Druid Hills High School Science Fiction Club, Smith College, Mythic Imagination Institute, Necon, and The Outer Dark Symposium families.

Thank you to my mother Margareta Martin, my family, and all the amazing longtime friends who have patiently waited for this book and pulled me out of ditches. I love you, Candy Billips, Mark and Molly Bode, Max Bernardi, Wendy Bowman, Shawn Carter, Marion and Cynthia Crowder, Daniel and KC Darkfield, Liz Dinsmore, Ginger and Ron Fox and my godchildren TJ and Shaelagh Fox, Julie Freeman Setzer, Phil Gilliam, Graham Humphreys, Kevin and Lori Jones, Rebecca Daugherty Kaye, Zada Law, Talloolah Love and Q, Chris and Laurie Mills, Shane Morton and Madeline Brumby, James O'Barr, Rebecca Perry, Matthew Porter and George Aguilar, Anjelah Ramirez, Bill Ritch, Maura Scherrer, Peter Straub, Lisa Twaronite, Jonathan Williams, Anthony and Betty Pitillo of Café Lily, and this list could last pages so I'd better save some of you for future books.

Finally, no acknowledgments would be complete without including a few friends and mentors who sadly are no longer with us especially Corey Frison, Dallas Mayr (aka Jack Ketchum), George Goodwin, Lonnie Harvel, Angelo Pitillo, and one of the bravest people I will ever be humbled to have known, a real-life "Fiver," Melissa Petrey Kern.

Publication Credits

"Black Stone Roses and Granite Gazanias" copyright © 2016, first appeared in *Mantid Magazine*, Issue #2.

"Boisea trivittata" copyright © 2017, first appeared in *Looming Low*, Volume I (ed. by Justin Steele and Sam Cowan, Dim Shores).

"A Girl and Her Dog" copyright © 2015, first appeared in *Xnoybis*, Issue #2 (Dunhams Manor Press).

"Grass" copyright © 2016, first appeared as a limited edition chapbook (Dim Shores).

"Jehessimin" copyright © 2018, original to this collection.

"Old Tsah-Hov" copyright © 2015, first appeared in *Cassilda's Song* (ed. by Joseph S. Pulver, Sr., Chaosium).

"Passage to the Dreamtime: A play in one act" copyright © 2017, first appeared as a limited edition chapbook (Dunhams Manor Press).

"The Prince of Lyghes" copyright © 2015, first appeared in *Cthulhu Fhtagn!* (ed. by Ross E. Lockhart, Word Horde).

"Resonator Superstar!" copyright © 2015, first appeared in *Resonator: New Lovecraftian Tales From Beyond* (ed. by Scott R. Jones, Martian Migraine Press).

"Sensoria" copyright © 2015, first appeared in *Giallo Fantastique* (ed. by Ross E. Lockhart, Word Horde).

"The Un-Bride, or No Gods and Marxists" copyright © 2016, first appeared in *Eternal Frankenstein* (ed. by Ross E. Lockhart, Word Horde).

"Window" copyright © 2016, first appeared in *Borderlands 6: An Anthology of Imaginative Fiction* (ed. by Olivia F. Monteleone and Thomas F. Monteleone, Borderlands Press).

Anya Martin was weaned on Friday Night Frights, has always rooted for the monster, and regrets abandoning her earliest career aspiration—digging for dinosaurs. She listens to punk rock with a heavy side of funk and experimental jazz, cooks dangerously hot curries, and hangs with dogs whenever possible. She's also half-Finnish, has an anthropology degree from Smith College, and earns her living as a journalist. Her novella *Grass* was a Dim Shores limited edition chapbook, and her play *Passage to the Dreamtime* was published by Dunhams Manor Press. Her fiction has appeared in anthologies and magazines including *Tales from a Talking Board, Looming Low, Eternal Frankenstein, Cthulhu Fhtagn!, Giallo Fantastique, Cassilda's Song, Xnoybis #2, Resonator: New Lovecraftian Tales From Beyond, Borderlands 6, Mantid, Daybreak Magazine* and *Womanthology: Heroic*. She blogs at ATL-Retro.com and produces The Outer Dark podcast, featuring interviews with contemporary Weird/spec-lit creators, with Scott Nicolay, for This Is Horror. Her author Website can be found at www.anyamartin.com and her Twitter handle is @anya99.

CPSIA information can be obtained
at www.ICGtesting.com
Printed in the USA
BVHW03s0904170918
527413BV00004B/12/P